LOVE
SONGS
TELL
YOU
LIES

By J.D.W

Cover illustration by Mark Powell- idmp
Graphics: Gordon Templeton

Printed in Great Britain by J F Print Ltd, Sparkford, Yeovil.

Serendipity

It is every reader's copyright.
Never give the plot away.

*Listen, hear the love songs played
by the man on the radio.
Honeyed words on honeyed tongues,
So easy it all seems.
And young love is made to go,
Down the street of broken dreams.*

*Honeyed words on honeyed tongues,
Love songs tell you lies.*

Prologue

On a hill high above the bay they sat entranced by wonderful views to the horizons east, south and west. All day the sun had blazed hot and now as it set a mist, suffused with shades of blue and green from the sea and red and yellow from the sun, was rising from the warm waters.

The heat of the day still pulsed from the dry, cracked earth. Zephyrs of cool air rising from the sea caressed them. Under a cathedral sky everywhere was quiet. There was no one on the world but themselves. Everything in creation was for their delight.

It was heaven on earth.

Low in the west a richly red sun was setting in billows of pale clouds. In the east a pearly half moon was already rising, its craters and mountains figuring clearly on its cold, wan surface. Above them through a strange other-world light created between the departing day and approaching night they could see clearly into the universe; into eternity.

With the blinding blaze of sunset veiled by flimsy clouds they could see above and beyond the sun. It was a rare and amazing view. They were so high they could discern the earth's curvature; the horizon curling away to the east and west. They were on a planet whirling in space.

This majesty did not make them feel insignificant. They were exalted: at one with the mystery of it all. In visual poetry, all was explained. Especially for them the divinities had created a perfect time and place: paradise.

They were in a dream world: and they believed it.

Love Songs Tell You Lies

Sometimes when you regard a stranger they can make you feel better. You like looking at them. If you are a man it may not be because it is a beautiful woman, or for a woman that it is a handsome man. They can be any age, any sex, anyone.

There is an air about them. You can tell they are smiling inside. Happy thoughts of a special someone? You feel good because they are feeling good.

For the huddled commuters in the crowded carriage it was just another same beginning to another same day. Not much to smile about, but looking at Kelly Webb they might well have felt one coming on.

Why so cheerful, sir?

I'm thinking of my wife and if you, sir, had a wife as beautiful you, too, would be feeling pretty pleased with life.

Walking arm-in-arm with Angela to the station Kelly had felt great. Just another start to another week, yet if he had won the lottery the night before he could not have felt better. Life was right on track and he reckoned he had sorted out what was important to him now; what really mattered.

So philosophical so early in the day, and on a Monday morning too! Counting his blessings was all due to the woman he had married. Normally he drove to the station, but this morning Angela was meeting friends and they were going to catch the train the other way to Brighton for a shopping spree. Another of her many friends was taking the children to school and they had set out with plenty of time to catch their respective trains. It was a lovely morning so for a change they left the car and caught the village bus to Reigate and walked the last quarter mile to the station.

Brighton: it triggered memories. They had been good times until it had all ended badly. This fleeting memory of their Brighton days as they strolled underlined just how good life was now. On the way they paused to look at an interesting house for sale. Just curiosity really, as they were very content with their 1930's semi in Meadow Gate village with its big mature garden. It was good to have time to

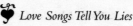

walk and talk, one of their favourite pastimes, and Angela looked gorgeous this morning – what's new?

Kissing her good-bye she had smiled at his zest, and it was as good as when first he kissed her. Yes, here was a man feeling pretty pleased with life; his life, his wife, his children, his house, his job, his just about everything!

Meet Kelly Webb, the luckiest man in England.

Settled into his seat he opened up the first of his morning newspapers. Rush, squash; the usual start of the day for commuters to London. It was not something he would admit to – the other passengers on the crowded train to Waterloo that morning would have thought him mad – but he quite liked the daily journey to work.

It gave him time to catch up on stories in rival newspapers, and time to people watch. He and Angela enjoyed people watching. They used to have lots of giggles when they were courting, sizing up people around them, and they still did it. So childish for a man within sight of middle age, but fun.

Middle age! Thirty-something is nowhere near middle age! Angela was out of order calling him a grumpy old man – old! – the other day when he was complaining about mobile phone loudmouths.

This morning he had got into a 'no mobiles' carriage but something just as annoying intruded – the two old buffers who invariably spent their journey gossiping about the office in penetrating voices.

Occasionally he had been amused by the sagas of office intrigue that occurred where they worked in the Square Mile. This morning however he was not in the mood and sighing tetchily tried to ignore their gossip and concentrate on his reading. He had dubbed them Basil and Bertie after a wet Saturday afternoon spent watching an old Hitchcock film that featured two silly-ass Englishmen on a train.

"Basil Rathbone and *Naughton* Wayne" Angela had admonished. "As a reporter you should get your facts right!"

Then to his surprise he heard one of them mention his name and realised they were reading his report on Jeremy Halpman in the Graphic. Folding his newspapers he settled back to listen.

"What he does he do all day," Bertie demanded to know, "peep

3

through keyholes?"

No need to. Not in Westminster. Always someone ready to tell you.

"How else can they find out? This Halpman story, for instance, how did this get into the papers?"

"There's always someone ready to sneak on you," said Basil, and rubbing plump fingers and thumb together added: "Money."

Yes, always someone. Not always for money though. Spite; revenge; ambition. They all have victims.

"They've got no principles," snorted Bertie.

Oh yes, I forgot principles. They have victims too.

The train was coming into the station and Basil and Bertie gathered themselves for another day of conflict in the corridors.

"Is no one's privacy safe from these muck-rakers?" Basil demanded to know.

No old chap, not if you have power over other people's lives. Then you are fair game.

Bertie snorted a laugh: "Mind how you go. He might peep through your keyhole one day!"

"I wish my life was that interesting!"

Don't worry, even if it was, you're safe. The naughty goings-on of royals, politicians, showbiz celebrities - and the occasional vicar. That's what sells newspapers. The oldest story is always the latest old chap.

Kelly entered the Graphic office breezily that morning. He doubted if those two old boys enjoyed going to work half as much as he did. It could not get better than this. He had the life to die for.

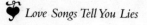 *Love Songs Tell You Lies*

The Oldest Story Begins

S hining low through the reeds the morning sun illuminated the opening scene of the oldest story.

She was wearing the white linen jacket in which she looked so good. It caught the sun so he could see her coming a long way down the path. A breeze stirred the reeds causing the sunshine to dance around her. The pyrotechnic display was brilliant but it was this woman who dazzled him.

She walked straight into his arms.

After coffee at the café they had made their very own, where no entreaty could get him to reveal where he was taking her, he drove West. Along a beautiful old-fashioned English road they bowled, uphill, downhill, zig-zag, beside a surf-dancing shore. When there was only half a mile to go he made her promise to keep her eyes closed so she did not see the signpost. Clasping her hands over her eyes she laughed.

"I'm being abducted!"

"That's the whole idea!"

At the signpost he turned down a narrow twisty lane and then she was allowed to look. They descended on the town down a steep hill under a dark tunnel of huge trees. Still she was mystified, and he was able to park in a side street, take her through a park by a river, and almost to Sidmouth's town centre before she began to realise.

"I know this place!"

"Surprise! You said you loved the town." Watching her face as it all dawned on her, he beamed with satisfaction. As they walked on into the town he reminded her how she had fondly recounted spending a childhood holiday there.

"You crafty devil!" she said, hugging his arm with delight. "Oh, it's a lovely surprise! Yes, my parents used to bring me here when I was little."

They arrived in a town centre reminiscent of an England of the Twenties. They wandered on through walled flower gardens towards the seafront along a path that had been made specially for lovers to stroll.

Amid surroundings easy and mellow, they passed through a pretty

5

churchyard. In the warm sunshine it was a pleasant, not a sad, place. As he went on ahead she stopped to read the ancient tombstones. Most inscriptions told of long lives for the times in which they lived; full three score and ten; time to live, time to achieve.

Then, on a tombstone close beside the path, one inscription warned every passer-by of the fragility of it all. Reading it she was suffused with sadness. It recorded the lives and deaths of three children from one family none of whom had lived beyond six months of age. Ellen, John and Julia Kent had died one after another in 1839, 1840 and 1842.

Turning and seeing her lingering he held out his hand. Hurrying on out of the shadow of death she clasped it and drew his arm protectively around her shoulders.

Soon they reached the promenade nestling between tumbling cliffs. Before them was a picture postcard English seaside town.

"Very sedate and level, just right for you city dwellers," she mocked, then mischievously challenged: "I bet you can't manage it to the top of that cliff!" Facing them was a climb so steep he had to lean back to see to the top.

"Easy! And I'll help a poor old lady up as well," he unwisely bragged, offering his arm.

He tried to keep up this cavalier banter, but the first steep steps up from the promenade exposed the city dweller inside the braggart. Soon she let go his arm and was well ahead, chiding him when she looked back down to see him pausing to recover his breath.

"Come on!"

"Just admiring the view!"

A feeble lie, although it was indeed a wonderful spectacle: wild tumbling coastline, groomed farmlands and the mellow town in a river valley; nature and man in perfect harmony.

"Oh, they have put a seat up here for you, you poor old chap!" Laughing at his plodding progress, she pointed and he could just see it halfway up the hill.

"Oh no!" he groaned when he finally puffed up to the seat. "It's rotted away!" Indeed, it was virtually a wreck and through its crumbling frame briars and weeds entwined. Despite the dereliction

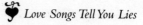

a plaque inscribed to the memory of a local woman still remained attached. He read out the dates of her birth and death: 1873 to 1940.

"If it's been here since 1940, no wonder it's a ruin," he puffed, still getting his breath back. "Pity it didn't last a bit longer!"

He flopped down on the grass and she joined him. He spread his arms wide to embrace the spectacular view before them: "Think of all the people down the years who have sat here – on a seat the lucky ones! – and admired this!"

"Hmm, yes, wonderful!" She answered abstractedly, because she was thinking of the other memorial down in the town for those three babies who lives were so cruelly brief. In contrast the woman named on this seat had lived for more than 60 years, yet her life might just as well have seemed as fleeting if not well lived. Clearly the memorial was for someone well loved, but being loved and being in love are two very different things.

If the woman could be here now looking out over her town and reflecting on what had been, or might have been, would her long life seem as wasted to her as were the lives of the children in the cemetery?

Her melancholy reverie was abruptly ended when he stood up, took her hands, and pulled her to her feet.

"Come on, I'm starving after all this exercise!"

With considerably more purpose in his step than when he had climbed the hill he took her back down to the promenade. Then with a flourish he escorted her through the entrance of the Riviera Hotel.

"Time for lunch!"

"Oh!" she gasped with delight at this second surprise, and her pleasure made all the careful planning worthwhile.

A waiter fussed them into their chairs and the two hours they spent over a leisurely meal was another memory of a summer neither would forget for the rest of their lives.

"Stylish enough for madam?"

"Well, the raspberry pavlova was not quite as good as mine."

"I'll have the chef thrown out of his cottage."

"This is a lovely day. Spare him."

"Now, show me those cliff-top gardens you remember so fondly."

To reach the gardens they climbed near-vertical stone steps from the beach and arrived breathless amid a blaze of flowers. People strolled or lazed in the kind of elegance suited to royalty. Mellow brick walls covered in fragrant roses enclosed a series of gardens, where in cosy bowers were seats for lovers and dreamers.

"Isn't it lovely," she enthused, as beguiling design enticed them from one garden to another.

Lovely indeed. If the man who had created these gardens had a woman in mind to grace them, here she was. They sat for a while on a sun-soaked promenade that allowed wonderful views of the beach and towering blue clay cliffs. Then soon she was exploring the gardens again, going down memory lane. They came to a stone balcony with a sheer drop to the beach far below.

"Oh, I remember this!" she exclaimed and rushed to the wall to look. Quickly he embraced her from behind as though to save her, and she laughed.

"I don't want to lose you," he said, squeezing her tight. "I'm not going lose you!"

She did not reply, and he could *hear* the silence.

"Do you hear me?"

Still she said nothing as she looked out at the hazy horizon. It was just as well he could not see her face.

"I don't want to lose you." He was insisting on a response, the boldest he had yet dared to be.

"When you love someone, you never lose them."

It was the kind of evasive reply he had heard before and, as before, he did not have the courage to go on. In her mood women are the stronger, and there was nothing for it but to wait for a better time.

"We'll never lose this. I'll remember it all my days. Thank you my darling. It is the loveliest surprise."

"Only half a surprise, so far. We have two days, remember?"

Then he took her back along the prim promenade and past a cricket ground from where an enthusiastic swipe might well put the ball in the sea.

"There!" He stopped in front of a mellow building. "The Fortfield Hotel. This," he said with a flourish, "is where Mr and Mrs Smith are staying tonight."

In their room she lay on her back on the bed, legs waving in the air, laughing fit to bust.

"Mr and Mrs Smith! My God! What did they think down there? Mr and Mrs Smiths in hotels are not Mr and Mrs Smiths at all! How the receptionist could keep a straight face, I don't know! Whatever possessed you?"

"I thought it was rather romantic. I wanted room five hundred and four, it looks like a hotel from that era – that grand Thirties staircase! – but they did not have that many."

"Romantic? Mr and Mrs Smith!"

"What better name? Mr and Mrs Jones, Mr and Mrs Brown, Mr and Mrs Whatever – all ordinary people. Mr and Mrs Smith however; ah, they are secret, naughty, wild, wilful, wanton lovers in love every one!"

Taking her in his arms he cuddled and coerced her towards the bed. "Down there in reception they knew that Mr Smith couldn't wait to get up the stairs to ravish Mrs Smith."

"Why five hundred and four?"

"One, two..." He undid the buttons on her blouse. "Three... hotels love the name Smith. They make a fortune from the name Smith. Four, five..." With practised hands he neatly undid her bra. He kissed her breasts, warm, life-giving breasts; God's gift to men.

"Mrs Smith, I love you."

Mrs Smith's skirt went next. She forgot the question. He did not need to bother with her knickers. She wriggled herself out of them, and with her joyful cry of 'knickers away!' flung them into the air with the abandon with which she spent the next hour.

More than an hour. Mr Smith only had two days and was determined to make the most of them.

Later, as they lay in the moist sweet smell of lovemaking she murmured: "Why 504?"

"Oh, it's a story," he replied, deliberately vague. He would explain later. The song from another age was perfect for this splendid

Thirties hotel.

Then she had a wonderful brainwave.

"You could write *our* story!"

"Our story? Two people in love. Not a very original plot."

"It's a wonderful story!"

"It is, to us."

"Why not to anyone else? Tell me!" she challenged.

"To write an interesting story you have to be unbelievable. You have got to make the characters do things that people never normally do, stupid things that real people never do. That's not real life. We are real.

"In a story the hero has to do something no sane man would do, for the sake of the plot, like risking what he already has for a bit more - money, power - that he doesn't need. He mucks it up, does stupid things.

"In real life he finds paradise and stays there with someone like you. In real life he would never be so stupid, would he, to risk losing someone like you?"

At this she stuck her tongue in her cheek, the way children do; uh, uh, here he goes again with the blarney.

"In stories the author makes the hero stupid enough to bugger up paradise. No drama here with us, no last-page twist, no story."

"Then make it a one act story! You are clever with words, you could write it. Please!" she urged when he just smiled, bemused by the sudden seriousness in her plea that had begun light-heartedly.

"It is not the kind of story that makes a story. It is just us. For us, it is great. But there is no plot - just us. A story has to have a plot, a third act."

"Who says so?"

"A chap I work with. He knows everything about real life. In real life there is no plot, just…real life. Life has no plot."

She pondered this. "But that is what all plays and films are about - people."

"Yes, doing things that make no sense just to make a story. This makes sense. There is no third act. Ours is a one-act play. Man meets Woman. Happy ever after." Ever *after* he emphasised.

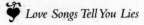

"Oh? Ever after?" Her mood suddenly darkened. "Don't get carried away!"

"Yes! Ever after!" He tried to make her look into his eyes, but she had buried her face in his shoulder.

In the late evening they drove up a narrow road past the walled gardens, now dark, deserted, silhouetted like a castle against a shimmering dark blue light rising from deep within the sea. They sought a place to park to look out over the sea, but at the top of the hill there was only a parking area among dark trees.

They sat for a while, totally hidden from the world under the trees in moonless dark. The warm summer air was filled with the primeval smell of woodland. In the almost total darkness he could barely see her but his senses savoured the essence of her; the warmth, the sweet kiss of her.

He switched on the radio. 'Friday Night is Music Night!' The familiar voice intoned the introduction.

"Your kind of music!" she chuckled gleefully. "The songs my grandma used to sing! Come on, sing-a-long!"

The fun of the let-the people-sing songs was infectious and she joined him in singing along with the radio singers. 'I'll Be Seeing You, in All the Old Familiar Places' 'You Are My Heart's Delight' 'We'll Meet Again, Don't Know Where, Don't Know When' 'If you were the only Girl in the World, and I was the only Boy'.

There was only the two of them in the entire world. They sang without inhibition, laughing whenever they lost the key, which meant they laughed a lot. Who was there to hear? Blessedly there was not one of those boors around who drone dreary put-downs to anyone who cannot sing like Sinatra or Pavarotti. The singers on the radio would have loved them if they could have heard their joyful row.

They laughed more than they sang. As far as they were concerned their performance was wonderful, therefore it was. They sang as people should, without inhibition, straight from the heart, the songs telling them – as songs are meant to do – what they wanted to hear, that everything would be all right.

Friday Night is Music Night had been out-sung for a good ten minutes before they finally ran out of breath.

He drove back to the Fortfield where they made love into the early hours. Finally, in each other's arms, they fell asleep.

And dreamt the lies of love songs.

They arrived back in her home town late in the evening. As usual, she refused to let him take her anywhere near her home and she asked to be dropped at a taxi rank in the town centre.

"It's been wonderful," she said. "Write our story one day, and when you do, be kind to me." Then a final kiss, and she got into a taxi.

Time for him to leave as well but, savouring the very last moments, he walked out into the deep silence surrounding the town.

The night was an enigma; deeply black but with everything clearly silhouetted in lunar light. Everything, houses, roads, hedges, trees, surrounding hills, glowed with the light of stars and moon. It must have been possible to read a newspaper in that astonishing luminescence. It was a warm soft night yet there was that hushed stillness that attends a frosty moonlit midnight. Just being here, awed, exalted, answered all the age-old questions of philosophers and seekers of truth. This was truly magic and he wanted it to last.

He walked on until he reached the hill overlooking their secret valley. There was no great height to the hill yet so flawless was the night sky, so immediate the stars, he was as close among them as any astronaut. Far off orange streetlights flowed like lava from the heights of a nearby island, endowing its brooding presence with a volcanic aura.

Under those fabulous stars, thinking of her, he was the greatest man on earth.

"Why isn't it a story?"

"There's no story unless someone does stupid things."

At least he got that bit right.

★

Toby Morrison walked nearly half a mile from his Whitehall office to make the telephone call. Before entering the booth his rabbitty pop-out eyes swivelled around to make sure there was no one nearby who knew him. It was ridiculously theatrical caution - after all, he was half a mile from his office but it was his nature to be cool and calculating. Not that he was feeling very cool now. Nervous perspiration glistened on the chalk-white skin of his plump face and made his egg-dome pate gleam.

Inside the booth he paused and yet again thought through what he was going to do.

This ultra-cautious man feared that if it became known a newspaper had been tipped-off about McCrae office gossip would re-cycle all that nasty business between him and the supercilious, overbearing, politician. They would put two and two together and make Morrison. First fastidiously checking that the telephone shelf was clean he smoothed out the scrap of paper on which the newspaper's number was written.

Then he picked up the telephone, holding it an inch away from contact with his ear to avoid germs, and tapped out the first moves in the series of events that would lead to murder and an increase in the circulation of the Graphic.

— 2 —

"**H**ello it's me, June." Kathy had been wondering when she would call, and she could catch up on the wedding details.

"Hello June, how are things going?"

"I'm off to finalise the details of the wedding. Want to come along, then a coffee? I'll tell you on the way."

"Love to."

"Right, I'll be round in a minute."

The two friends lived in a suburb on the outskirts of a small town and the church was in a hamlet just a short pleasant walk from their homes. Despite the proximity of the busy town the hamlet was in a quiet valley with meadows that had never been disturbed by the plough or sprayed with pesticides. Horses grazed unkempt tussocks of grass and wild flowers flourished in the pure earth. Through the valley a pristine river weaved secretively through rushes to a lake set on fire that morning by the sun. In all England there was no setting more sublime.

It was a place where some would see the world as perfect, and others sad that it was not.

Kathy had not asked where they were going, and it turned out to be the church. She had been married at the same church. It had been a wonderful day, and the weather then had been as beautiful as it was this morning. That was a lifetime ago, and in memory the sun no longer shone. Since her wedding the nearest she had got to the church was passing by in a car. Had her wits been more nimble she might have thought up an excuse for not going.

No, she was being silly. That was another life, long gone.

While the bride-to-be's mother conversed with the vicar inside the church Kathy wandered into the time-mellowed churchyard. Here in the centuries-old solitude there was a peaceful sadness that suited her pensive mood.

Faintly, like a long-ago, half-recalled memory, the murmur of the discussion about the wedding arrangements drifted from the church. Although for many years she had not let herself dwell on the past, overhearing the mother's conversation with the vicar took her, unwillingly, back. Recollection no longer brought any pain but her expression as she reflected was sombre.

When June had concluded the discussion with the vicar she rejoined Kathy.

"Oh, I do hope they'll be happy!"

Kathy knew June had reservations about her daughter's sweetheart so she answered encouragingly.

"They will, of course they will!"

"They're so young!"

"Don't worry – it will all work out, you'll see. They'll make a handsome couple, as they say."

"Handsome is as handsome does! He doesn't seem to stick at anything. Oh, he's a lovely lad, I know. He'll buckle down – he'll have to! He's had no end of different jobs. But you can't manage their lives for them, can you? Kirsty's dotty about him. It's a lovely church, isn't it? I hope it doesn't rain." June laughed at herself. "So many things to go wrong!"

She took Kathy's arm. "I'm glad you came with me. You didn't mind, did you?"

The invitation had been made on the spur of the moment, and she was suddenly anxious as she remembered. She had quite forgotten that her friend had been married at the same church. If she had taken a moment to reflect she may not have invited her along, in view of what had happened.

"No, of course I didn't. Don't be silly. I'm glad you asked me," and Kathy linked arms to reassure her.

The pair walked back up the hill chatting away, June's thoughts and feelings all out in the open, her friend's hidden.

★

Happy-go-lucky Joe Fowler liked the girls and the girls liked him. Two, three, or more dates a week with different girls was his usual routine. He was known for pulling the girls, and it was a reputation well earned because he worked at it. Nothing was ever serious; life was always a big laugh for this back street Romeo. Football and sinking a few beers with his mates never took second place to girls.

Debbie changed all that.

Joe first set eyes on her in his local supermarket where he was after packs of beer on special offer. Fancying the look of her – he had been eyeing another girl but she lost out the minute he spotted Debbie – Joe tailed her trolley until she completed her shopping and got to the check-out.

More than once his trolley – oops! – bumped into hers, and he had got her to respond to his cheeky grin. When Debbie reached the check-out another shopper with a laden trolley got between them. If he waited to buy his beer he would never catch her up.

It says something for the effect Debbie had on this young blood that he promptly shoved his trolley and its beer supply for the week-end to one side and abandoned it. Even so it was after-work Friday and the place was packed and she got far ahead of him. Any chance for chatting her up seemed gone when he spotted her waiting behind a couple of other shoppers at the taxi telephone outside the supermarket.

Wonderful luck Joe thought of it then, and it was if you agree with the homily that it is better to have loved and lost than never to have loved at all.

With the cheek of the devil Joe was beside her in a flash.

"Would you like a lift? I go your way." Debbie turned round and, if up to then the encounter had been just another of Joe's cheerful try-ons, the moment he looked into those eyes he was lost. What it was in those dreamy depths he could no more explain than could any of the many men who had felt what he was feeling at that moment.

All he knew was that his heart jumped – over the moon for all he knew – and he felt good, very good indeed.

"Oh? Do you? Well…."

Joe was not slow in these matters, notwithstanding the dizzying effect of those eyes. They made him feel great and boldly – bold even for him as this girl was upper class, out of his league really – he picked up the bag of shopping she had put down to make the taxi call.

"My car's over there."

Normally Debbie would never accept a lift from a stranger, but he was so obviously a nice young man she smiled her acceptance and Joe immediately felt in charge. He was too young for her, but long ago she had fallen into the easy mode of letting men fall over themselves.

Once he had driven out of the supermarket car park Joe asked: "Which way?"

"I thought you said you went my way?" Debbie could not help but be amused at this young man's blatant tactics; he thinks he is so good at this game! Seeing her reaction to his chat-up charms, Joe thought so too.

"Yes, I do. You live …." Joe made a gesture as though he was stumbling on the name, but he could not hide his broad grin.

"Turn left here," said Debbie.

"I thought I had seen you out where I live, Greenside," he said, cheekily keeping up the pretence.

"No, I live…". She paused; enough was enough. "You can drop me here, this will do," she said, when they were near the block of flats where she lived.

Joe, full of himself, was emboldened by her knowing smile.

"I was lying. I just saw you in the supermarket and wanted to get to know you."

"Oh, well, now you have," said Debbie pertly, opening the car door to get out.

Cocky as always Joe was not discountenanced.

"Fancy a drink sometime?"

Debbie, unable to remain aloof any longer, laughed. Joe's grin widened happily.

— 3 —

W hen it dawned it was a day that promised to be one that would always be a golden memory, but by the time it ended it was one he wanted to forget but never could. Images from that time remained ever-present in his mind, in his being, lurking just behind the façade of adulthood. Anything might awaken them, a place, a face; a pensive mood.

Tonight memories stirred uncomfortably as Hamish McCrae looked across the table at his wife. She was laughing at something Ross Buchanan was saying. Ross - typical of him - was flirting with her. The joke was just between the two of them, the others at the table being engaged in their own conversations.

Seeing the laughing intimacy that Catherine never shared with him, McCrae felt the sting of exclusion. It was not jealousy of Ross, who would never dare to play around with Catherine, much as McCrae suspected he would like to. McCrae was confident that Ross was held firmly in check in that respect. Even the affair involving Debbie, which McCrae shrewdly suspected had upset Ross far more than he made out, would not induce him to risk his relationship with McCrae by messing about with Catherine. McCrae was sure he was too valuable a business contact for Ross to lose for the sake of just another conquest.

No, it was witnessing that cosiness between them, the womanly warmth that Catherine never afforded him, that brought on the surge of self-pity that in turn triggered the dark memory.

He must have been about thirteen and on the cusp of manhood. As he had taken to doing lately he studied his naked body in the bathroom mirror before donning his riding clothes. Soft black hair had appeared in his groin and his cock, once just a dangly joke, a source of boyish merriment when he vied with his friends to see who could pee the highest, had now become of absorbing interest. Suddenly the bathroom doorknob rattled as someone tried to enter and he got dressed hastily, the blood rushing to his face. Whoever had tried the door had gone by the time he opened it and as he made his way down to the stables he gratefully felt the fresh air on

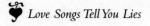

his burning face. If they had stayed and seen him as he left the bathroom his face would have surely given his thoughts away.

However, once out on the hills riding with Moira and his friends, he was again the braw lad who had stood admiring himself in the mirror; cocky, full of himself. He rode bolder and faster than he had ever ridden before, showing off for Moira, daughter of one of the estate's tenant farmers, who had also become very interesting.

They all rode to the top of Penn Hill for a picnic, full of chatter and laughter, their view unhindered by any man-made development for 20 miles across Lowland Scotland.

It was a wonderful day that ended with him winning the last half-mile gallop back to Dunglennie. As the others bade their farewells and made tracks to their farmhouse homes he received a special look from Moira, waving gaily as she rode away. The groom took his horse and with a last wave to Moira he strutted into the house. His father was in the drawing room talking to one of his tenant farmers. Looking up and seeing his son's face aglow with the beauty that heralds manhood parental pride and affection gladdened his heart.

"Good day Hamish?"

"Great, father! You should have come with us."

The master of Dunglennie and his son sometimes went riding together. They were the times - the only times - he was to remember fondly down the years. The master of Dunglennie was an undemonstrative man but there was a strong unspoken bond of affection between father and son. Hamish was eager to talk about the day's riding but his father was engaged in business, so he dashed upstairs to get out of his riding clothes.

After all these years he only recalled the outline of that day, the way dreams are recalled; just a few images that stir emotions. What happened could not possibly have spelled out to a young lad that his parents' marriage was sham; that his father had to endure the humiliation of his wife's blatant affairs with other men. All that was pieced together in the later years of lost innocence.

It was a recurring image that had come to encompass all the pain, all the bad memories. He was racing up the stairs and burst into one of the bedrooms. It was one that was not used regularly - there were fifteen at Dunglennie – and he must have been looking for something.

Mother and son were caught in a moment of time that stood still, a split second that remained framed in his mind for life. He could see it now, out of nowhere, triggered by what? The way Catherine looked tonight; the way the other men in the party kept looking at her?

His mother was wearing nothing except a diaphanous negligee that made him aware of her warm naked body. If she was startled by her son's entrance, she did not show it. Calmly she pulled the negligee around herself and asked him if he had had a good day. The man who was the room with her also behaved as though everything was normal and continued tucking in his shirt.

"Yes mother," her son answered.

Nearly 40 years on McCrae could hear his answer echoing in his head, mingling with the social chatter going on around him.

Then his mother gave him a brief hug, something he had rarely experienced from her.

The present moment – Catherine across the table talking animatedly with Ross and a woman seated next to him telling him why Britain should never have joined the Common Market – now seemed to be the dream; the reality was back at Dunglennie.

As she hugged him his mother's negligee fell open and he was bathed in her warm body odour, his face against her breasts. Then she pushed him away in an awkwardly playful manner saying: "Get yourself a bath and get ready for dinner." He had wanted the embrace to last, and he could not remember her ever holding him again.

As he left the room he heard the man say: "Well, he had to learn one day."

It was from then on that he came to know the real situation at Dunglennie. His mother had many lovers and his father, a quiet man immersed in his lonely business world, was the subject of patronising gossip; a cuckold.

Despite his obsession with business and running the estate his father always found time for his son. There was no better day than when they rode over the splendidly isolated hills on the estate; just the two of them, never needing to talk a great deal but nevertheless close.

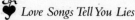

Then there were the other days, when he was embarrassed at having a father who allowed all those men …and then he was ashamed of those thoughts and overwhelmed by love for his father, and hate for his mother. He was too young to know how to deal with the situation, and as he grew older locked his feelings away.

There was a burst of laughter round the table and he had to pretend to share in the joke that he had not heard. This was no good, it was weakness, and he dealt with it the way he always did, by sheer force of will, the muscles at the back of his neck tightening with the mental effort of crushing the memory.

Then he caught the eye of a woman seated opposite. She was staring at him and he realised that his face must have reflected his emotions. Mustering up a false smile he joked: "Just thinking about my speech in the House for tomorrow," which fortunately made her laugh.

A glance at Catherine triggered again the image of that long-ago embrace; her warm breasts, the perfumed negligee.

Mustering his ice-cool mental strength he concentrated harder on the usual Whitehall and business gossip and society scandal being bandied back and forth. Politics, money and intrigue: now he was back on home territory and he entered the conversation around him with authority.

Catherine was still in head-to-head conversation with Ross and McCrae calmed his mind with thoughts of Debbie. Dear little Debbie, the one oasis of tenderness he would never abandon.

Or so he thought.

*

When Kathy and her friend reached the top of the hill overlooking the church in the valley, they parted company and made for their respective homes. Glancing at the clock when she entered her house Kathy saw she had time for a cup of tea before her daughters arrived home from school. She sat at the kitchen table to drink it and now just let the memories, set adrift by the visit to the church, flow as they would.

The local paper always published wedding photographs on a special page and every week one was singled out for printing in colour. That week theirs had been featured and they had made a handsome couple, as they say.

'Handsome is as handsome does.' Recalling her friend's remark brought on a rueful smile.

Oh, she had been such vain little so-and-so in those days! The world had revolved around her. Now she could smile about it, although with momentary sadness for her long-ago self; that pretty girl who had expected so much as her right.

At school she had considered herself the bee's knees, and eager boys had flocked around her. Robert had been the one all the other girls were after, but they had never stood a chance. There had been no question that they were the ideal couple. Some couples are so perfectly matched, so beautiful together, they seem destined for each other.

Her friend June's remark 'handsome is as handsome does' had disturbed sleeping memories and she recalled herself as a bride at the same church on a day as lovely as this.

It had been the culmination of her dreams. They had been made for each other; everyone said so, and she had never had any doubt that they would marry. Never in the whole of her young life, from playground flirting to teenage conquest, had she ever lost the boy she fancied.

Then he had walked out, leaving her for an unprepossessing woman who she would never in a million years have feared as a rival.

The parting words had been bitter, and so had the tears. However life, as it insists, had gone on. When God created this woman he had loveliness in mind, but he did not forget courage. She was not the sort to brood, nor to be a recluse.

Men were still moths to her flame, but she could not change herself. So choosy! There had been plenty of opportunities; still were in fact. None were ever taken up seriously. It was not because she had become a suburban nun, her friend Lesley's phrase for embittered once-bitten-twice-shy women.

She had been hurt, angry - furious; a sparky-eyed flouncing fury. All that, but never bitterness. There is a difference, if you have style, and that she had aplenty. Pride still ruled her life. Pride: that was the trouble with her. Yes, she was choosy; too choosy. Yes she knew it but, she told herself, you can't change your heart with your head.

On top of that, she had become very protective of her daughters. One upheaval like that in their young lives was once too often in her philosophy. She had never been prepared to lightly risk another, so being a mother had occupied the years that had flown. Regularly she assured herself that she was content with her life, and that was not untrue. She had a wide circle of good friends, as did her daughters. They were never short of companionship. Half a family they may be, but their lives were full. Life was good.

Despite what other people might naturally think, there had been no lasting anger; a shock to her self esteem certainly, but she had eventually accepted with honesty that there had never been love. Not the real stuff. Not good enough for her.

After the turmoil she had reflected on what love should be and had come to the conclusion that if it was not worth dying for, it was not worth crying for. Whatever love might be she could not explain, but she knew that it had not been there in her marriage. Respect, affection; anything and everything that was decent perhaps, but not the passion of love.

And for none of the men that she had met since her divorce, most of them introduced - presented for her inspection! - by well-meaning friends, had she felt anything worth dying for. Respect, affection, she had in abundance with friends and family. Any man who came along had to offer more. Her still young and undiminished spirit demanded more. She was worth more!

Finishing her drink, she regarded herself in the mirror. Suddenly that sombre face smiled back, and in so doing hinted at the secret of women that men are prepared to risk all to know. There was no self-pity, and no reason for any.

"I've seen worse on the television," she informed the mirror. "Not bad, with plenty of Polyfilla!" and her reflection thought that funny and winked back. Yes, she was still worth more.

"I'm still a vain little tart," she confessed to the mirror as the girls arrived home from school, bursting in and filling the house with life. "Take me or leave me!"

It was not just bravado. She meant it. This woman had style.

— 4 —

Peter Pattimore was getting some political advice over Commons coffee. Stalker, the link between the chief whip and new MPs, had called together half a dozen members who like Pattimore had directorships in the City for a cautionary chat. There had been too many scandals in the press recently involving money and MPs. One of the companies on which Pattimore was a director was Investmentguru which was currently in the news over takeover gossip. As the meeting broke up Stalker took Pattimore aside for a special word.

"Peter, this business of your company merging with Broadbent's goldrush.comm. He is not one to get too close to. His company's finances are stretched, and he's survived in the past with some dubious deals with dubious people. I know you two are old friends … but…"

"No, no," Pattimore started to refute that 'old friends' tag but stopped himself, as always never quite sure how to deal with that damn infuriating assumption. He drew a breath to steady his response. Right now he wanted to keep things calm, but he was bloody furious that Broadbent had primed the financial press that goldrush.comm was about to merge with his company. Most emphatically that was not going to happen if Pattimore had anything to do with things.

Everyone seemed to know about Broadbent saving his life, and Pattimore could hardly let the world know that he did not like the man. Broadbent's character was wild and bullish, with a streak of callousness that Pattimore had always found repellent. Pattimore had never told the story, but somehow everyone knew how Broadbent had saved his life in Bosnia. The times people had said to him 'you two are old friends', and he had had to clench his teeth to prevent an exasperated denial. Pattimore disliked Broadbent so much he hated having an obligation to him. Yet the man had saved his life and Pattimore felt as trapped by obligation as he had by that sniper on that bare Bosnian hillside.

Pattimore had been wounded and lay exposed in the open with

only the dead body of a Bosnian soldier giving him scant cover from the sniper high on the bleak bomb-blasted hill. Time was running out as fast as his blood seeping into the mud and snow.

While other members of the patrol kept the sniper focussed on them Broadbent drove round to the other side of the hill in a Landrover and got him from behind with a rush across 20 yards of open space.

They got blind drunk when Pattimore got out of hospital. Nothing however could change the truth; Broadbent was the last man to whom he would have wanted to be obligated. Under fire Broadbent could show extraordinary recklessness, which had resulted in successes like saving him. Yet Pattimore could never warm to the man, and what others might have regarded as courage he saw as a savage streak. In that mood Broadbent certainly did not care about his own life, but neither did he care about others and at times Pattimore knew that had included the safety of his fellow soldiers.

Because of what had happened on that hillside it was impossible for Pattimore to show his dislike, and it was a situation made worse because Broadbent thereafter assumed a patronising friendship with Pattimore, an attitude that he was Broadbent's man.

Broadbent left the service two years before Pattimore and had made quick money in business deals with the bullishness that had won him his reputation in the Army. Pattimore forged a new career in politics after leaving the Army and became Member of Parliament for the London borough of Notton Wood.

As human as the rest of them, he soon discovered the financial delights in being an MP and got on the boards of four companies by the end of his first 18 months in Westminster, which was how he met up again with Broadbent.

Time seemed to have had mellowed Broadbent's nature and Pattimore allowed himself to get involved in one of his business scams, cashing in on dotcom hysteria. Money was being conned out of investors by the truckload, and when offered a chance to grab some of it he was tempted. It was soon to his regret, because Broadbent had not changed.

The Bosnian obligation was still there and Pattimore made efforts to distance himself again, but business in the City involves liasing with many people with whom you would not socialise.

Very soon it was Pattimore, because of his high-level connections, who was of more use to Broadbent than the other way round. Now Broadbent played the old comrades card for all it was worth and Pattimore knew it would have seemed churlish to snub him.

So Stalker's advice was timely as Pattimore was deep in secret negotiations to have rising company, Safe Hands Finance, merge with Investmentguru in which he held 50,000 shares. Broadbent was also wooing Safe Hands to merge with goldrush.comm his company that was not doing well.

Pattimore had not wanted to be seen as doing the dirty on a chap who had saved his life. He had not been relishing the boardroom fracas that he knew was looming.

You get nowhere in business or politics being soft. Stalker's words gave him a sense of righteousness that would make it much easier. In business, your friends are where the money is.

What he had to do was to get the Safe Hands board to vote for the merger with Investmentguru and not Broadbent's goldrush. As part of the deal Safe Hands finance director Richard Tobler would become finance director of the merged company. With Investmentguru shares around 90p, the financial muscle generated by the merger alone would put another 50p on that. Pattimore had to persuade the other directors that the merger was also going to make them more money than Broadbent's scheme.

It was the toughest City firefight he had yet been in, but he held his allies together in the teeth of bitter opposition from Broadbent, and won the day.

Shortly after Broadbent stormed past a frightened secretary into Pattimore's office and pointed a finger like a gun at Pattimore's chest. "Pity I didn't just leave you on that bloody hill Pattimore!"
So ended an uneasy alliance.

That same morning, as Kelly travelled to work upbeat as usual, another commuter heading for the City was also in a good mood. This was Ted Black's last day with Investmentguru and an interview on the financial pages was nicely timed to persuade him that leaving

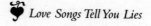

the damn company was the best thing he could have done. The interview was with Peter Pattimore, who was outlining his plans.

Pattimore had told the reporter how the merged company was to trim its exposure in the American and European markets, which were saturated, to concentrate on developing countries. The report highlighted the decision to make a big push into the Chinese and Far Eastern markets, making full use of the low-cost labour and excellent technical expertise available.

That had been Black's idea, one that he had promoted energetically for more than a year. There was no mention of him. Reading the article, it was as though Pattimore had masterminded all the planning. The article had a picture of Pattimore with Isobel D'Avril. The plain impression they gave was that they had thought it all up. Yet the bloody woman had been with the company barely six months! The change in the woman since Pattimore arrived took some believing. Almost from the day Pattimore had won the boardroom battle, she had started to strut around the place, fancying herself as one of London's Power Women.

It had been a bitter day when he had been summoned to a board meeting to be told he was not going to be the finance director of the merged companies. Before Pattimore arrived, the job would have automatically been his. Pattimore handed the job to his own man, some so-called financial wizard who had helped Pattimore and the other directors who had voted against Broadbent to make a lot of money in other companies. Dot-comm mania was the modern version of the South Sea Bubble and Tobler was the wizard with figures who could create the necessary financial illusions that would keep the share price inflated. Like Pattimore, the directors wanted that Midas touch applied at Investmentguru.

Black had been given a salary increase and patronising words as to how much he was valued, and left in his old job. Worse for Black was that right from the start he and Tobler had not got on. With Tobler in charge he found he was no longer in the inner circle that ran the company.

Bitter though all this was, the most shocking event had occurred barely a week after Tobler arrived. Jenny Edwards who was personnel manager and also dealt with any public relations matters, was made to take early retirement after 33 years with the firm. D'Avril was given her job with the grandiose title of public relations executive. Despite his disappointment Black was hopelessly besotted with Isobel. He took her out for a very expensive dinner, yet even as he congratulated her he knew things had changed between them.

It was sickeningly obvious to Black that D'Avril had only focussed her attention on him to further herself in the company. Now Tobler was the man the man who mattered and Black simply ceased to exist.

He was dumped, well and truly. From then on it was Tobler around whom she hovered. He was the man she needed, and the ruthlessness of it was chilling. Black would not have believed a woman could have such a shattering effect on a man; or how, embarrassingly, a man could feel so helpless against a woman. He did now, and he had no way of getting even.

Black had always been sympathetic to the philosophy of equality for women. That viewpoint was severely tested in the encounter with this sexual predator.

Jenny went quietly, needing time to sort herself out, and Black and some of her old colleagues met her later for a farewell dinner. By then they had a lot more to talk about regarding D'Avril. Everyone was eager to update Jenny with all the gossip since she left.

"Now she is all over Peter Pattimore," they told her. "Tobler's still her lapdog, but it's Pattimore she is after now. She's all over him, hardly ever out of his office. Everyone's talking about it! Jo has just been on holiday in Torbay and she saw them staying at the next hotel. Jo said it was plain as day they were only there for one reason – she said she knew they were not there on company business."

"You're best out of it Jenny," Black consoled.

"Yes, I have found a two–day a week job near where I live. So it's not too bad, what with my redundancy. In that at least they were generous. I hear you are out of it too Ted. What happened?"

"I had had enough. Yes, I've got an offer of a job from Tom Broadbent, I start in a couple of days. Couldn't wait to get out."

"Broadbent! Well, good for you. Well, I hope you are appreciated there – you weren't by Pattimore. Best of luck Ted."

"Thanks, and good luck to you Jenny."

Ted Black might have quit but he hardly turn a page in a newspaper it seemed without encountering Pattimore.

The man was suddenly famous and was being quoted, and his views aired in television debates enjoyed the importance associated with fame.

Despite his surge of bravado when he had walked out of Investmentguru Black was still bitter, still felt like a loser. Seeing Pattimore in the media so much was baffling until he read a cynical piece in a newspaper. A political journalist revealed that media publicist Maxie Persent was handling the image of Pattimore's companies and so, subtly, the man's public persona.

Clever, these PR people. Whispers are all they need to sire success. They earn their fees.

So that was it, Pattimore plays himself up into something – something from nothing – and cashes in. God, the man will get a knighthood next! What had he done to earn it all, except make himself a lot of money and get into the gossip columns? Not only was it all a load of bollocks, it glorified the bastard who had shafted him after years of solid graft!

Then Pattimore managed to be appointed chairman of a charity just before it played a huge part in helping refugees caught up in an East African earthquake. That was pure luck, and his PR man made the most of it by arranging television interviews on all the major channels.

Next he was appointed chairman of the committee set up to report on the debacle of London's Heron Island Millennium Theatre.

Right from the start it had bled millions, never more than half full for any performance except the VIP opening night. It was lambasted by the press and public who hated its weird design, drawn up by an architect as out of touch with harmony and meaning as a Tate Modern artist. Pattimore had pages of benevolent exposure telling the nation everything it agreed with.

Black simmered, but he was to get his chance of revenge, although only as a piece of flotsam on the stormy seas of bigger men's quarrels.

Broadbent needed Black because of his financial expertise, which was vital given the shaky state of goldrush.comm, but he could be of use in getting even with Pattimore. Broadbent knew how Black felt about Pattimore and D'Avril and saw it as a chance to hit Pattimore.

Choosing the right time over a drink Broadbent said: "The board have been hearing good things about you Ted."

"Oh?" Black was pleased. Lately he had become a man in need of some kind words.

Broadbent adopted a confidential demeanour. "Look, I know you were disappointed over that chief executive job." He lowered his voice. "'I know not everyone on the board was pleased at the way things went. Some wanted you in the job."

"I think Pattimore was set against me from the start."

Broadbent heard the bitterness in Black's retort with satisfaction.

"Well, you will do well here. Things may change, be patient. There's some unfinished business Ted."

Black was hooked like a fish, and over the ensuing weeks Broadbent played him expertly with hints. Then he landed him with an invitation to lunch.

"I'm being interviewed for a business profile," Broadbent explained in the taxi on the way. "A fellow named Reynolds, Andrew Reynolds, a reporter. I wanted you come along, you can help keep the conversation flowing." Broadbent managed a deprecating chuckle. "I don't want it to be 'me this, me that'. You can put in some background and, oh, just keep me on track."

They met Reynolds in the bar of the hotel where they were to eat and to Black's surprise he was introduced as 'our next chief executive'.

Reynolds looked very impressed. "Next chief executive!"

"Well, he deserves to be," said Broadbent, "It's on the cards, eh, Ted?" His words spun dizzily in Black's brain. Once more he felt like 'the man'. There seemed to be little he needed to tell Reynolds about the company despite what Broadbent had said. Then somehow they were talking about Pattimore and suddenly the reporter turned to Black and asked: "What did you think of him?"

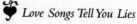

"Think of him?" Black did not know what was safe to say to that. Broadbent nudged him. "Oh, Ted can tell you everything about Investmentguru, can't you Ted? He damn well ran the place!"

"Bit of a ladies man, Pattimore, so I hear." The reporter was slyly stirring the pot.

"Ladies man?" Black hesitated, looking at Broadbent, who sat smiling encouragingly. Now Black was beginning to sense what was expected of him. The inner circle beckoned.

"Apparently their new chief executive does not get on too well with the new public relations director, Isobel D'Avril," prompted Reynolds conversationally. "Pattimore appointed her, I'm told, and Tobler - is that his name? - and the lady fell out somehow." The reporter shrugged, like he didn't care much either way.

"You can say that again - well, if you can call her a lady!"

"Oh?" This made the reporter immediately focus admiringly on Ted, as though impressed to meet someone who was in the know. "Really?"

All in the jokey manner of men swapping laughs, Black told the reporter about Jo Matthews, the typist who had spotted Pattimore and D'Avril together at a hotel.

"Jo Matthews?" Black saw the reporter jotting down the name.

"Yes, works in the typing pool. According to her it's an office joke how often D'Avril is away at the same time Pattimore is off on a business trip."

The reporter grinned. "Sounds a bit of a lad."

"He's a bit of a bastard!" Black managed a laddish chuckle.

By the time the coffee was served the reporter had enough easily-checked stuff on Pattimore for a bloody good story. Oh, he would make money on the profile on Broadbent; that had been ordered. Marketing the tip-off on Pattimore would be a nice extra earner. Making his departure, he thanked Broadbent.

"My pleasure Andrew," replied Broadbent, and meant it.

Reynolds wasted no time getting on the phone to the Graphic.

"Kelly? Hi, it's Andrew Reynolds. Yes, fine thanks, and yourself? Look Kelly, I've got a good tip for you, about Peter Pattimore. You know, the M.P....yes, that's right.

"It's a good one Kelly, you'll like it. Right, we'll have a drink and I'll fill you in. This is good stuff Kelly."

★

The Chief Whip swivelled slowly to and fro in his chair looking up at the ceiling as he listened to the details. He did not query them. Brown invariably got them right. Good man, Brown, exactly the man he needed. The Chief Whip always made it his business to try and find the facts before the media did. It was essential to know the truth if one was to have any chance of suppressing it.

"Thank you," he said when Brown had finished. "We'll have to wait and see if the papers get hold of it."

"I think they will," said Brown.

The Chief Whip nodded in weary agreement. "Will he leave Mrs Pattimore, do you think?"

"If he does, the publicity will be worse of course, being the way she is. Much worse."

"Hmm." There was not much else the Chief Whip could say. Old and wise as he was in the ways of Westminster, he could never quite understand why men supposedly clever enough to run a country did not organise their extra-marital affairs more efficiently.

The Chief Whip heaved a sigh. Once a fortnight followed by a good cigar suited him perfectly, and Mary never complained.

— 5 —

Today's headline is yesterday's work and Halpman was already old news in Kelly's busy schedule. He usually had two or three projects going at the same time and now he turned his full attention to the piece he was doing on the Peter Pattimore story. By lunchtime he had it all wrapped up, went for a snack, and when he returned checked it through. Pity he could not get a word with Mrs Pattimore. He had tried, but she had not returned his calls. It was a common scenario in political sex scandals. Patttimore had been targeted by power-freak Isobel D'Avril.

Kelly had been puzzled why a man as worldly-wise as Pattimore – ex-army officer, politician and sharp businessman – had messed with such a politically dangerous woman. Not much to get excited about in Kelly's opinion, judging by the photograph he had seen of her, and certainly not as attractive as Pattimore's wife.

Pattimore surely must have been very well aware that he was regarded as a trophy by D'Avril. Vanity? Or perhaps the drug irresistible to some men: sexual danger? Reasons, reasons. In the saga of the sexes they were invariably a variation of the eternal trio: lust, betrayal, revenge. No – nowadays it is the eternal quartet: lust, betrayal, revenge, money.

This cynical thought caused Kelly to smile the superior smile of one who thinks he knows it all.

Who was it, he wondered, who Pattimore had stolen from Black if it was not D'Avril? Not that it mattered to Kelly, he had got what he needed for his story, but it was because Black had been the loser, his job and the girl, that Pattimore faced public embarrassment.

Jealousy, hate, revenge: basic plotlines in life's script. Only this script had a twist ending that Kelly would never read.

*

Ted Black rang Peggy to invite her to lunch. Delightfully, she said yes – she didn't always – and that made him feel a lot better. Peggy, dear Peggy; the real love of his life.

Ted flung his arms wide to embrace her.

"Peggy!"

Peggy was used to being bathed in his adoration. It was years since their affair but Ted had remained devoted. As far as Peggy was concerned after that brief episode they would have each gone their separate ways, but Ted was a good friend of Nicholas, so they continued to meet socially. It was all very civilised, and they remained friends.

Peggy had arrived to see him in the foyer of the restaurant engaged in conversation with a good-looking woman.

"You look very pleased with yourself Ted," Peggy observed as the waiter ushered them to their table.

"I've got a new job."

"Oh?" Her tone was teasing. "So nothing to do with that woman I saw you talking to?"

"Nonsense!" Ted protested. "Just someone in business."

"Well you seemed to be getting on famously, I must say."

"Nonsense, nonsense! Not my type."

"Oh, and who is your type?" A mistake to ask, but too late.

"You know full well who is my type."

"Now, now, Ted," Peggy admonished, with a gentle wag of a finger. Ted in turn waved away her protest. He did so in that playful manner he had fallen into over the years, the loser in the game of love who remains devoted to a lost cause that – perhaps? – may not be entirely lost.

"You are my type." There, it is said yet again, just so you never forget my sweet Peggy.

Oh dear! Peggy thought, and smilingly protested: "It's six, seven, years!"

"And if it's another twenty six, seven, years, nothing will change – as far as I'm concerned." He laughed. "I hope Nicholas realises how lucky he is!"

Peggy moved the conversation on to more comfortable ground. "A new job? Who with? I thought you were settled for life."

"Oh, it's a long story. Broadbent offered me a job with his company, goldrush.comm. Bigger salary, better prospects."

"Goodnesss, it's all very sudden. How did this come about?"

"Oh, I'll tell you all about it, but not now. I'm not going to waste

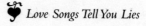

lunch with you talking about work! Now, I want to talk about you – much more interesting! How are you?"

Ted had no doubts about his feelings, and Peggy had none about hers, although if Ted knew what they were he would be crushed.

Peggy, always finding it difficult to be hard on him, had never managed to sever his hopes, and eventually had ceased to try. Their brief affair was not an unhappy memory for her, but it had certainly not been the great love that it had been for Ted. She had ended it rather basely, pretending that she did not want to risk Nicholas finding out, when the real reason was that she had found someone else, someone who for the first time in her marriage, she would go to; except, it was impossible.

Hope springs eternal in a would-be lover's breast, but vainly so for Ted because unbeknown to him Peggy was in love.

Until then, an occasional affair had always been under her control. Never would she have considered leaving Nicholas. It was a secure and comfortable life; he was a decent man. This lover changed all that as though by magic, but whereas Peggy would never before have left Nicholas for a lover, now she was willing the irony was that her lover would not leave his wife.

Nothing could keep them from each other however and they lived in a web of deceit which, like a web, was beautiful as long as it was not disturbed.

Kelly Webb's exclusive in the Graphic did more than just disturb it; it blew it away.

★

Frank transferred the call. "It's for you." Kelly's desk phone was beeping even as Frank called across from his desk.

"Wouldn't say who it was. Who she was," he added with a leer.

"Hello."

It was a pleasant upmarket voice that must have intrigued lady-killer Frank, for out of the corner of his eye Kelly could see him cupping his ear, eavesdrop style, grinning wider.

"Mr Webb?"

"Yes."

"I'm returning your call. It's Mrs Pattimore."

He was taken by surprise. After telephoning her several times without answer for a comment regarding her husband's affair he had finally just left a message on her answer-phone.

"You wanted to talk to me."

"Yes." He recovered and was back in gear. "Thank you for calling back. Yes. I did – I do. I had wanted to include your response in our story."

When she read the story had it been a total shock, or had the marriage been crumbling? This looked like it could be a follow-up story.

"Well, I have something to say to you."

"Right, then…"

"I am in London next week; Tuesday."

"Yes, all right."

"Tuesday, then. Eleven, at the Savoy?"

"Yes. Eleven would be fine. How…?"

"Just see George the concierge."

"Fine, eleven, then. Look forward to…"

The line had gone dead.

★

George the concierge was Mr Efficiency. Kelly's name instantly switched him into the right gear.

"Mrs Pattimore is in the coffee lounge, Mr Webb." With just a glance he summoned a porter to the desk.

"This way, sir." The porter led him to where Mrs Pattimore was seated.

On his way to the hotel Kelly had pondered on how to greet her. 'Pleased to meet you?' 'So glad you telephoned?' Such courtesies were hardly appropriate from a man who had been more instrumental than anyone else in Fleet Street in damaging her husband's Westminster career. So he just said hello and sat down. She did not smile and he felt, as he had on the phone when she had called him, that she was directing events.

In the photograph of her in the Graphic's picture library she had looked lovely; happy and smiling with her husband at some glittering function. Now she looked much older although the date on the photograph showed it had been taken only two years ago. How could two years have aged her so much? Were the lines on her face the ravages of anger and bitterness?

"I've ordered coffee," she said. "Is coffee all right?"

"Fine, thank you."

From her handbag she took out a bundle of photographs. "I've brought these to show you." It looked like any bundle of pictures that would be put in a family album when someone got round to it. Some were still in the folders they had been in when they came back from the developers.

She started laying them out on the table. When he picked one or two of them up he saw that they were indeed family pictures.

The waiter arrived with the coffee, and she put a £10 note on the tray in such a manner that he did not try to insist on paying.

"That was taken on our wedding anniversary. Our second, we spent it in the Canaries. Time flies!" These last two words were said almost to herself.

Val Pattimore was smiling at the camera and was proudly pregnant. Her husband was standing behind her, grinning over her shoulder, with protective hands on her bulge.

"That was when I was expecting Maria. There is Maria, on her first day at nursery school. That is Robert, playing football for our village team. He dreamed of being a professional, they all do I suppose. He always blamed us for sending him to a school where rugby was the game."

It was polite coffee table talk, without the polite smiles.

Kelly glanced perfunctorily at the other photographs, wishing he had not come.

She poured the coffee, but her movements were awkward and some of it spilled into the saucer.

"I suppose you could have used some of these with your article, Mr Webb. Some of the other papers had photographs of the children from way back. They weren't our photographs. Where do newspapers get pictures like that, Mr Webb? They always seem to. From friends I suppose. Though why would friends think it would help at times like that?"

Kelly sipped his coffee, staying silent

"Not saying, I see. A trade secret."

"What did you want to say to me, Mrs Pattimore?"

"Well, Mr Webb, when I called you I had a very clear idea of what I wanted to see you about, and what I wanted to tell you. I still do, but now I have come to think that whatever I might say will have no effect. In fact I am sure it won't. However, one thing that I wanted to let you know was that we have a wonderful marriage, but thanks to you the world will never think so. Not that I care about the world, but the children … " The sentence trailed away.

She touched one of the photographs. "Maria, there, dotes on her father." There was just the fraction's hesitation. "She still does but no thanks to your article Mr Webb. We are a good family, and they all now know the truth – which has made us a stronger family than ever, although I am sure you did not have our family's welfare on your agenda when you wrote it.

"I suppose if you were to say something to that, and by the look of it Mr Webb, you don't have very much to say, it would be, 'well, Mrs Pattimore, you have a cheating husband so he didn't love you.'

"But that wasn't the point, Mr Webb, even if it was true, which it isn't, which doubtless you will decide not to believe. And just because he was a politician doesn't make it the point. Oh, I know you think it does. Member of the Tory family values party, and all that.

"Well, what about our family values Mr Webb? What does your paper care about the value of our family? We value it. I value it. And whatever the public may think, it is our family, not theirs.

"You may contend that the facts of your story were correct Mr Webb, but facts don't tell the truth. What good do you think it has all done Mr Webb? I can't say that the people I see reading newspapers these last few days look any saintlier than they did before. Do you think all their marriages will be better after reading about mine? You see, the trouble is Mr Webb, you only deal in facts, and selected facts at that. But the truth, Mr Webb, the truth; ah, now there's a different story.

"Well, Mr Webb, I have said rather more than I intended. So sorry to have wasted your time."

She gathered up the photographs. "And I am afraid I have wasted your time Mr Webb because none of what I have told you is for publication. It was just for you. But then I expect you think you have the right to decide on that as well."

She stood up, and Kelly noticed she was unsteady. A secret drinker, perhaps? She remained still for a few seconds, steadying herself before turning to leave. Kelly was sure she would not have welcomed him offering an arm. Then, noticeably slowly, she walked away.

Kelly watched her as she made her way awkwardly across the vast foyer of the famous hotel and, strangely, felt better for having met her despite what had happened. He was a natural man, and womanly women always pleasured his spirit. Although her features had looked drawn, Mrs Pattimore still had that womanly quality, that powerful, beguiling mystery, that Kelly, for all his skill with the written word, could never have adequately defined. It was a quality that made him think of Angela, and whenever he compared a woman favourably with Angela, well… well, you are honoured Mrs Pattimore, and you, Pattimore, are a bastard and I am glad I shafted you.

He sipped his coffee. It was very good, but then for £10 you would expect it to be.

Walking back to the office, Kelly already had in mind another bastard to shaft. McCrae – now if only he could nail that one. It was beginning to frustrate him.

★

The tree-shaded glade was an oasis on the sun-blazed, harvest-shorn hill high above a shimmering sea. Here was their own private paradise, and they entered its shade gratefully. Feeling the cool air on her hot skin, the woman shivered with pleasure. As she stood head thrown back to let the air caress her face the man undressed her. They made love like teenagers, wantonly, selfishly; the latest actors in the oldest story.

Afterwards, as they sat on the high ridge to catch what breeze there was rising from the sea the woman was quiet in the man's arms for a while, then she suddenly voiced the question he was frightened to ask.

"Where's it going to end, my lovely?"

The man did not reply.

— 6 —

Joe's mother pierced the potatoes in the simmering saucepan with a knife. Almost done, and she set about laying the table. Joe's dad was working late tonight but her son would come flying in at any moment, wanting his dinner before dashing off again.

It was always like that these days. A son in love made life hectic for a mother! By now she ought to be used to it but although Joe had been in love as many times as any 18-year-old – about once a week since he was 14 – this latest affair was drama! What with football, rock band practice and girlfriends the lad was hardly ever in the house. Now it was even worse. Being his mother these days was like being a landlady, supplying bed and breakfast and evening meal!

Mrs Fowler drew in a breath and let it out as a sigh. She was not really happy about this latest passion of Joe's. She had refrained from saying anything since he had brought Debbie home, but she was not sure about this. There was that nagging feeling that it would all come to grief.

To Joe's mother it seemed that all the interest was on Joe's side. No, she was not really happy about this. Joe was always trying to please Debbie, spending all his money on presents and taking her to expensive places. Whereas Joe was a typical teenager, Debbie, compared to him, was a mature woman.

Oh, she was a nice enough, and that sweet helpless air about her would make a Sir Galahad of any man. He was a good lad and she did not want to see him messed about. The girl was really very sweet, but – there she went again, always that 'but' when she thought about the pair of them.

Joe's mother sighed again. She knew she must not say anything. Not that it would do any good. Joe was head over heels in love and when you are upside down you cannot see things properly.

Right then Joe proved it as he came flying into the house. Taking his coat off as he came through the door his outstretched arm knocked a vase of flowers over.

"Oh, you clumsy – dinner's ready!"

"I don't want any dinner."

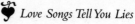 *Love Songs Tell You Lies*

"No dinner!"

"No time. Not tonight. Going out to eat." The reply came down the stairs from the bathroom as Joe changed, brushed his teeth and checked out his good looks in the mirror.

"It's on the table!"

"Oh mum, sorry!"

And that was it. With a quick hug and a cheeky grin Joe was off.

Joe's mother sighed again, philosophically, as she picked up the wasted meal and took it back to the kitchen. It is only mothers who can sigh thus when half an afternoon spent cooking is blithely wasted in this fashion.

With this blessed Debbie, she only hoped it was not going to end in tears. "Well," she said to the kitchen sink, "we'll just have to wait and see what happens, won't we?"

Joe knew what was going to happen. He had been planning it for long enough.

He had booked a table for dinner at a posh (and expensive) restaurant. He was sure this would please Debbie. She had real class. She talked a lot about the theatre, and parties she had been to and the celebrities she had met. Her tales fascinated him. He had been amazed that she had taken to him. Really, he had asked her for a date more as a dare. At any time he was cheeky enough and not afraid to put himself up for it, but he had expected the brush-off.

The age gap did not bother him – why should it? Mum had gone on about it. Well, she had only mentioned it once but mum had a way of mentioning things once that was just as effective as going on about it!

Joe saw the Mercedes parked outside the block of flats where Debbie lived. It was a classy area but a current-year Mercedes would stand out anywhere. That was the kind of car he was going to have one day! Joe pressed the buzzer beside Debbie's flat number and did a little jig as he waited for her to answer. When Joe was in love everything jigged. His heart joined in the jig when Debbie's voice whispered in his ear.

"Hello?"

"Hello. It's me."

"Oh!"

Debbie sounded surprised.

"It's me, Joe."

Again : "Oh." Now she sounded strange.

"It's me. Are you ready? The surprise, remember?" That much he had told her. Anticipation of this evening had been simmering inside him for days.

The intercom crackled and Debbie said something he could not catch.

"Debbie?"

"Oh Joe. Oh dear."

"What's the matter? Aren't you ready yet!"

Something was wrong. "Can I come up to wait?"

"Oh Joe, I can't … Oh God!" There was an awkward silence. Eventually she said: "Oh all right, come up."

The street door lock clicked open and he climbed the stairs with foreboding. What was the matter? He had arranged everything right, he was sure.

That something had gone wrong was plain from Debbie's face when she opened the door of her flat.

"Joe, I'm sorry. I can't come…oh dear."

"Why? What's happened?" Joe remained standing at the door. He had been invited into her flat before, but this time he was being kept on the threshold.

"I … I can't explain now. I'm sorry Joe, I really am. Call me…"

"You've forgotten!"

"No, well, no. Look, I'm sorry but…..actually, I'm not feeling too good," she added, the words trailing away as spur of the moment falsehoods do. She was squeezing the door closed and pulling back, embarrassed and shamefaced.

Joe could not do anything but stand there as the door was closed in his face. There was final insincere "give me a call" and the door clicked shut.

Ross Buchanan looked enquiringly at Debbie as she came back into the lounge. "Who was that? Are you all right?"

"Yes, of course"

"You look upset."

"No, I'm O.K. Give me a few minutes and I'll be ready."

"Don't be long. I want to catch someone before he leaves."

"Oh, who's that?"

"McCrae, Hamish McCrae. The bugger never stays long at these do's. Got to have a word with him."

"You know a lot of important people."

"Have to, if you want to get on. Hurry, Sweetie."

With Joe forgotten, Sweetie hurried.

Outside in the courtyard Joe could not bring himself to leave. He stood there, looking up at the windows of the flat, suspicious, jealous and miserable.

Then the lights in the flat went out. A minute of two later Debbie emerged into the courtyard accompanied by a man. In the dark Joe could only discern that he was tall, but somehow he looked like someone with loads of money. Proof of that was when they got into the Mercedes that glittered expensively under the street lights as it slid away.

More than once in his hot young life Joe had loitered on the streets where girls he had a crush on lived, but always in a fizz of passion that never lasted beyond the next sighting of a pretty face. Now he was hanging round in a sullen jealousy, discovering that love can be a physical pain. A second time he saw Debbie leave with the same man. Again he did not get a good look at him, but he was definitely someone with money - a Mercedes equated with wealth. Joe did not make himself known: there was just a glimmer of hope that it might be all right soon, and Debbie would come back to him. If he did anything silly now he could blow it.

Finally after many days of hanging about the street he tried her bell again, but there was no reply. Thoroughly despondent by now, and not knowing what else to do, he tried the bell of the flat opposite. The occupant told him that Debbie's flat was now empty. "She left a couple of days ago, a new tenant is moving in soon."

It was that bloke in the Mercedes! Debbie had found herself some posh git with money. Not knowing who the man was, not knowing where they had gone, Joe could nothing about it. Given the chance he would! In a twist of fate as random as meeting Debbie in the first place he did.

— 7 —

"Life does not have a plot." It was Bill in a discussion in the Hack and Headline. "There is no story. A story has to have a plot, a third act. Life is like this story, just a daily cock-up." Under discussion was Bill's scoop on Nicholas Cartier and Dolly la Rue that the rest of the media had followed up and turned into a saga.

As far as Frank was concerned it was the best story, plot or no plot, of the week. He would love to have interviewed Dolly, a sparky East End tart, the star of Bill's scoop

"Neat though, wasn't it," chortled Frank, who had ogled the luscious 17-year-old. "She was supposed to be the victim and it is the two blokes who got everything they deserved."

Nicholas Cartier? Even the seen-it-all Press boys were surprised that the patrician politician had dallied with the bra-busting Dolly. Dolly la Rue was not her real name "It's my professional name," she explained pertly to the world on television, and insisted on being addressed as such.

Her real name, as the Press quickly discovered after she and Cartier hit the headlines in the Graphic, was Tracey Potts. Her 'profession' was being nice to rich punters at the Golden Goose Club. Her boyfriend and self-styled manager was small-time spiv Terry Stewkes.

It was when Cartier came to the club with a crowd of upper-crust cronies that Stewkes thought of the scheme that was to ruin the venerable politician's career and scotch the knighthood that until then had been a matter of when, not if.

The scheme was also to ruin Stewkes' source of easy money, which was at least poetic.

Dolly and other girls at the club soon joined Cartier's party and the drinks were flowing profitably. Stewkes immediately spotted Cartier's interest in Dolly. That was when Stewkes started getting ideas above his station but not, as it turned out, above Dolly's.

"Play up to him," he urged Dolly. "He fancies you like mad. This is a chance to get into a bigger league," he wheedled when Dolly scoffed. She was barely 17 but unlike many another wonderfully-endowed young woman her brain had developed apace with her body.

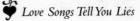

Dolly had no illusions about Stewkes but if she knew what his half-brain was planning, even she would have been shocked. It was not getting a leg-up the society ladder he was interested in, for Dolly or himself. It was blackmail he had in mind.

The way he saw it, it was simple. Bloody 'ell! – the papers were full of stories of politicians resigning, getting divorced, losing their political jobs, all over women. Women were the key to making money, and not just here in the Golden Goose.

It was a mad idea, but it is the lure of big money that gives men mad ideas and the lunacy to act on them.

Cartier as a sugar daddy? No real harm there, surely? Dolly gave it some thought: why not? She was game for anything. She had long known her power over men; but power over men in power, now that was exciting. Like Stewkes, she knew Cartier was going to be easy. And high society sounded fun.

So she set her sexual co-ordinates for Cartier. When he visited the club again he soon found himself sat beside the girl who was to become famous as the Wandsworth Wonder, Lolita of Lambeth or Monroe of Marylebone. (These were the places in London sub editors decided she came from to fit the headlines they dreamed up.) Cartier's intentions had been as innocent as a man's intentions towards a girl like Dolly can ever be. He loved his wife and would never have actively pursued another woman, and certainly not one that stood out, literally, as Dolly did. It was a surprise, and not an unpleasant one, that this bedroom fantasy seem to take to him. Not only was she sexy, she was also jolly good company and he loved her Cockney wit.

He could not recall giving her his number, but soon she was calling him. Just a quiet drink, even a stroll in Green Park seemed to be enough for her. Certainly she did not behave like a gold digger on the make. He was not a fool, if she had been after his money she would have got the old heave ho. She really liked him, that was obvious. It was true, she did. Dolly found the patrician, well-mannered Cartier rather cuddly, sweet. She was enjoying this taste of life Up West.

So was Stewkes. His scheme was going nicely. He had secret videos of them having a drink, snaps of Dolly giving Cartier a kiss. All he needed was something on Cartier in a bed with Dolly and he was in the money.

Dolly had no idea of Stewkes' real intentions. She thought it was just a scheme of his for the pair of them to get into a more lucrative strata of society. Life Up West was a bit of all right. Cartier took her to a quite different London, amazingly different considering it was only a few miles from where she had grown up. Yes, this she definitely liked.

Cartier, the poor man, never stood a chance but Stewkes never did make any money blackmailing him.

Enter Bill Cannon, investigative reporter from the Graphic.

The paper had got a tip-off that Cartier was cheating on his wife. It was a piece of cake to get the story. When Stewkes realised what was about to happen on hearing about Bill's enquiries he made what money he could with an interview for cash. He also gave the Graphic the pictures he had already taken, which included more kisses, a hug and a dance. With them and what Stewkes told them they had a story to publish.

It was disaster for Cartier. He could have survived perhaps if he had fought back. Despite how it seemed, he had not slept with Dolly. For him it just been the fun of her company. Someone working class would find an intimate contact with the upper strata of society fascinating, so why shouldn't that apply in reverse?

But then the really unbelievable happened: his wife left him.

Cartier was stunned. It tore the guts out of him. He had no will to fight, nothing left. Sticking it out, he would have likely survived politically, with maybe just a few months in the wilderness to be media-cleansed. That's the way it is usually done but he resigned, in the old-fashioned, no excuses way he had always accepted as the rule. In any case, he knew that the fact that his wife had left him was proof positive in the eye of the world and his mistress that an affair had taken place.

It was not what he deserved but it was what he expected. Dolly should also have got what was expected, and in her case what she deserved, namely a good slap from the Press and public.

It does not work like that.

Love Songs Tell You Lies

Although it was a disappointment, and she was genuinely quite sorry for Cartier, the whole episode was a big lark.

The cheeky little hussy not only arranged a Press conference but also charged each attendee a fee. The hacks would have given her a tough time anyway, but with the fee they felt even freer (and more inclined) to rough her up.

The effect on television was unseemly. The viewers saw a young girl being crudely harried. What delighted them however was Dolly's lively defence of herself. She decided to meet fire with fire and give these Press buggers some grief. The viewers loved her cockiness and the bright-eyed wit with which she handled the questions.

One brash reporter tried a gambit he thought was on Dolly's level. "The tabloids have described you as a cheap tart on the make," he called out.

"Oh they are behind with the latest news as usual," she cracked. "I'm moving off Cheap Street. The price is going up."

The cameras liked her and she was an instant hit.

Stewkes was quick of the mark and started marketing her like mad. Dolly found this notoriety was her element. Inside she was a hard little bitch on the make, but on the outside she was a luscious bit of stuff with a cheeky smile and a streetwise wit the public loved.

In a week she had made more money from interview fees and chat show appearances than she had in two years at the Golden Goose. Stewkes was ecstatic. But not for long.

He was small time and Dolly was big time. So when media publicist Maxie Persent came offering a contract that promised even bigger earnings she dumped the hapless Stewkes and told him where to shove his pathetic home-made contract.

Stewkes was a spirited little spiv. He got back in touch with the Graphic and sold them another story, this time a pack of lies that Dolly had deliberately set out to snare poor old Cartier.

"She's a little gold-digger," he said.

It was very effective and for 24 hours, until Dolly went in front of the cameras, it looked as though it had put her on the spot.

Not our Dolly; she was a little trouper. She was cut out for showbiz, where gall gets you further than grace and tat further than talent.

Dolly went straight upfront to answer Stewkes' jibes. It was her usual bravura, Cockney wit performance but what topped it all was her answer to a question shouted from the back of the Press pack: "Stewkes says you are a little gold digger – is that right, Dolly?"

With a perfectly timed pause Dolly turned sideways, thrust out her bold boobs, and queried: "Little?"

Then as the raucous laughter drowned out any remaining moral tone she quipped: "Nice girls come second." In an age when an otherwise forgettable politician at Westminster answering well-deserved criticism achieved months, years, of fame for the banal everyday riposte 'They would say that, wouldn't they?' Dolly's mot was sufficiently bon to give her a good couple of years being famous for being famous.

"Bloody good story," was Frank's summary of it all. "Everybody got what they deserved. Cartier, the old lecher resigns, Dolly gets a showbiz career, we get the chance to look at her boobs regularly, and that creep Stewkes got his comeuppance."

Dolly never lost her wits or her way. Before the poundage accumulated she married poundage.

The Graphic's fearsome columnist Penelope Hawn savaged Cartier. Hawn tore him apart for betraying a loyal wife and depicting her as the woman who now had to face the last years of her life finding her own identity, her own reason for living, after a lifetime as the dutiful wife of a career politician. Poor Mrs Cartier, another one of the hardly-noticed, never properly appreciated political appendages of so many selfish men in Parliament, etcetera; brilliant, biased, coruscating etcetera.

One columnist, a man, did point out that Cartier was a great loss to politics where there was a shortage of wise and politically honourable men. Among all the gleeful Dolly-oriented hoo-hah his article had the usual impact of a reasonable point of view: none.

And Frank was wrong; Cartier was the one who did not get everything he deserved. But then Frank believed what he read in newspapers.

"Life is not a morality tale and has no plot," said Bill. "Ours is just to do and sigh."

— 8 —

"Hello."

At the other end of the line his response was alight with pleasurable recognition: "Oh, hello!"

Peggy was silent for a moment, gathering herself. Her decision was still so fresh, it took getting used to.

Pattimore probed the silence. "Hello?"

"I'm still here."

"Good, better still if you were here. How are you?"

"You remember, you asked me to come and live with you?"

"An unhappy memory. You said no."

"Yes, well...I've changed my mind, if the offer is still there. Is it?"

Decency advised against, but decency never won another man's wife.

"Yes!"

Within the hour she was with him, her life irrevocably changed in sixty minutes.

As soon as she got through the door he hugged and hugged and hugged her until, with her laughing and gasping for breath, he had to let her go.

"I suppose after Val died, all I ever needed was a little push," she said.

"I was always ready to catch you."

He made a pot of tea and when they were seated to drink it, just like the two long time lovers they were, he said: "Now I want to tell you something." Smiling so she would not think it was going to be anything bad he proceeded to tell her.

"Val always knew about you."

All she could do was assimilate this in silence.

"Right from the start, almost. She knew about you, and in fact knew you, having seen you at some function somewhere."

Still she stayed silent. He continued: "That bloody nonsense. It was a business trip that at the time I wanted to keep confidential and that bloody woman" – he could not bring himself to say her name – "arranged the hotel for me and when I got there I found she had booked herself in as well. She just made out she thought it was what I wanted. I was annoyed but could hardly kick up a fuss. Nothing went on, I just changed rooms.

"Then all those grotesque lies she told about us having – uh! There's something wrong with the woman. Anyway, I just had to stay silent. Val was in no condition for any more pain. She knew, we both knew, that it was all lies and what anybody else thought didn't matter. And you believed me. That's all that mattered. So, it was to hell with everyone else!

"But Val always knew about you, and it was then she told me. I was, oh, stunned, but she said she did not mind. Because of…because of her illness, the physical side of our….well, she simply did not mind about you. In fact in a way she was pleased. She liked you, and when that wretched woman and her lies got us talking she said then she hoped you and I would, well, this, this is what she hoped, and she told the children never to blame me or you."

Now there were tears in his eyes. "Love is a very strange thing my darling. Very strange. Where would we be without it?"

Throughout all this extraordinary explanation she sat silent and amazed. When he finally stopped speaking all she could do, her own tears welling, was to reach out across the table and take his hand.

★

Cartier seemed much smaller than the man of a few weeks ago. Ted had felt guilty when pretending friendship while he and Peggy were having their affair. He felt worse now, offering comfort to the man he himself had cuckolded.

"What are we going to do Ted? She's gone."

"Give it time Nicholas. She's in shock. It's not as if you had an affair. It was just, well, all blown up by that bloody newspaper."

"That's not why Ted."

"Give her time Nicholas. She just needs time."

All these years he had wanted Peggy to leave Nicholas, now she had. Now she was free. Ted just kept talking. Peggy had left Nicholas. He had his chance at last!

"Nicholas, this bloody Dolly thing is not going to be enough to break you two up, not after all these years. She will come back. She just needs some space, some time." Black feared Cartier must surely detect the hollow insincerity in his voice.

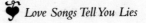

"That's not why, Ted," Cartier repeated. "That's not why!"

Ted shook his head in puzzlement. "What's not why? What do you mean?"

"Not Dolly, not that little tart. That's not why she's left me."

"I don't understand. If it's not…then…?"

"There's someone else, another man Ted."

Black sat stone still. Another man? Who? Ted's stomach was churning painfully, his head in a whirl. What was Cartier about to say?

Black echoed stupidly: "Another man?"

"Ted, she only stayed with me because she felt oh, God, because she could not desert someone who did not deserve it. The note, it was all so …but anyway now she's left, gone."

"When did you learn this?"

"Tonight, barely an hour ago."

"An hour? She's just upset, perhaps…." Ted's emotions could be likened to those of someone who has heard the lottery numbers and is positive they have them all, but the ticket is at home – they think! Peggy said she could never hurt Nicholas, but now she had left him because of his stupidity over that Dolly tart. Peggy was free!

"I don't know what to say Nicholas. Who, I mean…."

"I think you know."

"I know?" Black was uncomfortably aware that Cartier was regarding him closely.

"I think you know."

Black was unable to answer.

Then Cartier said: "You know him. Pattimore. Peter Pattimore."

"What!"

"Pattimore She's left me for Pattimore."

"Pattimore!"

Cartier mistook Black's shock as concern for him.

"Apparently it has been going on for some time."

The two men sat staring bleakly at each other.

Then after a moment Cartier said: "Thanks for your support Ted. It's good to have you around."

Around: the very last nowhere place Black wanted to be.

"Did you see this piece on McCrae, Kelly?" The SS Squad were taking a coffee break.

Kelly had earlier seen the item on the MP in the newspaper his colleague was reading. Hamish McCrae was once again being linked to another woman. Not quite an expose, just one of those 'look who's been seen with who' gossip column items.

"You're after McCrae, aren't you Kelly? What happened about that girl?"

"Disappeared. She wouldn't talk."

"This fellow Reynolds seems to get a lot of stories about McCrae," someone else remarked, referring to the by-line on the story they were discussing. "Who is he?"

Bill knew, as usual. "He's a freelance, sells to the highest bidder." Bill indicated the paper the other had been reading. "Usually that rag."

Andrew Reynolds been writing quite a few well-informed reports lately on McCrae. Kelly had a regard for freelances, himself having done that stint freelancing before joining the Graphic. It was a tough game with one rule: survival of the fittest. Their motives might be mercenary, but Kelly believed that as they prowled the corridors of conceit, they did more for democracy than a dozen politicians.

Reynolds obviously had a good inside line on McCrae. He was giving his rivals a run for their money and with a rueful smile to himself Kelly acknowledged the fellow's ability - or luck! But the game was far from over and Kelly was convinced he would get the big story on this one.

His conviction was quite illogical - he did not even know where that girl was now. Illogical, but somehow he felt lucky. Her name had slipped his mind, but it was in his notes.

Eventually McCrae would slip up. That girl may have disappeared, but there would be others. With someone like McCrae it was a certainty. McCrae was the most obnoxious man he had ever met. Sure, any foot in the door reporter gets plenty of mouth; it was part of the job. Notwithstanding, somehow McCrae had got to him.

On one occasion Kelly had tried to talk to McCrae's wife, but McCrae had prevented him. The MP had said in that sneering voice of his: "I don't want you to talk to my wife" when Kelly had tried to contact her.

'I bet you don't want me to talk to any of your mistresses either,' thought Kelly, 'but I will Mr Bloody Obnoxious McCrae. You can bank on it'. That very brief conversation had left him with a greater determination to bring McCrae down.

What had really got to Kelly was the girl to whom his colleague had been referring. Once he had traced her and they were face to face, he damn well knew, gut-feelingly knew, that she had had an affair with the sneering McCrae, but she just would not talk to him. She had been a nice young woman, with a vulnerable appeal. Kelly could see she was not from McCrae's social strata. There was a simplicity about her, an honesty.

Kelly had felt strongly about that young woman's plight. She had answered the door wearing a loosely-tied dressing gown, but Kelly had been sure she was pregnant. As they talked she adjusted her gown, revealing a glimpse of her breasts, full and rounded, oozing sensuality. The breasts of a pregnant woman.

Being near her had made Kelly acutely aware of the amazing power women can have over men. He was himself stirred and had felt protective.

McCrae, a man of fortune and power: she, innocent and vulnerable; basic ingredients for life's melodramas.

Reading that latest McCrae story revived those chivalrous feelings again. Why such a nice young woman would want to have anything to do with the decidedly unattractive McCrae was beyond Kelly. Concerning women when is male chivalry justice or jealousy? All Kelly knew was that he had wanted to rough up McCrae with a story all the more after meeting her. But she had kept him on the doorstep. Sorry, she had said. Thank you. No anger, no hostility; just weary resignation.

Sorry. Thank you. Door gently closed.

He had offered his name and telephone number. She had taken his card but he knew she would not call him, and she didn't.

I'll have McCrae one day, Kelly had promised himself. It was a promise he was going to keep sooner than he hoped.

Toby Morrison had read the same story about McCrae that morning. He had been dithering and it made up his mind.

★

"Good yarn on Halpman, I'll give you that," conceded the reporter, bringing Kelly's mind back to the present. "Looks like the woman he had it off with was on the revenge trail – or was she getting paid?"

"Yes, she did a deal with the paper," said Kelly. "It was easy. I was on their tail, and Halpman thought he had gone to ground and was safe, but she talked."

"The cow!"

Kelly's expression was theatrically worldly-wise. "Money."

"What would we do without it," said the reporter, grinning broadly. "And sex of course."

Bill slipped in his contribution: "Money and sex. Mix together, publish and be rich."

Kelly had not enjoyed doing the story. There was no ferreting out the facts; no challenge. The hapless Halpman had lost his marbles over a woman a quarter his age. The eternal middle-aged man daftness. The illicit pair had spent a weekend in a New Forest hotel and a waiter there had made an easy few quid tipping off the Graphic. As soon as Kelly was put on the story Halpman went to ground and his wife went to live with relatives. However the scarlet woman faced the music and confessed all to the Press. For cash – surprise, surprise.

One of Halpman's friends confronted Kelly to get the story killed. "It's just a piece of silly middle-aged nonsense," he had protested, trying to talk man to man. "It was only one isolated mistake. He is distraught."

"It's out of my hands, it's with the editor now," Kelly had replied.

"It was you that started it!" Halpman's friend retorted, letting his anger show now he could see supplication was useless. "Without you, nothing would have happened! His marriage would still be intact!"

No reply.

"It will kill the poor man," Halpman's friend had stormed. "He won't be able to take it."

Still no answer. Anyway Kelly had heard that kind of plea before.

Then realising he was flogging a dead horse the man made a contemptuous gesture towards Kelly. "God help you, you must spend all your time in the gutter!" He turned on his heel and stalked off and was not meant to hear Kelly's response, which was spoken to himself: "No, not all of it, only when I'm working."

"Nice way to make money," observed the reporter. "Modern blackmail – have an affair with a married politician and then sell your story. Neat, eh?"

"They ask for what they get," said Kelly.

"You know, a lot of these affairs are caused because the woman targets the man. Yet it is always the man who figures as the villain. That's not fair."

"May it ever remain so."

"Oh? Why is that Kelly?"

"Leave us one illusion at least!"

The reporter digested this, than agreed with bravado: "Yeah, they say men are being emasculated; let's at least keep the right to be the bastard!"

★

Catherine McCrae was admired her for her skills as a social hostess and political wife. She knew how it would be before they were married but she nevertheless did wonder during the first months whether it was worth it. She had not fully prepared herself for the conjugal aspect of her decision. Of course there had been intimacy before they married. It should have been warning enough that the price she was going to have to pay for the good life was too high. She had bargained that lying back and thinking of Scotland, or at least that particularly nice part of Scotland, would be an anaesthetic. She found out what so many women who marry for greed find out: it is not worth it. Feigning tiredness and headaches and with the help of a woman's traditional holiday from a boring husband Catherine avoided sex. It meant McCrae often had to wait weeks for what he considered his conjugal rights. Finally, after an evening of drinking, he returned home, his patience at an end, and tried to claim them. Catherine however was as physically robust as she was mentally determined, and fought him off.

Shaking with anger and disgust she spat at him: "Try that again, and I will have you for rape!"

Shocked and equally angry he bellowed: "You're my wife, damn you! Rape? You're ..." Words nearly choked him. This was unbelievable! "Rape? Damn you, woman, you're my wife!"

"That gives you no right to rape! So damn you!"

"Rape! How can it be rape? You're mad – mad! No one would believe you!"

"Wouldn't they? Just try me. I will not stand for it. Try it again, and I'll call the police. Rape! That's what you just attempted. Don't you dare! Don't you ever...." Now it was Catherine who choked on her words.

"Don't ever touch me again!" she stormed, and her husband now in name only realised that she meant it.

If she carried out her threat his political career was over. True or not, found guilty or not, he was finished. It was blackmail; not provable, not defendable. The perfect crime.

After that shocking night he was sullenly silent for a week. Then making a superhuman effort – with his nature that was it required – he tried to find the way back to what he thought they had, little as it was. But his ego-lumbered efforts at reconciliation were pathetic and hopeless.

There was no way back; there had never been any 'there' in the first place.

There were rows and threats and pleadings but she was a woman who did not desire this man. It was a wilderness and he was lost in it. She stood her ground, knowing that politically he needed her at his side.

"Take a mistress," she screamed at him. "Do what you like!"

Catherine had set out her stall. Things might be somewhat worse than she had expected, but otherwise her life in that privileged seam of society had the advantages she craved. Marrying McCrae had been a way into that kind of society and with greedy haste she had taken it.

She loved the estate, and in the Edinburgh and London social circles that she graced so effortlessly she made many friends. The contrast between her and her dour husband was very sharp. She was charming and attractive, he was neither, and the gossips were on her side.

Her charm helped McCrae enormously in his Westminster ambitions. When he had asked her to marry him he had been in love, but emotion had not affected his political acumen and he realised that the popular and socially affable Catherine would be a career asset.

He got that part of the package at any rate.

Thanks to Catherine's friends society reporters were never short of biased updates on the McCraes. Journalists know how to harp on about something in such a way as to leave no doubt without incurring a libel action.

Innuendo became information.

The world and his mistress knew only what they read in the newspapers. Don't believe everything you read in the papers. That is what everybody says, but it is not what everybody does.

Toby Morrison believed what he read.

～ 9 ～

The party was one of the regular political circuit affairs where, as Bill once put it, the great and good meet to find someone great in bed or good for a favour. They were networking in fashionable buzz language; scheming, in plain English.

The paste-on smiles were dazzling and everyone was having a great time oozing insincerity. Buchanan had been sure it would be the perfect atmosphere in which to do business with McCrae, but it was not working out well. Something was disturbing the politician's concentration, and he kept looking around. Buchanan was aiming to earn a big commission for getting a decent chunk of the Euro Air Shuttle contract put the way of his business associates, and McCrae who was both a director in EAS and had political influence, was the man to suck up to.

Buchanan was very hopeful of a result. Neither man had ever particularly liked the other ever since their public school days, but as greedy and socially ambitious people they had to bear the cross of suffering those with money or influence. In that spirit he and McCrae had shared a few bottles and bedded the same women. Never true friends – who was with McCrae? – they had nevertheless always understood each other as vultures of a feather. Thus Buchanan was confident he could rely on McCrae's help.

Normally McCrae was a single-minded listener when it came to political and business intrigue, always applying the predatory concentration that was his hallmark. Now however he clearly only had half an ear for what Buchanan was saying. Suddenly the politician started smiling, an event rare enough to halt Buchanan in mid-sentence. The reason was immediately evident, as Debbie came up to them in her hesitant, shy manner. Buchanan had grown used to seeing the interest Debbie aroused in other men, and he could well understand it – now. As a regular and very successful womaniser, he had simply entered into the relationship with Debbie in the impatient, let's get to bed, fashion of the day. Rather to his surprise, he found he had become quite fond of her.

Unlike the hard worldly-wise totty that is always to be found where

the high rollers roll, Debbie was endearingly different. She was slight, softly-built, with an eager-to-please smile. Other men, he soon noticed, also found her appealing.

McCrae's blatant interest caused a sharp stab of jealousy that surprised him. Buchanan hopped from bed to bed as frequently McCrae, but Debbie had become a bit special. In years of back-scratching Buchanan and McCrae had passed the occasional woman around. Certainly Buchanan would repay a favour by introducing a woman he knew McCrae had an eye on. McCrae in turn helped Buchanan in his business dealings. So far they had, as with thieves, stayed thick.

But in the case of Debbie things went wrong.

"You must introduce us," McCrae said, his eyes fixed on Debbie, and Buchanan did as he was bid, although with misgiving.

Buchanan was hoist because of the importance of the shuttle contract, and had to spend the rest of the evening behind a false smile as he watched McCrae dancing with Debbie. What made it harder was that he had to concede, with surprise, that Debbie herself appeared captivated by McCrae. Instinct proved to be spot on, as Debbie was taken from him with a brutal swiftness.

Leaving Buchanan seething, McCrae escorted Debbie to the foyer where he instructed the car jockey to fetch his car. The evening air was pleasant, and they chatted on the pavement in front of the hotel while they waited for the car jockey to bring McCrae's Mercedes to the door.

Almost as a routine McCrae would normally have suggested they went to a hotel. Instead he asked: "May I see you again?"

"That would be lovely," Debbie replied. McCrae smiled at her, and it was the start of a relationship that was as near to courtship that he could manage.

★

Julie clung happily to Joe's arm as they strolled along from Piccadilly towards the Green Park Underground. "It's been a lovely evening Joe."

"Yeah, it's been good," Joe agreed. So it had, and he gave her a hug. Julie was growing on him, and they had become close in the past few months. After the affair of Debbie, Julie was exactly the girl Joe needed. Her affection and loyalty was the stuff lasting marriages are made of; she was so different to the kind of girl Joe used to pursue. Julie was good for him, he knew that – his mum also knew it, or thought she did as usual! It had been Julie's affection that had helped him get over Debbie. Joe was still too young to appreciate the fact, but women have a God-given ability to get the Joe's of this world to rely on them. Anyway, Julie was a great kid and was going to make him a good wife. The fates arrange these things Joe. A lot worse can happen to you son, a lot worse.

"One night I'll take you to dinner, somewhere posh like this place," said Joe grandly, indicating the plush frontage of a hotel they were approaching.

They paused and Julie looked up at the hotel's facade. "Very nice," she was saying. "But it will cost a fortune!"

But Joe was not listening.

His fantasising had been stopped dead in its tracks. Standing on the pavement in front of him was Debbie, glamorous in evening attire. With her was a tall man whose hawkish face wore a haughty expression.

Then a gleaming Mercedes pulled up. The car jockey opened the door for them and doffed the brim of his gold-braided cap as he deftly accepted a banknote from the man. Then he stepped out into the road to see them out into the evening traffic.

By the time they got to the Underground Julie noticed Joe had gone quiet.

"Are you all right?" she asked.

"Yes, fine."

The man had been a lot older than Debbie and bloody ugly! Is that what money can do? From the man's appearance he was well loaded – the Mercedes proved that. Mixed painfully with his jealousy was anger that Debbie loved money so much she could go out with an ugly bugger like that, but his anger could not sustain. As they waited for the train Julie clung happily to Joe's arm, but Joe was thinking about Debbie and he would have forgiven her anything.

★

Within days the story of how Buchanan had lost Debbie to McCrae

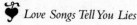

was making the rounds. When acquaintances, with insincere commiseration, asked him what had happened, slyly hoping to be entertained with a display of anger from a loser, he affected nonchalance. Debbie had not meant anything to him.

Until then Buchanan had never allowed himself to be greatly bothered at having to creep round McCrae, whose born-with-it arrogance, honed to perfection by wealth and power, made him insufferable even to people as insufferable as himself. Buchanan needed him, and while he was the man with the power and could do him favours he was prepared to kiss arse. Business is business.

In regard to just another woman Buchanan could have accepted the situation with insouciance. With his record, it was a certainty that he would have dumped Debbie sooner or later. Yet she had managed to briefly reach some part of him that was not all shit. Losing her to McCrae in such an humiliating manner had shaken his chauvinistic ego.

He was helpless to do anything about it. What he would like to do to that bastard, though! And, in a way that was to fill him with secret triumph, he got his chance.

For the very reasons that he had remained on good terms with McCrae he was friendly with Catherine. Buchanan was a lecher, and Catherine had always taken his eye. Buchanan knew that here was a woman who would not be averse to taking a lover but he had always considered it was a bit too close to home for an affair. Until now he had not dared risk this very useful political contact by seducing his wife. So he had contented himself with flirty looks and smirky smiles and she responded in kind, and no more than that.

Now all that was changed. Now Buchanan was a man who was determined to avenge his honour. The fact that he had none did not occur to him.

This was how he could get his revenge, and he set out to seduce Catherine, solely to get back at her husband. It turned out to be easy. Catherine was between lovers and because of the ease with which she could conduct an affair Buchanan got lucky.

It was a case of deceivers deceiving a deceiver, and for many years to come the events that ensued from that tangle of conceits and deceits were to be regurgitated at many a two-hour Whitehall lunch.

So the world had a pretty poor opinion of McCrae. He was a difficult man to interview, his attitude towards the Press supercilious. The result was that the coverage of his political life was mostly unfavourable. Between the lines readers were given to understand that this M.P was not a good advert for Tory family values. Indeed it was true that McCrae did not give up sex just because love had given him up. He carried on his sex life the way he carried on his political life, the latter behind the locked doors of the corridors of power, the other behind the discreet doors of tucked-away country hotels.

It was a sexual system that he had perfected. Nothing went wrong and it would have remained that way if he had not met Debbie. Had they known about her, McCrae's former mistresses would have been astounded. That little mouse! None of them, those bed-swap, sex-circuit women, had ever lasted more than a month or two.

The two were totally incompatible on paper; the one a naïve girl out of her social depth; the other a worldly self-obsessed man who treated women with scant regard. McCrae could not express even to himself why Debbie was important to him. The analysis of politics was more comfortable than self-analysis. It was as perfect a relationship as any could be with McCrae.

Then Debbie became pregnant.

She was delighted, thinking of the child as a bond between them. He was frightened, and dumped her. Losing her was nothing compared to the fear for his political ambitions. On top of a generous sum of money he added enough for the abortion he instructed her to have. Then, money having solved the problem, he turned his back on her.

A number of newspapers did their damndest to get the story, but could never safely nail it down. The only reporter who traced Debbie and almost got her to talk was a man from the Graphic. She had liked him. He was a nice man, not at all like the brash foot-in-the-door reporters she had seen in television soaps.

It had been very hard not to confide; he had a way with him. But she remembered to say nothing. Hamish had hammered that point

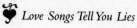

into her before they parted. So she had remained silent, hoping time would change things. No normal person would ever understand how such an emotionally desolate man as McCrae could come to replace all others in the life of this sweet young woman, but then such things are beyond explanation. She believed Hamish loved her and that this situation was forced on him. In time things might get better. There seemed no alternative but to hope they would.

The reporter had left his name, Webb, and asked her to call him if she changed her mind. But she never did, and had mislaid his business card long since. After that Debbie just disappeared from the scene and neither that nice reporter nor any of the other newshounds could find her.

～ 10 ～

Morrison was surprised himself how after all that time he was still determined to get even with McCrae. The insult had cut deep, but he thought the wound had healed. Not once had he mentioned that episode since and neither had any of his colleagues. He had always been a loner in the office. There had been no words of support from anyone, although he knew damn well that they had also had enough of McCrae. When he had stood up to him he was only doing what many of the staff would have liked to do if only they had the guts.

There had been an added nastiness that galled him: not only being keenly aware of a lack of support from anyone, but also sensing the suppressed smirks. It was jealousy, of course. He had been progressing rapidly and was getting noticed. People love it when someone like him gets in trouble.

Morrison had had the confidence of a man on the rise. He was running his section, and habitually sat in on top-level meetings. He worked all the hours needed to ensure everything ran to perfection. There was no one who could tell him how things were done in Whitehall. McCrae thought otherwise, and not only with regard to Morrison. Everyone was treated in a lordly manner, their wisdom and experience simply McCrae's scullery maids.

'Patience,' murmured senior colleagues, 'ministers come and go, but we go on forever'. Perhaps! But if they all keep coming, fumed Morrison inwardly, and each one behaved like the bull-brained McCrae, then it would be intolerable!

So he had stood up to the overbearing minister. Smooth, diplomatic; oh yes, he knew well enough how to make his point very effectively behind the Whitehall smile. He had expected support and approval, discreet but effective, from his colleagues. He misjudged that, but more to his misfortune he misjudged McCrae. Morrison found himself sidelined in the office. He was no longer called to important meetings. The word got back to him loud and clear that while McCrae was minister he was no longer persona grata. "I do not want that pompous fool in this office!" McCrae had

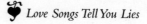

snarled, and that remark got back to Morrison thanks to gleeful colleagues. He had never thought much before whether he was popular, or even liked. Now he knew he was not. How is it you know when someone is hiding a grin when you pass by, or has just switched one off when you turn around? Morrison knew.

And his superiors were right; ministers come and go. Prime Minister Adam Crichel was leading a Conservative government reeling from one sex or cash scandal after another and it needed a new image. Haplessly, all he could think of doing was to re-shuffle the well-worn pack of usual suspects and McCrae lost his job.

After McCrae departed Morrison's career continued on its rise, yet the encounter with a man he found so obnoxious left a bruise. The incident still rankled. God, how it rankled! Obnoxious toad of a man! Quite extraordinary that someone like McCrae could ever manage to persuade a woman like Catherine to marry him. Not his money, he was sure of that.

Morrison had met Catherine several times at official functions and she was far too fine a person to marry for money – far too attractive, anyway, to need to. Far too attractive! How had she ever managed to stomach marriage to McCrae? It was baffling, but he knew women made these mistakes. He admired her for making the best of what must have been an awful situation.

Catherine McCrae had certainly made an impression on him. Once he had managed to arrange to be seated next to her at a charity lunch. It was an evening he was never to forget. Back at his lonely flat later that night he had drifted to sleep thinking of her.

After that humiliating episode with McCrae one of his fondest and frequent fantasies was discovering that Catherine was madly in love with him, and they indulged in a torrid affair. 'Why couldn't I have met you before I married that pig?' she sighed into his ear as they lay in bed.

Instead McCrae got the sack as minister. Morrison rarely saw Catherine after that, but he still had his dreams.

And something else: a photocopy of a letter in a neat, feminine hand. The opportunity to gain revenge on McCrae had actually arisen before Morrison had any desire for it. McCrae had only been appointed a few weeks when Morrison came across the letter. Up to then Morrison had not crossed personalities with the new minister.

For such an important letter, one that needed to be kept well away from prying eyes, it was an extraordinary slip on McCrae's part. But these things happen. It was among papers the minister had left on his desk. Quite what it was that made it jump into his eye, Morrison did not know, but it immediately looked very interesting. A family letter? He caught the words 'Your son is doing well' then the bit that nailed his attention 'if you are interested!'

He could not risk being caught reading the letter. Without any conscious thought in his head he was at the photocopier, had copied it, and the letter was back on the minister's desk. He had left the office sweating, heart beating as though he was a thief. It was astonishing what he had done, and knew he should not read any more of the letter.

He waited until he was home that evening before he did.

It was just signed 'Debbie', and had been written in short plain sentences as though the writer wanted to tell McCrae only what he had to know. She had moved to a different address. As she could not contact him at his home 'for obvious reasons', and he had instructed her never to telephone, she had to write to him at his office. She hoped that marking the envelope strictly personal was sufficient precaution.

Then unaccountably and stupidly he had left it behind with other papers!

The letter ended with 'You can send the maintenance money to my new address from now on.' and was signed without love and kisses.

Morrison knew he ought to destroy the copy of the letter, put it out of his mind. It was not his business. Instead he put it in a locked drawer, the neat and methodical man as usual. Everything properly filed away and no hasty action until he had made his mind up.

Then came the humiliating episode with McCrae and that made it up. The following weekend he went to the London suburb where Debbie lived and set about finding out more about her. It was something to do with his spare time as much as anything. Outside

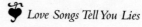

his job he did not have any interests. He did not go near the address on the letter but by visiting pubs and cafes in the vicinity he found out her surname, that she was on her own and had one child. It was so easy, never asking any direct questions, just chatting to the locals. He should have been a private detective. It was the most exciting thing he had ever done. It was a good feeling; he was secure, like a man in a dangerous situation but secretly toting a gun.

'You know what, Morrison,' a colleague had once said to him. 'If ever you commit a murder, it will be the perfect murder. I've never known anyone to plan and think out all the pros and cons of a situation as minutely as you do!'

The colleague had not spoken admiringly but Morrison had not noticed that. He had taken it as a compliment.

His colleague was right. Thought and counter thought, consideration and contra consideration. That was how he worked. When he had been stung by McCrae's insulting treatment of him he had intended to send a copy of Debbie's damning letter to the Press. Photocopying the letter on a machine in another office so as not to be seen, he was careful not to leave incriminating evidence. The times he had used the office copier and found the document copied previously – often confidential material – had been left in the machine.

Then he pondered again and again as to how he could get the letter delivered to a newspaper without it being traced back to the department. If it were, there would be only a short list of people who could have found it on McCrae's desk. Of them all, he would certainly be the first suspect to jump to everyone's mind.

Of course he must post it in a postal district well away from Whitehall, preferably even well outside London. Fingerprints! He would have to make sure it was wiped clean. But what if he had left ink traces on it when he first found it? These days forensic science was amazing. So he went back and carefully photocopied it again and again, searching for a copy that was readable but faint. That would do the trick. Or would it?

And so on and so on.

Then McCrae was sacked as minister and Morrison dithered for a

― 11 ―

They were having one of their regular girls' nights out, and it was well into the evening. Flushed with wine, loud and laughing, they had taken over their corner of the pub. It was a happy sight, and their merriment had attracted the flirtatious attention of a group of men. In particular one of them, who had 'ladies man' stamped all over him, had, despite a distinct lack of encouragement, become very interested in one of the women. Twice his offer to buy her a drink had been declined. When his mates ribbed him he affected nonchalance but it was nevertheless plain to see that his ego was dented.

Slender and very feminine, the woman he had his eye on was one of those women who arouse the envy of rivals with their effortless ability to look elegant in whatever they wear. In repose, in serious mien, the woman's charm was not showily obvious. In that mood, although certainly attractive, she was not eye-catchingly beautiful. Several of her companions had bolder good looks.

Tonight in this company however, she was neither in repose nor serious, and the qualities that drew men to her like bees to a flower were very evident. She was bright and animated and there was an allure in her glance, the divine feminine mischief that leads men to doom or delight; the look that is like the flash of sunlight that can mysteriously and instantly spark a dormant seed to life.

She had a way, especially when, as tonight, with her and her companions in a gay mood, of regarding a man with a certain smile; a smile that could arrow unerringly into his heart. Seeing her in this mood, even a man happy with his own woman might well pause for a moment to savour temptation, and most did.

The two groups were indulging in flirtatious cross-banter, and the good-looking man's attempts to make time with her had become centre stage. Taking it all in good heart for the sake of the occasion, the woman had nevertheless pointedly avoided eye contact with him tonight. One unwary moment on a previous evening in the pub had been more than enough.

"You men are all the same," one of the women accused the blithe bunch of men. "When you are out, you can't be trusted. I know some of your wives - I'll tell them a thing or two when I see them!" Their ribald laughter all but drowned out the protest of the man that he wasn't married, but one of the woman's companions heard him. "Oh, he's available - play your cards right Kathy and you could be in luck."

The response to that was an evasive grimace. She was now regretting that previous occasion, that unwise moment when she had not kept up her guard, but the man remembered it very well.

On that occasion too Kathy had been in jolly company and had turned and caught his eye. He was on close terms with his mirror and was confident of his technique at picking up women. She had been dealt his Sunday-best smile.

For just a moment, seeing his undisguised interest, she - perhaps with vanity - had returned his smile. She had then looked away, immersed in merriment with her friends, with whom she was clearly very popular. Brief as it was, that alluring glance had hooked him like a fish. For the rest of that evening he had tried to catch her eye time and again. To his vain surprise and unaccustomed disappointment she always looked away quickly, that blood-stirring smile now cool, eyes properly veiled.

This evening her companion, thinking it great fun, egged her on.

"He's not bad looking, Kathy. Jackie knows him, and she says he has a good job at County Hall."

The man guessed they were talking about him and, encouraged, again tried to insinuate himself with keen glances. When she still did not respond he found an opportunity to ask her friend if she was single. Deciding that she had teased Kathy enough, she lied: "She's getting married, and she already has four kids!"

Resigned at last to defeat, the man turned his attention elsewhere. Unfortunately for Kathy the man did not switch his attentions to the right quarter. One of the others, a plain woman named Bella, had been witnessing with a sour face his obvious interest in Kathy. On several previous occasions when Bella had seen the man in clubs and pubs she had made eyes at him, but he had never shown the slightest interest in her.

Once in drink she was noted for her loud voice and her propensity for making comments full of all-to-obvious innuendo regarding anyone or anything that had upset her. The man's total lack of interest in her upset her well enough, but the fact that he now plainly preferred Kathy to her was absolutely infuriating. It fanned a long-smouldering resentment, intensified by the bitterness of a woman who craved the sexual fortune her personality denied her.

There had always been an edge between them, even before Bella's husband, now long since the other name on their divorce documents, had become too interested in Kathy. It had all been imagination, both in the case of her husband who had not stood the slightest chance with the delectable young Kathy, and with his jealous-blind wife.

Unreasoning jealousy of Kathy had existed since their schooldays when the boy Bella fancied madly, Robert, had been Kathy's slave. It was all Kathy, Kathy - and how she used to put it on airs! Robert was putty in her hands. She never left him alone. He never really wanted her, otherwise why did he leave her? It was Kathy, always determined to get whoever she wanted; throwing herself at him!

When Kathy's marriage with Robert broke up, Bella's husband began making a fool of himself over her. First he tried to pretend he was offering friendly help, such as do-it-yourself work on her house, but once Kathy perceived his real intentions she cut him dead. Thick as a pile of bricks, he took some dissuading. By this time his own shallow marriage was tottering, due not to his behaviour towards Kathy but because he and Bella were two of a kind; ugly-natured and self-centred.

Nasty in nature, and greenly jealous, the soon-to-be-ditched Bella had been all too ready to believe Kathy was to blame, and not her husband. The two women moved on into different social circles, but it was a small town and because they had some mutual acquaintances there were occasions, such as tonight, when they could not avoid each other.

Here was Kathy spoiling it for her again! The burning jealousy of those immature times had remained but it had only smouldered, with no occasion to spark it. Now, having to watch the man she fancied showing such naked interest in that damn woman was stoking up more fury than she could contain.

While Bella simmered in her own bile, the rest of their crowd were merrily discussing the day's news of the wedding of an American billionaire to a nubile Hollywood beauty.

"Now I ask you," one woman sounded forth, "If he was an ordinary bloke, would he get himself a bride like that?"

"Well, if she was an ordinary-looking girl, would she get a rich bloke like him," countered another, and that set everyone off, eager to add their pennyworth.

"Can't blame him."

"Or her. Give me a chance!"

Under cover the of their lively discussion Kathy took umbrage with the woman who had joshed with the persistent man.

"Why on earth did you tell him I'm getting married? Four children!"

"I was only trying to help. I could see you didn't fancy him, Kathy. Sorry!" Not that sorry, as her friend was laughing. "I thought it would put him off."

Despite the loud chatter, one of the others overheard. "What's that? Kathy getting married?"

"Oh God, I wished I hadn't said anything!" Kathy threw her hands up in exasperation, while all her friends were immediately agog at what seemed a juicy bit of news.

"No! No! Of course I'm not getting married. Oh, for goodness sake!"

Everyone laughed at her embarrassment while her friend did her best to explain the misunderstanding

That was the point when sourpuss ruined the evening for her. "She doesn't need to get married," Bella said loudly.

If the remark had got swallowed up in the hubbub, it would have done little harm. But unfortunately someone on her fourth or fifth gin and tonic decided to ask Bella what she meant: "Kathy? Why not?"

"Ask Lesley!"

"Lesley? What's Lesley got to do with it?" the same woman

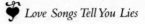

demanded, too tipsy to detect the awkwardness that had suddenly descended on the gathering. She turned to Lesley, Kathy's life-long friend, who was looking shocked at Bella's remark, and persisted: "What does she mean Lesley?"

Attempting to prevent any nastiness spoiling the jollity someone with quick wits shouted: "She's only interested in millionaires, and as there are not many of those around she'll have to stay an old maid – won't you Kathy?"

Everyone laughed too loudly at this, glad of a way to by-pass the unpleasant moment. They all knew exactly to what Bella had been referring. Most of them had enjoyed the hotch-potch of gossip years ago, that mishmash of baseless speculation that had convinced half the town that Kathy was having an affair with the husband of her best friend, Lesley.

The joke worked after a fashion and everyone managed to act as though nothing had happened. Soon afterwards the party broke up but on their way home they regurgitated the gossip of years before. With tremors the cracks in Kathy's settled way of life were widening.

Lesley drove Kathy and two of the other women home. Lesley and the others kept up a determinedly bright conversation, in an effort to disperse the embarrassment caused by Bella's bitchiness. Kathy was mostly silent, still seething at what that cow Bella had said. But she could not say anything to Lesley until the other two had been dropped off at their homes. As soon as they had, Kathy exploded.

"I could have killed that bitch!" she stormed.

It was the first time the matter had ever surfaced between the two friends, and although Kathy had never wanted it to arise, and certainly not in this fashion, now it had she was going to seize the chance to put the facts straight.

"I'm sorry Lesley. She is such a cow!"

Lesley took one hand off the steering wheel and placed it on her friend's arm reassuringly. "I don't worry about what she says, nor must you. She's always had it in for you."

"But you know what she meant."

"Yes, I do."

"Lesley, you don't think ...."

"No!" They came to a stop outside Kathy's home. Lesley turned to her friend and repeated with emphasis: "No, I don't!"

Kathy was near to tears. "Lesley, you mustn't think…"

"I don't!"

"Oh, Lesley!"

"I don't! I never have. Now, forget it."

" I wouldn't - I haven't - with anyone!"

Lesley squeezed her arm. "Then it's time you did."

"Have an affair!"

Laughing, Lesley shook her head: "No! Get married!"

"Married? I'm past it, on the shelf!" But it was not the time to joke. God, that bitch Bella! "Lesley, really… I'm so glad you believe me, because it's true."

"I know, I know."

"I'm so glad. I know you believe me, but even when you're sure, you're never sure." This absurdity made both of them giggle, and the giggling released a few tears from Kathy.

"Oh, you - you silly thing!" Lesley clasped her dear friend to her ample bosom, and Kathy was enveloped in warmth and kindness. "Don't talk about it any more. That's just what she would love - to think she had caused harm. But I'm right. It is about time. It's been eight years since Robert went you know."

"No, it's too late."

"Nonsense! Have an affair then!"

"No - all the best men are married anyway! Lesley, I'm happy as I am. A man isn't an essential ingredient for a woman's happiness you know!"

The old familiar spark was back and Lesley laughed. "You still wear your ring," she pointed out.

"Oh, that's for the sake of the girls really - shows I'm not an unmarried mother!"

"Oh!" Lesley dismissed that with a gesture. Nonsense!

Kathy looked at her ring finger. "Yes, silly, I suppose. It means nothing. Eight years is it? No, longer than that; eleven, nearly twelve!"

Lesley thought for a moment. "You're right. Goodness!"

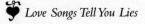

"Lucy's 16 you know; Anne-Marie's nearly 14."

"I know, Cherie's a year younger than Lucy. We're middle-aged! Time flies. You mustn't waste any more. They'll soon be leading their own lives Kathy. Time to start leading yours."

Thankful for being believed, because it had weighed on her all these years, Kathy opened the car door. "Goodnight. I'll give you a call later in the week." But still she felt concern for her friend. "Oh Lesley! I really am sorry, and thank you."

"'Night, Kathy. No more - forget it! That's an order! You mustn't let it upset you. Bella's a cow. I know nothing happened." She squeezed Kathy's hand and could not help adding mischievously: "Anyway, if he did, he showed good taste!"

Kathy could not reply to that as her babysitter, who had seen the car arrive, had come out of the house because Lesley was giving her a lift home.

After locking up and checking the girls were all right Kathy sat down in her kitchen and made a cup of tea.

In her head whirled the disturbed debris of the past. She knew that Lesley believed her but in these matters, in love and rivalry, however much you may trust someone, it still requires faith. Suspicion is rarely if ever routed by logic or facts. It was genuine friendship that Lesley not only believed and trusted her, but was concerned for her feelings.

Kathy was deeply moved and the flood of tears she had held back welled. As they coursed down her cheeks, they were somehow forgiving, undeservedly so because she had not told the truth, or not all the truth. Dear Lesley, I lied to you.

Yes, I lied to you Lesley. Not the real truth is a lie.

Life had gone on after Robert left, and in a typically defiant mood Kathy had held a party, just like the parties they used to hold. It had been towards the end of the evening, when the drink had relaxed inhibitions, she found herself in a secluded part of the house with Lesley's husband Alan. He started to dance with her, and suddenly he was kissing her passionately. Startled, and frightened in case anyone saw them, she broke away and managed to stay out of his way for the rest of the evening.

But he would not be deterred and, with Robert gone, it was easy for him, as a close friend, to persist. Clearly he was in love with her, or thought he was. Disconcertingly in the weeks following the party she found that her thoughts strayed more and more to him, and that passionate encounter. Eventually she weakened to his blandishments and met him for dinner in a discreet location. After dinner, on the way home she insisted it had to stop, but it was not to her credit. It had only been a near-miss encounter with people they both knew as they left the restaurant that had shocked her to her senses.

Thankfully, however, nothing had happened between them, although that did not make her feel very virtuous. Later Alan found the opportunity to shamefacedly confess that he, too, was glad that nothing serious had occurred. Kathy knew that he meant it, and their marriage was rock solid.

You are right Lesley, perhaps it is time, but finding the right man in a small town is not simple. Well, not for a vain little tart!

~ 12 ~

Politically McCrae was successful enough for most men and was now a leading figure in the Tory Party. Such personalities, backed by personal wealth and driven by unquenchable egos, usually end up somewhere. His social influence and money had served the party well and he had got the nod that in due time he would get a knighthood.

Yet all this was not enough for McCrae. He had had ambitions to be Prime Minister at one time. There was a big reshuffle going on, and he decided that he would publicly throw down the gauntlet for the leadership. He knew he would not get it. His acerbic tongue, cold personality and vengeful nature had long since ensured that he would have only his brilliant political brain for company and a cunning soul for a friend. But he knew he would get enough support from political bedfellows to provide him with bargaining power in the corridors of privilege and he could get into the cabinet.

As the premiership battle developed those votes gave him enough clout to do a deal: he would withdraw from the contest in return for a cabinet post. Ah, sweet drug of ambition! He was 50. It had been his last chance and he had nothing to lose.

Maisie Reynolds had read in the morning papers about McCrae's tilt for the party leadership. She was on her way to meet Catherine for coffee and a chat, but a piece of gossip she had heard about Catherine was more interesting than what her husband was up to. 'They' were saying Catherine had a new boyfriend, but no one could – or would – tell Maisie who he was.

Maisie kissed Catherine warmly when they met. "You must be so excited!" she said, pointing to the leadership battle story in a newspaper on the table, feigning enthusiasm for the sake of her friend.

Catherine laughed. She too had to put on a false show. Even though the sudden turn of events in her husband's affairs had surprised her as much as anyone, she was keeping her mind on what really was important to her now – and it had nothing to do with her husband, neither him nor his ambitions. Fortunately she had a cool brain, and although the turn of events in McCrae's career was an upheaval, she had quickly determined that it changed nothing. It was a shock, but everyone was in for a bigger shock. Loathing McCrae as much as she did meant Maisie had to work hard at drumming up that show of enthusiasm. Reading yet another political sex scandal story about yet another politician in her morning newspaper before leaving home had brought a shudder of memory of the time McCrae had tried it on with her. She had kept that nasty episode to herself. Had she told her husband Andrew there would have been hell to pay, but she had got her own back on McCrae often enough since.

Andrew was a freelance journalist working for racy tabloids. Apart from revenge, giving Andrew information about McCrae had resulted in stories that had beefed up their bank balance. Maisie had no conscience about this. Catherine knew what Andrew's job was and she ought to realise that what she told Maisie was likely to get in the papers.

The impatient shrill of a mobile phone intruded rudely into their chatter. "Excuse me," said Catherine, and flicked the phone alive without noting the number that was calling.

"Hello?"

"Hello sexy."

"Oh!" Startled, Catherine could not prevent a guilty glance towards Maisie before quickly gathering her composure.

"Oh, hello." Her mind raced. To give herself time to think she said meaninglessly: "Oh, thanks for calling back."

"You called me, darling? I haven't checked my messages." Then, taking in the implications of what she had said: "You didn't leave a message!" The caller's voice expressed horror. You know better than to leave messages!

Catherine put the receiver against her cheek and said: "Excuse me just a sec Maisie," making sure the mouthpiece picked it up.

"Oh God! Maisie's with you?"

After feigning listening to the caller for a moment Catherine said: "Yes, look, I'll call you back. Right? Thanks, 'bye." She put the phone on no-calls and slipped it into her handbag.

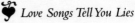

In the telephone box he had used for greater privacy – a conversation out in the open could have been overheard – Andrew slipped his mobile into his pocket. He dealt with the surge of alarm and guilt in his gut by making a joke face of relief in the booth's mirror.

Over the coffee cups Catherine continued smoothly. "Sorry Maisie. Now, where were we? How are you today? Oh, yes…" – picking up the threads of their conversation – "…yes, Hamish is very pleased. He was badly upset when he was sacked in the last re-shuffle."

"Well, let's hope it all works out this time," said Maisie, meaning it for her friend's sake.

"We'll see. He is as good a choice as any in the Party."

Yes, thought Maisie, if they have all tried it on with their wives' best friends! Maisie had resisted McCrae's attempts to seduce her at the end of a wine-laden country house party without turning the episode into a drama to save Catherine any embarrassment. To Maisie friendship meant it was kinder to keep some things to oneself. In Maisie's view, the hurt and embarrassment would have been unfair to share. And unwise to share with Andrew!

The two women keeping a secret from each other chatted on about this and that, and their meeting ended with Maisie leaving for the hairdressers and wishing Catherine good luck.

When Maisie had gone Catherine sent a text in their code to Andrew. Almost instantly he called back.

Apart from Andrew asking: "It's OK now?" it suited the conscience of both of them to avoid a reference to the incident and they quickly fixed up the time of their next liaison.

"Can't wait," said Andrew, and blew kisses into the phone.

★

Morrison met Catherine again at a Lord Mayor of London dinner. It was a nice surprise as she seemed to have dropped out of the political social scene after her husband's sacking. She felt sorry for this earnest, lonely, man. Without going further than the briefest of greetings she acknowledged his presence with a sweet smile. Like so many others who met Morrison she felt an irrational guilt because she did not want to linger and talk to him. It was unkind, but her conscience lost the argument without putting up much of a fight. Despite his grand status within the Civil Service the man's personality had the aura of the lonely bedsit.

Morrison felt the glow of meeting her long after the dinner had ended and in his bed that night he again dreamt adolescently. A few days later he learned that McCrae was in the running for the party leadership, and realised why his wife was back working the political-social round. It incensed him that such a pig of a man had such a lovely wife doing his PR.

What of that poor young woman left alone with McCrae's child, a scandal kept discreetly hidden by the power of his money? Was that the kind of man the public would want as Prime Minister? Not that there was much chance of that happening. Morrison knew that it was all a political game with something in it for McCrae at the end. However that might turn out, he decided that it was time to send that letter to the right person. In his mind to justify his action was that poor girl. This ultra–careful man also knew that after all this time there was no risk to him.

It was then he entered the booth half a mile from his office and picked up the phone.

"Hello?"

It was a camp, prissy, voice that its owner was trying to disguise with a ludicrous accent. ('It was straight out of the Goon Show' Kelly later chortled to his colleagues).

"Mr Webb?"

"Speaking."

"Mr Webb, you will be receiving a copy of a letter that will be of great interest to you regarding Hamish McCrae. It will be in a large brown envelope marked personally for your attention. Don't treat it is a hoax. I promise you, it is true." Then the line went dead.

Meticulous as always, Morrison had made sure that the letter did not get overlooked in what he guessed would be a mountain of letters arriving at a newspaper office.

If he got a tenner for every anonymous telephone call Kelly received at the Graphic from unbalanced individuals it would pay for an annual holiday for the family. This time however Kelly did

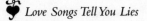

not replace the receiver with a routine yawn. Silly as the caller's voice had been, the reference to McCrae ensured he would read the promised letter with sharper interest than usual.

Morrison had made sure his letter stood out. The envelope was addressed to 'Reporter Kelly Webb' in large capital letters. Kelly read the enclosed photocopy of a letter in neat feminine handwriting. It revealed McCrae had a secret love child. Then when he saw Debbie's name and address he was knew this was a real lead. He punched the air, causing Bill to look up enquiringly.

"Something good?"

For answer Kelly just winked, his grin wider than a shark's. Within ten minutes he was on his way.

Disaster and death were on their way to the McCrae household.

★

Morrison was not the only person following McCrae's political manoeuvres with interest.

Debbie bought a paper as she walked her little boy home from school. When she got home and read it and saw her former lover's face in a story about the leadership battle momentarily she was caught with off guard. Up to then she had accepted her lot with quiet dignity. After all she had not been forced to become McCrae's lover. He had been married and she had no right to demand more of him. Yet seeing him living large while she and her son lived in obscurity brought on a rush of anger.

The uncharacteristic mood would have passed. Revenge and anger were both too extreme for her nature, but it shook her at just the moment Kelly Webb knocked at her door. She recognised him right away. It was the nice reporter with the winning smile. Seeing her Kelly again felt that protective urge.

This time Debbie did not close the door on him.

"You might as well come in," she said.

★

McCrae spent the day horse-trading. A lunch and a few phone calls and he was promised Transport. Then he gracefully withdrew, knowing that enough of his supporters would vote for Crichel. They did and Crichel kept the leadership, the crisis was over, and

Dunglennie Burn house staff started preparing the biggest dinner party at the house for many a year. McCrae intended to celebrate in style. For the time being he and Catherine stayed in their London home, expecting confirmation of his cabinet post soon.

After the last few days it was good to relax and McCrae was testy when Catherine told him that two reporters were at the door and wanted to talk to him.

"What do they want? It's Sunday, for God's sake."

Now that he did not need publicity reporters were the usual damn nuisance. He had spent the past week being interviewed in the papers and on television. A week of being pleasant and patient had been exhausting. Now that the job was in the bag, it was safe to revert to type.

"It's Sunday, what do you two want?" he snapped.

"Sorry, Mr McCrae." The reporter did not sound the least bit sorry. "We thought this would be a good time to talk to you."

Glaring at them, McCrae could see the other bloody nuisance was a photographer.

"Did you!" he snapped, "What about?"

"It's about a story we are doing on you."

"Yes, I would have guessed that, as you are here and I live here! What story?"

"It is about your relationship with Debbie Crawford."

McCrae had read that people hit by sudden trauma experience a split second of total nothing. Time, everything, stands stock-still. He had never really believed that. Now he did.

Rigid with shock he heard himself exclaim: "What!"

"Debbie Crawford. She says you were her lover and that you are the father of her child."

The reporter did not get a comment, at least not one he could print even in the Graphic. The photographer got a great shot of McCrae, face contorted with rage, because McCrae rushed them to the street and the photographer was then on legal ground.

Losing his temper with the Graphic journalists had been a stupid mistake. Then he made his second.

The Prime Minister called him in and asked, point blank, if what he

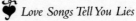

was hearing from party whips was true. No, promised McCrae, it was not. He was determined to stall, buy Debbie off, try anything, in order to survive this.

The Prime Minister, already punch drunk by a series of sex scandals in the party, decided to publicly stand by McCrae and pre-empt the story with a statement of support.

Then the Graphic carried its story, with bank statement details of McCrae's payments to Debbie, and a picture of her with her baby son. Even at that tender age, the poor little devil was a McCrae look-alike.

Even now McCrae was prepared to fight; that is, to lie and obfuscate. He never got the chance. He had not lied to the House. Others had survived worse sex scandals. But he had lied to, and embarrassed, the Prime Minister and that is fatal to any political career.

Crichel ditched him in a short, terse, phone call followed by the usual insincere first-names note of regret.

★

Morrison read the report of McCrae's downfall. As he did so the sly snake of his hatred writhed around the weak creature of his conscience and crushed the life out of it.

★

Kelly was first into the office. Bill O'Toole and Frank Farrell were the next to arrive. The ebullient Farrell slapped Kelly's desktop with his folded newspaper.

"Look at that smirk. The bugger's got a Westminster scalp."

"Good one," grinned Bill, "I suppose you are feeling very gung-ho this morning, Webb."

Kelly's smirk became smirkier.

"You deserve it," conceded the good-natured Frank. "You've really worked on that story. You were determined to get the bugger, weren't you?"

The cheerful mood was suddenly shattered.

"Just don't a expect a pay rise!"

The loud harsh voice heralded the arrival of Buller. The words were machine-gunned around at the group, but he looked hard at Kelly as he spoke. Buller was in charge of the features desk on the

Graphic, but the SS Squad had developed its own niche on the paper. Buller was anxious to assume control of them, but officially he had not yet managed to get it.

The small group of specialist reporters that formed the special investigative desk on the Graphic had been dubbed the SS – Sex and Sleaze – Squad. They specialised in scandal stories, and currently the Tory Party was paying their wages.

Buller had placed a smile on his face to deliver the words, but it did nothing in the way of public relations for him. Mother Nature, or whoever it is who does the design work on the human race, can be very slapdash. Physically he was an ill-favoured man, built awkwardly large with an ugly fleshy face. A domineering manner, cold eyes and abrasive voice completed an unlovely collection.

Kelly drained the friendliness out of his expression when he looked at Buller. With a slow contemptuous shrug he stayed pointedly silent, and deliberately held Buller's cold eyes a touch longer than was necessary. Buller had taken an atavistic dislike to Kelly when they first met, and that was OK with Kelly who felt the same primitive antipathy towards him.

"We've got the best story. They'll all be chasing us on this," chortled Frank.

Buller just grunted and strode off.

Kelly watched Buller stride away with a grimace. "What would make him happy, I wonder?"

Bill answered that. "A country to lead to disaster might do the trick."

"What do you mean?"

"The world is full of Bullers. Some, like Idi Amin and Saddam Hussein get lucky and are born into a country they can ruin. Buller had the misfortune to be born in Britain, and had to settle for a small arena, like an office."

Kelly laughed. He liked that. It was a remark typical of Bill, and one with more than a grain of truth. Buller was one of those people with Dobermannic natures who exist only to dominate and lay waste any opposition.

"He wants to be in charge of the SS Squad, not only general

features," said Bill. "It's an office power struggle. I reckon he will win. Don't go looking for trouble Kelly. He's well in with Smith by all accounts."

Kelly did not feel threatened. He knew he was good at his job, and was also well thought of by Smith, the deputy editor who had overall control of features and the SS Squad. Just recently Smith had told him that the paper's new editor had asked for his congratulations to be passed on to Kelly regarding a story. Smith had added: "It is not often he does that. Consider yourself honoured Kelly."

It was said in front of Buller and Kelly had felt the antagonism from the man like a force field. Buller was the kind of loud lack-talent that he abjured. The man had a fast mind and could leap ahead of what was happening in the office, giving the impression of ability and leadership. He made crash-bang decisions and if they turned out to be a waste of time and the newspaper's money he simply covered up with bluster and blame-passing.

An ideal general for the First World War. That was another pithy comment delivered by Bill when the paper was running a series on the butchery of 1914-1918 and Buller was heard across the office at full bellow. Kelly liked that description too. Buller treated the Graphic's younger staff over whom he did have authority like peasants. He would have made an ideal madman at Ypres. He even had the piercing send-men-to-their-deaths-without-question eyes of the sergeant major in that famous First World War recruitment poster.

Buller had tried to bully and belittle Kelly when he perceived Kelly's poorly-disguised opinion of him. All the other writers were young, except Bill, and mostly on short-term contracts. Buller barked and they were puppies.

Bill was a cool, easy, man who had developed his way of surviving the perils of the workplace: neatly side-stepping head-on collisions with a dry remark or a joke. He always outsmarted Buller with effortless ease.

Kelly was the odd man out as far as Buller was concerned. He was the one who neither hid his feelings nor kowtowed. Buller had made up his mind within a week of Kelly joining the paper that he was going to have his guts for garters.

On top of that atavistic dislike, there had been differences of opinion as to how stories should be treated. Buller felt the blood flood his brain when Kelly challenged his views. Kelly would stick doggedly to how he thought a story should be written, leaving out details that he thought were too salacious and tasteless even by the Graphic's standards. Ignoring Buller, he had also started taking his ideas of how a story should be done straight to the deputy editor and, infuriatingly, had received his backing.

"Maybe you ought to get a job on The Times," Buller sneered, during one of their tight-lipped discussions on ethics. Kelly had just come from a meeting with Smith and had again been praised for his latest story. Cockily Kelly had retorted: "I've a job to do here thanks."

Buller did not say anything, but his glare followed Kelly like a spectre.

Kelly had felt again the blast of hate and knew he ought to guard his back. But he also felt those good vibes from the editorial management. You don't frighten me Buller, his body language shouted large and clear, so sod off.

At the Graphic lots of people were vying for power all the time. Buller had barged his way to the position he was in. It was the Graphic's way to let staff kill each other off and the Doberman Buller was exactly the type to prosper in that environment. However he was all too aware that he had not got an office title formally in writing, and no long-term contract. The Graphic knew how to keep people on their toes.

Buller eructated, his habitual way of expressing hate.

'A job to do here, have you? Well Mr Smart-arse Webb, you won't be having a job much longer, that I promise you!

'If you think I am going to let a blue-eyed prat like you threaten what I have achieved, you are more stupid than you look Webb. I am an expert at this game my son, and I can tell you that this game is full of fancy writers. They come and go with the fashion of the day. Me? I know the score Webb. It's not what you know. It's not even who you know. It's who you shaft!'

Buller rarely smiled, and when this thought amused him the rictus that creased those ugly lips revealed how badly out of practice he was.

— 13 —

The house was silent. Catherine sat at the telephone table for a moment, composing herself before making her call. She knew exactly what she was going to do, and it was very simple, but nevertheless she wanted to make sure nothing would go wrong. So uptight was she, she debated which phone would be wisest to use, her mobile or the table phone. Chiding herself, what could it matter, she opened her handbag to take out the mobile just as the telephone on the table rang. In her tense mood, it made her jump out of her skin. There was no reason why she should not answer it, so, calming herself, she picked it up.

"Hello?"

"Hello? Hamish?"

She recognised the voice, having been to bed with its owner.

"Oh, hello Ross. Sorry, no, he's not here." With a 'goodbye' tone in her voice she said: "I'll tell him when he gets in."

The unexpected encounter left Buchanan with nothing to say.

"Right," he grunted and hung up.

Catherine put the handset down and paused to collect herself. Weird that it should have been Buchanan who called at that moment. It was the first time they had spoken to each other since she had told him it was finished between them. She needed a moment to compose her thoughts.

Making herself concentrate she took out her mobile and called Andrew on the number he had assured her was safe. Cupping the mobile conspiratorially to her ear with both hands she impatiently listened to the dialling tone.

Had he got the tickets? She must check on the meeting place and the time. Then she and Andrew would elope to a new life. Elope! Such a lovely, romantic word. She was leaving it all behind, and with not a scrap of regret. Just making the telephone call made her heart beat faster and she felt quite ridiculously happy when he answered.

"Hello?"

"It's me."

"Darling, I thought you were never going to call."

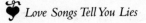

"You silly thing. Nothing would stop me. Have you got the tickets?"

"Yes. All fixed."

"I can't wait."

"Where are you are now."

"At home."

"Home? Isn't that… a bit risky isn't it?"

"Hamish is not here. I'm by myself."

"Still, you should …oh, well, I suppose it doesn't matter now. So, Friday, Heathrow, Terminal Three, in that cafeteria you said - yes, I know the one - midday, to give us plenty of time."

"Yes, Terminal Three, Friday, twelve o'clock."

"This is amazing, isn't it? A month ago, I would never have thought… ..you won't change your mind! You're giving a lot up."

"For you darling, I don't care. I would give everything up. Hamish and I have never been happy. That girl - I knew all about his affairs but they meant nothing to me. There has never been anything to keep us together, but until now no one I would have left for. Now there is, and I love you, love you, love you darling. I can't believe it has all happened."

"Nor me. I love you too. You had better go, it's risky you calling from home."

"It's all right, Hamish won't be home for ages. Love you darling. 'Til Friday." She blew kisses into the mobile, slipped it into her purse, and went upstairs on wings.

Hunched over her mobile with her back to the door Catherine had not heard McCrae arrive while she was speaking to Andrew, and McCrae had not realized she had been using her mobile. She had been oblivious to everything at that moment. In any case she would not have seen McCrae because he had pulled back out of sight when he overheard her first 'darling', and had then listened to the whole of the rest of the conversation in a mounting rage that became so intense it hurt his chest.

Shocked as he was, his mind stayed ice-cool.

Pausing just long enough to allow Catherine to enter the bedroom, McCrae quickly crossed the room and picked up the telephone on the table. First hiding his own number, he pressed last number recall and Buchanan's familiar voice answered. Without a word McCrae put the phone down, feeling the slow burn of murder beginning in his gut.

Fifty years of conditioning take some altering. Now the resident rage was back in charge. There was nothing he could do about the events that had ruined his political career, but he would not tolerate this. They would find they were making a fool of the wrong person. He re-crossed the room to the door and this time opened and slammed it shut noisily. Making plenty of noise he went to the drinks cabinet and poured a stiff whisky and threw it down his throat.

It never occurred to him that he had no right to demand fidelity from Catherine, the McCrae of a dozen mistresses. This was the McCrae who was losing everything; being made a public fool. Anger and self-pity controlled him. He refilled his glass to overflowing.

Having heard the door bang Catherine appeared at the top of the stairs, looking anxious.

"We're due at eight," he reminded her.

Catherine took a deep breath to calm her fluttering heart. "There's plenty of time. I'll get ready."

McCrae emptied his glass in one swig. Life has a habit of continuing whatever happens and it did now, although on automatic. They had a dinner engagement this evening and after another drink he followed Catherine upstairs to change.

At their bedroom door he stopped and watched Catherine dressing. Her figure had not changed since they first married. Her limbs were glistening white, strong, smoothly muscled. She was beautiful and had moved him deeply when they had first met, before reality had asserted itself. It was doing so now despite his pent-up anger; indeed, perhaps because of it.

He had intended to wait until the dinner was over to confront her with her perfidy, but it was all too much to control. His voice strangled by fury he finally exploded.

"Are you having an affair?"

Her expression at this bolt from the blue was all the evidence he needed.

Transfixed with fear by his murderous eyes, Catherine could not speak.

"The call you were making just now! I heard!" It was a snarl; a savage, primitive snarl. "I *heard!*"

Still she did not answer, and her shocked silence was corroboration. He stood quite still on the other side of their bed. He felt as though he was in a different zone to his wife. He saw her but as in a dream, where he could see her but not touch her. Somewhere in the background was another man who could have her whenever he liked, but he was denied. Denied his rights!

Still half dressed, crushed by the sudden accusation, she looked frightened and vulnerable. Never before had he seen her thus, or found her so inexplicably desirable. His rage and distress unlocked his imprisoned self. The longing for her was more than he could withstand. Momentarily released from his emotional straitjacket he started awkwardly towards her, reaching out. Overwhelmingly he wanted to tell her he loved her, to experience the sweetness that comes with that confession. Catherine's coldness had for too long created between them an impassable wasteland.

She sobbed fearfully and moved to keep the bed between them.

"Don't be so stupid!" Childish tears stung his eyes. It was so unfair! He was not going to hurt her!

He loved her and yearned for tenderness. Why couldn't she see this? Why did he have to *say*?

Then he stopped, his outstretched arms falling back, the bonds that had held him in check all his life tightening again. He pulled himself together. He could not win if he was weak.

"I know who you've been having it off with." He choked on the words. Now anger gave her courage. It was all over. Pretence ended; the façade torn down. Her eyes blazed.

"Having it off! That's how you think of it, all you could ever think of it! We make love. That's something you could never do, make *love!*"

She grabbed the rest of her clothes and got past him to the door.

When he found her a few minutes later she was in the living room, dressed ready for going out. It was unreal, but they were going to continue with the evening. In truth Catherine felt safer, knowing they would be in company. They got in the car and he started the engine.

"Why?" He sat, gripping the wheel as though strangling someone. Now that she was going to leave McCrae, all that money and position suddenly worthless, Catherine felt nothing. She did not look at the man she had used so cruelly for so long. Neither pity nor triumph. It was like someone else's life she was leaving behind. She stared straight ahead into the neon-flecked darkness and did not answer.

McCrae rammed the gears in and drove savagely.

Suddenly she screamed. "Look out!"

McCrae hit the brakes as his attention was wrenched back to the road ahead.

"Bloody fool!" The shout came from one of an alarmed group of people in front of his car as it jerked to a halt a yard on to a pedestrian crossing. Angrily, stupidly, McCrae tried to drive on before the people had properly got out of the way. There were more angry shouts and an irate face appeared at the windows, mouthing abuse.

"Get his number!" someone shouted.

"Apologize, for God's sake," Catherine urged, "and let's get out of here!" Eventually McCrae wound down the window to placate the owner of the angry face. It was a mistake, as the man smelt the alcohol.

"You've been drinking!"

"Sorry," said McCrae. "My fault, bad lighting here. Nobody hurt, right?" He tried to make the car creep forward but there were still people in the way.

Joe turned, alarmed for Julie who was just behind him on the crossing. First ushering her safely on to the pavement Joe strode back to the crowd which was ganging up round McCrae's car.

"Bloody fool!"

"The bastard's drunk!"

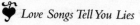

"Call the police!"

McCrae was saying something about it not doing any good behaving like this. As soon as he saw him Joe knew immediately who it was. That stern ugly mug was not easily forgotten. The gleam of the Mercedes was confirmation.

Then the same man shouted again: "He's been drinking!"

McCrae swore at him and tried again to drive the car forward. Joe leapt in front of it to prevent it moving. He felt he could have stopped a tank, so great was his fury. A couple of men stepped up to support him and Joe called the police on his mobile. A patrol car was just a street away and within minutes it arrived. Cursing under his breath McCrae got out of his car and forcing a smile went to meet the officers. Making a supreme effort to keep the fury of the last half an hour out of his demeanour he made himself known to the officer. Careful not to seem to be trying to use undue influence he endeavoured to keep far enough away so the officer would not smell the alcohol on his breath.

At first it seemed to be going well for him, but the obstreperous man came up to them and shouted: "He's been drinking officer. You can smell it. You've got to breathalyse 'im!" The officer told the man to stay out of it, but the man started shouting that if McCrae was not breathalysed, he would be making a complaint.

With reluctance, because the officer would have let the whole incident go without any further action, he made McCrae take a test. It showed he was over the limit, and he was arrested. Catherine had to go back home in a taxi, while McCrae waited until a lawyer secured his release.

The man who had been doing all the shouting overheard McCrae give his name to the officer, and was on the telephone tipping off a newspaper within minutes. They paid him £200 on a promise to keep it as an exclusive. It was early enough in the evening for them to check it out and it appeared in the next morning's edition. The headline of a leading Tory politician arrested for suspected drink driving a sold extra copies.

The following morning's headlines of his dramatic death sold thousands more.

After the warm day there was a slight chill in the air. Although still wearing the lightweight suit he had worn for the office Morrison did not feel the chill. As always just thinking of Catherine warmed him and tonight, so close to her home, he was burning.

More and more often this summer he had found himself hanging around in the vicinity of the McCrae household. A few times he had glimpsed Catherine entering or leaving or, thrillingly, at a window as she drew the curtains.

★

Released from custody with the aid of a top lawyer McCrae, using a reserve set of car keys, found his car and drove straight to Buchanan's flat, checking on the way that the gun he had put in the glove compartment was still there. Killing Buchanan would be simple for a man who had no need to cover his tracks or care about the consequences. McCrae had already decided on the way he was going to deny the world its chance to crow over his downfall. Then he could end it all knowing that he had ruined Catherine's chance of making him look a fool, leaving her to face society and the gutter Press.

When Buchanan opened the door to his flat, McCrae shoved past him, pulling the gun out of his pocket as he kicked the door closed. But the killing was not as simple as he had anticipated, and a nasty shock awaited him.

★

Tonight it seemed he was going to be disappointed. After waiting a hour the house was still in darkness and Morrison was thinking of returning to his car that was parked discreetly a street away when a taxi drew up. Catherine got out and hurried inside the house.

Morrison saw the house lights come on, and waited in the hope of spotting her at a window as she drew the curtains. With that he would have gone home happy.

Then a gleaming Mercedes arrived fast and braked hard into the driveway. Morrison saw McCrae get out of the car and stride into the house, leaving the front door swinging open behind him.

Morrison moved closer to the open door, wondering what was going on. There had been great urgency in the way McCrae had

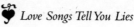

arrived and rushed into the house.

From the doorway Morrison heard their raised voices. McCrae was shouting and swearing and Catherine sounded frightened. There was crash of something being knocked over and the sound of breaking glass.

Morrison became a man transformed. The woman he loved and who loved him was in danger. Hurrying into the hallway he followed the sound of the argument. McCrae was in front of Catherine, and at first Morrison could not see he was holding a gun. A side table had been overturned and drinking glasses and cutlery were scattered on the floor.

Catherine was cringing before McCrae, her eyes wild with fear.

"Dead!" McCrae was snarling at her. "Dead! You will not be cheating on me again. Dead, you hear me?"

Andrew dead! Catherine cried out in despair. "Oh God, no! Please God, no!"

Then Morrison saw the gun.

McCrae had been about to turn the gun on himself and leave Catherine to mourn her lover's death. It was a split second from the start of a sequence of events that would have led to Catherine discovering McCrae's mistake and being free to run away with Andrew.

That course of fate was changed when McCrae was hit from behind by the ungainly bulk of Morrison.

Morrison grabbed at the gun and it fired as they fell in a heap on to an armchair. McCrae's expression was one of total stupefaction as he recognised Morrison. He struck at him with his free hand as Morrison desperately hung on to his gun hand. With the strength of fear and hate Morrison turned the gun away from himself. It went off a second time, sending a bullet up through McCrae's neck and into his brain.

McCrae's suicide had been done for him.

Morrison struggled to his feet. Everything was unreal. Time was suspended in the silence of death. On his face he felt the blood that had splattered from McCrae and he started shaking violently with horror. Then he turned and saw Catherine sprawled on the floor.

She had been killed by the first random bullet; her lifeless eyes were wide open. It was like a lurid illustration for a cheap crime paperback. For slowly passing seconds Morrison stood looking down at the woman he loved. His mind and emotions were utterly frozen, his body was shaking like a leaf.

Then like an automaton he walked out of the house to his car and drove home.

The world and his partner were agog. Murder, sex and high politics: all the ingredients for a bloody good story.

Ross Buchanan and socialite Isobel D'Avril, whom he had been dating, were found shot dead at his London home. A couple of miles across the capital the prominent Tory politician Hamish McCrae was also dead, and his wife Catherine murdered.

Statements by the police confirmed that the deaths were being investigated as being linked, as ballistics were later to prove.

Sub-editors like sex. It is a word with more impact than any other. Every newspaper had 'sex' in their headline on the story.

'Minister in Sex Drama Shoots Wife'; 'Sex-Mad Minister Shoots Wife Who Strayed; 'Top Politician's Wife's Sex Life: Four Dead.'

"Why? Everyone knew he did not care for Catherine," a confidant of Catherine's was quoted by one newspaper. "It makes no sense. It is so cruel."

Newspaper pundits surmised the answer to that puzzle. McCrae could not stand the ridicule of being dumped by his wife for Buchanan. They tapped out a picture on their laptops of an arrogant man who had lost the political prize he craved because of his selfish sex life. Then when he realised he would be a laughing stock if his long-suffering wife was to walk out on him for another man he killed them both. Isobel D'Avril just happened to be in the wrong place. Kelly recalled his encounters with McCrae, a man who appeared to have it all but really had nothing, and saw no reason to disagree.

The Graphic news room buzzed all the next day as staff put together a follow up. Kelly had not got involved in this but he gave the reporters some details he had collected but had not used and so

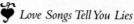

were not in the newspaper's library.

"We've also got some exclusive details from someone close to the McCraes," one of the reporters told Kelly.

"Who?"

"A freelance, Andrew Reynolds."

"Him again!" Kelly was impressed. "He has bloody good contacts as far as McCrae is concerned."

"He should have. His wife Maisie was a good friend of Catherine McCrae. He quotes her - exclusive to us. He does not want a by-line. But he will be happy enough - we're paying him a packet."

Knowing he would not get to read the full Graphic story until the next morning Kelly asked the reporter to print it off and he read it on his homeward train.

Maisie was quoted: "Catherine had found real happiness. Until then I think she had always accepted her lot. She knew what kind of man Hamish was and in her way had learned to be content with what she had.

"Then her friends knew she had discovered true love and she was prepared to give up everything; all that money and position.

"It is a terrible tragedy. You might have expected anything else, but not this."

Looking at the photograph of Catherine that accompanied the story Kelly wondered how anyone with her looks could ever have married McCrae in the first place, money or no money. This job was making him wonder why beautiful and talented people did what they did, but it was not giving him any answers that made sense.

Folding the proof-page, Kelly looked at a woman seated opposite; an ordinary housewifely woman who was deep in thought as she gazed abstractedly out of the window. People watching again, he wondered what was she thinking about: what to get the family for dinner that evening, or counting the minutes until her secret lover took her in his arms?

I'm sure you are not thinking anything of the sort lady, but then what do any of us know of each other? The pretty young girl he often saw on the train came to mind. Now there, you could expect it. She would tempt any man.

Disconcertingly the woman looked up and caught him studying her. Fortunately she smiled, as nice women do, and it transformed her, revealing an unexpected beauty.

See, you never know Maisie. In love and war the unexpected is all you can expect. There's more goes on than you know Maisie Reynolds.

Kelly returned the woman's smile, and so doing enjoyed the predatory conceit a man indulges himself at such times.

Now, *that* was to be expected.

Morrison read the reports of the McCrae murders and 'suicide' and joined the ranks of those who hope there is no hell.

Andrew Reynolds read them and knew there was.

"A bloody good story," observed Frank. "We won't top that in a hurry."

"The supply is endless, Frank," Bill assured him. "Endless."

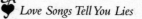

— 14 —

"Eastwinter as editor of the Graphic!" The speaker was so flabbergasted at hearing this news from his companion he failed to control his laughter in the manly mode he cultivated and it came out as its natural poofterish squawk.

It was the usual drinking lunch the two members of the staff of London Media needed to recharge their egos.

"Eastwinter! Those hoodlum hacks on the Graphic with Mr Morality as editor? You're having me on!"

"Apparently he wanted the job."

"Really?"

"Surprising isn't it?" The sleek informant who had delivered this gem about Henry Eastwinter smirked, well pleased. Being the first with such juicy gossip gave one a satisfying boost.

"Old Chillywinds! Bit of a comedown, isn't it? I mean, I would have said The Times, Guardian – never the Graphic!"

"Well, it's true."

"How will he fit in with that mob, I wonder? His style is hardly theirs. It will be like having a bishop as editor of the Sun!"

This evoked a snigger and a shrug from his companion.

"I don't know, we'll see… he's a hard man and he will shake things up at least."

"Yes, but can you imagine – Chillywinds directing those sex scandals they specialise in?"

"Yes, and it's ironic. His own mother was involved in a scandal. Remember?"

"Oh? No, when was that? What happened?"

The sleek one was enjoying this attention from his fellow ego.

"His parents split up. Chillywinds was only a lad at the time. Very sad. Affected him quite badly apparently."

"Well, it would of course. What happened?"

"Oh, I forget the exact details, it was gossip, but everyone knew – except you! Didn't get into the papers, but it was common knowledge Lord Emburey had been having it off with Chillywinds' mother."

"Emburey? The former chancellor? Now chairman of the Emburey Group!"

"Yes, that Emburey. Lord Bonkalot."

"Of course! I remember a bit about it now. That's right, Bonkalot – that was his nickname. They actually called him that on that radio satire programme, A Week's Not Long Enough."

"Did they? Good programme that. Chillywinds' parents split up, then later Emburey ditched his mother."

"What happened to his father?"

"No idea. Never heard."

"Cruel irony, that. The rogue gets remembered, the victim – phut!"

"So perhaps that accounts for all his coruscating articles and editorials, banging on about standards and principles. Very much the old-fashioned family man."

"Well, that could explain it I suppose…" The second drinker interrupted himself, and started on a new tack. "I can tell you something about Chillywinds. You remember Tony Church? No? Well never mind, he was not long on the paper. He was a pushy little sod. Came from some Brighton rag. He was working on the desk that Chillywinds was running then, a society gossip column thing – who's staying at which country mansion. In other words upper crust knocking shops!

"Well, they had a story about McCrae, you know, the M.P., and some woman he was knocking off – I don't know the details, but anyway Chillywinds did not want to use it. McCrae and De Haan – Ben De Haan – were as thick as thieves; both are on the board of Leisure Land – yes, you didn't know? Members of the Mutual Backscratchers Club."

"De Haan? He owns the group!"

"Yes, well practically – nearly all the shares, anyway. Yes, De Haan, Chillywinds' boss – and Chillywinds was ambitious …" The speaker stopped there: enough said? "Upsetting McCrae would have done him no good with De Haan. It probably was – it must have been – something like that"

"Not very principled."

"Huh! Principles?" The sleek one sneered. "The road to Ambition

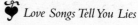

is paved with principles!"

"Yes, well, what happened?"

"What? Oh, yes." The sleek one gathered himself, having been carried away with his digression. "Well, this Church fellow used the story while Chillywinds was out of the office, on holiday. Chillywinds was furious. What they reckon is…"

"Who's 'they'?"

"…the people in his office who told me - this is top stuff I'm telling you - what they reckon happened is: Chillywinds had promised McCrae it would not be used, and this Church fellow flouted his order because he thought it was unethical not to use it.

"When Chillywinds got back to the office he had Church sacked. Chillywinds has spent years cultivating powerful friends in politics and business and the newspaper backed him. Church only had the IoJ or the NUJ - if he is a member of either - and had no chance. Church was a cocky young sod, but he didn't deserve that. But that was Chillywinds, ramrod righteous."

"I've often wondered what sort of private life moralists like him lead - he can hardly have an affair himself, can he?"

"No! Anyway, he wouldn't. Very married is Chillywinds. You'd see why if you met his wife. She's a beauty - now she could tempt someone! But could you imagine any woman fancying Chillywinds!"

"Well, his wife did and she's a beauty, you say."

"True! Maybe he should be nicknamed Hotwinds!"

"Ramrod righteous. I like that, you should use it in one of your articles."

"Good idea. I'll find someone to stick it on!"

Those alcoholic egos propping up the bar of The Reality Refuge, the name of their local boozer which the owner had very cleverly copyrighted as a trade name, may have been surprised, but Eastwinter reckoned taking the Graphic editorship was a good career move. During a big senior executive re-shuffle he had sensed the danger of being dealt a mediocre hand.

At a turbulent time in the group it was a very useful temporary safe haven. Eventually he had his eye on the editorship of the group's flagship the Sentinel, and via that to group managing editor. He knew that taking the Graphic editorship had surprised many people and he liked that. It was no bad thing to get a bit of media exposure oneself occasionally. He had reasoned that if he could make a good job of it, was not afraid to get his hands dirty as it were, it would do his career a bit of good.

Meanwhile his rivals could cut each other's throats fighting for the too few prestige posts presently available within the group. There would be better chances later with a number of top men nearing retirement and he was a patient man.

More importantly, he was on the best of terms with De Haan.

★

When Kelly got back to the office there was message on his desk to ring the editor's secretary. Bill, who had taken the message, saw him reading it and quipped: "I'll organise a whip round for the wife and kids."

Kelly laughed, but was unable to stifle a foreboding. He had been gung-ho practically from day one on the Graphic turning in cracking good stories, exactly the kind the newspaper revelled in. But life in media world these days was only as long as your contract, and sometimes shorter. It is fashion, not principle, that often determines the fate of the poor bloody media infantry. The current fashion was to have five minutes to clear your desk. It was witless, savage, but gave those who do the firing a power buzz. So it was a very popular way of getting rid of people.

Bill knew how he himself would feel and guessed Kelly felt the same.

"It'll be a pay rise," he added encouragingly. "You've been doing great."

The fact that the editor was Henry Eastwinter added to the trepidation any member of his staff might feel when summoned to his office. Chillywinds had a reputation for being a hard man to please and it was reputation he made a point of fostering. That stony demeanour advertised the inner man accurately. It would not have troubled the advertising standards authority. As Kelly set off to the editor's office someone remarked: "Well, at least Kelly will be able

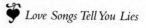

to tell us what he looks like. I've not even seen him yet."

"Rather grim by all accounts," said a colleague. "Well named, too."

"He's managed to get himself a nice young bit of stuff though," Frank suddenly interjected, to everyone's surprise.

"The editor? Never!" Bill was laughing. "That crusty old bugger? - he's married anyway."

"Isn't that why old geezers like him want young nooky?" Frank considered that to be pragmatic reasoning.

"What makes you think he has?" challenged a reporter.

"I saw her leaving his office. He was at the door and she was kissing him goodbye. Tall, actressy, centre-fold stuff. Looks like a model."

The reporter burst out laughing. "That's his daughter you fool!"

"His daughter!" Frank was flabbergasted. "Never! Twenty-five-ish, gorgeous figure, long black hair, bedroom eyes …"

"That's her. That's his daughter, you plank!"

"How did an old crabface like Chillywinds father a daughter like that? His daughter!" Frank brightened as he instinctively homed in on the essentials. "Single? What's her name?"

"Charlotte. But you needn't get any ideas Farrell. Daddy dotes on her and would not allow a ram like you anywhere near her."

"If he has a daughter like that, he can't be all that bad," reasoned Frank. "Anyway," he objected, "Fathers don't have a say in who their daughters date, not these days."

"They do if they are the editor and the date is a randy hack on his staff."

"Who're you calling a hack!"

Eastwinter's' reputation had the effect of a dismal weather forecast but Harry Haynes, a reporter who had once worked on another newspaper with Eastwinter, soothed the office unease.

"His reputation is worse than his bite. He can be a bastard, but long as you do the job, he's all right. Remember Buller's glee before Chillywinds came? It should have suited him, having another like himself in charge. But it doesn't seem to have made any difference. Chillywind's made some changes, but Buller is still where he was."

Haynes turned to Frank and interrupted his daydream of the editor's daughter. "You won't catch old Chillywinds playing around.

He is happily married. Dotes on his missus."

"Well, maybe he has his bit of stuff well hidden away." Frank always tried to believe the best of people.

"Not Chillywinds," said Haynes. "He is a big family man is our editor. Very old-fashioned views on marriage."

Henry Eastwinter's views on journalism could also be thought of as old-fashioned. Whenever he was invited to give an after dinner speech, his favourite theme was that journalists had a duty to maintain standards in society. Being editor of the Graphic made no difference to his lofty ideals.

Staff soon felt his presence. He was not frightened to set standards and none of the campaigns he had orchestrated had given him as much satisfaction as the current media microscope on sex and sleaze in politics.

He had been born blessed with a brain that found prep school, Charterhouse and Eton an easy journey from childhood to maturity. His entire life had been lived in an environment that suited his nature perfectly. It was a life that was elitist, intellectual and cloistered. He was a tall, angular man and those who were minded to try and describe him would have found that 'austere' and 'distinguished' were the most diplomatic adjectives to use. Privately they would probably choose 'haughty' or 'cold'. That frosty face tended to cool any inclination to be friendly. Eastwinter - well named they thought. Yet in this opinion they might feel rather guilty. After all he was clearly an accomplished man, one who ought to be admired. Clever and well mannered - although didn't those manners rather make them feel put in their place?

When he had decided he wanted to be in journalism, attracted by its power to influence, his father had arranged for him to be suitably groomed for a high-profile career. Having a father with influential business friends is worth a couple of laps start in life's race. Where most journalists have to start on a regional paper and work towards London and Fleet Street, Eastwinter only had to spend a token year on a West Country weekly. A national newspaper group owned it and used it to groom staff for its London office.

At the end of the year he moved on to writing a society column for the group's national daily. In the West Country he had interviewed a man who was an adviser with the Rural Development Commission. He told Eastwinter about the basic piece of advice he always gave to anyone worried that they might not have all the skills needed to run their own business.

"I tell them you can always buy expertise. The secret is to make sure the price is right."

It was a simple truth and it stuck with the youthful Eastwinter, not for running a business but for furthering his career. As soon as he got to edit the society column he took care to hire the best brains and talent to contribute to it. A general is only as good as his troops. He spent the newspaper's money blithely. At the time the finances of newspapers were a fantasy. Many were owned by organisations that stood their losses from the profits of other enterprises within the group. Long before there was a financial reckoning Eastwinter had moved on, the glory his, the debts the company's. Hire the best continued to be his successful policy. Guided by that wise advice from the Rural Development Commission adviser he set about becoming a shaker and shaper of society.

More sharp advice came from a wizened wise old newshound who had taken a shine to the earnest young Eastwinter.

"We shovel shit in this business, so shovel thoroughbred shit. You'll get more pay and the importance of important shit will rub off on you. There are no kudos in journalism getting sued by Bill Bloggs. If you have go to be sued, be sued by someone famous.

"Remember Sir Harold Butterfield? 'Course you do. Twenty years on telly chatting with the rich and famous, gets a knighthood. No dangerous assignments, no digging the dirt.

"Remember Billy Coomber? No, I can see you don't. Best investigative reporter on the Street for 20 years, more scoops than any of his rivals. His stories righted wrongs. Got the sack and ten grand pay-off."

As young men do, Eastwinter assimilated that philosophy his way. He filtered out the two bits he liked: importance and pay.

The best thing that happened to him was the best thing that happens to any man – a warm and womanly woman: Sophie. Had

Frank known Charlotte's mother he would not have been mystified as to the origins of her beauty. Being Frank (being any man for that matter) he would certainly have appreciated why old Chillywinds must be happily married. Even in middle age Sophie Eastwinter drew plenty of admiring male glances.

Eastwinter was delighted with Sophie from the moment they met. Not only was she a beauty, he found they shared so many interests. Their marriage was perfect. He had the perfect family as well; Charlotte and her brother Simon had both grown into young adults of which any parent would be proud.

Simon was the physical copy of his father but with a sense of humour and a happier attitude to life. He loved variety and had five different jobs within the first two years of leaving university where he had mainly studied the art of enjoying oneself. He was never likely to give the world grief, sit in judgment or end up on a newsstand in a lurid headline. He was the son his father might have been brought up in a happier family.

Charlotte was just as personable, but with more of the thrust of her father. She had inherited his intellectual genes and she breezed through university. On graduating she moved seamlessly on to a City job as an analyst with an investment firm specialising in futures and combined this with freelance work for a spread betting company.

Eastwinter was emotionally scarred by the bitter divorce of his parents. Determined himself to be a good father, he never stinted time or energy to help his children, especially his beloved Charlotte, in whose face he saw his mother.

The Eastwinters' social strata was one in which Charlotte thrived. Helped by her parents' contacts she soon began to taste – and like – the exotic flavours of London's social and political life. Having inherited her father's single-mindedness, and a cool brain that could calculate people as accurately and efficiently as it did facts and figures, she fitted in nicely. Those who mattered were cultivated unerringly. It was invariably a rapid conquest, as her looks inherited from her mother and grandmother usually ensured a first round knockout. However her most valuable asset was every successful woman's deadliest weapon. She was sexy.

It was not, as women as smart as her quickly realise, a man's world that women had to conquer. The way she worked it out was that it was a woman's world as long as the man was allowed to do the swaggering.

Why does a man work to be rich, except to attract women? Why does he wheel and deal, meddle and murder, slave and save but to make a beguiling bed for his woman? Wise women approve of this arrangement. A feminist would not have approved but tradition suited this feisty lady very well, and she set about enjoying it to the full.

Her career raced along, but at nothing like the rate of knots of her social life. The men she brought home to dinner lulled her parents into the belief that when she did marry it would be wisely. Much more fun were the men she did not bring home.

～ 15 ～

"**K**elly! Come in. Sit down." Eastwinter's expression was as affable as it got for people of Kelly's ilk. The knot of tension in Kelly's stomach started to unravel. First names! "Congratulations Kelly, well done."

Kelly looked puzzled.

"You've won an award. Didn't you know?"

Then it dawned on Kelly. More in hope than expectation he had entered for the newspaper industry's Cadbury-Hobbs awards in the investigative writers' section.

The editor pushed a letter across his desk.

"Didn't you know? They didn't tell you!"

Kelly read the letter: The award committee was delighted to inform the Graphic editor that Kelly Webb had won the investigative journalist section. Still taking it all in, Kelly passed the letter back.

"I leave home before the post arrives."

"Well, I'm delighted to be the first to tell you Kelly. Congratulations. Well done! I think this calls for a toast."

Kelly sat in a happy daze while the editor's secretary poured two drinks.

"Here's to more award-winning stories from you Kelly," toasted Chillywinds. "You've been doing some good work. The McCrae story was first class. Perhaps that will win you a prize in the next competition!"

Kelly felt the pleasant warmth of the spotlight and liked the feeling.

"A thousand pounds first prize as well," said Chillywinds. He doffed his glass. "Well done."

Kelly raised his cut glass tumbler in response and downed the contents in one gulp. The whisky felt good and settled in his gut where it created a sweet fantasy of invincibility.

He looked around the editor's office tasting not only the whisky, but power. It was better than money. To be close to the insiders was to feel that power. 'Kelly' it was, not 'Webb'. Yes, this was what some men craved and were prepared to risk so much to achieve. For them, there was nothing better. Except sex. For that they would risk all.

Back at his desk, Kelly rang Angela. "Darling, was there any post for me this morning?"

"Some."

"Bring it to the phone please, will you? I want you to open a letter for me."

"Now?"

"Please, darling. It's important."

"Oh!" Sounding a bit worried Angela put the phone down, and returned in a few minutes. "Which one?"

He got her to describe the letters, and when she came to one that sounded likely he told her to open it.

"It's from a firm called Cadbury Hobbs."

"Read it for me, will you?"

He waited, grinning expectantly into the phone, listening to the slight rustling of paper at the other end. Eventually: "You've won an award!" Angela was squeaking with delight.

When she had calmed down he said: "Look at the prize. That's yours. You can spend, spend, spend on clothes."

"Wonderful!" she kept repeating, "marvellous!" and "you are clever!"

"Tell me all over again tonight," he said.

"Drinks on me, chaps," he said as colleagues crowded round with congratulations.

Bill and Kelly walked together back to the office from the Hack and Headline where Kelly bought drinks all round after winning his award.

"New chap joining us tomorrow, I hear."

That was news to Kelly. "New chap? Why do they need any one else? It's getting busy I suppose."

"Hadn't noticed. Maybe they are grooming him to replace one of us!"

"What would be the point of that? We're the best Bill!"

"And some of us win awards! No, there's always change, power games, intrigues, at the Graphic. There is a lot going on Kelly. New people at the top and new people make changes."

"Not us, Bill. We're too good. We fill the damn paper!"

"We'll see."

Kelly laughed. Nothing could cloud his horizon these days

Yes, he felt pretty good about everything in his life. There was that great feeling of being right on course.

It had taken a bit of steering in stormy waters after that bad time in Brighton. But the Brighton setback had been a kind of blessing. It had strengthened him. Certainly it strengthened his marriage, or rather made it stronger, as there had not been a thing wrong with it and never would be.

He had got the break he wanted early in his career. Soon after he finished his training period with a small weekly he got a job on the South Coast evening paper The First Star.

It had been great on the weekly. He had been full of youthful fervour. He worked with good colleagues, covering a newsy area close enough to London to get some of his stories in the London Evening Standard and in the nationals. That had been lucrative and fun, plus good training for knowing what was a good story.

There followed nearly three years on The First Star, still with that enthusiasm that comes with a love for the job and a talent for it that you know makes you one of the best. The days sped by in a blur of work, dreams, ambitions, love and, finally, upset.

When he started he was one of three young reporters on the paper. The other two were Charlie Brown and Tony Church. Tony was a bit older and he had already been there a year when Kelly and Charlie arrived.

They knocked about together, doing the Sussex fleshpots. There were always plenty of girls, invariably different ones every night so as to be fair to as many girls as possible.

Tony was the serious one, Charlie the daft one, with Kelly somewhere in between. They were good years. Work was a doddle because they enjoyed it. The fun of it all was considerably increased, thank you very much, by that extra money they made flogging their stuff up the line.

Their dreams and ambitions were enjoyed endlessly over endless pints. Work, dreams, ambitions - then love, when Kelly met Angela. "She's a knock-out," he enthused to the others. From then on there were only two different girls, because wherever Kelly went, Angela went too.

Charlie always boasted he intended to play the field until he was 50

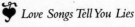

and then settle down with an heiress.

"You're like a boring old married couple," he scolded, making the latest girl on his arm giggle. "And what's all this 'just a half'?"

"Saving to get married, aren't I," said Kelly, love making him impervious to scorn. Six months later Charlie had to give up all hope for Kelly when he married Angela in her home village on the Sussex Downs.

Oh yes, those Brighton days were great days. They were good at their job and they became the golden boys on the paper.

Great days, and the cavalier attitude to life of Kelly and Charlie made sure they got the most out of them. Social life and work life were fun. They were adept at dodging the boring jobs, the re-writes and the parish news beats.

The news editor liked them, noting that they worked well together and needed the minimum supervision to produce the goods.

They were the blue-eyed boys and got cocky with it. Three Musketeers. As long as they produced plenty of good stories, and they did, they were given a pretty free hand. Charlie and Kelly revelled in the scope for making the extra money from selling their stories to the nationals. This was supposed to be a sacking offence, but it was a lax rule and the liveliest reporters ignored it.

"If we don't sell our stuff, the local agencies will," Charlie argued. The thought of some freelance buying a copy of the paper and reeling off their work over the phone incensed him.

"They may make an extra phone call or two, but really we are handing them money on a plate! It doesn't do a scrap of harm to our paper. Everything we write appears here first - the day before! So what's wrong with it?"

"Nothing!" agreed Kelly bullishly and Tony, who always seemed to go along with their reasoning, did not disagree.

It was extra money that Kelly in particular went after as he and Angela saved the deposit for their first home.

The lads were in love with the job, and there was never any suggestion they did not work hard for their paper. Whenever they argued the point over many a happy pint, they never failed to remind themselves that knowing what constituted a good Fleet

Street story meant they wrote good yarns for their own paper. A convenient morality, but it was true nevertheless.

Then came the upset. Wise executives build a management-buffer between them and the people who do the work. It increases their importance and their power-security. If things go wrong there is someone other than themselves to carry the can. They use words like accountability, efficiency and productivity; jargon that justifies spending a thousand pounds on management salaries to save a few quid in wasted time among the working staff.

The trio's mistake was in enjoying their job and making no attempt to disguise the fun they got from it. Youthful arrogance or youthful honesty, either way it caused a constant drip of mutterings from dull reporters stuck in dull routines.

Eventually one sour remark hit home. 'Who's supposed to be in charge here?' That woke up someone in management that another decision ought to be made, as one had not been made for some time. It was decided that tighter controls were needed on the three. The news editor knew they were good reporters who he did not have to chivvy along. To his credit he stood up to management and argued that they were good at their job, and did not abuse their freedom to roam. A compromise was arrived at where they had their own office and worked as a team on off-diary stories. Tony, the elder by a couple of years, was made a kind of team leader, answerable to the news editor.

They had been genuine in their congratulations for Tony. "Who wants to be a bureaucrat?" Charlie joked to Kelly in the pub that evening. Tony was not with them, but then that was not all that unusual lately. Tony had always been the quiet one of the three, a bit of an outsider. It was something Kelly only noticed later, looking back. The laughs and the mischief were always initiated by Charlie and himself.

Tony had tended to always do things by the book, taking proper hours for lunch and staying on in the office even when there was nothing to do. Work done, Kelly and Charlie were more likely to be round the local snooker hall.

After he was put in charge they expected everything to carry on

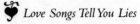

much as before. After all, Tony was much their age and they were a damn sight better than he was in coming up with a story. But inside the ambitious Tony, who they had regarded as a mate, there was a blossoming bureaucrat. Being put in charge revealed the real person. He thought he had been promoted as head of a major department the way he behaved. Before his promotion they had worked together as young people do, free and easy, throwing ideas about like confetti. Now, despite the fact that there were still only the three, he set up a command structure. They had regular meetings.

"Conferences, for God's sake!"

Charlie was incredulous.

"He is only two feet away at the next desk. We used to get an idea, sling it about between us, and have it done by our second cup of coffee!"

Tony had watched and learned however. He had seen how those in charge of the paper, the layers of management, worked. If management had been like Kelly and Charlie, 'Where's the story? Write it!' there would not be enough work to keep them occupied. The secret of security in management, Tony correctly concluded, was to set up structures. This created a system of control that gave a manager existence, importance, protection. The structure might or might not improve efficiency. Probably not, but it would protect management.

Tony had yet to learn how to smile and give assurances that nothing would change before making changes. He issued memos to Kelly and Charlie when he could have got some coffees from the machine and had a chat.

"In the time it takes to explain it, I could write it," complained Kelly.

But Tony had got it right. He had watched closely those who had climbed the editorial ladder, and had learned.

Where once they had been three mates working well together, now Tony was the boss and acting like it. He was too inexperienced to handle it well, and they were too young to take it well. He was too serious; they were not serious enough.

The Three Musketeers became two Cavaliers and a Roundhead.

Unwisely, Tony dug his heels in and tried to exert his authority. Unwisely, they resisted. So Tony tried to get support from the management, but he was just told to 'make it work'. Now Tony was on the back foot. The other two twigged this and they made little effort to hide their satisfaction.

Tony finally got the chance for revenge when they sold a story to the Daily Express. As usual, the story had appeared first in their paper, but Tony reported the matter to the management. It is all about timing in politics, office variety or otherwise.

One day you may get a rollicking. On another day, for the same misdemeanour the boss will decide on dismissal. Kelly and Charlie were not too worried. They anticipated a lecture, and then it would blow over. "We'll just do it quietly in future," Charlie said with a confident grin.

Kelly and Charlie were sure they would only get a reprimand, and it would all be forgotten. They were good at their job, and cocky with it. The paper was not going to lose two of its best reporters just to back that prat Tony.

The pair were summoned to the managing editor's office. They paused outside the door to wipe the grins of their faces and look suitably contrite. Two minutes later they were back clearing their desks. That was another lesson: management looks after its own.

"They can't sack us for that," stormed Charlie. "Everyone does it. Even the boss flogs stories to nationals, or he did when he was a reporter. We'll fight this," he vowed, still incensed as they reviewed the disaster over a pint.

"There's nothing anyone can do," said Kelly. "Maggie Thatcher killed off the unions. How many are left in the NUJ or the Institute? Are you in?"

Charlie shook his head.

"No, so you've got no cover. Forget it, mate. I'm ready to move on anyway."

By the end of the evening and three or four pints later, they had got life into perspective again.

Charlie gestured obscenely. "They can stuff their job – right up!"

"It's time to move to Fleet Street anyway," said Kelly. "That's where we were going, remember? It's the best thing that could happen!"

They laughed scornfully at the sodding world and clasped hands across the table. Sometimes ambition needs a shove.

Angela was brilliant. Furiously she slated the fools who ran the paper. "They don't deserve you," she stormed. "You were the best reporter on the paper!"

That made him brim with a superb feeling of invincibility and he hugged and hugged her for a good five minutes!

The sacking had come at the wrong time. He and Angela had scraped together the deposit on a new home and had only been settled in three months. Angela worked extra hours to a month before Jo was born to make sure their mortgage got paid. Kelly went freelance but it was unreliable and hard hand-to-mouth money. It took him two years, during which time Thomas was born, but he finally landed a short contract on a national.

"I would not have done it without you darling," he told Angela as they enjoyed their first evening out since his sacking to celebrate. Whatever the world chucked at you life was very sweet if you had someone like Angela on your side.

Charlie had left for a job on a Kent evening. His last scornful words were: "What is it about people that changes them when they get a little bit of power?" He and Kelly kept in touch, occasionally meeting up for a pint.

After a few short-term contracts on national newspapers Kelly was offered a job on the Graphic. There his talent for investigative reporting soon earned him a place on their elite team. It was a harder and tougher world, both in regard to the work and the people he worked with, but now he reckoned he was well able to take care of himself.

When he telephoned Charlie for a chat he reminded him of his parting words. "I tell you what, Charlie, you should see how people change when they get a lot of power!"

Kelly's youthful idealism had lasted longer than most; cynicism cuts in sooner rather than later in the media business, but the Brighton incident had underlined the fact that journalists are same as everyone else.

∼ 16 ∼

Gazing westwards from his homeward evening train Kelly understood very well why John Betjeman had been moved to write such evocative lines about London's suburbs. The sun was going down in a Turner landscape. The haze of factory smoke, car fumes, and general pollution the capital had energetically produced during another day of making money had been enchanted by the forgiving sun into the stuff dreams are made on.

A young woman in the seat opposite was looking out of the window. She was smiling to herself, the sun warming memories perhaps.

Kelly had seen her on the train quite often. She was very pretty and with the Betjeman sunshine caressing her face, lost in thought, she was herself an inspiration for a poem. So lost was she in reverie he was able to look at her openly, pleasurably.

Then she suddenly turned and caught his eye. He smiled and she smiled back with the reserved recognition of regular commuters. He looked out of the window into his own thoughts. Millions of solitary men were out there, millions of women alone. Everyone looking for the perfect partner, and so few succeeding. With all that willingness and all that choice the success rate should surely be better. Perhaps it needed a mathematician to solve it. Reality divided by dreams equalled…? Or should it be dreams divided by reality?

The young woman became lost in her thoughts again and on such an evening there was, surely, love in the air? It is what such evenings are for. Whoever she was thinking of was a lucky man.

So was he! Thoughts of Angela gave him a great idea. Kelly scrolled up his home number on his mobile phone and called her.

"I love you," he said as soon as she answered.

There was silence, then a throaty voice replied: "This is the Meadow Gate police station Guv."

"What the hell are you doing with my wife?"

"Looking after her a bit better than you have been doing lately, Guv. Always at work, never home until seven o'clock or even later.

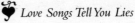

You keep saying you love her, and she says she loves you. But sometimes she thinks you love your job a bit too much."

"Not guilty. It's a lie. And I'll prove it. You tell her that I will be home in a jiff. Tell her to bung any burnt offerings she might have been preparing …"

"…burnt offerings! You cheeky!…"

"… in the bin, put on something that shows off her gorgeous figure to perfection and will make all the other fellows in the Whitewaters want to shoot themselves because they are not me, and then get one of her friends to baby-sit tonight."

"Right-ho Guv. Consider it done. See you in a minute. Oh, and Guv…"

"Yes?"

"…I love you."

This time the young woman had been watching him. He had whispered very quietly into the phone but she had guessed from his face he was phoning someone special. She looked away quickly with a smile. Pretty enough to attract any man, and that smile would haplessly ensnare the willing victim. Kelly felt the old Brighton Kelly stirring and it was very nice. She really was a little charmer. Yeah, he was feeling pretty good tonight!

Angela saw him coming up the path and opened the front door with a flourish.

"I'm ready and waiting," she said. Kelly was halted his tracks, absolutely gobsmacked. Angela always looked good when she dressed up, but tonight she looked as though it would be kinder if she did not tell him how much her clothes had cost.

"Gordon Bennett!" was all he could manage.

Angela kissed him, well pleased with the effect she had on him. "You said spend it on clothes."

"But not take out a mortgage!"

"You always tell me to buy the best!"

Kelly gallantly pooh-poohed the small fortune the clothes must have cost, with: "Only the best for the best" and punctuated every word with a kiss.

"Worth every penny of a thousand pounds - when we get it!" he added, holding her at arms length to admire her. "You look million quid!"

"I didn't spend it all! You've got some change."

"Then we'll blow it tonight!"

"And I've bought you a present." She handed him a boxed set of CDs and when he saw the title Hits of the Thirties and Forties he was delighted.

"Brilliant, thank you darling. And some Al Bowllys!" he chortled.

"You must have just about every song and artist from that era by now."

"They knew how to write them in those days."

"We get good songs nowadays."

"Not the same. Those songs…they hit the spot, connected, made people feel better - told them what they wanted to hear."

"But very old fashioned," she teased.

"Then I'm old fashioned, and I'll serenade you tonight."

"Not in public!"

"Certainly not! They don't pay, they don't hear."

They laughed as he hugged her. He could not sing for toffee, but loved to warble the tunes from those days, and they often provided him with the words and music to waltz her to bed.

"Sexy!" Thomas and Jo were at the top of the stairs giggling as they spied on their parents embracing.

"Denise is baby-sitting. She will be here soon, so get ready," Angela called up the stairs as her husband bounded up to deal with his offspring.

"There's plenty of time."

"There isn't. Hurry up!"

Angela had got the car out of the garage and Denise had arrived by the time he was ready. "You call that hurrying up? You men talk about women taking hours to get ready!"

Kelly took over the driver's seat. "They wanted me to help with their homework. Do you know, Jo is getting damn good at maths. Too good, she's leaving me floundering!"

"She takes after me."

"Oh, big head!"

"It was my best subject!"

He took one hand off the wheel and pulled her to him. "You're my best subject."

He could not change gear with his arm round her, and the transmission jerked as they went round a roundabout in top.

"Darling, this is doing the engine no good!"

"Blow the engine! It's doing me good."

"My word, what has brought all this on?"

What had brought it on? At the back of his mind all day had been Mrs Pattimore. He gave Angela another squeeze and then had to take his arm away to change gear and slow into the restaurant's driveway.

He had long ago resolved never bring his work home. He realised well enough that he made a good living doing stories of trouble and woe. They often involved families just like his. He always pushed that out of his mind and focussed on the facts, and stayed focussed. He had a job to do, and did it well. The world was not his responsibility.

"It's spring! That must be it. April in Meadow Gate, thereby hangs a song." April already! "We have got to start thinking of where to go on holiday. Last year we dithered, and the summer went."

"You dithered! Always so wound up in your work!"

"You're right. Work is a four-letter word. Time goes too fast when you are happy. And we are happy, aren't we?"

Angela gave him a hug that was more eloquent than 'yes'.

With that little matter settled to mutual satisfaction they walked arm in arm into the restaurant. They were shown to their table amid greetings from people who knew them, or more accurately who knew Angela. She was a very popular woman in the Meadow Gate area. Locals hardly ever saw him, away at his job so much. Angela was involved in lots of things, among them the PTA, the community hall committee and Scouts and Guides now Thomas and Jo were at that stage.

Tonight she looked stunning in her new outfit. As she exchanged pleasantries with acquaintances at other tables Kelly counted his blessings.

Of those, at least, he was certain.

— 17 —

Senator Booth dominated the conversation of the Graphic staff in the Hack and Headline. He was being interviewed on the lunchtime news.

The senator was constantly setting new standards in sex scandals. Over the past year he had hit the headlines regularly, denying one blatant affair after another. The evidence was always inescapable, and the impression was that he was never trying too hard to escape it. It would, after all, be quite difficult for any man to show genuine outrage at being accused of sexual athleticism.

The heavies on the Graphic were rarely envious of other reporters. They always reckoned to get their share, and more, of the juicy stuff. When other newspapers competed for the same stories, the Graphic reporters could usually give measure for measure.

This latest Senator Booth saga was something else however.

Frank sighed. "I thought we had some right clowns among our lot but this guy is the answer to a reporter's prayer."

The near-daily reports from across the pond amounted to a real-life cartoon strip. 'Superstud Senator' was the theme of most headlines, as one buxom lovely after another revealed their sexual encounters.

"Superstar Senator, in my book," said Frank admiringly. "Compared to this American guy our politicians are wimps. How many women is it now?"

The Booth saga, always simmering, had been on the front pages for months, over a year in fact.

"On Broadway it would have made a fortune," quipped Kelly.

Bill dryly topped that. "On Broadway, it *will* make a fortune." Bill was right on that one but first Booth went for a bigger audience.

In the past the senator had survived several sex scandals. They cropped up whenever he ran for office, yet somehow he had always managed to get elected. His antics in bed and broom cupboards should have long since finished him off as a politician but it was the age of 'anything goes' and such things were daily on the telly.

Now his political ambitions were becoming ludicrous: he wanted to be President of the United States. At his party's summer convention

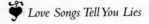

prior to the autumn presidential election he had announced he was seeking nomination as his party's candidate. Because of his reputation this otherwise domestic news made the world's Press. To the amazement of non-Americans he got support from enough state delegates. Sophisticated street-wise Americans, living in an America that was more or less permanently politically punch drunk, would have bet on it.

Then the senator announced he would contest a state primary to show his 'election worth' and convince his party he was the man for their final choice of presidential candidate. The move ensured he would continue to be news. Raking up his lurid past was near-nightly entertainment on television news the world over.

Now a woman party worker, leggy and bosomy like all the other accusers, claimed he had sex with her in a toilet cubicle at party headquarters. She was Maria Guerecki, the latest of the always generously endowed young women to come forward to denounce the senator.

One snippet from across the Atlantic that provided material for chat shows and gags for comedians was a street interview in which a man declared : "It proves the man has balls!"

"So, that makes him eligible for president." That was Bill's contribution. It was as sane as any, either side of the Atlantic.

★

Kelly could not for the life of him manage to infuse any enthusiasm into his greeting for the man they appointed to be Buller's deputy. It was not that Kelly was worried about any 'new man'. He had always kept out of office intrigue. The times he had seen people het up, flouncing about the office, and next day - what had it all been about? He was going to get on because of what he could do. He would write his way to the top. He was never going to be a Tony. Life was too short; the job itself far more interesting.

It was a worthy philosophy, but not one to rely on too much if there is someone in your office like Barry Green. Right from the start Kelly did not take to him. Practically his first thought was how eminently suitable the man was as Buller's deputy and that was not a nice way to greet anyone, even silently.

"Welcome to the SS Squad Barry," said Bill.

The new arrival nodded hello to everyone and then asked: "Why is it called the SS Squad?"

"Sex and sleaze, and we are the squad who get the job of writing about it."

Green greeted this with a mechanical laugh: "Sex and sleaze squad?"

"Well, we do stories of a loftier nature, but sex and sleaze is the name of the game at the moment," Bill explained with a mock gravity.

"It helps if you have no taste, no standards and no morals," Frank guffawed. It was a friendly gesture. Welcome to the gang.

Kelly had watched Green's reaction to these comments. His laugh had been devoid of humour and his smile was fixed. It chilled Kelly's response, though he was aware a new man might just feel ill at ease. What is this churlishness Webb! He sensed Green seemed to pick up the cool vibes. His smile was as perfunctory as Kelly's as they shook hands. It had been bloody unfriendly to a new arrival, but Kelly did not regret it for long.

Bill was very sharp. After a couple of days he said with a keen look at Kelly: "You don't like this new bloke, do you."

Kelly was evasive. "He's all right."

"You haven't met him before have you?" Bill knew that journalists moved around in a small world, taking their rivalries with them.

"No. But he reminds me of someone I knew in Brighton."

Bill did not understand, but did not pursue it.

Charlie understood when he and Kelly met up for a drink.

"It's the first thing I thought of as soon as I met him – Tony!"

Charlie got the picture vividly. "Oh God!" he groaned. "Maybe he's come back to haunt you in another body!"

Over the next few weeks Kelly knew that his instinctive reaction to Green had been spot on. Charles Dickens would have relished creating a character based on Green's oily personality.

— 18 —

"Here they come, lock up your lovers." Archie Archer was pleased to see Frank and Kelly come into the bar with a crowd of reporters and sub-editors from the Graphic. As usual he was propping up the section of bar he rented, and was just beginning to think that he was going to go home that evening without being able to exercise his wit. It was his pleasure to wind up the younger journalists on the paper with his 'in my day' rants. His style was growlly and po-faced. It was an act but he was so good at it that it really did upset some. Occasionally he leavened his tirades with a smoky grin but not often enough. Certainly not for Frank who groaned as he and Kelly and several of the Graphic staff stopped by for a quickie before catching their trains. Frank found old Archie's harangues wearisome.

The ageing hack had a knack of delivering his jokes at other people's expense with an edge. When he was on the outside of a couple of pints the edge cut. Not many could parry that sharp tongue good-naturedly. Once he had been one of Fleet Street's top reporters. He had been there, done it, fiddled the expenses and reckoned he was now entitled to hand out stick. So he handed it all round, but he most enjoyed targeting the new bloods, all on big pay contracts. They had a killer instinct with the written word, but they were rarely a match for Archie when it came to the verbals.

"It's 'lock up your daughters'," ventured a reporter pedantically.

"Not with this lot," snorted Archie. "It's lovers they are interested in – and whose marriage have you buggered up today, chaps? Or have you been busier than usual, and buggered up several?"

"It's news, remember news Archie?" someone from the back of the crowd enquired sarcastically. These days Archie edited the readers' letters page, but the jibe did not disturb him.

"News? News is for newshounds. You lot are news mongrels! So whose lives will you turn upside down in tomorrow's paper? And another politician, no worse than any other, just unluckier, has to resign?"

Kelly clapped Archie's shoulder. "Now there's a quaint old fashioned attitude. Resign? Maybe they fell on their sword once, but nowadays it takes a lot of lies ands scandal to get a politician to admit anything, let alone resign."

"Must be disappointing for you lot."

"They take on the job, its power and perks, they've got to accept the downside."

"So nothing's private if you're public?"

"If someone has power, the public have a right to know everything about him, down to the size of his socks."

A woman writer on an up-market rag butted in, deciding to side with Archie just for the hell of it.

"Why? Why do we have to know every-bloody-thing Webb? We're not talking sock sizes, we talking moral judgements. Oh, your readers need all these scandals to make a balanced political judgement, do they? That's why you publish all this sleaze stuff is it? If you believe that, you believe anything!"

"The voter votes in the whole man, and is entitled to know what he is getting for his money."

Archie got in a swipe: "The gospel according to Webb!"

"According to Joe Public: which papers have the biggest circulations? Those that reveal the sock sizes!"

Frank guffawed. "Or in the case of Senator Booth, the size of his jockstrap!"

Another woman at the bar who worked in a city investment office had been bursting to have her say and finally exploded.

"Archie's right. You bloody men are obsessed with sex! Why do you reporters have such a nasty view of life?"

Bill turned to her with a kindly expression. "It's in our job description."

"God, I wished Bonker Booth was over here," sighed Frank, lost in wishful thinking.

"He can stay in bloody America," snapped the city investment woman. "We've enough over here. Anyway, is your sex life the business of your boss?"

Bill pounced on that. "Yes, it is if it's in work time. If you sign up for a job nine to five, what you do nine to five that affects it is your boss's business.

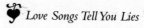

"A politician signs up to the job 24-7. Whose back he scratches, who scratches his, whose bed – and so on …." Bill let it trail away. Enough said?

Frank rounded on Archie. "What did you do if you came across a bit of scandal in your day, Archie, ignore it? You'd be some journalist if you did! Your generation were so soft-hearted?"

"Sex out of hours – it always happened. But we did not fill the paper with politicians' sex lives – and we sold a fat sight more papers in those days. We had some real news sense – not like you lot. Circulations were greater then for all newspapers."

"That's because of television," said Kelly.

"Different times, different standards Archie," said Bill.

"Lower standards!"

Bill shrugged. "What are we supposed to do – go around looking for good in everyone in public life? These guys hire PR people to do that."

"The lower our standards are, the higher everyone else's!" The reporter who delivered that thought it rather clever and was aggrieved it was lost in the general hubbub.

The pub had one wall decorated with an Hogarthian-style painting of a 17th century hostelry, with gape-mouthed drunks and painted whores rollicking their way to hell. As Bill listened to his fellow hacks ranting and hooting with chauvinistic mirth he looked up at the picture. Fancifully he allowed his imagination to continue, like a film camera changing the scene, out over modern-day London. In his mind's eye he saw all that debauchery was being re-enacted in modern dress, and with an enthusiasm and invention not one whit less profligate.

Another of the pub regulars joined in the fun. "You reporters are all hypocrites," she scoffed. "Come on, how many of you can say they havn't had an affair?"

This was greeted by a male chorus: "Mind your own business!"

"Oh, different now is it? You can ask rude questions, I can't."

"We're an ugly bunch," said Bill wearily. "But the others are even uglier. The ugly in pursuit of the uglier, as Oscar Wilde might have said."

"An affair? Not our Kelly Webb!" Archie roared. "This is Mr Happy Family."

Kelly groaned, finished the dregs of his drink, and headed for the door. He guessed what was coming. He chuckled as he made his way through the evening scrum to the Underground. He had once earnestly and unwisely admitted that he liked his lot.

Yes, he had admitted, he liked his job. He enjoyed commuting to work, and he liked being married, living in the suburbs and with a mortgage big enough to sink the Bank of England. Yes, he liked London and, yes, he thought the stuff reporters like him wrote was important. In short, he liked his life.

He also had a lovely wife he loved and two super kids.

God, that had been a mistake! Archie was not the sort to let him forget that alcoholic confession.

Frank followed Kelly out of the pub and caught up with him. Archie leaned on the bar and watched them go with a wide grin of victory.

"Old Archie loves to give us stick," he grumbled. "He's only having a laugh I suppose. But a lot of people do it seriously - blame us, I mean."

"Who else? Like Bill said, we're an ugly bunch."

"Yeah, but the others are uglier."

"We write about it, and make a living from it. Don't let it get to you Frank. I reckon most people are on our side, it's just that they are the majority, and majorities are always silent."

Frank felt a surge of nobility. "The public blame us for the rubbish they read. It's 'those muck-raking reporters' again. People who complain about the stuff we write won't buy papers unless they are full of stuff they can complain about."

"Young man," said Kelly, thinking of Basil and Bertie, "I am impressed with your analysis of the British newspaper reader."

"A quick one after work does wonders for the brain."

"Don't weaken Frank. That's the secret."

Catching his usual train with nice timing Kelly settled into his seat. That was enough soul-searching for one day. Never mind the ethics as long as the pay's good.

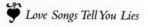

"Someone's happy."

Seated opposite him were two women, homeward bound after a day's shopping in the City judging by their collection of bags and parcels. The one who had spoken had espied him smiling at his thoughts. Responding to their chirpy good humour Kelly broadened his smile.

"It's nice to see someone with something to smile about, love," said her companion who had the London evening newspaper on her lap. She tapped it. "There's not a lot to smile about, not when you're reading the papers."

Kelly sighed inwardly. Not again! What was it about today?

"It's all we ever read about," added her friend in a sniffy tone. "We were just saying." She did not need to say what, that certain tone of voice said it all. Her eyes nailed Kelly with an invitation to join in the discussion.

"There's a lot of it," he agreed warily.

She was delighted to get him talking.

"I agree with you love. You're quite right, there's far too much. Who wants to read about people's sex lives, and all those goings on?"

Illogically they both squawked with laughter at the thought. That gave Kelly the chance to try and disappear behind a grin. No escape there however, not now they were enjoying themselves.

"Don't you agree?" she persisted.

He said yes, he did, hoping agreement would spare him as cowardice may spare the coward. It didn't.

"You wonder what sort of people would write such things, don't you?"

He nodded and kept the grin determinedly in place. It was no protection. The pursuit was relentless. They had taken a fancy to him and he was done for.

"What do you think?"

It had been a long day, but from somewhere he found the strength.

"Well, I suppose they are only doing their job."

"Doing their job?" The first woman pondered this with a grimace. "But why can't they do their job and write about the good side of people?"

Her friend came to his rescue. "Don't get on to the poor man. He's not to blame."

"Of course he's not. Sorry love. You're not a reporter are you?"

"Ooh, he might be!" laughed the first woman.

"Oh my Gawd you're not, are you?" The thought made them laugh even more.

He lied with a smile.

"'Course he isn't. He's got a lovely smile though, hasn't he?"

They had almost had him cornered, and he saw the chance to escape. "I see you've been busy spending."

"Yes, up for the sales."

"Where from?" he enquired politely.

"Brighton," one of them replied.

"Brighton?" He had escaped but was careless. "I used to work there."

"Really? What doing?"

Damn! He was caught again!

The first woman chided her friend. "Don't be so nosey!"

"No, it's not being nosey," her friend persisted good-naturedly, giving Kelly a cheeky smile. "It's not, is it love?"

Kelly could hardly disagree. Turning mischievously to her friend the woman mused: "I reckon he's a film star, don't you?" That made them laugh!

"Well, as you say he's got a nice smile," her friend added. "'He could be on the telly couldn't he? He could take me out any time!" Her bosoms danced merrily in tandem with her chortles.

"Now we're embarrassing the poor chap. Leave him be!" chuckled the other.

"Sorry love," said the first woman, but she was reluctant to stop the fun. "Tell us though, what do you do for a living? You've got us all curious."

Kelly could not avoid an answer and was about to accept defeat and tell them when he looked again at the attractive woman nearby who he had been admiring before the two had started speaking to him. The woman was dressed very tastefully and Kelly loved well-dressed women. Angela was one of those lucky wives who are

positively encouraged by adoring husbands to spend, spend, spend on clothes.

"Fashion," said Kelly airily. Well, news follows fashion. One day this scandal is in fashion, another day, that.

"That sounds like a good job," one said, making the assumption that Kelly hoped she would.

"But they say it's very bitchy, the fashion business," said the other. Her friend looked at Kelly. "Is it luv?"

"Ferocious!"

They loved that and chortled some more. With no idea of how he was going to go on from there he was lucky. After a few Ahs and Ohs one of them suddenly reverted to the original topic.

"It's the same in Brighton," she said. "The paper there is always full of rubbish." That tickled Kelly which in turn delighted the woman. "Something's made him laugh," she said and Kelly finally made good his escape, laughing all the way.

"Isn't he lovely?" said her companion as they chuckled along.

Walking from the station past the innocent frontages of the suburban houses Kelly played a mind game, pondering on the lives lived behind the net curtains. When he and Angela were dreaming of their first house, they liked to go for walks in the suburbs and discuss what they would buy one day. At the same time they would have fun speculating on the sort of people who lived in the houses they passed. Angela insisted on her theory that just as people are supposed to end up looking like their pets, so they became typical incumbents of a certain kind of house.

In that big old rambling house there is a large happy family and the father is a doctor or a headmaster, she might assert with the utmost certainty. Kelly would join in the game. That bungalow? Oh look at the neat little garden - a nice old couple for certain. Who lives in that brand new detached house? A couple with no children and high-flying careers, absolutely certain!

They always explored the same neighbourhoods they liked, so later they occasionally saw the inhabitants through a window or in the garden. Then they would gleefully remind each other how wrong their guesses had been. They thought it was great fun.

You never can tell by appearances mused Kelly as he walked to his car through Reigate's mellow suburbs. Most English, most respectable of homes. The people who lived in them valued their privacy, indeed guarded it fiercely with hedges, walls and curtains. Their love lives did not sell papers - except the Surrey Mirror perhaps! Only the scale of their lives made them different, not the difference of their lives; but then an erring husband hiding behind one of those respectable frontages was unlikely to affect the course of history.

⁓ 19 ⁓

Linda Merchant arranged for flowers to be sent to her mother so that they would be there before she called that evening. It was a peace offering. She knew her mother would be disappointed that she was going to stay in London again for the weekend.

There was no need for the flowers. Her mother was delighted that her daughter had found someone. "But it has been two months since you popped down," she complained the last time Linda telephoned and said she could not make it. "This Robin must be very special."

"He is mother," Linda had replied, as though just saying the words gave her pleasure. His first name was all Mrs Merchant knew about her daughter's latest love but she sensed that Linda did not want to be pressed on the subject. Whoever he was she was pleased for her daughter who had been hurt more times than any girl should be.

When Linda eventually brought him down to see them would have to be soon enough to find out who he was. Nevertheless when Linda had called that evening to say she would not be down as promised, her mother was just a trifle piqued.

"When *are* you coming down my dear? We are beginning to have to look at your photograph to remind us what you look like!"

"Mother! I will be down, but…."

"I know, you are seeing him again. That's lovely. We have been thinking. If you can't get down to see us, why don't we come up to see you?"

"Yes, I suppose so."

"You don't sound very enthusiastic! We could all go to a theatre, dinner, or something."

"Oh, perhaps."

"He sounds very secretive!"

"It's not that."

"No, no. It's just me being nosey. As long as you are happy."

"Don't worry mother."

"It's a mother's privilege. Anyway, one day perhaps we will be allowed to see this amazing man." Linda's response was a hesitant laugh.

Mrs Merchant knew she was not going to get an answer yet. One day, in Linda's own time.

"Anyway, thank you for the flowers. 'Bye love."

"'Bye."

Linda's father heard the farewells.

"Was that Linda? What did she say?"

"Oh, nothing much." Except between the lines, thought her mother. You are keeping something from us Linda. "I'm beginning to think we will never know who this latest great love is."

Mr Merchant put his arm around his wife.

"She has not been lucky in love, has she?"

"Hmm, no, well it can be a bit of a lottery."

Mr Merchant grinned broadly and squeezed her.

"I got all six numbers!"

★

Robin Lane braked the car sharply to a halt and regarded the hotel sourly. Even before he had set off with Elly he had regretted asking her to spend the weekend with him.

At the time it seemed an ideal opportunity, as he had long fancied Elly, nicely nubile and fun-loving. With Mrs Lane conveniently away the same weekend on one of her many charity events he had jumped at the chance and booked the hotel. Then bugger! they had scheduled a meeting to decide on which MPs would be going on the trade delegation to Japan. It was one of the Westminster jollies he had had his eye on for some time; he had always wanted to try those Japanese massage parlours. He would rather have been at the meeting to make sure of a place on the trip.

"It looks rather nice," said Elly, peering through the windscreen. "There's a small hotel….."

When Lane's response to this whimsy was just a grunt she thought: Oh! Oh! Throughout the drive Lane had been monosyllabic and she had been unable to lighten his moodiness try as she might.

It was going to be a lot worse when she told him the bad news: it was the wrong time of the month. She was right.

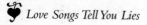

"The curse!" Lane threw up his hands in despair.

Elly sat on the bed hiding her face, trying to prevent herself laughing.

"You agreed to come on this weekend when you are out of action!" Lane stomped up and down the bedroom. "I've put off important meetings for this weekend!"

"You invited me, remember!" Elly retorted spiritedly. "Look, I'm sorry darling, but they were not due, I promise you."

"Let's have dinner," he snapped, his hard features made uglier by frustration.

By the time the desert was served he had calmed a little, and was even beginning to see the funny side of it. A phone call from London telling him it was OK, he was on the Japan jolly, had helped.

"We'll go back early tomorrow," he decided without discussion.

"Why? It's going to be a sunny day. There are some nice walks round here."

"Walks? I did not come here for a walk!"

"Do you good. We can go back in the evening,"

"Well, I suppose I will have some energy to spare now!"

Elly used the bathroom first and when Lane came out of the shower she was sitting pixie-like on the bed.

"I should have brought a good book," said Lane as he got into bed.

"Tell me…" Elly paused, considering how to phrase her question, then with a giggle blurted: "Do you ever get fed up with sex?"

Lane stared at her. What sort of bloody stupid question is that!

"What? With no sex, yes!"

"I do."

"Well, you'll be happy tonight then!"

"Have you ever enjoyed being with a woman, on a date, without having sex?"

"No."

"That must be boring."

"Not as boring as not having it!"

"Think, though – tell me, don't you enjoy it better if you have, well, something more than just … just this? A sex arrangement."

Lane reply was a long puzzled look. What are you on about Elly?

"I mean, just putting it about. If it wasn't me, it would be someone else. It's like… like a treadmill. I'd like to be liked just for… well, for me. Not just what's in my knickers."

'Knickers' caused Lane to snort a laugh.

Funny how the mind works. Out of the blue had come a memory snapshot of Tod. Thinking of him had prompted her questions.

She tried again. "Isn't there anyone you remember fondly even if they were not that good in bed?"

"They're all good in bed when they're in bed with me." Lane laughed, his bragging putting him a better mood.

Elly did not reply immediately, still thinking of Tod. Dear Tod. No Casanova, but we had such a lovely time together. He was fun. I think if I was to get into a serious relationship it could be with him rather than a lot of brain-dead stallions I've known. This thought surprised her.

She returned to her questioning. "No one?"

It was his turn to be surprised by his thoughts. After a moment of silence, he started to say: "Yes, someone…"

Elly turned to him, eyes avid with curiosity. "Who?"

Uncomfortable with her questioning Lane tried to veer away.

"Yes, someone I suppose. I don't remember. I don't think about it! You think too much. Just take what you can while it's on offer."

"Really, no one special?"

"No one in particular. Sex, that's what there is between a man and woman! What else joins them?" He sniggered. "Sex makes the world go round."

"That's love."

"Same thing."

"You really think so? Doesn't it all sometimes get a bit all the same, not much difference when its just sex?" She looked at him, and seeing that face, that greedy, self-centred, face, she was glad things had turned out as they had.

Lane switched off his bedside lamp and lay down.

"I don't know - I've forgotten!"

Elly laughed, not caring in the least now. "Blame Mother Nature, not me!"

She slipped under the covers and wondered where Tod was now. It must be two years or more now since she had seen him. He had had a thing for her, and she had slept with him because he had been so besotted. Patronising really, but he had been a dear man. He had made her laugh, and it was afterwards, when she had dumped him, that she missed him. His lovemaking had been hopeless at first. So excited and inexperienced he had ejaculated before entering her and had been so crestfallen. But looking back she realised that they had had something really nice going for them. He had got better in bed, but it was just being with him that had been so good. Somehow she was always glad to see him; felt right being with him. Now, thinking about him, she imagined him as a husband and knew that it would have been good; it would have lasted. Tod was the sort any woman with sense and good taste married.

Who was he with now? Lucky girl!

She stole a glance at the disgruntled Lane's scowling face. Apart from greedy sex, what else did he have to offer a woman?

The Curse? Tonight it was The Blessing! With that smiling thought, she was soon asleep, and dreamt of Tod.

Something more important between a man and a woman than just sex? Despite himself Lane lay awake for a long time thinking about that.

And about Linda.

Thinking weakens a man. A week later Lane was back in the real world. He knew it was time to end it. That meant the warning signs had been loud and clear. For him they had to be; he was a man who saw the world through the end of his penis, and these days all he had seen was Linda. This time however the Press interest was getting too hot. How do those bastards find out? Stupid question, they always do sooner or later. His own fault, his rule was always to dump them before people started talking. Linda was a bit special, though. Poor kid, she didn't deserve all this.

Press bastards! Bloody nosey Press *bastards!* They don't care, the *bastards*, about all the trouble they cause. *Bastards!*

The way he felt about Linda, well, he had taken more of a chance.

135

You can't just walk out on a wife, just like that. She had all the money. The hassle! Thelma would fight him like hell, especially over the money. He'd look good, wouldn't he, claiming a settlement, like some Hollywood toy boy!

What the hell. It was all a game.

He turned into the road where Linda had her flat. He was not looking forward to this. She was not like his usual women. There was something about her that was very appealing. She had introduced him to the human race and he had become a temporary member.

Until now his affairs had been with high-society women whom he regarded as top price call girls. Debs, young actresses, Chelsea girls. Dumping them his exit line was "Women are my hobby," and that was the smart prat reputation he enjoyed among cronies.

Suddenly there was a spout of selfish rage. Why the hell should he have to give up the tasty Linda just because a nosey hack – a nosey *bastard!* – wanted a story? Because that was all it was; they were just looking for a juicy headline. Why him, when parliament was full of prominent politicians having it off?

Not safe any more though, not with that bugger from the Graphic poking about.

Viciously braking to a halt in front of the block of flats where she lived he marched into the building. Let's get it over with. He should have finished it with a phone call. That is how he always did it.

Linda's face lit up when she opened the door to him. Lane was surprised at his feelings when he saw her again. All his other women had been the female equivalent of himself, and he never had any difficulty in dumping them to protect his image. But this Linda, well something about her had got through to part of him no other woman had touched, and it felt good, very good.

The *bastards!*

"You won't be rushing off right away, will you," Linda implored, having grown used to the pressures on her lover to be everywhere but with her. "I've made us a nice meal."

She led him into her small dining room where a table was laid for two.

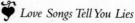

Lane had allowed himself just a few minutes for this visit, just enough to tell her it was over. But even before he saw the beautifully laid candle-lit table his real affection for this loving young woman and his hatred of the Press had bolstered his resolve. Those shits were not going to dictate his life!

He looked into Linda's smiling eyes and for once in his life wanted to be with a woman without sex on his mind. He wanted to stay; he was bloody well going to stay!

"It'll be lovely," enthused Linda. "My speciality, beef stroganoff!"

"That's wonderful," he said, and kissed her. "Of course I'll stay."

A couple of quick phone calls to cancel engagements and he sat down to enjoy one of the nicest evenings he could remember.

He raised his glass to Linda. "To us, and bugger 'em!"

Linda did not understand this, but raised hers in response .

"I love you." When he did not answer she looked at him, hesitant at first, then the need to know was too strong: "Do you love me?"

Love? That had never complicated his sex life. If he had been asked that by any of his other women it would have annoyed him.

"Yes."

His answer, arriving of its own volition, astonished him, and astonished him also because he meant it. Almost. As much as he ever could. For three hours he forgot money and politics and his wife. But only for three hours.

As he left the flat the spectre of reality was waiting.

He did not spot the car parked across the road with two men inside. Had he noticed them he would have seen the telephoto lens poking from the car window like a nosey nose.

These days the Press can take pictures without flash in almost any light. He came out nice and clear.

In the next edition of the Graphic the picture filled most of the front page with a lead to Kelly's story on an inside page. Lane entrenched; brazen and blustering; the real Lane was back in the real world.

For the first time in his life Lane felt sad at the ending of an affair, but he was not man enough for love.

For Lane the real world was money.

Disguising his shame with spurious anger at the Press bastards he telephoned Linda. He was brutally brief, finishing the call too quickly to hear her crying.

"The world is changing," he told his cronies. "There is too much of this media shit. They are cutting their own throats, all this morality stuff. I reckon all I've got to do is hang on, say no more than I have to, and it will be all forgotten in a couple of months.

"You get murderers writing books and getting paid to go on TV. I'll write a book and they'll make a film of it!"

Many a true word is said by bastards.

★

"Another victim for Mother. Lane's for it," said Frank, gleeful at the prospect.

Mother was the nickname, which no one dared use in her hearing, for the paper's columnist, the multi-award winning Penelope Hawn. Frank was right and Lane got a mauling from the keyboard of Ms Hawn. It was a memorable word-whipping that flayed his reputation to shreds. Most columnists showered him with opprobrium, but her column alone would have been enough to ensure he was not chosen by his constituency party to contest the next General Election. One almost felt sorry for the man, forced to spend the remainder of his Tory party term hastily securing directorships and consultancy posts to ensure he died as wealthy as he would have done after a career in politics.

Ms Hawn had honed a fearsome, coruscating style that earned her £200,000 a year. No newspaper had ever spent money more wisely. No sooner had some hapless philanderer fallen out of the wrong bed to read all about his wicked ways in the morning papers than he would read her column to get a second pasting. Wronged wives were her favourite.

"You can't go wrong with a wronged wife," was Frank's copyright quip. In the space of half a fag the lady, whose plump motherly face atop her column had inspired the nickname, could deliver five hundred words of invincible invective.

She was a witch of words, an ogress of opinions and tackled anything and everything if - very unlikely - there was no errant male around to string up by his jockstrap. It was always wonderful stuff which lesser writers would have been glad to produce once in a while let alone in almost every issue without fail. With consummate skill she could maintain a riveting moral tone throughout a whole column of fury.

She was the best. She could kick straight to the groin with one word, uppercut with a sentence, head butt with paragraph and lay the poor sap out for the count with the final full stop. She had turned ranting into an art form. No one could live with her. She was a celebrity in her own right, and as such could be shot down as she shot them down. But there was not a gun in town fast enough. After reading one of her articles slamming a bishop for his views that the church should not allow homosexuals into the clergy Frank protested: "she hammered the teaching profession a year ago because they wanted to encourage more homosexuals into being teachers. She's a hypocrite! She kicks whatever backside is around, if she has nothing else to fill her column."

"Have opinion, where's the subject," grinned Kelly, who was a devoted fan of Ms Hawn.

One of the aforementioned lesser writers joined in on Frank's side. "She writes three or four columns a week, each with at least four opinions. Say 12 a week, take off four weeks holidays, that is 570 opinions a year. Nobody can have that many honestly held opinions about anything!"

"She's a woman, W.O.M.A.N," Kelly persisted, staunch in his admiration of Fleet Street's most readable hack. He wagged a wise finger at the two younger men.

"As long as there are women like Penelope around shooting from the hip and saving the world, you can sleep safe in your beds at night."

"Maybe," muttered Frank, "but only by myself."

"Women writers are always playing the bastard–bashing game," complained Frank's ally.

Frank agreed. "Why is that, Kelly, seeing you know so much about women?"

"Did I say I know women? No man knows a woman! They are a

beautiful mystery."

"With knife-edge tongues!"

"Hell hath no jury like a woman scorned."

"You've been practising that Webb. Anyway, you've got it wrong. Fury, not jury. Hell hath no fury, etcetera."

"I'd sooner face hell's jury than a woman scorned." Kelly smirked victoriously. He was too good for these youngsters.

At the coffee machine another reporter quizzed Kelly on the Lane story.

"What happened to the girl, what's her name…?"

"Linda Merchant, you mean?"

"….yes, where has she gone?"

"Don't know. To ground somewhere. Never found out where she lived. She'll pop up again, no doubt."

"Telling her side of it for money no doubt, slagging Lane off, getting her revenge."

"Maybe. A woman scorned. Wouldn't blame her."

"You're a bit of a Sir Galahad I reckon Kelly," chuckled Bill. "All these wronged women you avenge."

"Yeah, not fair really is it? We don't seem to take up the sword for wronged husbands very often do we, if at all."

"Kelly Webb, the expert on adultery."

"That right Kelly?" stirred Frank.

"Chance would be a fine thing," replied Kelly, giving the standard answer.

"You're too old for that game, aren't you Kelly?" Frank kept a straight face.

Attempting a swift rejoinder Kelly failed to get his sums right.

"Ten hours in the office, eight hours sleep, three hours commuting, two hours eating. What chance do I have?"

A sharp reporter did a quick finger count. "That's 23 hours Kelly. You can do a lot in an hour. And how do we know you need eight hours sleep?"

Kelly's attempt at answering that was swamped in laughter, and he gave up. When the conversation is about sex, with men it's never sensible.

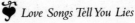

When Linda Merchant was found dead it should have made national news. Big news, in fact. The headline would have been 'M.P.'s Reject Lover Kills Herself'. All the ingredients of a good story were there. She had been the lover of Robin Lane, the man a tabloid sub-editor had dubbed the Minister for Sex.

When the Graphic's story with pictures of him leaving Linda's flat had finally nailed him there had been no escape. He issued a statement saying that he and his wife were reconciled and they just wanted to be left alone. His public posturing of remorse enabled him to remain an M.P while he sought more directorships and other ways to get rich.

Linda, young and besotted, had believed he would eventually leave his wife but then the young and besotted will believe anything. It got pages of coverage, fuelled by Lane's horribly insincere grovelling regret in television interviews as he tried to save his political skin and the weird reaction of his wife Thelma to his infidelity.

In one story she was quoted: "Marriages are made stronger by infidelity." More proof for the world and his partner that Mrs Lane was plain daft came when she left her husband, but only to travel as far as the nearest religious retreat where she was reportedly examining her soul to discover why her husband went astray.

All this diffused media focus on Linda. One or two writers did sympathetic articles on her. Penelope Hawn's was one of her brilliant best.

Inarticulate and unsophisticated, there was not enough about Linda to keep a story going. She was rapidly shuffled into obscurity which, thanks to fate's callous kindness, was the best thing. When Lane told her he was staying with his wife she was too proud to weep for the cameras. Instead she wept in her small flat in Horsham. Her death could have melodramatically resurrected the whole story but there was one missing ingredient. It was the reporter on the local weekly who had made so much money tipping off the nationals when Linda was in the news. She had moved on, along with most of her colleagues, and no one among the young new staff twigged that a young woman who had committed suicide was the once briefly famous Linda Merchant. Her parents did not want

~ 20 ~

The number was one he did not know. The bloody Press again?

"Hello?"

"Robin Lane?"

"Yes."

"William Joyce, of Joyce Choice PR."

"Yes?"

"I'd like to take you out to lunch."

Bemused, but Lane said OK. PR people would not be PR people if they were not persuasive.

When they met at the restaurant Lane quipped sourly: "Is this a free lunch?"

Joyce laughed. "Well, put it this way. It could be profitable."

"Who for?"

"Both of us."

The waiter took their orders. The preliminary courtesies did not take long. Joyce's time was too valuable to waste.

"You have had some bad Press," he said.

"An understatement. Look," Lane too had no patience, "how much? And why."

"Why? Why do you need us? Well, you don't if you want to sink out of sight. But I have been watching you on the telly, I have reached the opinion that you are a survivor. But you need a public relations firm to manage your career."

Career? Lane had thought he had been looking at the remains of a career. Not Joyce. As he read about Lane's troubles and public disgrace he had been weighing up the possibilities of profit, for him and the penis-propelled politician.

"Yes, all right. But how much? And I don't see what you or anyone can do about my career. Sacked is sacked. In time I will get back, if I have a mind for it. Maybe I will, maybe I won't, but I don't need any help. There's nothing you can teach me about survival in Westminster."

"No, not Westminster."

"What then?"

"The nation's front room."

Lane did not answer and waited.

"People hate you right now, and that's where we start. You have to meet that head on, television interviews, radio, newspapers."

"And you are going to turn me into a saint overnight."

"No, not at all. No attempt to make you look better – make you look worse more likely. Let the media dogs loose on you."

"Charming. And for this, I pay you? Thank you and good ...."

"No, they pay you. We negotiate a good fee."

Lane shrugged at that. He knew people sold their stories. "That will give them free reign."

"Yes. They will go for your jugular. They'll love it. The public will hate you."

"And to improve my public image, what will you be doing?"

"Nothing."

Lane leaned back and regarded Joyce. "Nothing? That it? Let them hang me out to dry?"

"At first, yes. We need to get some stories in the Press that demonise you."

Lane opted to stay silent and just listen to this nutter.

Joyce spelled it out: "The more people hate a public figure, the more they want to read about him. It is the public who judge, and to judge they must read, and to read they must pay, and so on. The worse you are, the wealthier. Simple as that these days."

Eventually Joyce paused and grinned at Lane. "And I'm on 30 per cent."

Two days later Joyce picked Lane up to take him to the Radio Two studios to be interviewed on Who's Who Today.

Joyce handed him a printed itinerary. "Read that on the way. It's a summary of the questions they will be asking. It will be no holds barred, just as we wanted. And tomorrow you will be interviewed by Sir Haut-Sinclair. And the article, that's settled."

"What article?" Joyce had so many schemes going Lane was losing track. "The article about your rise and fall in politics And I've got our price, five K."

Lane whistled. £5,000, for a piece of PR. The world was mad. He

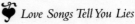

was enjoying this.

"Which paper?"

"You are going to love this - the Graphic."

"The Graphic!" Joyce was right. Lane did love that. The Graphic! They shaft him, make him notorious, then they cash in in that notoriety! It's a funny old world in media land.

Joyce pulled up at the BBC studios. He turned to Lane and they sat grinning at each other.

"I said you'd love it," said Joyce. "And that's only the start. Ever fancied having your own TV programme?"

Lane fancied it.

It took Joyce only a month to fix it up.

★

It was a typically bright fresh day for late Spring; much too nice to be doing this. The appointment was not until later in the day but Kathy decided to fill in the morning with a walk through the wildlife area leading to town to catch her bus. The footpath did not run between the town centre and the suburb where she lived, but whenever the weather was nice Kathy loved to walk that way to her office in the town. Lesley gave her a lift and dropped her off at the start of the footpath. Lesley's drive to work took her that way and she was used to this request.

When she reached the Esplanade sunlight was being bounced about on a vigorous surf and she thought, as she so often did, how lucky she was to live in such a nice part - the best part! - of England. But for how long?

The number 10 bus ran the length of the Esplanade before turning inland to Dorchester. Along the Dorchester road the bus passed the pub where their crowd had had their regular night out the week before. Quite an evening, one way and another. That cow Bella! But there had been a one good outcome, as she had been able to clear things with Lesley. And all that chatter about dating agencies and affairs. Looking back on her life - with this frightening problem on her mind she had started to do a lot of reflecting these days - had she made the most of it?

Some of her friends had happily embraced the way of modern woman, taking as many lovers as they could. They enjoyed life. Well, they said they did. Life's too short they were always saying, although quite what that had to do with finding love she had never worked out. Perhaps Lesley was right. Perhaps it was time she …perhaps she was too damn choosy! Life did not come to you. You had to go and grab it!

Oh God, listen to her!

The number ten bus was an excellent service and took passengers right to the main doors of the County Hospital. As ineluctably as life's ticking clock it arrived and she alighted.

If she were to start changing her life, she first had to learn if she had one.

★

"Kelly, do me a favour."

Kelly wondered what Penelope Hawn would sound like if ever she spoke without a fag on her lips. The smoke deposits of a lifetime gave her a throaty drawl. Kelly thought it was sexy.

"You only have to ask."

"You sweetie, my most handsome fan," she cooed into the telephone from her smoky den. Kelly made no secret of his admiration for the column written by Fleet Street's most irascible writer. "Look, you did the story on Robin Lane. What happened to the girl, Linda … I forget her surname?"

"No idea. Why? What's Lane been doing now?"

"Can't you guess? What all these bloody bedhoppers do, he's written a book. The sod's got a £250,000 advance.

"I'm going to crucify the bastard!"

She did too, savagely, dismembering him limb by limb. The article put thousands on the book's sales.

★

"Kelly, any ideas for some really nasty thing – not murder but almost anything else – that I can do to make loads of money? It's got to be something really tacky. Something that makes me a public bastard."

Kelly swivelled his chair and regarded Frank as a teacher might regard a stupid boy, over a pair of imaginary specs. It amounted to the only answer that Kelly was going to make to such a question.

"You see, I have come to the conclusion that honest graft will never make me rich. I need some street cred. I need to become famous

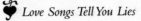

for being a total bastard, then I will get on the telly making millions in celebrity this and celebrity that."

"You're already a total bastard Frank, when it comes to women at any rate - so you would have us believe."

"Yes, but not enough people know. I need wider exposure, an agent. Look at this Lane bastard. Now he is on a TV programme about swapping wives. The lucky sod."

"It's a pound to a penny Lane will have an affair with the swapped wife," quipped Bill.

Bill would have won the bet, because that's what did happen. Then - surprise, surprise - the dotty Mrs Lane had dinner with the other wife to see where her marriage was going wrong. This time she was canny enough to arrange that the dinner was filmed for television and she got paid it for it. The television company made a mint out of another programme about how they made the first programme and in this they included explicit sex shots of Lane and the swapped wife that they had retained to use for another money-spinner.

Then came yet another spin-off with the two wives talking about it all and comparing the bed performances of their husbands. Then the wronged husband committed suicide so there was a few more quid to be made from television news that used bits from all the programmes.

"You said he would have sex with the other wife," said Frank. "What will happen now Bill? I'll have fifty quid on whatever you say. What odds that Lane gets his own programme?"

Bill shook his head. "Won't be worth a bet, it'll be odds-on."

Again, Bill was right.

Lane became host on a television programme negotiated for him by Joyce. It was a master stroke. It was called Tarts and Scoundrels with Lane talking to anyone who had disgraced themselves publicly. Everybody who was nobody clamoured to be on it. Eight million people watched it every week.

Then there came a sequel with the same motley crew of public dross locked in a mansion for a month with hidden cameras to watch them night and day. Especially night.

Eleven million people watched that.

— 21 —

When she came out of the hospital an empty Number 10 bus was waiting by the main doors like a hearse. She was the only person to get on. It was the same driver as on the way up, and like just about every man who saw her he remembered her and smiled in recognition. There was no response and he noticed her serious expression.

This was a hospital, and he wondered.

The sun of the morning had gone, replaced by cold gloomy rain. The bus took on damp passengers on its way through Dorchester town centre and joined a huddle of traffic on the way back.

She looked at her watch; the timing was about right. She would get to town at just about the right time to meet Lesley.

Lesley wanted to be with Kathy at this time. At first she was going to take a day off work to take her to the hospital but Kathy had insisted on going alone.

"All right, let's meet at Sibleys for a coffee when you get back," Lesley suggested. When Kathy arrived at the café Lesley was anxiously waiting.

All day long Lesley's anxiety that had been mounting. She waited until the waitress took their order and then took her friend's hand: well? Then to her consternation Kathy burst into tears.

"Oh Kathy!" Clearly Kathy needed time to answer, and Lesley waited fearfully, clasping Kathy's hand across the table. Finally, pulling her hand away, Kathy dabbed her eyes with a tissue and Lesley saw the beginnings of a smile.

"Oh Kathy, tell me," implored Lesley, not at all convinced by that tearful smile.

"It's all right. It's all right!" All the way back Kathy had kept the wonderful news bottled up. It was benign! The lump had become hard and sometimes painful. But it was benign!

The joyful news had had to stay locked inside her, with no one to tell. Now, telling Lesley, it had all came out quite ridiculously in a flood of tears.

"Oh that's wonderful!" Lesley was beaming, but with tears in her eyes too.

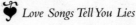

Tears at a happy time like this; but only a woman would understand. Now they were chatting away like mad – or Kathy was, telling Lesley everything that had happened at the hospital (including how dishy the specialist had been!) – and when they did finally get around to their tea it was stewed and cold.

Tea, at a time like this! This called for something with style, and they ordered a bottle of wine.

The taxi got them home just in time for their children's tea.

Kathy's daughter Anne-Marie scolded her: "Where have you been Mum!"

"Oh, to hell and heaven."

"What are you laughing about? Mum, you're drunk!"

★

The Graphic used it big as they did not have many good stories that day. That puffed up Frank. He was full of himself over his scoop. Most copy national reporters produce stems from tip-offs, stories originating from other people's groundwork. To get a story that is all your own work from the very beginning makes you feel good.

Frank's scoop was basically another 'vicar runs off with a parishioner' but it had some interesting special effects. The parishioner in this case was a leading light of the local amateur drama club, a healthy, lively, young woman who had tempted the too-good-looking-to-be-good vicar.

Many of the locals had been whispering about it, and it was not the first time they had relished rumours about the vicar and local women.

Frank got to hear about it when he was in the village pub. Typically Frank was visiting a woman in the village, the wife of an engineer who spent nine months of the year earning a fortune in the employ of an oil sheikh. It was way out of his usual hunting grounds but Frank found her rather tasty.

Her house on the edge of the village was nicely situated for him to be able to slip in unnoticed of an evening. After one such tryst he left earlier than usual and decided to rebuild his energies with a quick one at the local pub. It was then he picked up the juicy gossip about the vicar having an affair with a villager's young wife.

Up to then the vicar was in clover. So was the erring wife, who had had the best of both worlds. Her accountant husband was only a squib in bed, but he made a bomb in the City and kept his wife in the style to which she aspired. The vicar did not have much money, vicars don't, but he was a devil between the covers.

The vicar's wife pleaded with Frank not to print anything and was naive enough to think he would not. A loyal friend in the village told Frank that she was a good wife and mother to her three children, a plea she made to appeal to his better nature and persuade him not do the story. A good wife and mother – that made it an even better story, and Frank laid that on thick in his copy.

It was true, she did do the good wife and mother bit perfectly. But the vicar's wife was no fool. She had long known about her husband's game. If it was stopped he would be home all the time, and there would no opportunity to carry on her affair with her lusty farmer.

Her husband's affairs kept him busy and out of the manse. She had the children, loved gardening, living in the big old manse and singing in the local choir. That, and the farmer, and her life was perfect.

No one else had ever poked their nose in and made an issue of it. They could have made a fuss as her husband was, after all, their vicar and was supposed to set an example but no one did anything about it.

So the situation suited the vicar's wife very well, but Frank's story blew the lid off. The accountant gave his wife an ultimatum: the vicar or him. It was a cruel decision to have to make. Her husband did earn a lovely lot of money, but then the vicar was lovely in bed. She cursed that blasted reporter.

She was not given any time to think about it. The bishop told the vicar he would have to resign.

The vicar realised the game was up and opted to run off with the accountant's wife.

The accountant was distraught; not only did he lose his wife but she took most of their money with her. The vicar was upset, as he had liked being a vicar, and now had to earn a living doing something

Love Songs Tell You Lies

boring such as a nine to five job. The accountant's wife was not as happy as she thought she would be, as she was not that religious and in any case she soon realised that an exciting affair was more to her taste than domestic sex.

The vicar's wife had been happy and now was very unhappy as she had to leave the vicarage and her beloved garden. Her farmer had always been able to pretend to his wife that his involvement in the church was why he was always at the vicarage. The local council provided the vicar's wife with accommodation but she had no say in where it would be. It turned out to be seven miles away in the wrong direction and her farmer lover did not have the imagination to think up excuses to tell his wife why he had to keep being away from the farm so long.

The vicar, his wife, the accountant, his wife, and the farmer were not the only losers. The fiasco also cost the taxpayer money, because the vicar's wife had to go on benefits as her husband's maintenance money and help from the church was not enough.

But Frank was happy. He had got a great story and the editor's congratulations.

The only thing that spoiled it a little was that Frank guessed that he would no longer be welcome in the village. Pity, the oil worker's wife had been rather sexy …oh well, Frank was young and resilient. And getting to the village had meant a long trip.

— 22 —

William Hally did not discover that his wife had been having an affair until after she killed herself. Anthea Hally was found dead in a flat in Knightsbridge and police enquiries elicited the fact that she had rented it. It was a huge shock and a deep puzzle that resolved into one question: why did she rent the flat secretly? That led inexorably to one answer: that she was having an affair. With whom Hally never expected to discover, and did not want to.

Matters were not helped by the attentions of the Press. There was sympathy in the reports, but also hints that they may not have been as happy a couple as they had appeared. There was emphasis on the way Anthea had immersed herself in social work and good causes, and he in his career. Even the emphasis on their childless marriage, factual enough as it was, seemed to have significance when carefully included in the reports.

Friends told him that reporters had been trying to find out more about their marriage. Perhaps he was being over-anxious, but he telephoned Carol to talk about it.

"They are bound to be nosey," she told him. Her voice was level and cool, and it calmed him. "I had a call from a reporter, but what of it? You and I have always openly been friends."

He saw her point. "Yes, and you and Anthea always got on well together." He relaxed somewhat, as she seemed to be putting it all into perspective.

"A reporter? Who was it?"

She paused to recall the name. "A man called West or Webb – something like that. From the Graphic."

"What was he enquiring about?"

"Just general questions – about Anthea."

"Why you?"

"Why not me? I expect he was asking around, not just me, other people who knew you both"

"Yes, I suppose so."

"Just carry on. Don't worry."

Just carry on. Whatever happens in this world, that is all you can do. He had no bitterness about the past. As the years had gone by he had learned that there are many marriages in which there is no love, where people carry on being married, for appearances, or perhaps, even sadder, just because there is not a more attractive alternative.

He had been lucky. For him there was an alternative, although Carol had not come into his life until quite recently. Until then he had grown to accept the emptiness of the marital bed. They had tried to talk about it, but clever as he was with words in Parliament, or in any kind of political and social debate, he could not find a way to discuss that subject with Anthea.

They made a perfectly good social couple. Anthea filled her days with the social life and good works that went with being a leading politician's wife. She made a career out of it, which suited her and, he would not deny, him. He accepted that it took two to make these things work and had assumed that he was one of those men who did not turn women on.

Innocence is a strange word to apply to a worldly-wise politician, but the few sexual encounters he had experienced had not taught him very much about women and nothing about himself. So, innocently, he came to believe that he was to blame for the absence of any spark between him and Anthea.

So he concentrated on his career, and Anthea on her charity work and organising events in the local Tory party. It meant that they seemed to be a close couple, even if that was mostly at Tory functions.

He might have gone to his grave knowing and believing nothing else about men and women if he had not met Carol.

It had to be someone like Carol. Political power and intrigue tempt the temptresses. However the air of solid marital respectability that surrounded him had always fooled any woman that fancied him. Except Carol: she was different. With her strong character she was much more like a man in getting what she wanted. At school she had excelled at sport, and had been a heroine to her friends and an icon of desire to the boys.

This Junesque young woman learned from men and it was

invaluable to her career. Successful men, she noticed, never let sexual considerations, however tasty, get in the way of their ambitions. An incident in her office soon after she left university and joined the firm stayed with her as a lesson in life.

The middle-aged manager of one of the small business investment departments was heavily involved in the latest of his many affairs. He carried them all on in the City, with its many hiding places for such things, while his other life, a wife and family, was safely distant in the Home Counties.

This time the woman was not a young secretary to be lightly dumped when she became too possessive. This time it was a mature woman who was divorced, only a few years younger than the middle-aged Romeo, and to her the affair was much more than a fling.

The woman took a liking to Carol and eventually confided enough for her to realise that both lovers found themselves caught up in what was more than a casual office affair.

One day the secretary told Carol that she was going to tell him he had to decide – her or his wife.

"It can't go on like this indefinitely," she said. "I know he feels the same as I do. If we don't do it now, we will regret it all our lives."

Regret was indeed to last all her life, but not as she had expected. Carol spotted her leaving the boss's office, and her face was a mask of shock.

Carol led her as she would a blind person to an empty office where it all came out in a flood of tears. It was a simple story, a woman's dreams of second chance happiness being blown away by the cold wind of reality.

Oh, he came up with pious reasons, and talked of the children and responsibility. Why, he pleaded, could they not stay as they were? He simply wanted his comfortable life and his exciting affair. Typical man, he wanted his cake and to eat it.

"I've been such a fool," she said to Carol, genuinely amazed at herself that she could have been so wrong about something of which she had been so certain. When she had composed herself, she left the office and did not come back.

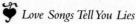

It was powerful image and when Carol met William Hally and his aloof, beautiful, wife Anthea and realised their marriage was empty she decided to take what she wanted.

Power, success and money are an infallible recipe for sexual success – so envious people with their noses up against the windows of life always assume. Anyone who possesses even one of them surely has much less trouble finding love than ordinary people. Yet lonely hearts clubs have among their membership highflying, successful and physically attractive people. The rest of the world is puzzled by that. William would have understood. So when Carol set out to get what she wanted he had no defence. By nature he was a cautious man. Caution; it allows a man to live safely; but love needs heroes. He threw caution to the wind.

With Carol he discovered he was not a failure as a lover, and the discovery was amazing. He felt no guilt, not even when he saw Anthea was friendly with Carol. They shared the same social circle, and that made it so much easier to conduct their affair.

Then came one of those turnings in life that are not signposted: Anthea committed suicide.

It was Carol who advised they took things carefully for a while, and did not see each other. There was shock, but no desolating grief. He did not like himself, but the rational man reminded him that he and Anthea had only been a partnership. The politician in him joined in the debate, telling him that Carol was right. If the lid was blown off his affair, how the media would love reporting that his wife had been duped so cruelly. The woman she welcomed as a friend steals her husband. The world would naturally assume that was why she had killed herself.

Death has to be tidied up. He paid monies owing on the flat in Knightsbridge, that had been in Anthea's name, and arranged for the sale of the furniture. There was no need for him to return to the flat again but the estate agent called and said that among the furniture they had been instructed to sell were some personal effects. Would he go and pick them up, and Hally sensed that they felt it was more appropriate that he did so personally.

The door to the flat was ajar when he arrived, and he assumed the agent or the caretaker of the block of flats was inside.

There was a small 'oh!' of shock when Carol looked up, holding a bundle of letters in her hand. William stopped dead, and they stared at each other for several long seconds without a word. In those few moments Hally understood everything, and she knew he did.

As they drove away from the flat, a man got out of a car parked opposite and went to the caretaker's flat.

"Was that the woman who used to visit when Mrs Hally was here?" he asked the caretaker.

The caretaker, who had already spoken to the reporter and knew he was on a promise, nodded. "Yes. She was the only visitor. They seemed to be the best of friends."

"Thanks." The reporter slipped some notes into the caretaker's top pocket. He did not count them for half an hour and when he did, thought: what does it matter now? The poor woman's dead.

William drove Carol to a place by the river where they could sit and talk it out.

"I was collecting a few personal things," said Carol. "I always had my own key." She saw him looking at the bundle of letters in her hand. "They are mine," she said, and that was all that was needed.

In the end it came down to one question: why? For answer she opened her bag and took out a photograph and held it for him to see. It was of a beautiful woman, blond, her figure seen to bold advantage in a tennis outfit.

"She happened," said Carol, before putting the photograph away.

It was all being explained to William in vivid acts and symbols rather than words.

"I never dreamed that she would …" Carol could not bring herself to say 'kill herself'.

"So I was just a means to an end," said William, piecing together the jigsaw. It was simple enough. A child could do it.

She reached out but did not quite touch his hand, "No. not at all. I am fond of you."

The compassion triggered his anger. "Oh, for God's sake! Spare me the…" The words strangled him.

"I'm sorry," she said.

He stared at the river, beautiful on the surface that shimmered with London's lights but black and cold beneath; much like life. Poor Anthea. His mind was telling him he should be outraged. But he could not feel outrage. Who was he to feel any moral fury?

Who was he? That was quite a question in the circumstances. He was a man who could not marry a normal woman, who could not even meet a normal woman to have a normal affair, and now was a cuckold, but a cuckold who would be a laughing stock if anyone knew.

"Well, you'll have a good story to sell the Press, won't you!"

"Just drive me home," she replied in a tight voice, and he did so, in cold silence.

The reporter who had watched them leave the block of flats was damn good at his job. He had a lead, and never lost the trail. It took him two days to piece it all together. Everyone has friends, and with friends in politics who needs enemies? Even though neither Hally nor Carol helped him with an interview or even a 'no comment' he put together a great story.

The day Kelly Webb's report appeared Hally resigned.

— 23 —

It was the Hack and Headline debating society in full swing. It started off with a reporter relating how his neighbour, a middle-aged housewife who had never written a line before, had not only managed to get a novel published but it was also a best-seller.

"I've written no end of short stories and not one of them has been accepted," he complained.

"I know, pisses you off doesn't it," Bill sympathised. "People always assume that if you are a journalist, you could write a book. I have given up trying to explain that journalists encounter real life, not the material for a novel. They think because you write so much about human folly, you must have lots of ideas. But everything we write about is just the same old all-too-believable crap."

Now Bill was on one of his hobby horses.

"It is always people just doing the same old stupid things, mucking up their perfectly good lives for greed, sex, whatever. They just shoot themselves in the foot. No one else pulls the trigger. Plot? There's never a plot."

Kelly put in his pennyworth: "It's the oldest story in the book."

Buller plonked his capacious arse on a desk and regarded the SS Squad. His habitual sneer was more pronounced this morning, indicating he was in a good mood. That meant some nasty banter.

"Doesn't your wife get worried at all these sex and scandal stories you do, Webb?"

Whenever women got into the conversation when Buller was around, the results were usually smutty. Kelly glared, staying pointedly silent. That was never going to discomfit someone like Buller.

Buller's teeth were bared in a bullying grin. When he took a dislike to someone in the office, he just loved having a go at them.

"Well, it must give you a lot of ideas. Maybe she thinks you get some perks of the job." That was a good one and Buller brayed. Green joined in dutifully.

Kelly held Buller's mirthless eyes with a contemptuous expression:

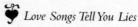

"I suppose you have to pay for it?" It was a crude lack-wit riposte but Buller brought out the worst in people.

Buller snarled a sneer, but the jibe had hit the nail on the head and he savagely relished one day hammering it into Kelly's coffin.

"Well, Smith must reckon you're an expert on the subject."

"Yeah?"

"Yeah. Well, he seems to think you are so good at it, he has told me that it is you he wants to go down to the West Country and interview Shirley Love. Insists on you. She is going to tell all about her first husband Jack Lee's affairs with half the women in Hollywood, naming names. All juicy stuff. Right up your street, Webb.

"Smith says she will also tell tales about affairs with top toffs including politicians. Seems she put it about a bit herself. She was a mate of Raunchy Wright who ran the House of Happiness at Hampstead."

That caused a masculine bellow from nearby desks. The House of Happiness had kept the tabloids in yards of juicy copy in the late Eighties. Someone sold a tip-off and within hours paparazzi photographers were paying hundreds of pounds to rent windows overlooking the place. Many an unsuspecting celebrity, Member of Parliament and government official were nabbed on their way to taste the forbidden fruits Raunchy's girls offered.

"Smith reckons you will get some useful material for future use, as well as the story our Shirley wants to tell."

"Where is she?"

"East Devon, here's her number." Buller put a scrap of paper on the desk. "Nice little holiday. It means you'll spend a couple of days down there. She's still quite dishy. Good thing your wife trusts you."

Kelly ignored the piece of paper. "I'll talk to Smith about it," he said. Buller was in charge of features, but it was still a grey area as to who was in charge of the SS Squad. In any case Kelly was getting more and more of his assignments directly from the deputy editor. Just underlining this he knew would infuriate control freak Buller. Kelly had not reacted to Buller's first comment because he had been taken by surprise. Now his anger surfaced and underlining his contempt for Buller and his own independence, he snapped:"Leave it with me; like I said, I'll talk to Smith. And you can leave my wife out of it."

Buller shrugged insolently before walking off.

Kelly turned to Bill. "What is it with that bastard?"

"He's a bit crude."

"A bit! The man's got problems. You can tell that whenever he talks about women."

Bill left it at that for the time being. Later, when Kelly had cooled down, he related a story about Buller that Kelly had to admit was surprising. It did not change Kelly's opinion of the man, but it was surprising.

"He won a prize for the story," said Bill. "It was not just one story, he made a series out of it, all about women's rights." Bill told Kelly how Buller had written an exclusive on a woman married to an extremely rich businessman from whom she was getting a divorce. "The fellow – I forget his name, I'll look up the cutting – had millions, pots of it. Buller discovered that the woman was going to walk away with nothing, scorning his money and all that, probably letting the trollop who he was bonking have it all. All she wanted was for their children to be taken care of financially. She meant it too. She had pride. Buller got the story from somewhere and it was brilliant. I remember it. It was not just a good story. He excelled himself. It was very powerful piece. The woman was defended there, Kelly, I can tell you."

"What happened?"

"Oh, she got half his money or at least a lot of it after Buller's story. It was the rich husband shamed – that was the story. It deserved to win a prize for Buller. He made it a paean for women. It was all about real equality, not just the law."

Bill got the cuttings later but never got round to showing them to Kelly, who was out of the office so much. Carl Landings, that was the name, and his wife was Nancy. It had been a very bitter affair. They say love is magic mused Bill. It must be; it can turn itself into hate – just like that.

There was another tale about Buller that Bill could have related if

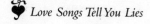

he knew about it, but neither he nor anyone else at the Graphic did. His colleagues may have believed Buller did not possess the finer human emotions but Dandy Nicholls came as close as anyone to proving them wrong. As she was not a notorious socialite, the Graphic hacks were unlikely to know her name. Dandy was a junior barrister when Buller met her at Spartacus, the health and sporting club that people on the up joined because its members were the kind of people from whom they were likely to profit. So much easier to make money or gain influence when you play tennis or polo with those who possess plenty of both, and talk of little else.

Buller was a member on Graphic expenses because the club's membership listed hundreds of the up and coming members of the political and social upper strata. Readers admired and envied these glamorous lives, and enjoyed reading about their scandals. It was Graphic money well spent, and the titbit about Hally and club member Carol had been picked up at the club bar.

If the Graphic crew were ever to try and visualise the type of woman suitable for the bull-natured Buller, they might well have come up with someone like Ms Nicholls. Amazonian, strikingly blond, she had a strong presence that did her in good stead in courtrooms.

In her teenage years she had been a county-class tennis and squash player and if she had not decided to concentrate on her legal career might well have progressed to represent England. Her physical strength and self-confidence made her not merely the equal of but also, in an indefinable but very definite way, superior to many men she attracted.

Men soon learned that they were suffered on her terms. Very quickly most of these admirers instinctively understood why this woman would never be their one and only, or indeed any other man's. Yet, when she wanted one, she was never short of a male escort.

Buller was not athletic but he was strong in the arm and surprisingly sharp on his feet, attributes that made him good at tennis. Dandy saw him play and invited him to a game of doubles, and he eagerly accepted.

Only after the game was arranged did he learn that her partner would be Nat Dobbs. Dandy's sharp senses immediately picked up an antipathy between the men when they met with curt nods and antagonistic body language. The situation gave her a buzz. Watching lumbering great men crashing about the place, quarrelling and generally occupying the arena of life with displays of stupidity was one of the recreations she and her special coterie of friends enjoyed. Partnered with one of Dandy's friends Buller played terrific tennis, boosted by his dislike of Dobbs. He played like a demon and Dobbs and Dandy were beaten.

"My word," Dandy said admiringly after the game. "That was the best tennis I've seen for a long time!" Buller's Graphic colleagues would have been open-mouthed with had they seen him then. He was grinning like a teenager.

Dandy, who found few men who were as good as her on the court let alone better, suggested they played again. One game led to another and a few drinks usually followed the tennis.

Buller was rarely successful with women, not surprisingly as he showed none of the chivalries women hope to find in a man. Now the sourness that had accumulated in his soul over the years regarding women was sweetened by his feelings for Dandy.

"I think you have made a conquest there," said Dobbs as he and Dandy shared a drink at the club one evening. They were two of a kind; self-absorbed people with bankable looks.

Dandy grimaced. "A conquest?"

"Yes, I think so. You two have played a lot together since that game." Dobbs sniggered, knowing Buller had no hope.

"It's just tennis, he's a good player! What on earth are you thinking?"

"What he's thinking."

"Fat lot of good it will do him," Dandy retorted sharply, finishing her drink.

She saw the look of satisfaction on Dobb's face at her response. By now Dandy was well aware that it was not just a matter of dislike: the two men hated each other.

"What is it between you two?

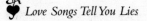

"Oh…" Dobbs held up his hands. Where do you start? There was a show of exasperated anger as he started the tale of antagonism.

"He once did a story in some bloody rag he worked for then – he works for one now, but this was even further downmarket – on one of my friends, Carl Landings. Poor Carl had to pay out millions to Nancy, his ex-wife, who played the innocent. But she had had lovers, you can bet on it – I know she had them." Saying that triggered a give-away smirk. Trying to ignore Dandy's probing look he attempted to continue. But she would not let him escape. "Oh yes – and how do you know!"

Dobbs confessed with a grin. "Yes, all right, but Carl knew and we sorted it out. We've done too many deals to fall out over that. That did not alter anything. Nancy was no innocent, that's the point. There were plenty of others, you can bet. The fact was Carl did not owe her anything. She had no moral right.

"Oh, it was a mess. I tried to stop the story – I knew someone on the paper's management. She did not deserve all that money – anyway I knew that the real reason Buller was doing the story was because he was after Nancy. Real hot for her, he was. I'm not stupid! At least he got what he deserved in that respect. She played him along to get a sympathetic story, then dumped him. You couldn't blame her! Give her credit for some taste!"

Dandy laughed. "Well, you keep them happy!"

Dobbs smirked. He had a reputation as a ladies man and worked diligently at deserving it. Although he was married he never allowed the elite of London's bedroom beauties to be denied his attentions. How he managed to keep his wife in ignorance of his extra-marital activities amazed most observers but not the cynics – they simply assumed he did not. If wives such as America's Hilary Clinton can stand public infidelity, how many such as Liz Dobbs lived with their lot? Women play a far more significant role than men in holding dodgy marriages together than the world and his mistress can ever know, and certainly could never understand.

Dobbs was on Sleazey Street with a rich wife who, for some reason perhaps only understood by her psychiatrist, stayed with him. A feminine mystery, but his reasons were simple enough: her wealth opened social and political doors where he found all the mistresses he could handle.

"He knew I had something to do with trying to stop the story, and I told him what a bastard he was. Told me to watch out, that he'd have me in the paper. It was nearly a punch-up! I expect he thought I had something to do with Nancy dumping him. I hope he did! I hope the thought gives him a permanent gut ache. He has never tried anything on me yet – never been in a position of power on a paper I suppose. Nasty piece of work, a bully."

"Well, watch him." Dandy said that with emphasis. She had seen real hate in Buller's eyes.

"Don't worry. I can deal with anything Buller comes up with, if he tries anything. I have the right kind of friends."

Quaffing the dregs of his glass Dobbs stood up. "Must go."

"What's the rush for?" she enquired. Then, with a knowing smile: "Who's the rush for?"

Dobbs grinned and winked.

"Tell me!" Dandy loved gossip of that kind. She and Dobbs swapped sexual secrets, just for the buzz.

Happy to oblige a soul mate Dobbs whispered a name into her ear. Dandy was surprised. "Really? Isn't she the daughter of…?" Dobbs nodded, placing a 'shush!' finger against his smirk.

"Well! well! At least you won't get in the papers!" said Dandy, kissing him chastely, and they were both laughing at their shared secret as Dobbs strode away, two people who had the world on a string.

Buller, who had arrived at the moment to play a doubles with Dandy and two of her friends, saw them close together; saw the kiss. It was a picture of two as an item to the lust-blind Buller.

A blood rush of jealousy forced rash words into his mouth.

"That prat always seems to be hanging around you," he said.

Dandy was shocked. "Nat is an old friend," she snapped, realising from Buller's savage expression that Dobbs had been right. She stood up and glared at this impertinence. She had hoodlum eyes when she was mad.

"If you don't like my friends, I won't spoil your day by having you

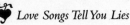

play tennis with them," she hissed.

Buller stood rooted to the spot of several long moments. Then he strode back into his car and screeched away, sending gravel flying. Now he knew he had to do something about that ponce Dobbs. Time to finish some unfinished business.

Exactly how he did not know – yet.

Carol, who had heard the loud voices as she came out of the changing room, still towelling her hair, came up behind Dandy. "What was that all about?"

"That fool!"

"What's up with him?"

"These bloody men! He thought – he thought wrong! He got the wrong idea! I told him to piss off."

"Why? What wrong idea?"

Dandy smiled at Carol, a special, secret smile. "He was jealous."

"Jealous?" The penny dropped. "Oh, I see," and it was Carol's turn to smile, though with some sympathy for the man. She did not know Buller from Adam, but she was thinking of William Hally, left behind by the speed of change of society's moral fashions.

"Men!" Dandy threw up her hands angrily. "They fancy a woman, decide they want her as a mate, and when the female of the species has other ideas they have the bloody cheek to get angry – they are doing you a favour by choosing you. God! Bloody ape men! They still live in caves, some of them!" By the time she reached the last word she had worked herself up into such a state Carol could not prevent herself laughing.

"Have some pity for the poor man," she said, placing her hand soothingly over Dandy's and entwining fingers.

★

Kelly was the target of risque jokes and offers from other reporters to do the job if he did not want to. He had to admit that it was a doddle, no hard work involved, but two days stuck in the West Country sounded boring. He telephoned Shirley Love and made an appointment.

Whenever possible he preferred to use trains because it gave him time to write the story on the way back. He had worked out an itinerary that entailed spending a day with her, travelling down straight after work the previous evening to the end of the line on the Dorset coast. There he could hire a car to drive to her place the next day and there would be time after the interview to catch a late train back. That would mean only one night away.

"When I get back, my darling, we are going to have a weekend break together," he promised Angela when she said: "Oh, off another little holiday?"

It was a tease, as she knew he hated all the travelling his job entailed. "I see airports, the inside of taxis, and then the same in reverse order," he would protest.

"A weekend break, just you and I."

"My word," she said. "First a romantic dinner, then a romantic weekend!"

A romantic weekend. There were going to be times when both would wonder whether it would ever happen.

★

Kelly thumped the last letter on his keyboard with an end-of-day, bloody-good-story-finished satisfaction. When he looked up he saw that he and Barry Green were the only two remaining in the office.

"Another scoop?" Green enquired.

"Yeah." Kelly's non-committal response was brusque.

"You have become quite the star reporter," said Green. He smiled as he said it. It would have been better if he hadn't.

What could Kelly say to that? It was not well meant, of that he was sure. "Just a good run," he grunted. When he and Charlie had likened Green to Tony back in Brighton it was apt. Tony, as Green was doing now, had fawned his way to a position of petty power. Subtly Green had become Buller's acolyte. He had steadily assumed more and more desk work, always willing to field the kind of routine chores that good reporters dodge. No one stayed later than Green in the office.

If that was how Green wanted to climb the greasy pole what was it to him? Why let it bother him?

"Staying late again," Kelly observed. "I don't know what you find to do."

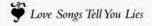

"There's all this filing for Buller."

"He will be pleased." With that Kelly sauntered off.

It had not been fair or clever; it was how you made enemies. He should worry! He was twice the reporter of either of them. There was no way he had anything to fear from the likes of Green, or Buller either.

Green's malignant glare bore into Kelly's back.

— 24 —

Kelly knew exactly what he was going to get Angela for her birthday. He had left that morning without a word, knowing she would assume he had forgotten as usual. Last year he did forget, and not for the first time, and he had promised her he would definitely remember this year. Forgetting birthdays was his woeful failing, one which she, bless her, never really got annoyed about. He always bought her something later to make up. "It's my only fault," he would wheedle. "You should have some fellas I know!"

"I might think about that!" had once been her tart response and he had dashed out to buy her an armful of flowers. There was only one fella he wanted on his wife's mind!

She would be doing the housework at this very moment, feeling smug, certain that he had forgotten as usual. But he had plans, and the first move was to get to the Oxford Street branch of Marks and Spencer at lunchtime and buy two hundred pounds worth of their shopping vouchers. He was going to add an expensive box of fancy chocolates, and had ordered a bunch of flowers to be delivered, stipulating that they must not get to the house before six. By then he would have arrived home and announced that they were going out to dinner.

Well pleased with his planning, he strode down Oxford Street.

Suddenly he heard a familiar voice. It was the street singer who had caught his ear on another occasion. And singing the same song.

Lonely man in lonely town.

Kelly paused to listen for a moment and dropped some loose coins into the fellow's box.

In her eyes the divine mischief
That makes heroes of all men
You're on the street that leads to grief
Where even wise men go again.

The words were sung to the kind of old fashioned melody that Kelly, an enthusiast of '30's and '40's music, liked.

He walked on, with the song,

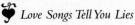

Lonely man in lonely town,
Aimless heart, aimless feet.

fading into the hubbub of London. Nice song, but lonely man he was not – and certainly not tonight!

Nipping neatly between the crowds of shoppers he turned into Marks and Spencer. Then his footwork was not so nippy and he bumped into a young woman.

"So sorry," he apologised, concerned as he had knocked into her quite hard.

Then he exclaimed in surprise: "Well I'm blessed, it's you!"

She was the girl he often saw on the train, the one who had smilingly watched him as he had made that telephone call to Angela. She recognised him with as much surprise.

"Sorry," she said, with an awkward laugh.

"No, no! It was my fault. In a hurry. Stupid, in this crowd." He put a hand lightly on her shoulder. "Are you all right. It was a bit of a bang. So sorry."

She shook her head. "Yes, I'm all right."

"I was hurrying to get a present for my wife – her birthday," he said, as they negotiated their way through the throng. There was a gap and he ushered her ahead. It was natural gesture to shield her with his arm.

"Fancy it being you I nearly knocked over," he said. He saw she was also heading for the store. "You are a Marks and Spencer shopaholic too? My wife swears by them."

"No, well yes, sometimes. I am just going for lunch in their café."

"My wife says that if they close our local Marks, we'll have to move to another town. Actually I was going to get a snack too."

Then on impulse he said: "Let me get you something."

A bit cheeky perhaps, but permissible surely in the circumstances. Anyway, it was an opportunity to satisfy his curiosity as to who she was, having seen her on the train so often.

And she was delightful.

Giving her no chance to say no, he steered her towards the escalator, keeping up the chat.

"Choose what you like," he invited when they were seated,

proffering the menu. "Compensation for damages!"

That made her smile, and it was delightful to see. As she studied the menu he was able to openly enjoy her youthful loveliness.

As they chatted, he instinctively used his reporter skills and found out quite a bit about her. Her name was Sadie and she lived in a suburb down the line from Reigate. She worked for a fashion company just round the corner from Oxford Street. He told her about his surprise for Angela.

"Very romantic," she said approvingly. "Women like romantic men."

Mingled with the aroma of their coffee he could detect her scent, a clean, youthful fragrance. Fleetingly, accompanied by the pleasant sadness of joy remembered, there was a mental snapshot of those Brighton days when he pulled little darlings like this every night. Well nearly every night - all right, Friday and Saturday nights mostly.

"And you? What sort of men do you appreciate?"

She laughed shyly. "Yes, I like romantic men too. I think all woman do."

"I'm sure you get a lot of romantic surprises."

She blushed at the compliment. His admiration was so frank she could not meet his eyes and she felt her blush running riot. Her embarrassment swelled his male ego, but it was not kind and Kelly changed the subject.

After some more chat he noticed her looking at her watch. "I have to be back at two," she explained, so he paid the bill and accompanied her to the street door.

As they parted outside the store Kelly quipped: "Well, it was nice bumping into you!" A corny joke but it sufficed to produced that delightful smile again.

As she walked away she could not resist a backward glance through the crowd, and saw that he was still watching her. As she hurried back to her workplace, she felt the cool air on her burning cheeks. Her feelings surprised her as he was quite a bit older than herself, but he had been rather nice.

Kelly returned to the store to buy the vouchers. From the time he first bumped into the girl to when he left her half an hour later he had not noticed Buller.

Buller had been about to enter the store when he spotted Kelly and the girl. When Kelly ushered her ahead it looked to Buller that he was putting his arm around her. Buller made an automatic assumption. Webb was playing away from home.

Following them through the store to the cafe Buller had seated himself at a table from where he could observe Kelly and the girl but Kelly could not see him. Well, well, well! So Webb plays around does he? Buller was not stupid; he could read body language when it was writ as large as this. The randy sod could not take his eyes off her. He was practically over the table!

In the lunchtime crowd it had been easy to follow them unseen back to the street. Times he had done this kind of thing on a story. That thought had triggered an automatic action and Buller felt in his breast pocket.

It was there, even though he had not used it for a long while, now that he was not doing any reporting. He took out the miniature camera that had played such a big part on those dig-the-dirt stories he had done, and done bloody well, during his clamber up the greasy pole of yellow journalism. He had been an expert in getting the kind of undercover picture that when used in an expose story always helps to create the impression that the person in the photograph is furtive, and has been caught doing something wrong. He had no trouble getting close to Kelly and the girl without being noticed. In that crowd it was a piece of cake.

The camera's design enabled Buller to take pictures of people one-handed without that tell-tale crouch and focus associated with photographers that might have alerted them. With a self-satisfied smirk Buller got several shots as Kelly ushered the girl through the crowd. That smirk became a leer when he studied the printed results. One picture had caught Kelly leaning close to the girl, his arm apparently around her shoulders and looking as though he was about to kiss her.

Buller put the photographs in his wallet and tucked the scene away in his memory along with all the other nasty bits of information he had on so many people. Right then he could not think of what good it would do, but come the right time ....

Revenge often requires patience.

For the rest of the day Kelly was busy catching up on bits and pieces. Occasionally he thought about the girl in Oxford Street. Sadie, that was a cute name. It was going to be even nicer to see her on the train now he had an excuse to talk to her. He had not lost the knack! He jotted down her name and where she worked and slipped the note into his wallet.

Just a reporter's habit.

～ 25 ～

Sophie Eastwinter was enjoying her solo lunch more than she thought she would. Originally she was going to lunch with Henry, then something that came up at the office meant he could not make it. As she was already on her way to town, she had decided to continue with the lunch and called a couple of her friends to join her but they had all been otherwise engaged. So here she was lunching alone, but she was enjoying herself as the waiter had seated her in a corner from where she could observe most of the other diners.

It was absolutely the 'in' place for media people and politicians and she lingered over her lunch to enjoy some people-peeping.

Now who is that with Roger Markham, who played the errant husband of Lady Violet Dallow in The Victorians, the BBC series she had enjoyed so much? Sophie knew Markham's wife slightly and she certainly was nothing like - or as young - as the girl-about-town Markham was with.

Sophie had become pretty adept at spotting naughty goings on among London's glitteratti since being married to Henry. She had enthusiastically helped with more than one useful tip in his career, especially when he had edited a gossip column on a Sunday newspaper. Now he was editor of a racy tabloid, she must remember to pass this on to him tonight!

She continued her enjoyable peeping. Over there was Roderick Chambers, an Opposition expert on European matters, and his wife Eleanor. Chuckling she hummed 'Chicago, Chicago, I Saw a Man Lunch With His Wife!'

Ah, that is Nat Dobbs, unmistakable with that blond mane. Now he is notorious. Now who is he dining with! Opposite Dobbs was a young woman whose face she could not quite see.

Sophie shifted her viewpoint to get a better look and her jaw dropped when she saw who it was. Charlotte! In any other situation she would have gone over immediately to speak to her daughter but she was so surprised - Nat Dobbs of all people! - she remained at her table unseen by the pair.

Any onlooker would have seen that the pair were very interested in each other. Dobbs' amorous body language was writ large for any gossip columnist's spy to read with ease. Charlotte looked vivacious and she was talking animatedly. She was plainly enjoying the company of her companion.

With a shock Sophie realised that here she was spying on her own daughter! Then just as she was on the point of making her presence known to Charlotte they left the restaurant. From her table Sophie had a good view of the restaurant's foyer and saw her daughter kiss Dobbs goodbye; a lingering kiss full on the lips.

On her way back to their Guildford home Sophie could not get that scene out of her mind. Holding his hand, kissing – and very definitely that had not been a social kiss – what was going on? Lunch with a married man. Usual enough in this day and age perhaps, but Sophie was not one to fool herself. One did not say thank-you for lunch with a kiss like that! First thing she was going to do was quiz Charlotte about it. There were things she had heard about Nat Dobbs, and they were not things mothers like to hear. Yes a quizzing was definitely on the cards!

★

Frank was finishing a phone call when Buller returned from the meeting with Smith. Except for Frank and Green, the others had left. It was late and Buller observed sarcastically: "Someone's keen, or knowing you, you were calling a woman."

"Wrong. She called us."

Buller lumped his backside on the edge of a desk and glared. Well? Frank read from a note he had made of the call. "Patsy Goldman, once a parliamentary secretary. Wants to tell us – exclusively – about a series of illicit weekends she had with a celebrity and holidays abroad."

"Who? When?"

"Nat Dobbs. Two years ago."

"Dobbs?"

Buller's reaction was ultra sharp. Surprised by this, Frank regarded him quizzically. "You know him?" Personally, Frank meant. Anyone who read newspapers, especially gossip columns, knew the name

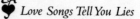

Nat Dobbs. He was a socialite ne-er-do-well, a professional charmer who made a living investing (and often losing) other people's money in grandiose investments.

Buller shook his head brusquely, but his eyes were agleam with interest. "What does she say?"

Frank was intrigued at Buller's reaction but made no comment. "Basically that's it. Will sell us her story."

"What story? Why isn't she his secretary any more."

"Didn't say, but she's got a child. She's a single parent."

"His?"

"I asked her that, of course. She more or less said it was, but she was not specific. Wasn't giving too much away before we talked money. And Dobbs is married. Sounds a good story."

"Call her. We'll have a look at it." Buller kept his voice calm. But excitement was drumming in his chest. Dobbs, eh? Right into his hands and at the right time!

Changing tack, Buller picked up a photograph from the desk. "Who's this?"

"Pictures for a story Kelly's working on. One of the hostesses at the Happy House."

Buller grunted. "Very nice. Sort of job you wish you were on, eh? I bet you could do with that massaging your bits. Wasted on Webb. He wouldn't know what to do with it."

"He doesn't need any extra. You should see his wife."

"Webb?" Webb with a good-looking missus? Buller's tone was disbelievingly sneering, but despite himself curiosity got the better. "What's she like?"

"A cracker. Very sexy. I reckon she could have been a model."

Buller' expression was 'You're kidding!' "Where have you seen her?"

"At a party. When he brought her up to London."

Remembering that party and what happened afterwards Frank felt bloody stupid all over again.

Nothing would ever induce Frank to tell Buller or anyone else about that awful episode. Being Frank, it had not taken him long to be his old self again but he was horribly embarrassed at the time. Our lad about town had never before been out of face when it came to an attempted pull that goes wrong. Some you win, some you lose.

He could understand Buller's surprise. When he was introduced to Angela at the party, he had been pretty surprised himself. Anyone over 30 was past it, of course, and when they were sensible family men like Kelly, a man who admitted he liked the commuting suburban life, they definitely had an image problem.

How did old Kelly manage to land a beauty like Angela? Maybe the girls down in Meadow Gate bumpkin country did not get much choice. His next logical thought was that she would be an easy target for a young bedroom blood such as himself.

The logic was entirely Frank's and it led him boldly on.

He downed a few bevvies to tone up his natural charm. He always found that to be a potent preparation to seduction. No woman seemed to be able to resist it, although on this night none of the other women at the party saw much of him. Sorry girls, another time perhaps. While Kelly was busy circulating he homed in on Angela and chatted her up shamelessly.

Angela was amused, and perhaps flattered, to be reminded that after having two children she was still attractive. Not that she really needed much reassurance on that score. More than one hopeful man had made a pass at her and discovered that she was not the least bit interested in that game.

Frank reckoned he was on form. The party was a posh do and the drinks were of the best quality. They certainly did wonders for Frank. Tonight he was superstud. Whenever Angela did get away to talk to others, there he was again. She could not escape, but anyway he was an amusing young man.

He found out all about her. Being a reporter was very useful for chatting up women. You got their telephone number before they knew what was happening. He was an expert. Smart, too, so he did not ask for Angela's. He knew Kelly's home number would be in the office directory.

"Nice to have met you," Angela said as she and Kelly left. Kelly was occupied with saying good-byes and Frank gave Angela his best bedroom leer.

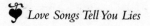

"Perhaps we'll meet again when you are in London."

Angela somehow missed the leer completely and her response sandwiched between making her farewells to other guests was incautiously polite.

"Yes, that would be nice."

That did it. It meant she was hot for him.

The next time Frank had a day off in the week he went down to Meadow Gate. He telephoned her mid morning, when he knew the children would be at school. "I am in town," he said breezily. "Thought perhaps you would like a coffee."

Angela was taken by surprise. It took her a few moments to remember him, "Oh, are you down here on a story? Well…" It was inconvenient, as she was up to her eyes in housework. "I've got a lot on today. Would you like to come round here for a coffee, if you have the time."

"That would be nice." Frank got the address, hailed a taxi, and was round there in five minutes.

They chatted as she made the coffee then they sat at the kitchen table to drink it.

"What story brings you down here," she asked. "We don't have scandals in Meadow Gate!"

"I'm not on a story."

"Oh, what brings you then?"

"I came to see you." Frank was confident. He had been ever since the party, and his confidence gave him ease. All Angela had seen until that remark was an affable colleague of her husband with whom she was having a friendly chat. Frank, thinking as usual with the wrong part of his anatomy, had interpreted her smiling, friendly manner as another success in the offing.

"Oh!" Alarmed, Angela looked up to be confronted by Frank's best seductive expression. Douched with shock she hastily retreated to the sink and busied herself with cups and saucers. Keeping up a now very polite conversation over her shoulder while trying to think of a way of getting rid of him, she was not aware of Frank coming up behind her. He, macho-brain man, had read the look of panic on her face as she had turned away as a sign that she was stirred by his interest.

It was a turn on, and he took her by the shoulders and kissed her neck.

"Please! What are you doing!"

It was Frank's turn to be douched with cold shock.

Putting the table between them, Angela her voice tight with affront said: "I think you had better be going!" If Frank had a cyanide pill in a false tooth he would have used it. As flummoxed as a newly-sexed teenager, he just about managed a choking 'terribly sorry' and scooted.

All the next morning in the office he thought Kelly was just waiting his chance to corner him. By midday he realised thankfully that Angela could not have told him.

But this was not just one of the lost items in the win some, lose some saga of his happily wasted youth. Frank did a bit of growing up; not much, but enough, and he telephoned Angela. He persevered in the teeth of her chilly response and persuaded her to meet him so he could apologise personally. There was no need she insisted, but relented as he pleaded. She could understand how he felt, working as he did with Kelly.

They met on safe neutral ground in a Reigate High Street coffeehouse. Frank spent ten minutes saying what a fool he was and how sorry he was, and repeating this with variations.

Some of the basic Frank surfaced when he ended his embarrassed babbling with: "It really is a compliment to you, Angela, in a way, you know," and tried out a grin.

"Right," she said, smiling by now, but realising it was time to stop him right there. He was reverting to type.

"Quite unforgivable," he said.

She had to laugh. "You're forgiven."

Feeling more like his old self, which was mixed news for women, he felt a good word for Kelly would be politic.

"He's a good bloke," he said.

"You don't need to tell me. He's the best."

Frank then learned to his laddish surprise how strong her marriage was. "There's never been anyone else," she said. "There never will be."

It was not meant reprovingly, but it was said with such feeling Frank

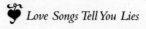

felt the sting a man experiences when a beautiful woman he fancies belongs undeniably to someone else. And to boring old Kelly!

"You almost make me want to get married," said Frank, thoroughly relieved now and welcoming the chance to joke.

"I just feel sorry for other women," she said. Her smile was the smile of a confident and secure woman.

"Well, you need never worry about Kelly. With you at home, he would never be tempted to stray." Frank grinned, thoroughly back to his old self.

"Don't worry about it," said Angela seeing it was time she left. "There's no need to say anything more."

Coming back to the present Frank grinned at the look of surprise and doubt on Buller's face.

"Take it from me," he said. "His wife is a cracker. His friend Charlie came up to London the other day and we all had a drink. They were trainee reporters together. He reckons Kelly used to be able to pull the birds better than any one else in the crowd they knocked about with. They used to get him to pull enough for all of them!"

Frank, as a fellow worldly wise in these things, grinned at Buller, who was staring in disbelief, and said: "You never know, do you?"

No, you don't, thought Buller. So Webb can pull the birds, can he? And he still does – Oxford Street! That sort of game can get you into trouble Webb. Like it is about to get this bastard Dobbs into trouble if I have anything to do with it.

Taking the note about Dobbs from Frank, Buller went straight to the deputy editor.

Yes, there was always a way! Buller had plenty more material from his earlier efforts to nail Dobbs.

"He has slept with more women than President Clinton," he promised Smith, who agreed to put a reporter on to it.

He decided on Kelly Webb.

～ 26 ～

"Hello? Kelly?"

There was no need for the caller to introduce himself. "Charlie!"

"How are you, Scoop?"

"What? Oh!" What he meant dawned on Kelly. The award.

"Congratulations."

"Thanks. Yes, it was a surprise, but it's nice."

"I'll buy you a drink and we'll catch up."

"Do that, next time you're in London."

"I am in London now. That's another bit of news. I've quit the paper."

"You've what! Why? I thought you were doing all right."

"Yeah, well. Tell you all about it over a drink. Tonight, if you can make it."

"Excellent. Hey! Now you can come and work for the Graphic. The old team!"

"No. I've got a job. Tell you all about it later."

They met in the Barbican Bar. Kelly put Charlie's drink in front of him, still shaking his head in disbelief.

"Public relations! That's the last thing I thought you would do."

"Why? It pays more than digging out stories, checking and double checking facts for newspapers run by profit-not-principles businessmen, and it's easier."

"Charlie, old mate! I never thought PR work would be your style." Then he remembered one of Charlie's alcoholic statements from the Brighton days. "You said PR people were the whores of truth!"

"Did I? But that doesn't make any sense, does it? What does 'a whore of truth' mean?"

"I don't know. You said it! And you said it nobly. You were good. You are good."

"There are too many shits in journalism Kelly. Pious in print, prats in private."

"What happened?"

"I fancied a cushier number. I mean, Kelly Webb, we haven't all got

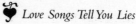

your determination to uncover the dark secrets of the wicked bastards who run the country! It was O.K., but in the end you have got to be a Tony to get on."

"Thanks! I'm a Tony, am I?"

"Don't be a…that's just it, you're not. That means you are on the outside, as I was. Just producing good stuff is not enough to get on, and that is all I wanted to do. I got pissed off with the hypocrisy.

"You have to stay on the edge to get the best stories, run a bit of risk. Right? If things go wrong you need management that knows this, not buggers with big salaries and tiny brains.

"I was chasing a story about a new road they wanted to put through a piece of common land. It was a tatty old bit of land, but it was still public land and had long been thought by locals as earmarked for a park, or wildlife area. No money in that though, is there? There was a consortium of local businessmen set to make big money if the new road went ahead as it would link up to land they owned which they wanted to turn into an industrial estate. Without that better road access they could not get planning permission.

"The paper was not allowing me to really get stuck into what I was doing. Then I found out that the editor was having meetings with the businessmen – one of whom was on the board of the newspaper. He didn't know I knew, but I started to get stroppy about the story. Oh, he published the views against the road, mostly in the letters page, but somehow the views in favour of the road got better coverage, more positive. Very subtle, but I could tell.

"And then I noticed, I could feel, an antagonism towards me. There was dishonesty in that newspaper.

"I thought, why bust your gut – no one would care anyway. You can care too much, bust a gut for bugger-all reward.

"You can write a hundred great stories with no thanks, and then one that causes some pompous local bigwig or businessman who is well in with the people who own the paper to complain and that's the one they judge you on. The one they sack you for, if they want an excuse."

"That's life, Charlie."

"Yeah, maybe. So, I went for the easy life and the easy money."

Charlie was grinning again and Kelly responded, glad to see in his friend the spark of the old Brighton sod 'em all!

"So you are going for the cushy life. Good for you Charlie."

"Ain't that the whole object?"

"You know, you could be right."

Three hours and half a dozen pints later Kelly was bloody sure Charlie was bloody right, and kept telling him so. Stuff 'em, old mate. Look after Number One.

Another recollection animated Charlie.

"You remember old Len? He was finished, bloody ill. He worked for the Printed Word Group division on the next floor - we used to see him as we went in and out, remember? He was falling asleep at his desk. I know he had to go, but all they offered him was the exact amount of compensation he was due under the old, out of date, terms of his company pension. £4,000. He needed more, and not only that, he was insulted, hurt.

"You remember, he had worked for them for 40 years for God's sake! All that company money - what was it, £20 million annual profit the year we left? £20,000 would not have even dented the directors' lunch allowances for a month. If Len had been with another firm they would have made a story of it. Think of all the copy he must have churned out, and with Len they would have been stories that helped people.

"Not like us - yes, yes, I'm right Kelly, we shafted people, admit it!" Kelly had raised himself to protest, but fell back grinning, too weakened by alcohol to do battle. All he managed was: "What's that got to do with the noble art of journalism?"

"It shows journalists are no different from anybody else."

"Should they be?"

"That's for you to answer now Kelly. I'm out of it. I'm going into public relations. An honest whore."

"That's economics Charlie." Kelly was not too sure why he said that. He had been trying to find his way back to the original argument.

"So's looking after Number One Kelly!" Charlie was quite sure why he said that.

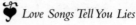

"Honesty is a much interpreted word Charlie."

"What's that supposed to mean?"

"No idea Charlie. No idea at all. Another?"

"There is only one honest answer to that my old mate – yes!"

On the train back home Kelly was lost in alcoholic reverie. They had been great days; no regrets. It was good in Brighton, being young and cavalier.

Sod 'em all, sod 'em all, we don't give a shit, sod 'em all.

He chuckled, remembering their version of the song.

Nothing worried them. Every day brand new and fun; every tomorrow looked forward to. Yes, it had been great.

Filled with light and comfort the train slid through the blackness. He hoped Angela would still be up. A nice cup of tea and a chat with her would be nice; just the ticket. Really, he just wanted to sit and look at her, to listen while she told him about her day and what Jo and Thomas had been up to.

Yes, Charlie, I remember old Len well enough. Poor fellow's dead now, so it doesn't matter. The strange thing was the people who had turned a hard face to Len's needs – after 40 years! – were the people who took their fat salary cheques from a newspaper. And that newspaper made its fat profits from taking high and mighty moral stances on social issues. And yes, Charlie, they do hobnob with businessmen more than their own staff.

No, Charlie, that does not seem so strange, not as you get older and wiser.

Yes, he used to think that journalists should be better than most. Ah, he was young then, wasn't he, with the impossible idealism of youth.

Angela was still up. He gave her a big, big, hug.

"What have you been doing to this hour!"

"Whining."

"Wining, and dining too no doubt!"

"No, just whining."

"Now what are you laughing at, you drunken stop-out!"

God, what would he do without this wonderful woman?

"Umm! I love you."

"Phew!" Fastidiously she waved away alcoholic fumes. "Drunkard!"

He took a big sniff of her. "You haven't been drinking have you? You have, I can smell booze!"

"You can smell yourself! Phew!"

"Never mind, I love you, whether you are drunk or sober. And I'll show you how much my scrumptious little bit of scrumptiousness." And he did, he thought magnificently. At home at least he was a hero.

★

Sophie Eastwinter let her husband settle down after their evening meal before bringing the subject that had been buzzing in her head ever since her mother and daughter heart to heart with Charlotte.

"Mother!" Charlotte had protested. "It is just a few lunches, all quite innocent. Don't be so old fashioned!" Old fashioned maybe, but still within her sell-by date and her mother could see quite well that her daughter was protesting too much. They may grow up and lead their own lives, but they are still your children!

"You know this millionaire chap, Nat Dobbs?"

Henry looked at his wife with surprise because just that morning he had given the go-ahead to negotiate with the woman claiming to have some juicy details about the man.

"Nat Dobbs, socialite, married a millionairess, yes, I've heard of him. Why?" Before his wife could reply he added: "And about to learn a bit more it seems."

Now it was Sophie's turn to be surprised.

Realising they were somehow at cross-purposes, her husband explained: "We are doing a story about him right now." He put her in the picture about the woman's claim that Dobbs was the father of her baby before asking why she was enquiring about Dobbs.

"Well," said Sophie, now glad she had ignored her daughter's entreaty for the matter to remain a secret between them. "I think Charlotte is having an affair with him."

Her words were a mortal blow to Eastwinter's lofty ethics.

★

"Right, that's enough for one day." Kelly turned off his word processor with and stretched his aching shoulders.

"How come you can get away so early," grumbled a colleague who

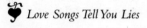

was still hunched over his desk, halfway through a story.

"Efficiency, that's the secret," said Kelly, and with a taunting grin was on his way.

It was nothing to do with efficiency. He had plenty to do but had decided at lunchtime that he would get away early. The sun was shining; it looked good out there and he suddenly had a desire to be kicking a ball around that evening with Thomas.

He knew of no better way to unwind the tangles of a day than to play football with Thomas and his friends. Even when Thomas was in playschool he liked to kick a ball about with them when he got home from work on The First Star. It was more fun than jogging.

"You're early," Angela greeted him. "What's brought you home so early?"

"I fancied a game of football with Thomas."

"Oh my goodness, all Fleet Street comes to a halt because of that?"

"Darling, you are out of date. They don't say 'Fleet Street' any more."

"What do they call it then?"

"Dunno – Media Mall?"

"Well whatever, you can forget football. Thomas has a lot of homework to do. So!"

Kelly knew better than to argue with So! Instead he sneaked upstairs.

"Forget the homework," he whispered to his son. "I'll help you finish it later. Get the football and we'll have a kick around."

They were sneaking down the garden path when Jo poked her head out of her window. "I'll tell on you!"

Caught red-handed, her father was crafty. "Come with us," he urged and, giggling, she did. On the way to the park they gathered up some of their school friends and a spare dad to even up the sides, and had a great mixed sex game of football. They returned home happy and excited, nearly talking their heads off, and drank gallons of squash.

Angela gave him stick over the meal table, but the children defended him, which made a nice change as they were usually on mother's side.

"Right, you can see they get their homework done and get to bed on time. I've got to get to a golf club committee meeting!"

Kelly, who had long since forgotten work, politics and sleaze, happily did as he was ordered, except the children did not get to bed on time. Instead they stayed up until just before their mother came home trying to talk their heads completely off. Her scolding was a complete waste of time, and only created a gale of giggles that further delayed them getting to sleep while their father scuttled downstairs chuckling.

"I can't trust you!" Angela scolded, as Kelly made the coffee.

"You can trust me with your life my darling."

"Mmm, can I!"

"Always, always," he wheedled, snuggling up to her.

"Good," she said, mollified. Her closeness was lovely. Warm, sexy; a man's reason for living.

"Always! Always!" God, he loved this woman!

"I'm peckish," she said, and made them a snack. "Healthy eating," she said, popping a tomato into his mouth. "To get you in the mood," she added cheekily. "This will help you."

"Help me?"

"Tomatoes; they are called love apples."

"Are they? Love apples! I don't need any help in that department! Not with you for my wife."

"Wow, you are in a romantic mood. Early to bed tonight!"

"Splendid notion," he agreed with a very wide grin. "But first, a little courtship? "

It was a beautifully warm night and they went outside, arm in arm, to drink their coffee at the garden table. He got out his old wind-up gramophone and played some of his prized Al Bowlly records, and they had a romantic waltz. Through the trees, caressing them softly like quiet music, drifted a breeze that brought with it memories of other happy times. This evening their world was perfect.

"The alyssum smells lovely," she said, inhaling sensuously.

He leaned over and kissed his wife. "You smell lovely too."

She covered his hand with hers. "We're lucky, aren't we?"

"Yes."

They sat for a long quiet while in the velvet dusk, the air soft and warm, a perfect environment for those fond memories to drift through their minds.

The telephone ringing in the house broke the spell.

"Oh, who can it be, this late?" Angela asked as she got up to answer it.

It was good ten minutes before she returned.

"What do you women find to talk about!" chided Kelly.

"Oh, how did you know it was a woman?"

"Because it took you so long to say whatever you had to say."

"Very funny! It was Susan - you know, Susan Squires." Kelly nodded. He knew Susan, always first with the gossip.

"What did she want?"

"Well, you know her friend Laura? Well, apparently Stephen - her husband - is having an affair. With some woman in his office. Laura is suicidal says Susan. It's awful, isn't it? They have two lovely little children."

"Very sad," said Kelly, typical of a man not knowing what else to say.

"Don't you go saying anything!"

"Me? Now why would I say anything! Susan will do enough of that, I reckon!"

"Don't be mean about Susan, she's worried about Laura! No! Of course darling I know you wouldn't say anything deliberately, but you might - without thinking," Angela added hastily.

"Goodness, what do you take me for? It's none of my business. Why would I say anything?"

"Well, you see Stephen at the golf club sometimes ... oh, of course you won't! Poor Laura. Oh, it's just like you read about in newspapers. You must come across it all the time. Do you ever worry that what you write will hurt someone who is innocent?"

"It's a job."

"Not a very nice job at times I suppose."

Then, sorry she was being so clumsy, she added quickly: "I'm sorry darling. You do a wonderful job. I'm sorry darling, really."

"Don't be silly, it doesn't matter."

"I saw your face, you looked ...."

"My face? You leave my face alone madam!"

"I most certainly will not. It is a gorgeous, wonderful, beautiful face and I am certainly not going to leave it alone!" Whereupon she proceeded to give his face a thoroughly good seeing-to with dozens of kisses.

Overwhelmed Kelly accepted defeat and took her hand. "Time for bed."

The silly romantic mood of this evening reminded him – as if any reminder was ever needed – why theirs was such a happy marriage. With his arm firmly around her he walked his wife to bed.

"This is one Meadow Gate marriage Susan will not be gossiping about!"

On a beautiful night such as this, with a woman as lovely as Angela, any man would have meant every word.

With or without love apples.

★

First thing the next morning Eastwinter summoned Smith.

"Where are we with the Nat Dobbs story?" he demanded.

Smith outlined the situation. "Webb is contacting the woman, perhaps already has"

"I want it killed." Seeing Smith's surprise, he added less brusquely. "We are spending too much money on the same kind of story. They're getting too same-ish."

Smith was taken aback, but nodded tamely: "I'll tell Webb."

"No!" Eastwinter did not want any discussion in the newsroom. "Call him and Buller in."

Kelly got to the office first and explained to the editor – who barely listened as he waited impatiently for Buller to arrive – that he had contacted the woman but was not going to get far until they started talking money.

Then Buller walked in but had no chance to speak before Eastwinter delivered his decision. Kill the Nat Dobbs story.

Buller was so surprised he protested too strongly and the editor snapped: "Kill it! I want it dropped." Then with a touch of caution – remembering he did not want the matter being bandied about in the office – he added: "There is a good reason. Just leave it, and I don't want any discussion about it in the office." Reporters talked shop all the time and he did not want the story being picked up by another paper.

Kelly too was surprised that the story was being spiked. It was strong and right up the Graphic's street.

Buller glared at Kelly, jumping immediately to the conclusion that somehow Kelly had influenced the decision. They had been discussing the story before he got to the office, and why had Webb been called in first? The creep had had something to do with this. Right from the start he had showed no enthusiasm for the story.

Buller was furious. He had had that bastard Dobbs right in his sights! "Well, that's it," Kelly said as they left the editor's office. "Nothing we can do about it."

Buller snarled and strode off. No, but there is plenty I can do about you Webb, you arsehole creeper. Plenty!

When Buller and Kelly had gone Eastwinter sat back and thought over what he had just done.

Of course it would not necessarily stop it all appearing in another paper as the woman would no doubt try to sell the story elsewhere. Keep her dangling without a firm answer and if she could be fobbed off for long enough Dobbs' brief involvement with Charlotte would have ended and it would be unlikely her name would be dragged into it. Knowing the lecher, no doubt there would soon be another woman to satisfy the paparazzi. If there was, she would be the one the Graphic would feature.

No ethical problems there that Eastwinter could see.

★

Kelly intended to get the last train available to the West Country, stay overnight, get the interview with Shirley Love done the next day and be back by that evening. Then Angela called and said they had been asked out to dinner that evening with friends.

"I hope it did not cause you too much trouble."

Angela said this through pursed lips as she applied her make-up ready for the dinner date.

"You come first darling," Kelly replied gallantly. "I've altered the appointment for the next day."

They had a nice evening, and did their favourite thing and strolled home afterwards in the moonlight.

"We should do this more often darling," said Angela.

Kelly agreed with a kiss.

"We'll make it a date, every moonlit night – but June to September only!"

They strolled on in silence for a while and then Angela kissed him. "Happy darling?"

"Very."

Under that magnificent night sky he was the greatest man on earth and he wanted it to last for ever.

The result of all this was that he set off for the West Country a day late.

And every day fate has a different schedule.

27

The first part of the journey was fast; then the train reached Dorset and, as if passing into another world, ran to a different time scale. Every few minutes, like a milkman's horse that had been years on the same run, the train stopped at tree-shaded halts with not a soul in sight or somnolent village stations where at most one or two passengers alighted. It took nearly as long to get from Bournemouth to Weymouth as it had from London to Bournemouth.

As he walked out of Weymouth station he heard gulls screaming, and from the nearby beach the happy sounds of holidaymakers were carried on a salty breeze.

Fresh from the squashed-up Home Counties the sudden huge open space of sun, sea and sand that burst upon him on the seafront was exhilarating. People were strolling lazily, and on the beach a scattering of picnicking families were enjoying a warm day for early May.

The town had just been a convenient destination, somewhere to stay en route to the assignment. He had not given any thought as to what to expect when he got there. This serendipity was sweet, like an unexpected drink to a thirsty man. For the next couple of hours he sailed a deckchair on the sunlit seas of happy memories. Those carefree days with his best mate Charlie. With his eyes closed this was Brighton. The smells and the sounds! Girls, girls, girls. Yes, he had done all right in that respect! Then he had pulled the best one of all, Angela. A picture of her splashing in the Brighton waves came to his grateful mind.

Late afternoon sun on his face was melting tensions he had not even realised were there. He made his mind up right then. When he got back, it was going to be a real old-fashioned fortnight by the sea with Angela and the children.

Pleasant reverie was rudely interrupted by a clatter right beside his ear and he opened his eyes. Young men, already sporting summer tans, were beginning to pile up the deckchairs for the end of the day. Daydreaming over he strolled along the seafront looking for somewhere to stay. Feeling decidedly out of place wearing a suit among holidaymakers in daft baggy shorts he made another decision. When they went on that old-fashioned seaside holiday, he was first going to spend some time in the gym. He pulled his stomach in, testing for flab. Yes, definitely some time in the gym!

Eventually he found a guesthouse displaying a 'vacancies' sign. The landlady was a cosy woman who greeted Kelly warmly. There was a chuckliness about her that tickled him and he felt at home right away. Chuckly, and with rather a saucy eye, she was the sort of woman who made men smile. Feeling very welcome he booked one night, telling her there was the possibility of a second – although he would not be hanging about if he could manage to get this bloody job done quickly.

"That's a shame," she said in a tone of voice that should have been accompanied by a wink. "I don't get many handsome young men staying – they're usually all spoken for, with a wife and loads of kids in tow!"

They both laughed as she ushered him towards his room. Young man! She was in need of glasses! He took off his tie and dumped his travel bag. It was too early yet to eat so he decided to have a look around. First, he studied a tourist map in the hallway of the guest-house from which he could see the town was built on an island.

"Yes, water, water, everywhere," chuckled the landlady. "We've got the sea in front, the lake at the back, the harbour that end and salt flats the other. If we get global warming we'll all be 20 feet under water they say! See you later my lovely."

There had definitely been a naughty look in the landlady's eye. He was not imagining it. Nothing made a chap feel better – or stirred the ego more vigorously – than a naughty look in a lady's eye. Showed he wasn't losing his touch – or perhaps it did, as she was not that young! Good humour fizzing through his veins he strode off along the promenade smiling to himself, and nicely stirred.

Approaching him a couple of on-the-town teenage girls seemed to catch his mood. "Got a friend?" one of them giggled. They skipped on, looking back at him and laughing cheekily.

The landlady was right: the town was situated twixt the blue sea and the green-blue lake. It took him only a couple of minutes to walk through the town from the sea to the lake. Unspoiled nature ran virtually to the centre of the town. There cannot be many towns in this crowded island, he marvelled, where untouched wildness can be found at its heart.

There was a footbridge over a river flowing through a prairie of reeds into the lake. He crossed the bridge, disturbing a host of pigeons and gulls that people were feeding and peevish ducks waddled at his feet.

He followed a narrow footpath that was disappearing deep into man-high reeds. Within moments he had left a busy town centre to enter a place that seemed untouched by man, almost primeval.

It was now very soft and quiet. From the West rays from the falling sun touched the tops of the browsing reeds. Shimmering bursts of light were sent in all directions as a gentle breeze ruffled through. Here and there a delicate brush of colour from wild flowers and strokes of green from new-season shoots showed among the wintered silver-grey of the reeds. He stood still, letting the peace all around ease into him. It was the silence of the wild, lulling; a silence emphasised by a murmuring breeze, rustling reeds and bird song. It was very still now, so near yet so far from the real world. This sudden plunge into an oasis of unexpected peace was luxury for the senses. Standing quite still he drew a deep breath and savoured sweet serendipity.

A tiny creature, a mouse, perhaps a baby rat - Kelly, a Home Counties commuter, hours spent on the Underground, man had little idea - deemed it safe enough to wander across the path right at his feet. Standing absolutely still Kelly watched it feed on something it found engrossingly tasty. From time to time it suddenly became alert, sensing something that alarmed it. Then it would relax again, totally unaware that a vast creature loomed above. Thomas and Jo would have loved this.

Then Kelly became aware of someone behind him and turned to see a woman who had come up quietly. She smilingly indicated that she too had seen the fragile creature. They stood watching it in silence for a few moments more until it had finished its snack. With a final, almost casual, look around, it ambled off into the grass at the side of the path.

"Well," said Kelly. "He was not worried about us, was he?"

"No, he wasn't."

Kelly looked around, hoping to see another of the charming creatures. "It is not often you get such a good look that close."

"You do here, quite often," the woman replied. "You see quite a lot along this path."

"When it didn't run away I thought perhaps there was something wrong with it."

"No, if you are quiet you can get quite close. But not with the water rats, they are sharp. They seem to have radar that detects humans a mile off."

They were walking on together as they chatted.

"Are you a holidaymaker?" he enquired politely.

"A holidaymaker? No, I live here."

When they arrived at a second bridge he could see houses on a hill rising out of the lake. "That's a nice place to live, on that island," he observed.

She stopped to see where he was pointing. "No, that's not an island, that's just part of the town, Radipole."

As she looked out over the water he was able to regard her. She was what, 35? slender, with silky celtic-blond hair. Her clothes looked expensive and she wore a lightweight summer jacket with a casual elegance.

A light breeze scattered a confetti of May flowers from a hedgerow over her. Smilingly she made to catch some. "My wedding day!" she joked.

She looked – he found himself searching for the exact word – nice, classy. Turning suddenly she caught his gaze and smiled. It was the smile of a woman who knows she is being admired. It brought a mischievous vivacity to her eyes before they were turned, properly, away.

It was the moment that has been repeated a billion and one times in the story of man's downfall.

"Even though you live here, you still like to walk through here?"

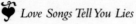

Obviously! Floundering, it was the best he could think of to keep the conversation going.

"I come through here on my way to work."

"I see. A lovely walk. You are lucky to live here."

"Very. I would never live anywhere else."

"Pity about the road." As they crossed the bridge, the sound of speeding traffic could be heard.

"Yes, they have just built it."

"It's new?" He looked around, surprised. "You wouldn't think they would put a road through here in this day and age, with so much concern for the environment. This must be a wildlife haven."

"It was in the town plan for 50 years, so they say."

"So they had 50 years to see sense!"

She invited him to look at the lake with a gesture. "There's still plenty left."

"People pay to come here on holiday. You are paid to live here."

She smiled, but did not reply and he sensed she was amused at his feeble efforts to make conversation. Walking on, she enquired: "Are you on holiday?"

"No." He did not want to change the subject and get talking about London. In case he had seemed too abrupt he added: "I'm here on business."

They had arrived at a kissing gate. He pointed. "Where does that path lead?"

"To Southill and Radipole. The one you want is that one, it leads back to town." Polite dismissal.

"Thank you." Then, although it was hardly appropriate having only walked with her for a few minutes, he added: "Goodbye. It was nice to have met you."

Again, she acknowledged the courtesy with that certain smile of a woman admired, and turned to walk the other way. He watched her until she was gone from view round a bend; walking easy, savouring the evening.

The road back to town was around the lake and beside the main road. They had used every inch of land without actually filling in some of the lake. There was just enough room between the dangerous new road and the lake for a footpath. The road had taken what must have been important hinterland for the lake. They were just as stupid in Dorset as the Home Counties it seemed.

There's still plenty left.

A philosophical lady. Yes, he could see that there was indeed still a lot for which to be grateful. The town was sited precariously in a watery landscape that would be hard to spoil further.

They had walked together so easily. The recollection of her walking away was suddenly very vivid; easy, good to be alive. He felt the ingrained City tensions that still lingered easing pleasurably. Hmmm…he thought of Angela massaging his shoulders for him of an evening when he got home from work.

He looked back over the lake gleaming in late afternoon light. Birds caressed themselves through the air, flying just for the sheer luxury of it. It was a privilege to be alive on such a lovely day.

Another image came happily to mind. It was of all of them traipsing over Box Hill, Angela, him and the children. He loved Box Hill and the views it gave of Southern England. Sometimes he went alone just to enjoy those views. There may be men as lucky as him, but none luckier. This evening he was feeling very good about himself, about his lot. Far away from the office, in this tucked-away slow-coach-to-nowhere corner of England, he had found something good, something far from the madding-hours of his life; a different perspective. This warm sunlit meeting with the woman had done him a power of good!

Kelly from Brighton. He could teach Frank a thing or two! Yes indeed, a power of good!

Back at the guesthouse he freshened up and put on a clean shirt, leaving off his tie. He strolled the promenade among the holiday throng for an hour with hands in pockets, up and down, easy and slow. Everyone was in the holiday mood and he could feel it all around, as a sweet melody is heard from a distance.

At eight he found a pavement café and asked for the menu, but had only just started to browse the variety of dishes on offer when he folded it. Who needs a menu at the seaside? Fish and chips of course, what else?

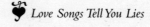

After finishing his meal he sat for a time watching people strolling the promenade. Walking back to the guesthouse he breathed in the happy holiday smells: sun tan lotions - it had been an unusually warm start to the year - beer, hamburgers and fish and chips. The woman on the footpath had left a much more upmarket fragrance lingering. Like her clothes, it had been - he sought just the right word - elegant, classy. They had walked along the path together so easy, so natural.

'Nice to have met you.'

Yes, it had been.

28

Buller had been delighted at first that Eastwinter was to be the new editor, however when he realised that having a hard man in charge was not going to smooth the way for his ambitions he became surly. No one noticed Green's reactions as he kept his thoughts hidden as usual but his stunted soul did a jig on learning the name of the new editor.

Because of a drink-talkative family friend of the Eastwinters he knew all about Lord Emburey and the inside story of the Eastwinter family scandal and he also knew all about Lord Emburey's predicament over the City Investment Group's pension fund money. Green could not believe his luck when he learned who the new editor was going to be. The long-ago Emburey scandal of illicit sex and cruel abandonment had been tearfully related to him by a raddled woman who had been a close confidante of Eastwinter's mother. The lady, inebriated on free drinks at a public relations do Green was covering, told him how Emburey had abandoned Mrs Eastwinter senior, who never recovered from the trauma of first leaving her husband and family and then being tossed aside by the lecherous Emburey. Mrs Eastwinter had just died – of guilt and a broken heart, according to her sad old friend, who in telling her tale spat out her anger at Emburey.

The conversation had not had financial possibilities for Green at the time and would probably have lain undisturbed in his memory. Then only a couple of weeks before Chillywinds' arrival at the Graphic he had picked up the story about the pension fund scam. Even then he may not have recalled the story the woman had told him and put one and one together to make a profit if Henry Eastwinter not been made editor. Then everything dovetailed. He knew he had the pension fund story to himself and had been quietly substantiating as much of it as he could before revealing it to the Graphic and taking the glory while one of the reporters did the rest of the work of putting it all together.

Since the news of Eastwinter's appointment he had mulled over all the possibilities of what he knew, and that plan had been changed.

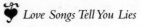

Now he waited for a chance to present the story direct from himself to the new editor.

Analysed through Green's mean view of the world it was a certainty that a chance to damage Emburey would be grabbed by Eastwinter and he would bathe in the editor's gratitude. In media world a mean view usually focuses spot on.

The landlady served Kelly a traditional English breakfast. A couple of rounds of toast and a bowl of cereals, was all he ever bothered with at home. What the heck, he was on holiday! Eating more eggs, bacon, sausages and fried bread in one sitting than you did in a month at home was what you did on holiday wasn't it?

"That will give you strength," said the landlady. That's all she said, the words innocent enough, but her chuckle made them saucy.

A salty breeze skittered along the promenade and the sun was still shining. He was more in the mood for a holiday than work, and he walked along the seafront to pick up the hire car thinking about where to take the family when he got back to Meadow Gate.

Once he was clear of Dorchester he found the road an old fashioned gem, an exhilarating drive high over unspoiled countryside. He had the road almost to himself for mile after mile. This was crowded England? Where was the traffic? He could not remember when last he had enjoyed a drive so much.

He was soon enjoying the company of the voluptuous Shirley Love. She turned out to have a great sense of humour. Her tales were outrageous, but told with non-malicious fun. She kept him chuckling all afternoon, with a glass of wine permanently in her hand.

The one-time screen sex goddess had used up four husbands who were not short of a bob or two, but none had the real money someone with her lifestyle needed. Kelly saw what had attracted them. There are plenty of well-endowed and shapely women around and in common with healthy men Kelly was grateful. He would enjoy the view but always return home.

Shirley Love's shapeliness was the kind that was apt to make a lot of men forget about home.

Indeed, judging by what she told him – the names of whom he jotted down for later development – many a Westminster Man had. Even in what Kelly judged to be the downhill side of forty there was plenty of her left worth seeing. What could not be obscured by the poundage, and likely never would be, was her comfortable sexiness. Kelly could imagine – and before the afternoon was through he enjoyed imagining – the pleasure to be had among those curves. Her body would be, Kelly fantasised, like a large warm bed with white silk sheets, into which a man could snuggle and discover delights and then, after nice snooze with her bosoms as a pillow, discover them again. Only fantasy, but all around her like soft lighting glowed a sexy geniality that was a very pleasant reality.

Kelly wondered what her reaction would be, being likened to a big bed with her bosoms as pillows. The thought tickled him.

"What?" she queried, seeing his amusement.

"Nothing," but his grin grew bigger.

She wagged a finger at him: "I think you can be a bit naughty!" Judging by the twinkle in her eye she was hoping she was right. Then looking around at the slightly faded grandeur of her surroundings she sighed.

"I love it here, but it takes a lot of upkeep."

She lived in a 16th century farmhouse, salvaged from the marriage to Jack Lee, husband number one bless him (they were still good friends despite all his affairs while they were married).

Husband number two, Lorenzo Love, the Hollywood icon whose name she had kept, had given her a flat in Nice that she liked to maintain so she could get to Cannes (so useful for contacts in festival time). Numbers three and four had left her with only two or three million and at prices these days that had not gone far.

"So my agent said I really had to write my memoirs," she explained, charmingly rueful. Leaning over to top up his glass she was so close that as he raised a defensive hand saying "No more for me thanks" he inadvertently touched her bold breasts.

"Oh such a sensible chap," she said, leaning closer rather than away from his hand. "You are driving of course. Are you always so sensible? Of course you are, I can tell. Not all men are so

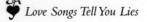

responsible, you know." There was that waggish look again, then she was off on a tale about the life hubby number three (or was it four?) had led her. Oh, awful! But such fun judging by the giggles.

Well before it was time for afternoon tea, served by a maid despite the poverty looming on her horizon, Kelly had more than enough for his article. In addition he had jotted down a few juicy titbits about politicians she had known, intimately in most cases.

"It's funny," she said as she poured his tea, "You think you have got it right, quite sure in fact, and then…"

She looked at him as though he might have the answer to whatever she was asking herself. The introspective moment lasted just that long, a moment, and then she laughed. Love! Who understands it?

"Are you married Kelly?"

"Yes."

"I thought so. I can tell. I can always tell. And happy too, right?"

A sheepish grin answered that more eloquently than words.

"Yes, I can see you are. You keep it that way Kelly. Take it from one who knows. In the end, all this " – with a gesture she encompassed the house and everything else in her life including, presumably, the few million pounds she no longer had – "is no substitute, you know. No substitute at all."

Oh yeah? The lady was a big fibber. Given the chance she would be into husband number five, and then six. Seven, eight and nine if she lived long enough.

"There's no telling with people." It was the best philosophy Kelly could manage at short notice.

"Oh yes there is. I can tell you are the faithful sort. Right? Yes you are," she insisted when his grin grew even more sheepish.

"Mind you. I'm not complaining. They were such fun. It's no good complaining, or looking back, is it?"

Kelly tapped his notebook. "You gave as good as you got."

"I did, didn't I! Well, what was I supposed to do? I was never good at being the little wifey. Not me! I don't know what it is all about – except one thing. You stay true to yourself. You can't expect to live by one rule and obey another. You know what I mean. I don't feel bad about what I have written. Oh, I have not revealed everything.

Some of them were dearies. They don't deserve…but I've seen the rotten side of many who, well, you'll see in the book.

"These people in the public eye, these politicians. I don't have any sympathy for them. They get voted in as one thing, little wifey by their side, all that sort of thing, so they must expect what they get when they hanky panky about. You can't sit there handing out moral judgements if you are playing around, can you? That's one thing about showbiz. It doesn't take moral stands. We play anything for money, hero or villain!"

Chuckling, she poured another.

"But you …" Kelly stopped himself. This was not Newsnight or Panorama. He was not going to grill this woman. Let her say what she liked. It was good copy, fun for a change in a media world of sleaze and spite.

"I haven't mentioned names dearie. But a lot of well-known people will be reading it and seeing themselves. Maybe they'll be wondering who else can recognise them! Make 'em worry a bit, eh?"

Kelly grinned along with her chuckles. He liked this risque lady.

The westering sun was shooting arrows of gold low over the Devon hills. Kelly looked at his watch. "I'd better be off. I was hoping to get back to London tonight."

"Oh, must you? I was just beginning to enjoy our little chat. You can stay over tonight if you like."

Taken by surprise, Kelly declined.

"No? Are you sure?" With a bright smile she was looking straight at him, and the message was clear. Was it shock he felt, or a tingling in his loins? Both, probably, and it was far from unpleasant. Certainly those juices were flowing faster than ever. Since arriving at her house he had enjoyed the view, and not only from the windows over the East Devon countryside. Shirley Love was one of those women who not only retain their attractiveness to men as they grow older, but improve on it.

And are more confident of their sexuality. And often more generous with it.

"You are very welcome." Ostensibly she was saying he was welcome

to stay. Ostensibly.

Quite unable to say anything appropriate Kelly floundered. So the lady took charge. "Well, there no need to decide now. Let's have some tea and I'll show you around."

Somehow the tour of the house seemed to involve her taking his hand frequently to lead him and standing rather close while she pointed out this and that. Then tea was two on a sofa; a nice *little* sofa. "You must stay Kelly. It is much too late to get back to London tonight."

"I really should."

"It doesn't always do to be sensible you know!"

"Well, ah…." Kelly felt agreeably weak. This ego massage was very nice.

When he finally re-organised himself and smilingly insisted he had to leave she was quite unabashed.

"No, of course not. You have to get back, I understand. Your editor will be wondering where you have got to! But we must meet up next time I'm in London. Yes, yes, it would be nice. I'll call you at the office? Give me the number."

After she had noted it in her pocket diary she tucked a piece of notepaper into the top pocket of Kelly's jacket. "Here's my mobile number." Those warm bedroom eyes held his. "In case you need anything else from me."

She saw him off in the drive. "Are you sure you will make it back tonight? You can stay if you like, there's plenty of room. Well, I hope you've learned from all this Kelly!" She laughed again. "Oh, I'm so rude. I'm sure you don't need me to keep you in check. I am a very good judge of character."

Holding a glass of wine in one hand she waved goodbye with the other until he could no longer see her in his rear mirror.

'It doesn't always pay to be sensible.'

Kelly laughed so much the car wobbled over the central white line. Hard luck Frank. If you had got this job you would have stayed overnight - all week, probably. It had certainly been an entertaining afternoon. He felt in his top pocket and pulled out the paper with her phone number on it. Underneath she had written: 'Don't forget!'

He put it back in his pocket. Well, he might have to call her to check a detail on his story. He looked a sensible chap, did he? Now that was a doubtful compliment if ever he had heard one! A very good judge of character was she? Maybe, but not a very good judge of husbands!

On the other hand, perhaps she was. Good, that is, if you want to maximise your divorce pay-offs!

He had another look at his watch. The last train from Weymouth to London was about eight. Perhaps he should have stayed overnight. He could still turn back. He was going to have to shift to make it to Weymouth to catch the train. However he encountered no delays as the traffic was light, and when he got to the Yeovil-Dorchester stretch he again had it almost to himself right to Dorchester.

Keep *him* in check! That was one saucy lady! She had fancied him! Kelly put his foot down. To a Londoner that road was pure pleasure. He was feeling the way a man who is fancied by a tasty lady feels. Bloody good, thank you mate!

He did not get to Weymouth in time for the train, yet on that wonderful high clear run to Dorchester he could have easily made it time. The promenade was still busy with people with nothing to do but to enjoy doing nothing and all the time in the world to do it. He breathed in deep, dispelling any last vestige of London smoke from his lungs.

"Hello my lovely. Staying another night are we?" chuckled the landlady. "Come on in love, and I'll make you a nice cup of tea."

Her smile was warm and welcoming. Kelly met that saucy smile with a broad grin. Here was another risqué lady; he was beginning to like this West Country.

Kelly wondered, as he drank the umpteenth cup of tea of that ego-tickled day, whether Shirley Love would call him when she got to London. His youthful Brighton alter-ego told him she would. It must be something in this West Country air.

Whatever it was, it was nice!

⌐ 29 ⌐

"**I**s there a follow-up on the Pattimore business?" Smith asked
after Buller had outlined other stories they were working on.
"Nothing, as yet."

"What about the wife? What happened when Kelly Webb saw her?"

"Nothing. According to Webb she just complained about Press
treatment, but there's no copy. Waste of time and money. Getting a
bit cavalier, is our Webb. I reckon he needs a bit more supervision,
more time in the office."

The deputy editor looked steadily at Buller. He was pondering.
Turning people against each other, backing one or the other, was an
important part of office politics. Perhaps some time he had to sort
this antagonism between these two. Not just yet though. Eastwinter
seemed to be very cool regarding Buller and had once remarked
favourably on the work Webb was doing. Just a hint, a nuance, but
this was office politics. An ear for hints and nuances was vital.

"Well, if he says so, it's probably right. He knows his job."

Buller, wrong footed, said nothing. He too knew all about office
politics. This was not the time. Kelly was the paper's hot property.
Since winning the award Smith was giving him the freedom to
work on whatever story he liked, when he liked.

Smith reached for his telephone, bringing the conference to a close.

"He's ambitious, and ambitious men are self starters. Let him have
his head. We'll get better results."

So saying, Smith smiled at Buller. Thinly.

Buller came out of the meeting boiling with fury. He had thrown
his dice and lost. Green looked up and put on an expression of
concern. He did not know what had transpired, but he could see
Buller's fury. That had to be a good sign.

Buller strode off and Green smiled at his departing back. The
opposition was defeating itself. He was beginning to feel more and
more secure just watching and waiting.

Now he was on the inside track and forging ahead.

When Buller had calmed down enough, he found a quiet corner
and rang Kelly's home number.

"Hello?"

"Ah, Angela. Buller, the Graphic."

The friendliness he put into his voice did not alter the expression he could not see on Angela's face. She had only met him once at an office function and immediately disliked him, an opinion formed without her knowing that Kelly did not get on with him. Kelly made a point of not bringing the office home.

"Kelly is not there by chance, is he?"

"No." Angela was surprised.

"O.K. Sorry to bother you. I thought he might have gone home early or something. We can't contact him."

"No, sorry. He's not here."

"O.K. Don't worry. We are getting used to it! Never seem to know where he is, these days." Buller injected jocularity into his voice. "What does that husband of yours get up to Angela!"

"Up to? What do you …"

"It's O.K. He'll call in."

Buller put the phone down, the seed sown. Then he took the Oxford Street photograph and put it in a plain envelope, already addressed following a visit he had made to personnel to get Kelly's home address.

I know what you have been up to behind my back, Webb, you smarmy sod. The editor's blue-eyed boy wants to come and go as and when he pleases, up to God bloody knows what. I don't need it spelled out. Well, two can play at being clever my son. I don't have blue eyes Webb, but I do have eyes that don't miss a thing; not a bloody thing. When it comes to shafting you are messing with an expert.

He waited a couple of days then dropped the letter in a post-box. Oh yes, he knew human nature. When wives get suspicious, that suspicion grows in their minds like a fungus. Human nature. You can't get away from it. Webb would try to guess the origin of the photograph when he was confronted with it, but he would have no idea at all. Not a clue. There was a great satisfaction in shafting Webb this way.

With an expert Webb. A bloody past master.

★

Kelly called Angela just as she was busy getting tea for the children and at the same time getting ready to meet the girls at the golf club. "I'm going to be late, darling," he said. "So I'll be staying overnight. I know, I know," he soothed when she started to complain that he always seemed to be away these days.

Angela did not have a chance to say anything else. He seemed in a hurry, ending the conversation quickly with some excuse. As she was also in a hurry, she had to let him go. She did not remember the call from Buller until after he had hung up. What did it matter now? No doubt Kelly had since phoned his office.

The call from Kelly and their incomplete, muddling, conversation, upset Angela. These last few weeks, probably longer, they hardly seemed to have had five minutes for each other. When was the last time they had had a good talk, as they always used to? Some time with him, that was what she craved; time to show him how much she loved him.

Angela could not erase the guilt, which she felt most keenly at family times like this as she watched the children settling down to do their homework. She was a woman who had everything. Kelly had not deserved the way she had behaved. After a few kitchen chores she made herself a cup of coffee. She sat at the kitchen table cradling the cup in her hands, gazing unhappily into the recent past. It was going to make no difference to what had happened, but she decided to be honest with herself about how it had all begun.

The way she had behaved had encouraged Bretts. That's how it all started.

Fiona was the reason, but that was no excuse. It had been a girls' night out, the first one they had held for a long time. She and Gilly had been having a coffee and chat in the Café Rouge when in walked Dot with, would you believe, Fiona!

It was like old times. Fiona had disappeared from the coffee mornings crowd at least a year before and their girl get-togethers had petered out. Fiona had always been the instigator of them, and the show-off life and soul.

Fiona loved being outrageous. She had married and divorced twice, and the cause of each divorce she blithely admitted was her fault. You did not have to be very perceptive to see she enjoyed the confession. Her mission in life was to have as many affairs as she could, and she kept pretty busy.

"We must have a get-together," she had enthused. They all agreed it was a good idea and arranged to call each other to fix it up.

"Same old Fiona, never short of a word," chuckled Gilly as she and Angela continued with the rest of their shopping.

Which remark reminded Angela how Fiona used to make patronising jokes at her expense because she and Kelly were so solid. 'Old Faithful' had been her nickname for Angela. Their girls' nights were fun, and she had never wanted to spoil things, but Fiona's 'jokes' had always secretly annoyed her.

"Never short of word," agreed Angela, "But I hope it's all talk. If half of what she says is true, every husband in Reigate – and Redhill – must be locked up quick!"

Gilly laughed. "Angela! If half of what Fiona says is true, it is too late to lock them up!"

"Then lock her up before she does any more damage!" Despite herself Angela could not help but laugh. Fiona was a bit of a card. Old Faithful! Better than being Old Floozie!

★

Normally breakfast was a coffee and a couple of slices of toast. It must have been the Weymouth air as the next morning Kelly tucked into another plateful of sausages, eggs, bacon, mushrooms; the works.

After that breakfast, which was all he was going to need until he got home to Meadow Gate, he decided to take a last stroll along the promenade. It was a wonderful morning, the sun eye–dazzling bright. There were families digging in their beach claims already, and it was not yet half past eight. Thomas and Jo would love it here. Kids are soon at an age when they don't want to go on holiday with their parents he recalled a wise old head saying. A family holiday is our next priority Angela!

A few holidaymakers were already paddling in the sea. It was probably freezing, still only May. Daft, but it was what you did on holiday. He agreed with them. It was a lovely day for doing daft things. The day and the place. A day for an adventure.

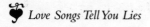

It all made him loth to leave without one last look around. He would catch a mid morning train, quit the office early and take Angela for a drink that evening.

After strolling the promenade and turning into the town centre he espied a crowd on the bridge over the river he had visited the other evening. It must have been the unseasonably Mediterranean-warm morning that had brought them out so early. He made his way over and watched as delighted children tossed pieces of bread to the gulls. Somewhere in that vastness of reeds that tiny mouse - or vole - was tucking into its breakfast as well.

"Oh, it's you again." She had come through the crowd on the bridge and there she was, pausing and smiling at him.

"Good morning." It was the woman he had met the previous evening.

"You won't get much business done feeding the birds."

"I'm not - just dodging them. Do you have to run this gauntlet every morning?

She looked at him questioningly

"You said you came to work this way."

"Oh did I?" She looked at him, and there was a certain something in her eyes, a smile; something intriguing.

Then just as easy, as naturally as they had the other evening, they were walking on together.

"Oh yes, I do. Quite often. I sometimes think it would be wise to bring an umbrella!" She laughed, looking up carefully at the wheeling gulls. "But they haven't caught me yet!"

They had passed under a bridge and were nearing the town centre. "They don't work you very hard then."

"Oh they do. Not a minute. I just had a bit of time before I catch a train."

"To where?"

"London."

She stopped as they reached the shops. "I go this way. The station's that way."

"Yes, I know."

"Well, goodbye."

Where did it come from? It was an impulse, quite crazy, that was to leave him spending the next three hours wondering what on earth he was doing.

"Do you get a lunch hour?"

As stupid questions go, it was a prizewinner. No, this is Back of Beyond Dorset. Workers don't get lunch hours here. They work chained to their desks and someone comes round to feed them.

She had been about to walk on but, turning, stayed. She regarded him quizzically. "Yes." There was that look again, knowing, smiling; full of the power of a woman. "Why?"

She knew exactly what he was going to ask. Now he was committed. There was nowhere to hide. A thought flashed into his mind, an escape clause, that at least he was a hundred miles from London. No one knew him down here and he need never have to come back and run into this woman again, have to avoid her eyes, the presumptuous stranger she was about to put in his place.

"I thought perhaps…" He was making a gauche mess of this, Kelly Webb of all people; the Brighton pull 'em expert.

She waited.

"Perhaps I could buy you lunch."

He was just saying the words in the disjointed manner of someone who would rather stay silent, but now with no option.

"That would be nice." She smiled and words promptly failed him altogether. Now where was that Brighton laddo? He had been better at this when he was sixteen.

Fortunately she had the essential word. "Where?"

"I don't know the town. Somewhere you like."

Pointing towards the seafront she said: "See that building? W.H. Smith's. Right behind in the next street the end building opposite is a café overlooking the seafront, Sibleys."

"Right, Sibleys." He etched it into his memory.

"I'll have to do a bit of shopping first. Quarter to one?"

"Fine." The world was slowly coming back into focus. Just in time he remembered to ask: "What's your name?"

"Kathy."

Then she walked on and did not look back.

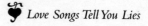

A snatch of the latest hit song burst out of a café door:

Walk, walk, your sexy walk.
Talk, talk, your sexy talk.
Blow me away!

Neat timing. With her, walking was an art form.

Still hardly believing what he had done – what the old Brighton Kelly had done – he spent the next couple of hours wandering around the town. He had been in plenty of seaside towns within reach of London. This one had a hard to define difference. It was a kind of tucked–away forgotten–England town, where time had slowed down around the 40s and 50s and had not got much further since. These were the streets and buildings you saw in old black and white newsreels; a town agreeably out of date.

In the bustling shopping street there was a carnival air as several buskers vied for the loose change of shoppers. There was a Cuban ensemble that he had seen several times in London and he sat at a street café table for coffee to enjoy their show.

Then he heard that song again.

Just along from the café there was the young singer from Oxford Street strumming his guitar. These fellows must travel the length and breadth of England mused Kelly. At that moment the Cuban band took a break and the young man could be heard. He was singing that song again, his clear voice enabling Kelly to understand the lyric.

Walking a cold and empty street
Darkened windows looking down;
Aimless heart, aimless feet.
Lonely man in lonely town.

The plane takes off.
It touches down
In yet another hotel town.

You wheel and deal;
More money's made,
Then you watch the daylight fade.

From your hotel room
You phone home.
Then once again you eat alone.

Too soon for sleep
The clock ticks slow;
You seek a downtown club you know.

It's an accidental meeting
As she steps from a door;
One of a thousand moments fleeting
That pass to tempt no more.

In her eyes the divine mischief
That makes heroes of all men;
You're on the street that leads to grief
Where even wise men go again.

She turns to go, and turning, stays.
You should walk on, it's late.
Into those beguiling eyes you gaze
And man, you've met your fate.

You stand aside; apologise.
She smiles with courtesy.
And then begin those tangled lies
That will never set you free.

Walking a cold and empty street,
Darkened windows looking down;
Aimless heart, aimless feet.
Lonely man in lonely town.

Kelly finished his coffee and left the café, the haunting melody following him. It had no words for him: lonely man he was not. This town had a buzz that he liked.

He bought an ice cream on the promenade and under a bright blue sky that was to bless almost every day of that wonderful summer he spent a happy hour sailing a deckchair with Angela and the kids on the sunlit seas of memory.

In good time he went to Sibleys and sat at a table to wait. He chose a table for two tucked into a corner from where he could see her enter. The place was busy because of the lunch hour. Every time someone came in he looked up expectantly. Perhaps she would not turn up at all. Perhaps she had decided not to show up. It would be the best thing really. Arranging to meet her had been a moment of…

Then she arrived, easy and smiling, as though meeting an old friend and he was glad.

"And what's your name," were her first words as they sat down.

She had not told him her surname, so he just said: "Kelly." It was only going to be lunch. In two or three hours he would be back in the old routine with this a fading memory; just first names would be best.

All morning he had rehearsed a polite conversation but his mind now was a void. Left to him the encounter would have been a disaster.

"Kelly? That's a nice name."

Then something remarkable happened. Somehow they dovetailed. Right away they were talking nice and easy, no strain, about this and that and nothing in particular. Even the pauses were relaxed. Talk flowed sweet and easy with this woman.

Newly-met strangers' conversation usually consists mostly of questions, and they quickly empty each other.

They asked each other no questions. A few facts surfaced naturally during their conversation; she had two children, Lucy and Anne-Marie, and he told her about Jo and Thomas. She did not mention a husband. He did not mention Angela.

"Oh!" she said suddenly, looking across to the beach. "It ought to be against the law! To dress like that! When you look like that," she added to answer his enquiring look. She was putting on an extravagant exhibition of horror.

The object of her scorn was a man naked except for a pair of shorts that had one leg red and one leg blue. They were fashionably knee length, which the wearer would have to take on trust as it was obvious that for many years he had not seen the world beneath his ballooning paunch.

"When they come on holiday, they lose their shirts, their trousers and their manners," she sniffed. "They wouldn't do that back home oop North!"

"He won't be a Londoner." He got that in quickly. "No Londoner would ever behave like that."

"I should hope not!" she retorted with asperity. Then with a cheeky grin she added: "But I wonder what the people of Skeggy or Clacton think of Londoners, eh?"

Meadow Gate was nothing to do with London, but right now being a Londoner was suitably anonymous. He did not enlighten her.

"That's where they all go on holiday, isn't it? And Sahfend."

"They love 'em."

Putting on a music hall Cockney accent she mocked him, chuckling at her own talent: "Luv 'em, do they? Even if they dress like that on Skeggy's prom? They just luv 'em?"

Londoners sorted, she flicked a disdainful hand at the sight of more offending paunches puffing by. Indeed the parade of Prom Blobs did make him think of saucy seaside postcards.

"We are all shapes and sizes," he ventured in their defence.

"Oh, not their shapes! All shapes are great. It's nothing to do with their shape. We're all a shape of one sort or another! It's the way they dress. Dreadful!

"Terrible taste! No idea at all. It's the men who are the worst. That lot" – a disdainful gesture included just about every man on the promenade – "should have to get a licence to wear shorts in public! I wouldn't give that lot permission to leave home!"

This woman was fun. He was enjoying this. Unable to keep up her haughty act, she dissolved into laughter over which he was to discover she had very little management.

Then she spoiled it.

"What time do you have to get your train?"

Before the meeting, he had worked it out carefully. She had said quarter to one, after getting some shopping. That meant a 12.30 to 1.30 lunch hour. The train station was only a few minutes away so he had decided on the 1.48 departure.

"You had better be going, or you'll miss it," she urged.

Suddenly his mind was not working properly again. In a minute of two, they would go their separate ways. They had talked so easy time had flown but they had learned very little about each other. There was no way he could make contact with her. They were not going to bump into each other again just by chance. His brain, working on partial power, had failed to remind him that she lived more than 100 miles away, far from a route he had ever taken before or was ever likely to take again. This was deepest Dorset, the back of beyond.

She stood up. "Thank you for the lunch. It has been nice meeting you." Now cool, ladylike.

"Look," he blurted. "As it happens, I am down this way again next week. Perhaps we could… it would be nice if…"

"Oh?" She had a way of making that small word speak volumes. Now it said: Really? Fancy that now!

"Do you often have to come to Weymouth?"

"Well, ah, well one day next week, yes, as it happens. Perhaps we could have lunch again?"

"That would be nice."

"Right." Delighted, he almost added 'wonderful!' but cut that as being a bit over-the-top. "Well, why not here again? In your lunch hour." Brilliant, Webb! Lunch in the lunch hour!

She nodded graciously. "Yes, lovely."

So are you.

"Right. What day?"

"What day are you coming?"

With an effort he got his mind working somewhere near to full power. "Yes, right – Wednesday?"

"Wednesday. Are you sure?" The lady was taking the mickey!

Kelly mustered a suave smile. "Yes, of course. Wednesday, next week. Same time as today?"

"All right. You'd better go. Your train! Look it's nearly half past. I've got to rush too."

There was no time to wait for his change from a fiver. He left the waitress smiling, with an unexpected bonanza in the tip bowl. She did not know it, but it was going to be the first of many tips from this couple who were to make the table in the corner their own special place.

The train slid from town alongside the prairie of green-grey reeds growing in the silver lake. 'What day?' What an idiot!

She had smiled as one who was watching a fool flounder. Yes, but that meant she knew he had been lying and had still agreed to meet him. That was all right. That made him smile.

To be more exact, it made the old Brighton Kelly grin.

∽ 30 ∼

To Kelly, perched in front of his screen and concentrating, it was just another raucous Buller bawl from somewhere in the office. He would not have reacted if he had not caught Bill's eye and seen his 'well, well, this looks interesting' expression.

"What's up?"

"Buller and Green. There's a tussle going on there. Buller and Green just had a 'discussion'."

"Buller and Green?"

"Yes. Power struggle."

"Green has only been here two minutes. Buller will squash him. Power struggle over what?"

"They" – the word was said with a capital T – "want to create a new department, all the feature writers and us lot under one person. Green is favourite to be that person, and Buller does not like it."

"You're kidding. What's so special about Green?"

"Don't you know anything that goes on in this office?"

No. The world outside is more interesting. Dorset is particularly interesting.

"What don't I know?"

"He comes with credentials. He was involved in a power struggle at the Sunday Post."

"What happened, if he is here?"

"He lost."

"Lost? That's 'credentials'?"

"People like that either end up stabbed in the back in some office corridor, or they end up on the board of directors. It was experience. Green knows how to operate in office intrigues. I know some chap who worked with him, and he says he is a smooth operator. Well, he said 'slimey', but…."

"You reckon Buller will lose then?"

"That's my bet, Kelly. Who do you think?"

"Well, in so much as I care at all, I hope Green wins. What am I saying? Neither!"

"You should care. People who don't get involved in office intrigues are apt join the great unemployed first. You should keep up with office gossip. Well, no, how could you? You are never here."

Kelly put his feet on his desk, Brighton-style, and treated Bill to a barn door-wide sod-em! grin..

Bill shrugged. It's your funeral mate.

Green did not like the growing antagonism between himself and Buller. He had tried to play his cards to keep on the right side of Buller, who he perceived as a man of his ilk. Quite apart from that, it made sense. Buller had his feet under the table long before Green joined the paper. If Buller remained a power on the paper Green would be wise to keep in with him, but he felt things were going wrong.

Buller was turning against him. Green did not like it, but there seemed to be nothing for it but to paddle his own canoe. He was disappointed, but not so surprised. There had been other times when he had found himself in the same office with people he had recognised as bedfellows. He had sidled up to them, assuming there would be a brotherhood, only to discover they had only one person in mind: themselves.

That was exactly what he himself was like, but it still surprised and disappointed him. In that respect at least he was human.

Smith was now the man with the power to influence promotion and Green concentrated on getting himself well in with him. Quite what had caused the bad feeling was hard to fathom; in an office who knows what slight, real or imagined, starts a war? Green could see Buller no longer looked happy around Smith and that was all he needed to know; when people fall out, there are opportunities.

If Vicky's 'Lost Love' series was a success Green wanted the credit. It would do him a lot of good. He needed to put his stamp on it. He had talked to Smith about it at every opportunity until finally Smith accepted it was his project. So, now the next thing to do was to set up meetings. They were essential for ambitious people. Meetings make people look important.

★

"It is unbelievable the hassle it takes to get something accepted on this paper!"

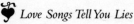

The drinkers in the Hack and Headline focussed on the speaker, one of the paper's feature writers, with interest. Strife – someone else's – always has promise.

Vicky Carew was steaming! Frank fancied her and oozing concern enquired: "What's up Vicky?"

Vicky had flounced furiously into the pub with her announcement and was so wound up she managed to flounce just standing still, her dark eyes flashing. Frank purred sympathetically.

Vicky threw her hands in the air. "I put up this idea for an article, an interview with Benny Lord on his secret lost love. Something no one knew about, not even his wife. I got him drunk one night. I could see it would make a great series. I want to get other famous homosexuals to confess to a secret love."

"Juicy! Great idea," chortled Frank, eyeing her great qualities. "So what's the problem?"

"Buller's the problem, Green's the problem, that vacillating twit Smith is the problem. I thought of the idea. Then Green grabbed it and took it to Smith. Somehow now it's Green's big project, his idea. Buller's opposing it – don't ask me why," she added, then provided the answer anyway.

"It's because Green is getting thick with Smith. Buller feels threatened. God! I don't know why our reporters bother to leave the office. There's enough soap opera to fill every issue right here!

"Office egos! God! How anything ever gets published in this paper I'll never know. It first has to be approved in turn by 20 overpaid idiots in suits! I'm going to write a novel set in a newspaper and it will be called Where Egos Fly!"

"You'll find it hard to get anyone else to make such a confession," said a reporter.

"You reckon?" Vicky dismissed the doubter. "You wait. As soon as the series comes out, readers will be queuing up to tell us their own sad tales. Men fancying men, women lusting after women. You wait and see."

Frank had a great thought. "We might get a repeat of that American episode where a man shot his homosexual neighbour for revealing on television he loved him. Juicy!"

Green finally got the perfect opportunity to talk personally to

Chillywinds. He found himself alone with the editor in the lift and told him he had a rather special story he was working on. The mention of Emburey's name ensured that Green got Chillywinds' full attention.

"Perhaps I could have the chance to tell you when you have a moment," Green suggested unctuously.

Inside the hour Green was summoned to Eastwinter's office.

Careful not to give any indication that he knew the story would have personal significance for Eastwinter, Green sketched its outline:

Lord Emburey was involved – perhaps was the central figure – in a major scandal involving the switch of pension fund money in Emburey plc to bolster up a network of failing enterprises within the group.

"It could be bigger than just Emburey," said Green, "There are several companies within the group, and on their boards are Harold Labouche, Sean Hannibal and Randolph Hendry. Hannibal is a close friend of Princess Edwina and Hendry is MP for Cliveden North. And Labouche …"

There was no need to say more. He had survived sex revelations, but if the former chancellor was involved in a financial scandal involving those big names it would be a Bank Holiday in Fleet Street.

Some might be speculation, but the facts that Green could prove would certainly finish off Emburey.

Hidden behind his façade of the innocent informer Green had difficulty in hiding his smirk when he saw the expression on Eastwinter's face.

"Write what you've got," Eastwinter said eventually. "I'll take a look at it."

Then, as Green was at the door, Eastwinter said: "Nice work," although his eyes remained as cold as always.

Those two words, rare indeed from Eastwinter, were music to Green's ears: a fanfare for his ambitions. Nice work, and he had got it.

*

Leonard Wakefield read Vicky's interview with Benny Lord in his neat, bleak bungalow and wept for an empty life. They were deep-rooted convulsive sobs, shocking, frightening and cathartic. He had never cried before. Real men don't cry his father had always drilled into him. 'Have a good cry' he had often heard women say. 'Do you good'. Real men don't cry, although would those women have considered him a real man? That was highly unlikely, not in those days and probably not even now.

But they were right about tears. Hours later he felt released, stronger.

He read through the article again and noted the panel at the end that invited readers' own stories. He sat into the early hours composing a letter to Vicky Carew.

⸺ 31 ⸻

Fiona was her old self, still posing as a femme fatale and centre stage. The group had their reunion at Toffs, a popular café with the local Thirty-something crowd, catching up on all the gossip, mostly Fiona's, as she was the one with the most outrageous stories to tell.

"I've been nearly married since I last saw you all more times than I can count!"

"Not like you to let anyone get away," joked Dot amid laughter.

"It's not the marrying. It's the divorce. That spoils the fun. It's like a hangover, fun getting it but as you grow older you think twice before you get drunk. So I've decided that nearly marrying is the safest option. That way you get all the fun and none of the hassle. Men are more fun if you don't marry them." She giggled, and leaned forward conspiratorially.

"I tell you who would be a lot of fun - fella called Bretts."

"Who's he?" Dot wanted to know.

"He's temporarily working as a coach with The Dream Factory."

They knew what that was, a club formed recently to help local young actors. "Absolutely gorgeous," Fiona drooled. "He's on my hit list!"

That got everyone wanting to know more.

"Well, you don't know what you're missing. When you see him, you'll start taking acting lessons. Tasty! I've enrolled in his class."

"Fiona! You'll get yourself in the News of the World!"

By then the gang had quaffed a couple of drinks apiece and were getting nicely warmed up.

Suddenly Fiona shrilled: "There he is!"

Dot looked around. "Where?"

She pointed at a group of men just entering. Their eyes hit on him right away. He walked in as though walking on stage.

"The one with the blond hair."

"Yummy. Tasty. Bring him over Fiona," said Dot.

That was the point where things started to go wrong for Angela.

"Fiona behave yourself!" she joked. "Remember, we are respectable wives!"

Fiona had been at full stretch in her naughty girl role and something in Angela's tone stung, making her feel foolish. That was not a feeling the outrageous Fiona liked and she hit out.

"Oh, I forgot, Miss Goody Two Shoes is with us. Angela, you are so boring!"

That did it. Fiona's sharp-edge riposte came at the moment Angela was recalling Fiona's 'Old Faithful' jibe and it had a double whammy effect. Angela in her turn over-reacted.

"No goody about it, Fiona. Anyone can get a man if she throws herself at him!"

"Now, now, you two." It was getting bitchy and Gilly hastily played the diplomat.

Her efforts were wasted on Fiona. "All right, Angela. If it is so easy, let me see you do it."

"What?"

"I bet you won't go and persuade Mr Tasty over for a drink."

"Oh God!" Angela choked on her laugher at such a ridiculous proposal.

"Well, if it is so easy…" Fiona smiled, oh so superior.

"I don't want him over here, Fiona. If you do, you go and get him."

"I bet you ten quid."

Gilly was trying to lighten the situation with jokey encouragement when suddenly, to their utter surprise, Angela put her drink down and said: "Right!" and plonked a ten pound note on the table.

"Come on! Come on!" she heckled until the ruffled Fiona put a tenner beside it.

Then with the others gaping in disbelief Angela walked purposefully toward the blond hunk. They watched as she stood with her back to them, talking to the group around the new man in town.

"She's done it!" squeaked Dot as Angela was seen returning with the man himself and his two companions in tow.

"Well ladies," said one of the men. "What can we get you?" Then as smooth as you like the men were seated at their table.

Gobsmacked as she was, Fiona was not slow. Bretts was neatly manoeuvred so he found himself sitting beside her. She hogged him all the rest of the evening, but he was happy to stay there. It gave him a nice view of Angela, off whom he never took his eyes.

As Angela discreetly picked up the two tenners she gave one of the men a surreptitious wink. He was Billy Mann, whom she knew well. A bright chap, Billy, and always ready for a laugh. A quick whisper in his ear at the bar, and Angela had the tenners won.

Angela's happy marriage was put further at risk when it was time to go home. She stood up to leave. "I'll call a taxi," said Gilly. "We'll share it."

"Certainly not!" Bretts was up and at their side. "I'll give you a lift." As they left amid a chorus of goodbyes Gilly whispered in Angela's ear. "Look at Fiona's face!"

Angela had already noticed. "Good!" she said, with alcohol-fuelled triumph. She made a point of giving Bretts a beaming thank-you smile just to rub it in.

"Angela!" Gilly smothered a giggle. "Mind you don't get yourself in the News of the World!"

"You watch out Gilly! My house comes first, remember. It's you who is going to be left alone with him after he drops me off."

"Oh my God! Fiona will be hopping mad!"

"Don't worry, our Fiona will get her man," said Angela. "But it has just cost her a tenner!"

They had a good laugh at that. But Angela was wrong.

Bretts was out to get Angela, and it was going to cost Angela a lot more than a tenner. But he was a patient operator. He just dropped her off at her home with his best smile and a polite 'nice to have met you' and then took Gilly home.

⟶ 32 ⟶

He got to Sibleys much too early. He waited at the same corner table where they had sat the week before and watched the door. There was the same uncertainty as when he had waited the week before, even though they had made an arrangement. If she did not turn up, he would have no way of getting in touch. He would have to assume she had changed her mind, but he would never be certain. Surely she would not have agreed to this meeting, with no intention of turning up, knowing he had to travel over a hundred miles. Surely she could not have really believed his lie that he had to pass that way on business.

Then there she was, and he finally noticed the sun was shining as it had been all morning. The insecurity of the situation was one he was to feel many times throughout that splendid summer. Always the link was tenuous. Obviously he was not able to phone her at home and she did not have a mobile. Every meeting had to be guarded, with an eye on the passers-by because of her many friends in the town. Every arrangement had to be carefully mapped out. If something went wrong, getting back in touch was always going to be difficult; indeed well-nigh impossible.

"I'm glad you came," she said as soon she had sat down and they ordered coffees and a snack. She was looking frankly at him and smiling. It was open, honest. No coquetry, no pretence. She was pleased to see him. It sent a jolt through his heart, making it beat faster, while at the same time his uncertain mind was calmed. She tossed her head, fussing her richly youthful hair to make sure it was keeping faith with her hairdresser.

"I'm a bit late. I had to buy some things. I'm glad you waited."

"I would have waited all day." The words came of their own, astonishing him.

"Oh!" She gave a little laugh, and managed to remain suitably demur, but there was that look he had seen on the footpath when she had turned to catch his admiring gaze. It was response that released dreams like balloons into a summer sky.

The scene was set.

"How long will you be staying in town?"

"As long as necessary."

Her eyes smiled. She sipped her coffee. "Will you be here this evening?"

"Yes."

"That will be nice."

So they arranged to meet at the Jubilee Clock at seven o'clock.

"Is that the very ornate one on the prom?"

"Prom! We call it the Esplanade down here. This is the posh part of England!" Putting on a comic Cockney accent she said scornfully: "It may the prom in Sahfend or Skeggy, but in Weymouth it's The Esplanade."

'I'm glad you waited.' Those words when she first sat down had made his heart race. Now her joking made him laugh and their mutual nervousness calmed to the kind of secure, relaxed, ambience in which relationships blossom.

Time flew, and then she had to get back to work

"Seven o'clock, then."

"Seven o'clock."

In the evening they found a pavement café and sat watching the holidaymakers stroll by.

"Well, we try to keep it posh," she exclaimed. "But look at them!" The object of her horror was again a group of holidaymakers promenading. "Would they walk down their own high street looking like that? You can laugh! It is not kind to your fellow man to walk around looking like that. At home they would not do it. If they did they would be arrested."

"They can't all be the perfect size, whatever that is."

"It's not their shape or size. I like people all shapes and sizes. It's just that there's no style!" It was said with horror, now she was on what he was to learn was one of her high horses.

"No style! Those shorts! Another inch lower on that one and we'd see what he hasn't seen for years. And with her we are seeing what he probably hasn't looked at for years!" She held her brow at the very thought of it.

"You'd arrest people for not having style?"

"Arrest them, and deport them back to Beermingerm, oop North, whatever." She chuckled, adding: "But not London."

"You thought I was a holidaymaker, remember?"

"Sorry." She did not look the least bit sorry.

"I should think so. Anyway, they bring money into the town."

"Some things money can't buy. We welcome grockles, but not the bits of them you shouldn't see."

"Grockles? What on earth are grockles?"

"Well, we're like a pair of grockles sitting here," she said, enjoying his bewilderment. Then she educated him in the local language.

"A grockle is a holidaymaker. It comes from an old West Country word meaning 'friendly stranger'. You're a grockle," she chuckled.

"I'm not a stranger, not any more am I?"

"No, but friendly I hope!"

There was half an hour or so before he had to get his train and he paid the bill.

"Let's walk round by the Harbour," she suggested.

They were strolling and chatting when she suddenly exclaimed: "Oops! Someone I know."

He carried on walking casually as she stopped and chatted to two women. From a short distance he waited until she could break away. The three were immediately into the excited so-important chatter of women. The other two were clearly pleased to see her, something that he was to often note when he saw her – always from a distance – with her friends. She seemed to be a natural centre of attention, the spark in any group, her presence pleasuring women as well as men. Times he was to notice the envious eyes of men, feeling the pride in himself and the pity for them.

He could hear the women urging Kathy to go with them for a drink. She obviously could not easily refuse, and turned a secret look of regret and goodbye towards him as she walked away with them. Fortunately they had made arrangements to meet again and he carried on alone to catch his train, happy with that last look.

But it underlined a situation as fragile as an eggshell.

★

Angela made the coffee after dinner while Kelly did the washing up.

"It's a long time since you did that," she chided playfully.

"I try not to be Domesticated Man."

"Never mind all that macho rubbish. I love you just the way you are. Mind you, you are hardly here these days to do any washing up. Can't you take a few days off?"

"It's difficult right now. I will, as soon as I can."

"Soon!" She would not let him escape without a promise and browbeat him with kisses until he agreed.

"Good! About time!" Content with his promise Angela did the drying up and then they took their coffees and sat down to catch the early evening news.

Angela snuggled up to him as the world and its troubles were paraded. An item about the divorce rate and single parent families on the increase came on and she snuggled even cosier and kissed him.

"We're lucky, aren't we?"

Following was the latest news on Senator Booth.

"This is getting like a regular evening soap opera," said Angela. "Never mind Coronation Street. Washington Street!"

A clip from an American talk show was included. A journalist was interviewing a group of women who all claimed to have had sex with the senator. There were ear-splitting gee-haws and shrieks from an hysterical studio audience as the women vied with each other on the number of times they had been laid by the senator.

The sex scandal was descending into farce. The nonsense was completed with an excerpt from an interview from a talk show with the senator's wife who said: "I am proud to be married to Robert. What woman would not be happy to have a husband with such sexual stamina!"

At this audience began a'squealin' and a'hollerin' with delight.

"The woman's mad. They are all mad over there," said Angela scornfully. "'My husband's a sex fiend, and I'm proud of it!' 'I'm a stupid woman and my husband's a pig' and everybody cheers! Our politicians are bad enough, but at least they resign. We have some values left "- she wriggled round again and gave him another kiss - "thanks to the Press, my hero! At least that couldn't happen here. Mind you, that nasty Lane fellow didn't get his just desserts, did he?"

It was not so long ago, in those conscience-free Brighton days, when Kelly would have had a cavalier answer to all this. A sex-mad senator and sex under a White House table, in a loo or a broom cupboard, would have been a big laugh. Being young makes life wonderfully simple.

Not so long ago.

But in another lifetime.

★

When they met again they met as lovers. There was no barrier, no shyness. It was in their eyes; in their ease with each other when they met where they had arranged, at Wareham.

"I know too many people in Weymouth," she had told him, explaining why Wareham.

When he got off the train she was waiting and she walked straight into his embrace, she confident of him, and he holding her as though there was no one else in his life, or hers, or ever had been.

"I knew you'd come," she said, making the words a bond between them.

"I knew I would."

They walked into the old town, so small, so unspoiled by modernity, much of it was still inside ancient earth walls.

Blazing June had arrived and noisy show-off youths were jumping off a bridge into a river and they sat on the quay to watch them. The river swirled muddily as the braggart youths, torsos bare but still wearing their jeans, vied with each other to make the biggest splash. Eventually, triumphant as from a victory, they squelched off laughing. Within a few minutes the river erased all evidence of their triumphant moment and ran clear.

They walked on alongside the river on a narrow path raised three or four feet above flat and watery countryside.

"We haven't much time," she said. "I have to be back at tea time."

He held her, and the teasing breeze caught her perfume and whirled it around his head.

"Then we'll have to make the most of what time we have."

She wriggled against him, chuckling.

"Don't we fit nicely!"

In full agreement he pulled her closer.

"Oh!" She moved back sharply. He looked around; had she seen someone she knew? But they were alone on the path. Then he saw she was holding her hand to her breast, grimacing.

"What's the matter?"

"It's all right. It just caught me."

"What?"

"It's all right."

"Are you sure? What is it?"

"Nothing. It is a lump on my breast. Oh, it's all right!" she hastened to reassure him. "Really. No, really!" She was moved by his concern. She took his arm, laughing, eliciting a doubtful smile from him.

"It's all right. I've been to the doctor. It's benign." She caressed his face tenderly. "Really, don't worry. "It's benign. I've seen the doctor – a specialist. He said it's benign. It just catches me sometimes."

He still could not say anything. His heart was racing, jolted by a potent mixture of relief and joy.

They walked back to the town. "The day's gone so quick," she said. "Don't forget the time and place," he said. They had previously made their arrangements to meet again. He had written them down. Once they had parted, he could not contact her.

"I won't. I'll count the days."

They were the only people on the sleepy station. When it was almost time for her train she said: "Best wait on the other platform." It was the cautious game he was going to get used to.

Alone on the other platform he watched as her train pulled out for Weymouth, leaving an empty station amplifying his loss. Ten minutes later his train arrived, to carry him over the spirit-liberating waterscape at Poole.

As the train slid towards London he recalled that moment on the path beside the river. It still quickened his heartbeat that without a moment's shyness or reservation she had confided in him something so deeply personal. It was trusting, intimate, her hand cupping her breast. Knowing it was benign, that she had been spared the cruel affliction of so many women had created a radiance in her smile.

He held his hands against his face and breathed in the lingering

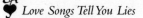

smell of her scent, seeing in his mind's eye her hand at her breast. It had been a powerful moment; loving, erotic.

And they had indeed fitted nicely.

★

It was such a lovely morning Angela decided to walk with Jo to school. Because of a special staff meeting lessons were not starting until ten that morning. It was the perfect chance to talk, as with plenty of time they made their way slowly chattering on like middle-aged gossips. Kissing Jo goodbye at the school gates she strolled home savouring the sunshine. Savouring her life: most women would do anything for a marriage and family like hers.

She made a coffee and opened the post. Among the machine-franked junk mail and the usual bills there was an envelope with only a photograph inside. Before she looked closely at it, she shook the envelope expecting an accompanying letter to fall out but there was nothing else. The photograph was of a man with his arm around a pretty girl outside a shop and apparently kissing her. It was such an odd item to find without an explanation she continued to be preoccupied with shaking the envelope for the expected letter and did not at first look properly at the photograph. It was several moments before she did and with a shock realised that the man in the picture was Kelly.

★

Eastwinter's secretary put the call on hold. "Harold Labouche on the line for you."

"Labouche?" Eastwinter took his time before reaching for the telephone. The thin smile on his face was like a brief shaft of cold sunshine in winter.

Labouche. Green was right. Labouche and Emburey and the pension fund money. Eastwinter had no doubt at all that the conclusion he had jumped to was the right one. This was going to be very satisfying.

"Put him through."

Labouche enquired about Eastwinter's health and his family, and then invited him out to lunch.

Accepting the invitation, Eastwinter's smile turned carnivorous.

⟶ 33 ⟶

In the coming months Kelly reaped unforeseen benefit from having established for himself some independence as a reporter. As long as he produced good stories he had become accustomed to being left days, weeks even, to work untroubled by close supervision. Keeping in contact with colleagues who sometimes worked with him on a story was informal, and the mobile phone was the usual link. Office meetings were irregular, held infrequently and at times to suit the work schedule of the SS Squad. He put this circumstance to use. It was surprisingly easy to get down to Dorset to see Kathy almost whenever he liked. His routine of coming and going did not seem to change as far as the office and Angela were concerned. She never rang the office anyway, always his mobile, and even that was very rare. Calls from the house phone to a mobile were expensive.

"Let the office pay for the bills," he would say, and made a point of calling her. He could be away several days on a story without causing comment. From now on he simply sweated blood to get results in as quickly as possible, and leaving him time to get down to Dorset where his heart now was.

This woman was indeed fun. She showed him the county's best places to dine but also where they could buy the best fish and chips to eat on a seaside bench. Whether they were eating fish and chips out of paper or in a restaurant with a fancy menu in French, her joke was always the same: "I was born for this, you can't afford me!" They went to Salisbury Races for the first Sunday meeting ever held at the track and a great crowd attended and basked in the sun that shone warm and brilliantly. All the women looked Ascot-splendid in their best outfits, and she outshone them all.

"I was born for this," she said. She was sat, or rather perched like an artist's model, at a table sipping her wine, all posy in that way of women wearing their best and knowing they look good.

"You can't afford me!" she laughed, when the horse he put a fiver on for her in the first race trotted up second from last.

"I think you could be right," he said. "Given the chance you would

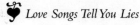

be a very expensive woman."

She gestured airily. "Money? What's it for! If I had plenty of money, I would spend it. But once it had gone, this" – she waved a hand that encompassed the crowds of dressed-in-their-Sunday-best families, the perfect Englishness of the countryside, the whole lovely day – "would still be free."

"It cost a tenner to get in," he quibbled.

"You know what I mean."

Yes, looking at her, he did. She was a free spirit.

★

Fiona did not give up on Bretts. She found a simple way of enjoying his company: she helped him in his quest to seduce Angela. Bretts was the type of man women like Fiona thrive on: always looking for sexual trophies. Fiona knew that right now she was not the trophy in the lecher's sights. To have any chance with this one, she would first have to get his Angela fixation out of the way.

Anyway, the truth was she found herself enjoying this situation. If she could get him into bed with Angela, think of the superior feeling she would enjoy. The once so-goody-goody Angela as bad as her! She arranged more girls' nights at Toffs. Every time Bretts managed to be around to offer Angela a lift home.

"They get on rather well, don't they," Fiona said to the others with a you-know smile.

It left the women gossiping. Angela? Never! Well, on the other hand, you never know….

She had gone for him that first night. Maybe it was not only to win the bet?

★

They sat on the hillside, looking down on the church in the valley. "This is a place I especially wanted to show you," she said, snuggling into him. "We'll be all right here. No one I know comes here. I'm so glad I can share it with you. It used to be a lot wilder, even more beautiful, before they put the road through."

She told him what the valley used to be like. It had been a remarkably secret place even though it was almost enclosed by the town, the centre of which was only half a mile out of sight. It had never been ploughed or mowed. Horses kept the soggy meadows cropped, and wild irises used to fill almost the entire valley floor with a golden glow.

Years-old blackberry bushes alongside the river provided pounds of fruit she used to make into jams and pies. Then they were destroyed by heavy equipment used to build the road.

It had been a wild poetic place in which people could walk peacefully alone right from the centre of town to the open countryside beyond Nottington.

As she drew the picture, he could see that no one with a soul would have allowed a road to be built in such a place. This town had had something unique, remarkable in this day and age. Now it only had a road and a precariously lingering remnant of former magic.

"But we've still got this," she said. "Can you imagine? The Romans used to bring their boats right up that little river. Until they built the road, it probably hadn't changed for 2,000 years. When I was a little girl we used to make paper boats and race them downriver to the lake. We never could see who won, or where they went. They got lost in the reeds." She laughed. "Just paper boats, but so… oh!" She lapsed into reverie, smiling at her thoughts. "So important."

After a few pensive moments she pointed to a tiny hamlet.

"That's my church down there. Pretty isn't it."

"Your church? You go there regularly?"

"No, yes – not regularly." There was a long hesitation, then: "I was married there."

"I see."

She looked at him, an anxious questioning look. Did he want to know more? He pressed his face in her hair and took a breath of its fragrance.

"That makes it even prettier."

They sat in silence for a long time. Then she said: "I wish it had been you."

In response he held her closer. He felt her wince.

"What's the matter?

She moved his hand away gently. "Nothing. It's all right. It just hurts sometimes."

He recalled the moment on the path in Wareham, when she had held her hand to her breast. That had been a memorable moment, loving. This time he was hit with a sudden shock of fear.

"It still hurts?"

That moment on the path had created a bond between them, a trust. Now he was alarmed. "It hurts? What have you done about it? Have you seen anyone about it? You must have it checked!"

But she was laughing, calming him. "It's all right. It's all right. I have seen a specialist. It's benign. I told you, remember?"

"They've checked?"

"Yes!" She was smiling at his panic.

"When? Recently?"

"Yes, yes, recently!" She kissed him, moved by his concern. "I have had two check-ups. The tests are fine."

"Good." He was reassured. "You must have regular check ups. It's important."

"I know. I know! Do I look stupid?" She kissed his cheek again. "You do love me, don't you." She did not need an answer.

He felt the fear in him dissolving. He pulled her down into the sunwarmed grass.

"X marks the spot," she murmured.

"We'll cover your county with them," he said. That was one promise he knew he could keep, and he did.

She chanced seeing him off at the station, keeping a discreet distance from the window of his carriage. They just kept smiling at each other as people hurried between them. It was so silly she had to hide a giggle behind her hand and he had to hold a newspaper up to his face in case the people sat next to him noticed him laughing too. She gave a secret wave as the train slid away and then walked home along the lakeside causeway.

She felt so happy. Sometimes she preferred to walk home along the causeway that was nearly a mile long and led virtually straight to her home. This evening it seemed to lead to a new horizon.

His alarm when she had winced at her pain stirred her more than words of concern ever could. She knew he had been reluctant to believe her when she had shushed away his concern. Despite her assurance, he had been unsure. She could sense that he was also unsure about them. Yet in a situation like this, how can anyone make a commitment? It was a dream world where truth and reality have to be ignored. In a woman's arms men made promises they always meant but could not always keep.

Let's just play paper boats while the sun shines.

— 34 —

Labouche had talked of everything except the reason for the lunch, which Eastwinter was rather enjoying. His steak was done to a turn.

Finally Labouche got down to business.

"I understand your position. You have a duty to your journalistic standards." Very smooth, thought Eastwinter, knowing precisely from which direction Labouche was coming. Since when have politicians revered journalistic standards? The roast potatoes were light and crisp, just the way he liked them.

"But, you know," the determinedly smiling Labouche continued, "in a way, you could be running the story for the wrong reasons."

Leaving that hint to brew, Labouche addressed his lunch as well. A waiter cleared the debris and another hovered with the desserts. Apple pie and ice cream for Eastwinter, cheese and biscuits for Labouche.

Eastwinter leaned back to allow the waiter to put the dessert in front of him, and waited for Labouche to continue in his attempt to bribe and corrupt. Eastwinter had rehearsed his reply, which would be an icy refusal to compromise his journalistic ethics. He had rehearsed some of his choicest phrases for the coming lecture. Few men could have savoured a sweeter revenge, one Emburey richly deserved and Eastwinter hungrily desired. He savoured the forthcoming moment, first letting Labouche crawl to the furthest tip of the limb he was on.

Labouche paused while he dealt with a piece of cheese. "What happened to …to your family, that was terrible but, well….It is very understandable…it would be very understandable if you were rather more determined to publish this than …."" The words died away; nothing said, everything said.

"What are you inferring?" Eastwinter cut in icily.

Labouche held up a white flag hand. "No, no…" The smile was as wide as a salesman's. Was this man ever going to infer anything, say anything? Keeping his salesman's smile in place (much longer and it would qualify for an entry in the Guinness Book of Records) he continued. "However, that is not the point."

"Which is?"

"Henry, this is a very complicated matter. I don't pretend to know exactly what is happening, but I do know that given some breathing space it could all be put right. No harm done. Now I know that will not – does not – change things from the point of view of a story, or makes it any more acceptable for you to…but if it all collapses now there might – quite likely will – be some hardship caused to the recipients of pensions in the fund. What I am saying is this: a story now could make it impossible to repair any damage. Later, perhaps, and a report then would be just as worthwhile to your paper and those responsible would not escape…but now, well…."

Eastwinter finished his dessert, wiped his mouth on his napkin. A cold smile bared his teeth as he prepared to savage Labouche. He was about to enjoy himself.

"Oh, before I forget, I've got something you will be pleased to hear." Labouche stopped Eastwinter with perfect timing. His marathon smile was now the sort people have as they wait for someone to open a present.

Eastwinter closed his mouth slowly, waiting for the present to be unwrapped.

"I was having lunch with Harry de Haan…"

Eastwinter interrupted: "Oh, you know him?"

"…yes, yes, quite well. I'm buying a tranche of shares in the company…"

"This company?"

"…yes, yes, but that's by the by, it's just that Harry wants to liquidate some money to expand in the Far East and he has sold them to me to raise the cash."

Eastwinter sat still.

Labouche was beaming, all innocence, affecting not to see the wary look on Eastwinter's face. Continuing seamlessly, he said: "Harry speaks very highly of you, and when Ben Gray" – mentioning the present managing editor of the group – " steps down at the end of the year, it seems he's got you in mind for the job. Cut and dried, so it sounded. And I agree with him."

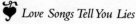

Eastwinter played the same game. If Labouche thought this was a trump card he was going to be disappointed. Eastwinter was already confident of his standing with De Haan.

"Yes, Harry and I have had had a few chats." He raised his eyes to Labouche with a sneer poorly disguised as a smile that said 'If that's all you can do'

Labouche returned an even better version of that smile. He did not lunch regularly in Whitehall for nothing.

"Well, anyway," he continued, "that's not what this lunch is really all about."

Labouche nibbled a biscuit, and sipped his coffee while Eastwinter wondered what was coming. At just the right moment Labouche engaged Eastwinter with what had now evolved into an Establishment smile. This man seemed to have every sort of smile in his repertoire – perhaps even one that was sincere.

"I have been asked – by the Prime Minister's office – to, well, sound you out in advance, as they are drawing up the list for the New Year Honours."

Struck dumb by this, Eastwinter fell into auto-survival mode and simply raised his brows interrogatively, suppressing the smirk that was trying to assert itself. Now in the driving seat, Labouche got right to the point.

"Your name has been put forward for a knighthood Henry. I've been asked to, well, you know, sound you out then…well, let them know…"

Eastwinter's attempt to play it all cool was totally demolished by this. His face burst into smiles. That rigid countenance had never been worked so hard.

"Goodness," he said. "How did all this come about?"

"Services to journalism, my dear fellow. It's only a recommendation at this stage of course – you know how it is done – but, well, if all goes well – and there is no doubt of course that it will. But they have to check, in case someone doesn't want – you know, saves embarrassment."

The rest of the lunch was taken up with Eastwinter telling Labouche how surprised he was, and how he was not expecting anything to come of it, but he was delighted just to be thought of in this sort of way.

"Well deserved, Henry," said Labouce.

"By the way, " said Labouche as they left, "Do think about this Emburey business. Just hold it for a while. In a week or so it can do no damage. It's the pensioners you have to consider – you understand? Not sympathy for Emburey mind you, even though he is on his last legs."

"Last legs?"

"Yes, don't know the details, but apparently he hasn't got long, poor chap." Nice kind touch that, Labouche thought, giving Eastwinter another reason –this one commendable – for holding the story back. He left the restaurant still wearing a smile; this one a self-satisfied version.

⌐ 35 ⌐

"Hello my lovely."

This time he had met her in Dorchester. "No one knows me here," she said. She was proved wrong almost immediately. In Antelope Walk a young woman shop assistant recognised her and greeted her with pleased surprise. There was that sidelong glance of warning and he continued on alone as though he did not know her. He waited in South Street and when she joined him again she looked heavenwards. Near thing!

It was to be ever thus he was to discover; always precarious. He could not call her, even if he knew her number. If her husband answered he could only use the 'sorry, wrong number' excuse once. A married woman cannot get calls from strange male voices. If she answered, she might be frightened, angry, that he had called her at home. There would not be a second chance.

But that was how his thoughts often ran when on the train back to London. Today, far from Meadow Gate, he was not a worried man. Today he was the old Brighton Beau.

Kathy took his arm in a snugly possessive manner.

"Come on my lovely, I will show you Dear Dorset."

Leaving Dorchester in a hired car he drove through a maze of hamlets to the coast road. Within a few miles of joining it they arrived at the sort of village he thought only existed in children's picture books. There were no straggling bungalows on the approach. One minute rolling countryside, the next a cosy huddle of mellow stone cottages.

The magic continued round a tight bend that insensitively sensible local authorities would have either smashed wider or plastered with regulation traffic warning signs. Blessedly they had not and vehicles, second class citizens here, just had to squeeze through as best they could. Even more unlikely, cars were parked untidily wherever the drivers liked, much as they must have done before the war. Amazingly for such a tiny community, a greengrocer, butcher and a higgledy-piggledy general store all plied for trade along with a Post Office-cum-shop. For all that this village knew, supermarkets were on the moon.

He brought the car to a stop to wonder at it all.

"What this place called?"

"Abbotsbury."

"There's a nice little tea shop. There's another!"

"There are three or four. All nice."

"Coffee?"

She wrinkled a choosy nose. "There's a place I like in Charmouth. It's lovely."

Anywhere like this with 50 miles of London would be a tourist treasure, not to be ignored.

"This looks nice," he urged.

"Another time. I've got lots to show you."

He was to understand how people in this county could be so choosy. Along the rolling coast road they passed through one perfect village and town after another.

"This is the place," she said as they approached a signpost to Charmouth. As a Londoner the first thing he noticed in the main street was that there was plenty of free parking. With no bother he was able to park right outside the old town house she indicated.

"Stow House. One of my favourite places."

It had been converted to a café, but was kept faithfully to its original and it felt as though he was entering a private home.

"Isn't it nice?" she enthused.

Tables covered with pristine tablecloths were laid ready for tea. Slices of home-made cake were displayed invitingly on a side table. The floor looked clean enough to eat off.

"Let's go in the garden." She led him to a walled garden that had a secret, intimate, atmosphere and they were the only people there. Yes, this was her style! Kelly smiled to himself at the expression of approval on her face.

"See? Now this is how one has afternoon tea, my lovely. Knocks your old Ritz and Claridges into a cocked hat - or should I say a cloth cap!"

The café owner brought them a plate of cakes and a pot of tea and a bold bird and tortoise that had the run of the garden promptly appeared to join in.

Enclosed within high mellow brick walls it was a time and place where any dream was perfectly possible. It was a lovely cafe, reason enough to remember it, but he was to remember it for a much better reason.

"Yes, very nice," he said, brushing the last crumbs from his cake down to the bird, "but the day is young. You said you had lots to show me."

"Yes. But not all today! There's plenty of time – when you come down again."

When you come down again.

No ifs. No buts. When you come down again. For the first time it was simply accepted he would. That was why he would never forget the Stow House garden cafe.

They drove on, but not for long. "Stop here. Come with me, I'll show you something a bit better than 'Ampstead 'Eath."

He locked up the car and followed her down a lane.

"This is how to see Dorset," she said. "Let's have a nice little stroll."

A little stroll seemed a good idea – for the first mile or so. After that her idea of a nice little stroll was not quite the same as a London commuter's. But he would not let it show and manfully accompanied her into a perfect world. For mile after mile they were the only people in that world, following the coast path along the edge of green, rolling, crumbling, cliffs.

"Upalong, downalong," she chuckled. "That's more Dorset for you."

More upalong than downalong! he thought.

"You are puffing a bit," she observed with glee.

"It's this Dorset air. Without a spot diesel, a dash of smoke and a seasoning of mixed pollution it just doesn't have the octane us Londoners need."

"You are going to have to get used to going organic my man."

They climbed airy hills to embrace huge sea-blue views, then scampered headlong down to wild deserted beaches.

Looking at this countryside made the spirit soar. The view was forever, the cliffs folding smaller and smaller right to the edge of the world. Nothing marred the perfection, nothing was out of place. The occasional farm was dotted here and there, just for artists to paint. Cirrus flocks of sheep flecked the distant hills and fat cows lazed on the lower slopes. In the valleys the greens and golds and blues of arable crops were as pleasing to the eye as fields of flowers. It was countryside that nourished every part: body and soul. See it, and you wanted to live forever.

They talked of this and that, and laughed just for the pleasure of it. Mostly however they were silent, she refreshed by the countryside she loved so well; he astonished that such countryside could still be left in a land so often run by fools for profit.

Upalong, downalong, sometimes winding precariously along cliff edges, and barely wide enough for one person, the path would then widen generously over grassy meadows. Then they could walk side by side and he could take her hand.

"This is England from a hundred years ago," he marvelled, looking around in amazement.

"Mind how you cross the road," she mocked instantly. "You'll get run over by a stagecoach!"

He soon got used to her delight in taking the mickey out of him. Truth was, he could have given as good as he got. You don't live and work in London without gaining a Black Belt in repartee. Sometimes he did raise a smart retort, but truth again was he took such delight in her delight, which she imparted to most of what she did, that he happily grinned and bore it. Life was fun for her, and being with her made just being alive fun.

She took great pleasure in showing him her county.

"I will show you all my favourite places. There are so many of them. This is going to be the guided tour you'll never forget."

She was right. Until his dying day.

*

Angela had been growing steadily more uptight throughout the day and when the telephone rang she snatched it up and snapped: "Hello!"

"It's me."

"Kelly!"

"Everything all right darling?"

She could tell that the tone of her voice had concerned him.

It was not the moment to talk about the photograph. Since its arrival her feelings had turned from shock to anger. Anyone who sent an anonymous letter, which the photograph was the equivalent, was beneath contempt. No way was she going to let it upset her. She would show it to Kelly and he would tell her what it was all about. She had no cause for worry. Her marriage was rock solid. She had not the slightest doubt of that.

The photograph had upset her for a time just as the sender had intended but it had not succeeded in its spiteful objective. Rock solid, and never the slightest doubt. She was a woman dearly loved and no marriage was safer or surer. Still, she wanted to know what Kelly had to say about it. She wanted to show him her love and her contempt for the anonymous mischief-maker. The sooner he came home the better.

"What's the matter?" His voice sounded … different, wary.

"Nothing. I was just surprised it was you. Will you be home tonight?" It was becoming a regular question. These days Kelly was away more than ever.

"That was what I was calling for. No, I won't be home I'm afraid."

"Oh, why not?"

"It's only for another day. Be back tomorrow."

"Another day! When? What time?"

"Tomorrow. Oh, late afternoon, tea time."

Just when she needed him! She suppressed her annoyance. "All right, but when…?"

"We'll go out. Book somewhere." His tone was conciliatory.

"You are away a lot these days."

"Sorry darling. Got to go."

He was gone.

Angela took the photograph out of the envelope and studied it. She wanted to tear it up, as she would like to tear up the sender. Destroying it would do no good. It would still be in her mind. She needed to show it to Kelly, clear the matter up. It was only fair – no secrets between them – but he was always away! So wrapped up his work.

He had sensed something when she spoke to him just now. There was something in his voice. Why? She had not been that dramatic had she? The last time he had called to say he was working away he had been the same, now she came to think of it.

Then she thought of Bretts. It caused a small shock, just like guilt. Nonsense! She had no call to feel guilty. What about, for goodness sake? But a small nagging voice was telling her: ah, but you know Bretts fancies you. Let him fancy away, nothing she could do about that. No chance, stick with Fiona mate!

Surely Kelly had not heard anything about him? More nonsensical thinking – he was practically a stranger in Meadow Gate compared to her! On the other hand it was a small town, and hearing things was what reporters were good at.

Dammit! She was angry! Kelly, for goodness sake come home!

Then another thought struck her, even more unsettling. Perhaps the photograph came from someone in Meadow Gate? A London postmark meant nothing.

★

Eastwinter wasted no time when he got back to the office. He called in Smith and told him to inform Green they were going to drop the story. Green, who had been enjoying face-to-face discussions with the editor about the story, was shocked but Smith's cold manner discouraged him from any query. Later when his puzzlement and discomfiture became more disquieting than his nervousness he tried to get to see Eastwinter for an explanation, but now Smith had assumed the role of doorman and stood between him and that cosy inner sanctum of the editor's office.

"If we don't publish it, somebody else will," Green grumbled.

"What do you mean? We've got it to ourselves, haven't we?" Smith engaged Green's shifty eyes with sharp suspicion.

"The whole Emburey group's management must know. These things leak, you know that," Green brazened.

"It's a risk we'll have to take," said Smith. "The editor has made his decision."

"The wrong decision!"

"Nevertheless, that's what he's decided."

However Smith's suspicions about what Green might do with the story made him go back to Eastwinter to warn him it could break elsewhere.

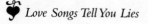

Eastwinter nodded. "I'm keeping it under review," he said.

Smith left, knowing he could get no further.

Eastwinter had not overlooked that possibility himself but if the story did appear in another paper, the blame could not be laid at his door. The pension fund fiddle, the real concern of Labouche, would soon be put right. And Green did not know what he, Eastwinter, knew - that in a week Emburey could very well be dead, and along with him the guts of the story.

In due time he might still run the story in the Graphic; honour served all round.

Eastwinter nodded to himself, his conscience settled very nicely.

★

That weekend Kelly made a special effort. On the Sunday he surprised everyone by announcing an expedition to Box Hill for one of their famous rambling picnics. Thomas and Jo brought two friends and accompanying one friend was her happy-dopey dog. It was brilliant: the children chasing the dog hopelessly, their laughter skittering far and wide over Surrey.

Water-colour clouds scudded over a softly green England that was having an afternoon nap in the sun. The view from that hill encompassed everything good and beautiful that English people extolled about their country. Angela loved this kind of simple day out. When he was sacked from The First Star they had had to find inexpensive ways of enjoying themselves. They loved walking the countryside and one day Kelly organised what he called a 'walking, talking, picnic' on Box Hill. They took baby Jo and it was a memorable day. It was the only kind of outing they could afford, but they both agreed that they preferred that sort of day out anyway. It had been one of those 'us against the world' gestures that had warmed their marriage through and through. Couples who do things like that usually collect their old age pensions together. Usually.

This day was as warm and sunny as that day had been, and the sandwiches and drinks as tasty. It was just that for him the old magic was missing.

The realisation was a knife, twisting.

∼ 36 ∼

Henrietta Chudley and Teddy her Yorkshire terrier accompanied her friend Audrey to the gate. Noticing the decaying debris of a once glorious display of daffodils Audrey remarked: "The daffs were out early this year."

"Oh," Henrietta replied, "they always are under that tree. It is a nice early spot for them."

She was reminded of a photograph of herself and Charles taken under that very tree when the daffodils were in bloom. She resolved to look out those old photographs later and enjoy a quiet stroll down memory lane.

"It is a lovely old garden Henty," said Audrey. "Nothing seems to have changed for years, for as long as I can remember."

Indeed, little had changed. It was the way Charles had designed it and he had thought a long way ahead so that all the trees and shrubs would create a haven. Nothing now needed to be done except cut the lawn and trim a shrub or two. Henrietta was pleased with her friend's observation because it illustrated how perfect everything had been with Charles.

Henrietta knelt and gave her dog a cuddle. "We miss him, don't we Teddy my boy."

As the years dulled the pain she had grown to be content, happy that she had had the kind of a marriage that, sadly, so many people do not enjoy; faithful, caring. 'The kind of marriage' was a phrase she knew might make some people snigger if they knew, because the sexual aspect of their love had been non-existent.

Charles had discovered he was impotent on their honeymoon. Curiously, it had never seemed such a terrible thing. It was hard to analyse, but his impotence had never been a matter of great anguish. It had happened, and they had tacitly accepted it.

Lack of sex had never affected the love and affection they had for each other one jot. Indeed she often wondered whether in some unexplainable way it had strengthened their bond. They were together for reasons stronger than sex - friendship, loyalty; total compatibility. They were a natural couple, inseparable, happy always

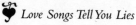

to be with each other, even without the much-hyped, endlessly discussed, worshipped, worried about, apparently worth dying for activity called sex.

It was another of Henrietta's friends, anxious to spare her the shock of reading it without being prepared, who drew her attention to Leonard Wakefield's interview in the Graphic. Henrietta heard her out, then read the article for herself. She read it two or three times, quite able to see it referred to her dead husband but somehow unable to take it in.

Vicky had done a good job of dramatising Wakefield's story. The essential ingredients were all there for a good read: a group of friends in a long-ago summer, inseparable, carefree, full of the future. There were the inevitable winners and losers in their games of love. For one member of that group of friends the loss was as painful but more total than for any of them.

Wakefield told Vicky: "In those days no one could say they were gay. Charles knew how I felt, he never said, never acknowledged, but I knew he felt the same. Like me, he was gay. But he married Henrietta. He just went along with it. It seemed to just sort of happen. She was besotted by Charles and in a way that dominated events. In the end he just seemed to accept marriage to her as the thing to do.

"Occasionally we met socially over the years and I knew the old magic was still there, but he stayed loyal to her. Nowadays people do not sacrifice themselves for the sake of convention but they did then and my life has been empty as a result."

Henrietta sat for a long time after her friend left, promising to come back later to make sure she was all right. She just sat, gazing unseeing into the garden. A flock of birds swept down on to the lawn and the movement awoke her from her trance.

Somehow it was thinking of the daffodils that triggered her to action. She picked up the telephone and called her solicitor. She was not going to have her Charles slandered, nor her wonderful marriage sullied by this fool. Her solicitor listened, already analysing, as he arranged an appointment, that any action was likely to be fruitless and anyway would be too drawn-out for someone of her age.

But taking this action was only a temporary balm to her pain. At one time years ago Wakefield had lived in the area. If he still did she was determined to confront him personally and she perused a local directory.

There was only one Wakefield, L, in the book and she called a taxi. Wakefield did not immediately recognise Henrietta after all those years. Taken aback with shock he just gaped at the sight of this extraordinary person on his doorstep, a deranged woman calling him wicked names. Then as she stormed at him, saying 'my Charles' time and again, he realised who she was.

Alarmed and horrified that she was still alive and that he had made a terrible blunder – he was not an unkind man and after all the years since had simply not thought of this possibility – he first tried to calm her with reason. When that failed to have the slightest effect he dredged up some spirit to fight back.

"What does it matter now?" he pleaded, his face gaunt with the despair of someone who has never lived and knows he never will.

"Matter!" Henrietta was enraged. "Matter! Who are you to decide what matters? Who are you to smear a decent man's reputation with wicked lies? Someone who cannot answer back!"

Defensively, Wakefield mustered what anger he could. "That's a typical 'normal' person's reply. How dare you say it's wicked!"

"How dare you decide what matters to me! You foolish, sad, pathetic man! My Charles was not one of you lot, this is all lies, lies! You'll rot in hell for such wickedness."

Wakefield was not going to listen to this! He started to close the door in her face. With the strength of fury Henrietta prevented him. As Wakefield tried to close it there developed an undignified, arm-flailing, tussle between the two old people.

Then just as Wakefield recovered from her surprising strength and pushed back harder Henrietta suddenly weakened and he tumbled past her down the doorstep, arms and legs skeletally askew.

Sobbing, Henrietta tottered home but there was more to come. Wakefield had broken an arm in the fracas and his neighbours had called the police. Chudley was not a common surname and Henrietta was soon traced and faced criminal charges. After the

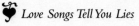

police interviewed her one of her friends insisted Henrietta contacted her solicitor.

A week of mental agony followed before her solicitor told her the police were treating the incident as an accident and no charges would be brought.

The matter did not end there however. The local newspaper ran an account of the incident and a freelance connected it with the piece he had read in the Graphic by Vicky Carew and sold it to the nationals. Henrietta stayed silent and protected by her solicitor, but he could do nothing about the torment circling endlessly in her head.

Henrietta received a good deal of sympathy from friends and readers' letters but it did nothing at all to lessen her distress. Indeed, the furore simply kept the story going. Eventually it disappeared from the newsstands, and Wakefield faded into the oblivion from which he had briefly and palely emerged. The distress in Henrietta's mind did not go away.

How could it? Once the prating imp of innuendo has been let loose it cannot be silenced.

The series was a milestone in Green's career at the Graphic. He now sat at his desk with an air of importance. An office desk is a strange item. Self-evidently it gives no physical protection, not from bullets, missiles; not even office draughts or spilled coffee. Yet some people sat behind them feel tremendously secure and powerful. That is how Green now felt.

"Wonderful series!" he enthused at an editorial meeting, and in a smart move doled out some praise to Vicky and the other writers who had contributed. Even a libel suit arising from another episode in the series did him no harm, even though he had vetted and Okayed the story. The high level meetings in which he was involved to discuss the case only served to get him more firmly established as management as he neatly laid the blame on the writer. The art of management includes the ability to pass the buck when unravelling your own cock-ups. He had long been an expert in passing the buck.

Henrietta Chudley became a victim of her rage. The wickedness of it all became a permanent lodger in her mind. She tried to treat the whole business with disdain, anger, but at her age she did not have the mental strength. Always in her memory of Charles hovered the spectre of Wakefield. She did not have the youthful strength to cleanse it with scorn, erase it with anger or crush it with laughter. Sometimes there was even guilt when she was especially low and, despite herself, wondered if perhaps there was some truth in what Wakefield had said about Charles. On those occasions she cried. It was a strain on her few friends who had survived the years and they stayed only as long as they felt they ought and the comfort they offered was increasingly dutiful. The story was forgotten by the readers of the Graphic by the turn of the page. It remained with Henrietta Chudley for the rest of her life.

— 37 —

Suddenly she had to have an ice cream. They were on their way to Exeter Races for the last meeting of their season. "Summer's nearly over and I haven't had an ice-cream!"

Never mind that they might miss the first race and never mind that summer had yet to start, it had to be an ice cream.

So there they were sitting on one of West Bay Harbour's massive ramparts with huge sloppy ice creams. It was hot enough for summer and they had to lick like mad to keep pace with the melting ice cream.

"We are going to miss the first race. I had picked out a dead cert."

She had an extra-long sensuous lick to give her time to reply. "There are no dead certs in this life my darling."

"You're wrong, it's a dead cert we will miss the first race!"

For answer he received a nonchalant smile.

Exasperated, he protested: "It will win!"

"You can pick winners can you?"

"Yes, I'm good at picking winners if you must know. I picked the winner of the Grand National and the Derby last year."

"Clever old you!"

"And I've picked you."

"Lucky old you!"

They were not the only people in a carefree-silly mood inspired by that superb May morning. Two lovers in the morning of their lives were strolling along the harbour wall. They were both very striking; a young man and his girl who would be centre stage wherever they went. Dressed light and bright for the splendid weather they would have pleased the eye of an artist. The young man was a prince; tall, rakish, his shirt open at the neck, his light-weight summer suit worn like a film star. He was a splendid young man, with a thick mane of hair, and the easy, careless confidence of a heartbreaker.

The girl was a flaxen-haired stunner, 17, maybe 18, gilded with health, beautiful without the aid of cosmetics. A smile from her and any youth would dream hero dreams. Yet of the two it was the young man who was unmistakably the centre of their world. That was plain. She clung to his arm, laughing at what he was saying. You never saw a girl walking so free yet such a prisoner.

As they passed by Kelly commented: "Love's young dream."

There was no answer and he glanced at Kathy. Her eyes were also following the young couple and she did not appear to have heard him.

"Handsome couple."

Still she did not answer and he snapped his fingers to get her attention.

Then, without a smile, still not meeting his eyes, she said tartly: "Handsome is as handsome does."

She knew he was looking at her, bemused. He put his arm around her.

"What's the matter?"

Surprised and puzzled, he saw real hurt in her eyes. Then suddenly and before he could comment further, her mood changed just as it was so often to do when things seemed to get serious. In a parody of her own accent she chuckled: "You're me 'andsome, and you does. Come on me darlin', we're wasting time!"

"We! Who was it who just had to have an ice cream, like a little girl?"

"What's this dead cert of yours called?"

"Always."

They did miss the first race, and Always had come nowhere.

"Oh you can pick them, can you?" But she was no better, and they spent the rest of the afternoon giving the bookmakers money and tearing up betting slips.

"Never mind, it's been a lovely day," he said as they sped homeward down the spectacular hill from the racecourse.

"It is still a lovely day," she enthused. "Look at the sun, there's half a day still left. Waste not, want not. I've wasted too much. Let's stop at Lyme Regis on the way back." When they arrived it was dusk, as a stop for tea at Beer and a walk along the cliffs had happily delayed them.

"Best time to come," she chuckled. "We've got the place all to ourselves."

On the way she had told him all about Lyme Regis and its history. He learned all about Jane Austen and the 18th Century gentlefolk who had elegantly patronised the resort.

"You can imagine them promenading here, can't you," she said, when they reached the seafront. "And tea dances - do you suppose they had them in those days?"

She did a couple of old time waltz whirls. Dah,dah,dah-*dah*, dah-*dah*, dah-*dah*.

He took her in his arms and to their own arrangement of The Blue Danube they waltzed along the promenade. Dah, dah, dah-*dah*, dah-*dah*, dah-*dah*; dah, dah, dah-*dah*, dah-*dah*, dah-*dah*, they warbled until they arrived laughing at the other end. Breathless, she turned round to lean back into his arms. Then, moving to the rhythm of a different tune, he whispered in her ear: "We may never, ever, change partners again ..."

He knew she was hearing what he was saying, and in answer she squeezed closer but stayed silent. With immense difficulty he suppressed a surge of frustrated anger. He was afraid, that was the truth; a man on a tightrope, oh so delicately balanced between success and disaster.

So, affecting not to notice her silence, he pointed to a massive buttress circling out to sea.

"What's that?"

"The Cobb. If lovers walk to the end of it and swear eternal love, they are never parted."

"That's the local legend is it?"

"Not really, I just made it up. It's a nice legend though, isn't it?"

They walked along the Cobb above a soughing silver sea. Eternal love; it was the perfect setting for such a legend, for a love as strong and enduring as the Cobb itself. They reached the end and, cut off from reality in a moon-gleaming, sea-murmuring limbo, he coaxed her gently down on to that mighty stone.

"What, here?" she exclaimed.

"Here."

"This stone is blinkin' hard on my bum, I might tell you! And oh God, we might end up in the sea!"

Just how hard the stone was he discovered when he fell back laughing.

"That's it, you've ruined the magic!"

She cosy'd up to him with conciliatory wriggles. "Don't be cross. We'll come back again, and bring a mattress."

High in the gardens above the beach an elderly Lyme Regis resident walking Teddy her terrier heard their laughter. It lit up memories of when she and Charles used to sit at the end of the Cobb on summer evenings. They had spent many a happy holiday in the town and she had decided to sell up and move here, in an attempt to ease the pain of recent events.

Remember the good times had been the parting well-intentioned words of her friends. Tonight, hearing those people laughing on the darkening Cobb, she remembered and was happy.

Down below the lovers she had heard, wrapped together in their coats, cosy as in a bed, sat for, oh, they had no idea how long, in a dreaming moonglow.

Then suddenly she demanded: "Where were you 15 years ago?"

"I'm here from now on, for always."

"Oh, always? Always? Wasn't that a certainty only a few hours ago at the races? And what happened to it, may I ask?"

"I'll be here from now on."

"Oh, miracle man. You'll be in two places at once?"

"And you, can you be…?"

"It's not me that's the problem."

"What do you mean?"

She stopped him. "No, not now. Not now. Let's have this at least."

Being here on the Cobb was a good analogy of his life; here and now was strong and sure, but all around the seas were ebbing and flowing.

~ 38 ~

Jeremy Halpman's head was throbbing; churning over and over again in his mind were the wretched details of the weekend he and Janet spent at that charming little hotel in the New Forest. Try as he might, he could not get rid of the images. He did not want to remember either that damn woman or the damn hotel. He finished the dregs of his glass with a gulp. It was his fifth, at least, and the memory still would not go away. Might as well finish the bloody bottle. Finish everything.

This damn headache! Where were those bloody pills? Two were no good.

How had it gone so wrong? From the moment he had met her at the local constituency party dance that, as the local MP, he was duty bound to attend, he had been besotted. The inner turmoil had been unbelievable. His comfortably-settled, years-in-a-rut, metabolism had been knocked for six. Nothing like it had ever happened to him, certainly not since he had got married.

Turmoil. That was what it had been. Not love, or passion; not as he would have thought of it. Just turmoil; ugly, like an illness. Silly, that was the truth of it. Just plain bloody silly. There was nowhere to go to escape. He was a laugh, a big bloody laugh. Media material.

The times he had read of colleagues in the House in similar situations, and had sighed and shaken his head at such folly. Middle aged shenanigans were the stuff of jokes, and he had joined in the raucous laughter as loud as anyone. They would be laughing at him now. Off-camera there was no mercy at Westminster.

Never understood it all before. Yet, there he was, telling lies to Rose so he could get away and enjoy an illicit weekend with a woman he had known for only a week.

This bloody head! Four pills and still they did not work.

Then it had all been a disaster. What had happened, or to be more accurate, what had not happened embarrassed him even now, and only he and she knew. At least that was not public knowledge.

Nothing had happened.

Yet that was worse than if something had. Philanderers are admired, let's be honest. Like that bloody Tory MP! Spread all over the tabloids as the man who had seduced another MP's wife and her daughters! The swine had merely looked superior when television reporters had harassed him with questions and he just coolly smirked a "no comment". The publicity made him a kind of sex hero, a superstud applauded with bar room guffaws across the nation. The cuckolded MP became the sad figure, and had actually ended up not being re-elected, as though being a cuckold these days was a crime! It seemed to be getting that way.

Yet when he had been caught in an illicit weekend, he had had to act as though it had happened. It hadn't, for God's sake, but he would have looked a bigger chump than ever if he had admitted it had all been an embarrassing disaster, a non-event.

They were not working, these bloody pills. Useless things. Where's the damn packet?

Not that he would have been believed if he had denied anything had occurred between them. To the media it was the usual story of an errant husband and they would have mocked him. Knowing that he was not even guilty of having it off with another woman, yet his life ruined anyway, turned a knife in his guts. The real truth had not stopped Janet, the cow, selling her story. Anyone reading it would assume they had slept together. She had talked once that bastard at the hotel - it must have been someone at the hotel - had tipped off the Press.

No doubt they had given Janet money to talk - she would not answer that question when he had raged at her on the telephone.

"I wanted the truth to be told," she had said. "I thought it was the best for both of us."

The sly insincerity of it had made him want to kill her. Yes kill her. He really could have, *would* have, had they been face to face.

The best thing for both of us! Lying cow! The best thing for her bank balance! What had happened to him? He was not violent or stupid. Now he was both.

"What bloody right did you think you had!" He had raged on and on, until she slammed the phone down.

So here he was. Rose had left him - kicked him out, which was why

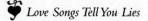

he was here at another bloody hotel. There was a four-figure sum to pay to solicitors just to tell him he had no case for libel and he was a man who had not even managed to be unfaithful!

Suddenly it was all too much. He started to laugh, and then was not laughing but crying. He sat there alone in his room pathetically grateful that this too, was something no one would ever know about. The head feels bit better. Better get some sleep. Nearly asleep already. Finish the bottle. Can do that like a man, at least!

He cursed the reporter who had written the story. He cursed the bastard who had sneaked on him. He cursed Janet. He sat late into the night, drinking and cursing, and none of it did him any good.

He had not even made a full page. No one would even remember the story in a month, only he and Rose. Poor Rose. He would just be another vaguely remembered public figure who had been forced to resign.

What the hell had been the point?

He was found the next morning by a waiter bringing the morning tea. This waiter was as smart as the one in the New Forest, and even while the ambulance crew were removing the body, was tipping off the Press.

In the following day's papers Halpman again did not make a full page. Somehow the death of this small-scale MP lacked the big headline.

★

In America The League of Red Blooded American Males voted Senator Booth The Man They Wanted to Lead America in the New Millennium. On the train home from the office Kelly was again within earshot of Basil and Bertie.

"It's getting so you are nothing as a politician in America if you are not a sexual athlete," snorted Basil.

"It's beginning to get that way over here as well," Bertie snorted in response.

They snorted a jolly good guffaw over that.

Kelly sighed. When you two start getting it right, God help us all.

⟶ 39 ⟶

Bretts was good at this seduction business. He had read the best scripts by the best playwrights hadn't he? Angela innocently played into his hands; not flirting by any stretch of the imagination, but certainly not discouraging him. Fiona kept a smile on her face whenever she met Angela, but Angela was not fooled. Fiona was miffed, and that gave Angela a kick.

She had not forgotten that day when Kelly's colleague Frank had called at the house. It had been a shock, not a pleasant one at the time. Later, when she had calmed down it had been flattering, she had to admit to herself, that a handsome young man had fancied her. This actor Romeo was Mr Eligible and he was hot for her. No chance, fella, but thanks for the compliment. A girl's ego needs a little boost now and then, and it was fun knowing that man-eater Fiona was fuming behind that paste-on smile.

Thinking this as she arranged her face in the mirror prior to meeting the girls Angela gave herself an approving nod. Well, you are only middle aged once!

Gilly picked her up in her taxi.

"You managed to get a baby-sitter all right then?"

"Yes. Josie, Ally's girl, is doing it. She's got college in the morning, so I mustn't be late."

"Won't Kelly be home to take over?"

"No, he's away for a couple of days."

"Again? That husband of yours is never home. I'll tell him off next time I see him. He's neglecting you."

"It's his work. There's so much pressure."

"Well, he'd better watch out, with Bretts about!"

"Gilly!"

That evening Bretts appeared at the club and when it was time to go home he was on hand with an offer of a lift.

"I'll leave you two, then," said Gilly mischievously.

"Don't you dare!" Angela whispered and made the amused Gilly go along with them. "Is that what I've come to," Gilly sighed mockingly. "Just a chaperone?"

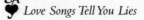

When they had gone Fiona over-acted the poor rejected woman. "Well, Angela is certainly showing me a thing or two about how to get yourself a man," she said with a phoney smile.

The others could not think of anything to say this time, and just looked at each other.

★

The lost battles at The Post and Worldwide had taught Green to be patient. Just wait, and often rivals kill each other off. Buller had seemed a certainty, but here they were making him department head instead.

"What will happen to Buller?" he asked during the morning meeting with Smith.

"He has left the paper," replied Smith.

"Left! What? How?"

"Walked out this morning. He was offered another role, but it was his decision."

Green looked suitably concerned, and maintained it expertly until he had left the deputy editor's office. Once he was out in the corridor he punched the air gleefully.

Back at his desk he right away started the pleasurable job of working out how he would run the department. High on his agenda would be sorting out Mr Kelly-sodding-Webb. That was going to be the most pleasurable job of all.

The appointment had been made all the sweeter when he had persuaded Smith to give him control over Webb. "He is out of the office a hell of lot," he had said. Buller out and him in, and having charge of both features and the SS Squad. All in a couple of months. You had to know how to operate in this game.

★

"You haven't opened your letter!" Helpfully Anne-Marie brought it over to her mother. "It's been on the kitchen table since yesterday!"

"Oh, has it." Kathy took the letter with an air of unconcern. "It's probably junk mail."

"Well, open it then and see!" Anne-Marie urged saucily, in a take-off of the way her mother chivvied her when she was lackadaisical about anything.

"Mind your business!"

Anne-Marie made off, giggling, leaving her mother contemplating the letter which she knew full well was not junk mail. It was a nondescript brown envelope but she could see from the yellow postage machine franking that it was exactly the same as the letter she had received from Dorset County Hospital fixing her appointment back in April.

They had said she would be asked to return periodically for routine tests, but surely not so soon as this? Certainly there was no other reason she would be getting letters from the hospital. Of course! They would make a routine appointment months ahead. Relieved by this reasoning she opened the letter.

The hospital wanted her to telephone and make an appointment to see the specialist again, not months ahead but as soon as possible.

★

Kelly was in Smith's office trying to keep calm and doing a bad job of it. For a week now he had been working on a story about top jockeys placing bets on other horses in the races in which they rode via an offshore betting company. It was a great yarn, and also a welcome change from the endless sex sagas of late. Now Smith, without explanation, was taking him off the story.

"It's right up my street. What's the problem?"

Rhetorical question. Kelly knew what the problem was. He was the problem. Smith and Green wanted him out. While the editor was away they were giving him a hard time.

"No problem," said Smith, not meaning a word of it.

"So? Let me work on the article."

"You have made your mark with scandal stories," said Smith. "It's got nothing to do with your ability, but we think Johnson is the better man for this."

"We? Who's 'we'? What do you think!" It was challenging, and Smith flushed as he felt the scorn. Kelly knew it was nothing to do with 'we'.

Smith said nothing.

Kelly rammed the words into him again. "What do you think!"

"Don't take it personally Webb."

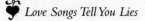

"Scandal stories?" Kelly was not missing anything here; quite obviously he was being pushed aside. His anger blotted out good sense, the mortgage payments, the weekly shopping bills.

"I have done every kind of story, home and abroad. What are you talking about!"

"It's not personal Webb. You are not the only good reporter on the paper." Smith put on a big smile. It was not reassuring.

He was about to say more, but Kelly got up and with a dismissive gesture walked out. The way he did it, it was he who was cutting the interview short. The deputy editor was made to feel foolish. It took several moments after his office door had slammed behind Kelly for the colour of Smith's face to change from the white of shock to the puce of fury. The editor was on holiday and Smith knew better than to sack Kelly without his say-so. No matter – Smith knew how to make it bad for Webb. Blue-eyed boy or not Smith knew that the editor always supported his department heads. They were there to bolster his importance. A man who had household staff knew the best order of things.

"What are you grinning at?" Bill enquired. "Pay rise?"

"Just feeling good," Kelly replied. His scorn made him feel clean. These days he was getting life into a different perspective.

'Webb'. '*It's not personal Webb.*' Back to surnames. Yes, in this life you needed to know what was important and what was a load of bollocks. When you had that sorted, you felt good. The Greens, the Bullers, the Smiths of this world only had power over men like themselves.

A man is what he does.

"Yeah, just feeling good Bill."

Bloody good.

— 40 —

He hesitated at the door. She took his hand. "It's all right." He entered the house carefully, as a polite stranger. She was smiling at his hesitancy. "Come in. It's all right, really."

When the front door was closed, she moved closer and snuggled up. "This is how it should be. Hello, my darling, my baby."

The large detached house had been built, he guessed, before the Second World War. There was a well-cared polished family-ness; a warm, homely smell and feel about it. He looked around, liking it right away.

"This is a nice house."

A memory of boyhood visits to the home of a well-off aunt and uncle came to mind. He had always liked their house, which had seemed posh by comparison to his own home. Yet posh was the wrong word here. The furnishings were polished and neat, but well used. It was mellow and warm, and brightened by the sun that somehow flooded the whole house. In imagination he could see the happy family of her friend who lived here.

"Make yourself comfortable. I am going to make you a lovely lunch."

"When will your friend be back?"

"There's no need to worry, really."

"What if she…?"

"We are very good friends. She understands. We've got all the afternoon."

The afternoon in bed had been her surprise when they met at Weymouth station.

"Make yourself at home while I get lunch."

Within a couple of minutes she was back from the kitchen with a tray of sandwiches and drink.

"That was quick."

"I was a fast order cook in a café." She laughed. "No I wasn't - I prepared them earlier!"

A picnic in bed in the afternoon; a fun and sexy idea.

She popped a tomato into his mouth. "They call them love apples. Now you'll be in fine fettle." She chuckled and offered him another tomato. His reaction stopped her.

"What's the matter?"

"Matter? Nothing."

"You looked … don't you like tomatoes?"

"Yes. Very nice. Nothing's the matter." He forced a re-assuring smile.

She changed tack. "So, you think it's a nice house?"

"Yes, it is."

"I'm glad you think so. It is a nice house, isn't it. Oh, it's lovely, being here with you. This is how it should be."

But she was still not satisfied with his assurance. "You went quiet. What were you thinking?"

"That I would like a cup of tea."

"So romantic! All he is thinking of is a cup of tea!"

With their picnic on a tray she led him upstairs. He hesitated outside what he could see was the main bedroom; his attitude: 'Should we?'

She ushered him in: "It's all right." She was close and warm. His reluctance was a poor weak thing.

From the bedroom window there was a fine view to the south of the lake, shining under a blazing sun, and in the far distance the town's skyline.

She switched a radio on. "We'll have some music."

Seated against the pillow like a sultan he watched her undress. He was a man and for him undressing had been quick and simple. She was a woman and it was a work of art.

It was an erotic art, starting with a delicate hint as she took her necklace off, promise as she removed her dress, sauciness as she smiled at him via the mirror, vulnerability when she shook her hair loose and harlotry when with a chuckle she flung her knickers across the room crying: "Knickers away!"

She put a hand on a naked hip and mimicked a pin-up pose, laughing. But in her eyes there was an uncertain mix of bold pride, knowing she was damn good for her age, and anxiety at what she would see in his. She patted her stomach, which was remarkably flat. "Not bad after three pregnancies!"

"Oh, I thought you had two children."

There was a pause. "A miscarriage."

He said nothing and just waited until she smiled at him again.

Then beckoned. "Come here my lovely."

She perched pixie-like on the bed. "My lovely! That's Dorset. You're learning the language!"

He took her foot, and nibbled her toes.

"Umm!" It was though she was savouring a tasty flavour. He lifted her leg and kissed the defenceless area at the back of her knee. It was a long, lingering kiss and the 'umm!' became a long lingering sigh which told him she was at his mercy. She reached down weakly. "Come to me." He brushed her strength-less hand away, kissing her fingers to soften the rebuff.

Her fingers stroked through his hair, coaxing.

"Come to me."

"Time," he said. "There's plenty of time. The man on the radio started the countdown with a song of love.

She reached for him. "Come to me. I'm flowing like a river."

Her skin in the warm sun dazzling through the window's lace curtains was softly white. Zephyrs of warmth from her body caressed his face like kisses.

"Come to me."

"Plenty of time."

"God!" Her sigh was almost anguish. "Like a river. Come to me!"

He did. But it was a long way to her mouth, and he kissed every inch of the journey.

Time. Plenty of time. They had all afternoon, most of which he spent inside her as they explored the secret places of heaven. The man on the radio was caught up in the mood and they were serenaded with love songs. They used up the programme and most of the one following before she finally slept peacefully in his arms. When she awoke she whispered in his ear. "Hello my darling. My baby, my darling."

For a while they lay in that serene time-free zone that lovers know. All the while the man on the radio played those dangerous love songs.

"I should have met you 15 years ago."

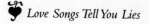

"Better 15 years late than never."

"Perhaps we were not ready for each other 15 years ago."

"Perhaps. Shall I tell you something?"

"As long as it not goodbye."

"Oh, never that. Fifteen years ago …oh, people are different at different times in their lives. We may not have liked each other 15 years ago." She paused. "We may not have been right for each other – no, I would not have been right for you."

"Why? Does that mean your taste has improved, or deteriorated?"

"I was very vain."

"Oh? What would that have had to do with it? You are very vain now – look at you posing a minute ago!"

"Don't be mean!"

"What do you mean, you were vain?"

"It doesn't matter. It doesn't mean anything. Kiss me."

He duly obliged, and more.

Later, as they lay curled together like foetal twins she said, as though thinking aloud: "People are often their own worst enemies."

"How do you mean?"

"Don't you think it strange, that so many of the people who use dating agencies are really very nice-looking people?

"I don't follow you."

She could not find the words for what she meant, nor indeed quite knew what she meant. Instead she asked: "Why is love so difficult to find, with everybody looking for it?"

"What brought that on!"

"Nothing."

"You're in a funny mood." He cupped her breast gently. "Everything all right?"

"It is now."

Soon she was flowing like a river again. They made a second disc jockey on the radio earn his every penny that afternoon.

The sun that had been warming on the west wall of the bedroom was now warming the east wall. "Do you realise," she said, "we've been in this bed over three hours!"

"Good thing I did not meet you 15 years ago. You'd be a widow by now."

"This is where I want you, where you should be."

"Your friend would get pretty fed up with that."

"Oh, that will be all right. We'll do it again soon."

"For the rest of out lives!"

"Mmm.." She stopped any further discussion along those lines with a kiss.

Suddenly she exclaimed: "Oh god! Good thing the window wasn't open. My knickers would have ended up in the garden. Explain that to the neighbours!"

The knickers she had tossed across the room had ended up caught on the window latch, on bright display to the whole street. It was a good ten minutes before they stopped laughing. The whole street must have heard them.

As she dressed he watched, fascinated by that feminine, total, concentration of a woman doing her make up.

"Just renewing the Polyfilla," she chuckled, catching him looking.

He drove to the station, leaving her at the house. She had said it was best, turning down his suggestion that he dropped her near her own home. So she did not want him to know where she lived. That was understandable, but he was never going to be such a fool as to call at her own home, or telephone.

Her discretion underlined again the uncertainty of their situation.

As he drove away he gave her one last kiss. "Too bad about the past 15 years," he said. "But we'll have the rest."

He tried to hold her gaze. "Do you hear me?" She nodded but said nothing. Her smile was wan and she remained silent.

Whenever he tried to close the net she always slipped away.

"What's this?" she queried as he put a card into her hand.

"It's the card of the guest house I stay in. If something goes wrong you could always leave a message." It had been something he had thought of before, but had been reluctant in case even having a card would make her feel pressured. "I'll always stay in the same guesthouse," he said. "'Bye, my love. Take care."

"'Bye, my lovely." Then through the open window of the car as he put it into gear she said: "Fifteen years ago I took the wrong

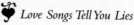

turning." She tapped the watch on his wrist to stop any query as to what she meant. "You must hurry."

He looked out of the train window as it climbed the incline towards the tunnel and to an entirely different and less magical world. Briefly the train was high in the air on a viaduct and he could see far over the peaceful town. He gazed until the tunnel blotted out the view, greedy for every moment of that so-English countryside soaked in hazy evening sun. He was becoming more conscious of time and the lack of it.

As the train slid through Dorset into the deepening dark the recollection of her downcast eyes nagged. This woman could so easily, with a word, or a dreaming faraway gaze, cast him adrift on a sea of doubt.

When he was with her in this hidden world of Dorset on the other side of the tunnel, he had no doubts; was full of purpose. Yet as the train left those potter-along stations behind and sped into the real world, he was all too aware of the fragility of the situation. He was a hundred miles away, seeing her only briefly, the contact so easily broken. Her husband had the base, while he was on the outside, hiding, with no plan of action. If they missed a meeting, he would be left in a maze.

What should be making a man bold was making him fearful.

★

"Write our story!" The notion had got stuck in her mind. She had been in mischievous mood as they lay on the bed, the sunshine of that lovely summer turning the curtains to a silver haze. "Why won't you? It's a lovely story." But now the idea was becoming intriguing. He held his hands out in surrender. "OK, OK. You're right, it is a lovely story."

"You don't mean it. Why not? Why isn't it a story? What makes a story for clever reporters like you?"

Someone's misery.

"Tell me!"

"It's easy for reporters to write a story. Someone always supplies them with the plot. Our's is not a story, the sort that sells books. No it's not," he insisted, quashing her affronted reaction. "A story has to have a beginning, a middle and an end; a third act. Anyway the best third acts are unhappy and we'll be happy ever after."

"We are not a story? A woman who is the happiest woman ever? A man who can love her for an hour, and then just a cup of tea and there he goes again? That's not a story?"

"It was that second cup of tea."

"You cheeky man! The tea is it? Not me, hey!"

The hour that afternoon did not start for at least five minutes. It was that long before she stopped beating him up and he had finished laughing.

Later as they lay in the sweet moistness of love-making she murmured sleepily: "Why isn't it?"

"There's no third act."

"You keep saying that."

"Happiness is not interesting as a plot. With us its: Act one: Happiness Begins. Act Two: Happiness Continues. Act three: Happiness Ever After."

"Oh!" There it was again. 'O' for off-putting. "You can promise that, can you?"

"That we'll be happy? Yes!"

First she kissed him to soften her words. "Don't make promises I can't keep." Suddenly her brittle bright mood cracked. "Oh!" This time it was like a sob, muffled as she was kissing him. "Don't let's talk any more. You will have to leave soon."

When she looked at him again, she was smiling. It was a puzzle and he had never been very good at puzzles.

— 41 —

Angela called up the stairs. "Tea time!" Thomas was down like a shot, and Jo came down shortly afterwards. "You've changed again," observed her mother, who saw her that daughter was wearing the new clothes they had bought the previous weekend. "Didn't you have your jeans on when you changed from school?"

"Yes!" The answer came in an uppity 'so what?' tone that brought a sharp look from her mother who, seeing Jo's expression, curbed her reaction to put her daughter in her place. Instead she enquired mildly: "Why have you changed into your new clothes? Something special?"

"Why the inquisition mother!"

"Sorry!"

"She's got a boyfriend," chortled Thomas, and laughed at his sister's furious denial.

Angela clipped her son. "Be quiet Thomas!"

Before Jo left the house Angela kissed her daughter. "You look lovely darling. Take care."

Take care – advice she ought to have taken herself!

The telephone interrupted her reverie. That would be Kelly. He said he was going to call her about this time, hopefully to tell her he was coming home tomorrow. Instead, to her annoyance, he said he was expecting to have to stay away for a couple of days again. Their conversation was short and awkward on both sides and she just said, all right. Be seeing you, he said, and hung up.

"It's getting a bit much," she had complained to Dot and Gilly over coffee only that morning. "Is the Graphic so short of reporters they have to send Kelly out on every job?"

★

"The wanderer returns."

Kelly crashed on to his chair and tossed his notebook and tape recorder on to his desk.

"Coffee?"

Bill nodded. He waited until Kelly returned with the drinks. "As you are never in the office, no doubt you haven't heard the latest."

"What?"

"Buller's gone."

"Gone?"

"Left. Five minutes to clear his desk."

"What happened?"

"He lost the office power struggle."

Kelly was indifferent, but nevertheless surprised. "Yeah? Who won? Ah, Green of course."

"Right."

"Survival of the fittest I suppose. Sometimes a changing environment suits the slithery and slimey. But not really much of a change. It depends how you like your nasty piece of work, large and loud like Buller, or thin and sour."

"There will be changes. Word is he wants to take direct control of us. He is working on Smith."

Kelly shrugged.

Bill shrugged in turn at that reaction. Whatever happens, it won't be the same for you Kelly, my friend. Not the same at all.

Kelly could tell what Bill was thinking. Don't worry Bill. I'm not stupid. He took out his diary and found the page where he had written the name: Norman Fell. That was the chap the guy from the Chronicle had given him. Kelly had sounded him out over a pint about any vacancies on the paper. His drinking friend had been obliging. "He is the chap to contact. I'll tell him you are interested if you like." Kelly thanked him. "It won't be soon," he had said. "There is still some time left on my present contract. But I will call."

Everyone has to have insurance.

He found the Chronicle's number and tapped it out on his mobile. He asked to be put through to Norman Fell. Time to move on.

★

"Imagine, if we had met each other first." She was lying on her back one leg waving in the air, regarding it from every angle with approval. "Look, no cellulite."

She turned her head to look at him. "Think of all the lovely afternoons. Wouldn't it have been wonderful."

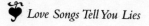

"Yes, if I had lasted 15 years." The leg was still in the air, and he took the opportunity to kiss the soft flesh behind her knee.

"You'd have got tired of me?"

"No, just tired. Would I have been allowed an afternoon off?"

"Well, I usually do the shopping one afternoon a week."

"The past is not lost. We just live it in future."

"Oh, Mr Magician!"

"We have the afternoons of the rest of our lives."

"Have we?"

"Yes."

It was said it with deliberate emphasis, which she deliberately ignored.

"Are you happy?" She was trying to make him look at her, to search his face for a truthful answer, but he was busy kissing the inside of her thigh.

She persisted and he gave in and looked up.

"Yes!"

"I don't understand that. If I were happy, I wouldn't be here with you."

He wanted the questions to end. They made him uncomfortable.

He tried evasion. "There is no explaining the unexplainable." Men in his position did not want to have to explain.

He escaped the moral trap as she sighed with pleasure. The kissing explored the inside of her thigh, lingered on the flatness of her stomach of which she was so vain, and caressed her urgent breasts. She was warm and flowing, flowing like a river; a flood that drowned all reason.

━ 42 ━

The Conservative Party was wiped out in the General Election. "They've bonked themselves out of Parliament," was how Frank summed it up with a sharky grin. "Now for some fun with the Labour Government."

Not, however, with Robert Jones, Labour Party Shadow Home Secretary. The Booth soap operetta had fascinated him as much as it had the rest of Britain. It had given him a good idea. While watching the almost nightly nonsense going on over in America the idea had developed.

In the last few weeks before the election, when it became pretty certain that his party was going to win, it became a plan of action. He felt confident it would work. There was that good gut feeling about the notion. When he had that feeling, he was usually right. And he was, and he started a new fashion in Westminster.

A week after the Labour Party was in office, and he had his new job in the cabinet safely in the bag, he issued an announcement. He was leaving his wife of 30 years and moving in with his mistress Alice Wright. As soon as his divorce was finalised, he planned to marry Ms Wright he said.

He posed for pictures with his mistress and it was a big story. But it lacked the one ingredient that had so damaged the Tory bedhoppers. The story had not been dragged naked from the bedroom.

The initiative was with him. With nothing hidden, it was all over in less than a week, and then the reporters really had nothing new to write about. He was on the moral ground. Maria his wife, a university professor, made no public comment as he knew she would not.

They had long since lost each other, absorbed in separate agendas of high-flying careerists. No one was to blame. They had remained civilised; and when he told her he was leaving for Maria, she agreed to stay quiet until Labour got in. Why not be practical? It was honest enough – a damn sight more honest than those worms from the Press and their mercenary morality!

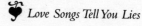

An admiring Labour Party PR person congratulated the minister. "You should have gone into public relations." For the day and age, there was no greater compliment.

Thereafter it was the fashion to bare adulterous Labour Party souls in public. They queued up to confess their domestic arrangements. The resulting repetitive stories proved to be as boring as the politicians themselves, and stopped selling newspapers. Even the male Labour M.P who appointed his lover as his Commons secretary got little coverage. The lover was also male but the story was only a one-day wonder. Two lesbian M.P.s arranged a Press photo-shoot with their lady lovers and that was another inside page story.

"Well, they did promise a New Labour," Frank had to grudgingly concede.

★

Kelly came into the kitchen pulling on his favourite old summer jacket, the one Angela had threatened to give to Oxfam 'only they would refuse it'.

"Ready?"

They were off to Reigate for some shopping, and caught the bus. Kelly had come home late the evening before and it had been so nice to see him, and it had been such a lovely evening with the weather forecast promising a fine weekend, that she had put off mentioning the photograph. She would do it, before the weekend was through, but not yet.

Having him home was lovely, and she had been reassured in way. He was just as loving, perhaps even more so. Yes, definitely more so. While he had been away the photograph had been a menace, sinister, needing an explanation. She would mention it, but she needed the right moment, so she could tell him without showing, well, anything that would make him think she had believed…oh, what a wicked person the sender was!

"Well I'm blessed!" Startled out of her reverie, she looked up at Kelly's exclamation to see a young and very pretty girl in front of them.

"Well, well, what are you doing in Reigate?" Kelly asked the girl.

"Oh, just shopping." The girl was indeed very pretty, with a charming smile. Kelly turned to Angela. "We are fellow commuters," he explained. "I see this young lady on the train.."

Angela had seen her before as well. It was the girl in the anonymous photograph.

"This is getting to be a habit," Kelly said, and the girl smiled. "What brings you to Reigate?"

"I'm meeting a friend here."

Angela stood by with a polite smile while Kelly exchanged a few more words with the girl before bidding her goodbye with a 'see you on the train'.

As they walked on he told her how he often saw the girl on the train. "You get to see a lot of faces, nod and smile but never know who they are from Adam – or Eve in this case! Sometimes you wonder what sort of lives they live, who they are."

"Well, you found out who she is, and where she lives. Very pretty, too." Kelly appeared to be oblivious to the arch tone in her voice.

"A charmer. The second best looking woman on the street right now. How did I find out? You are dying to know, admit it!" Kelly grinned teasingly. "I was in Oxford Street, buying your present as a matter of fact, when I bumped into her, literally. It was lunch time, so I bought her a cup of tea."

Confused, but doing a good job of recovering from her shock Angela said tartly: "Quite a long conversation for a 'bump into'. And what's her name, now she is not a face on the train?"

"Oh, her name? I'm not sure she told me. If she did, I've forgotten!" He put his arm round her. "I know your name, that's all I need to know."

With purpose in his step he headed towards the town centre and one of their favourite cafes.

"Come on, I'll buy my favourite lady lunch."

"Oh, we're being serenaded as well," said Angela as they turned a corner and almost bumped into a street singer.

"How odd," said Kelly. "It's the same fellow who was in Oxford Street the other day. He's following me!"

Laughing, he dropped some loose change into the fellow's collection box and they walked on, the words of his song following them.

Listen, hear the love songs played
by the man on the radio.
Honeyed words on honeyed tongues,
So easy it all seems.
And young love is made to go,
Down the street of broken dreams.

In the midnight room
The young girl cries.
Honeyed words on honeyed tongues,
Love songs tell you lies.

The oldest and the latest story,
Eyes wide open, but love is blind.
The fun, the sun, the glory,
Honeyed words are not always kind.

In the midnight room
The young girl cries.
Honeyed words on honeyed tongues,
Love songs tell you lies.

When they returned home Kelly did a bit of gardening while Angela made some coffee. It took a while for the realisation to fully sink in that Kelly had not been the least bit embarrassed at meeting the girl. He could so easily have passed her by without saying anything if he had been guilty of what the photograph suggested. Sometimes you cannot be sure whether something is right, but when you can see the truth it is unmistakable. Kelly felt nothing for this girl, except polite friendliness. That was plain. That Angela could see. That she had been sure of, standing there in Reigate's High Street, noting his reaction.

Even so, she was human, and before she tore the picture up and threw the pieces down the toilet Angela took one last, searching look at it. There was enough of the shop in the background to show it was Marks and Spencer, where Kelly said he had a snack with the girl.

Angela was filed with remorse, guilt, that she could even have considered such a possibility; especially in the way it had been drawn to her attention. Malice had clearly been the reason for the photograph being sent to her. With a sudden rush of relief and love she embraced Kelly.

"We are lucky, aren't we darling?"

He held her, surprised. "Yes."

Had there been something in his voice, or more exactly, something missing? She pulled back and look searchingly into his face.

"We are, aren't we?"

"Yes. Yes, we are. Very lucky. Why do you ask?" Kelly's own guilt made his tone less than convincing, and his effort to inject conviction into his words made it worse. Despite himself he avoided looking into her eyes by pulling her close again.

Angela sensed something was not quite …her stomach lurched. She quelled her panic. Had he heard some gossip? She had behaved badly, disloyally, but there was nothing serious to feel guilty about. She would make it up to him, even though he would not know why he was being treated extra nicely.

"I love you," she said. "I am a very lucky woman."

Kelly laughed and hugged her even closer.

"And I am a very lucky man."

They were closer that evening than usual. Both knew they had a very happy marriage; one knew why, the other wondered why.

That night Kelly excelled himself. He entered her slowly and lovingly, seeking to give and to receive; finding and giving delight in her every part. Her sighs of pleasure were whispered in his ear into the early hours.

★

In America Senator Booth contested the preferential primary to test his national popularity as presidential candidate. His opponents and the Press stood by ready to howl with laughter when he was thrashed. This was the man who had been unfaithful to his wife countless times. His exploits while in positions of political power had brought him close to being indicted for violations of the law and the Constitution. His wife's saintly performances in public were a joke to all sane and dignified American women. One scornful television pundit asked his viewers: Does this guy think he is running for nomination as president of Loonyland?

If he did, perhaps he was right. He won by a landslide.

"What are we supposed to be doing?" Frank wanted to know.

"Following fashion, son, following fashion." Bill delivered it in his gravest manner, but for once Frank did not laugh.

"You remember that joke, about what the next political story will be, three in a bed, lesbian cheating on lesbian? After Booth, what next? Is the joke getting truer, or just dafter? As fast as we nab one prat, another prat is elected."

"Just be guided by fashion, Frank." It was the best even Bill could come up with. He sighed. When Frank started getting serious, things were indeed serious.

"You know, by the time this parliament comes up for re-election, no heterosexual in the land will get a single vote," said Kelly.

That was easier for Bill. "No one would dare admit to being one."

★

On the Sunday Kelly took Angela out to lunch while the children visited their friends' homes. Angela updated him on the marital troubles of Jenny and Stephen.

"Stephen has been playing around again," she said. "It is such a miserable situation. As she says, she can't just walk out. She has the children to consider."

Kelly held her hand across the table. He stopped himself saying anything.

"He chooses such awful women it seems. It can't be love. You can't love two people, not the kind of love it should be in a marriage. It's always the man!"

Kelly tried a little joke. "Men were deceivers ever."

At any other time that would have cornered him. Angela would have pounced, and would have threatened him with dire consequences if he really believed that: plight his troth or woe betide! That was before Fiona had arrived in Meadow Gate and muddied the clear flow of Angela's life. Angela had no reason to feel guilty but she did, and that made her angry. She did not reply. She was in no mood for levity about fidelity.

They spent the afternoon pottering around the garden. In the warmth of the dwindling sun they sat on the garden seat under the rose arbour he had built. This was the life he had always dreamed of, would die to defend. He still loved it, yet at the same time would he give it all up?

Angela finished her drink. "I'll give Jenny a ring," she said.

Thomas and Jo burst into the garden, noisy, laughing. All he had ever dreamed of. There was no understanding it. Not any of it.

Deceivers ever.

'Write our story!'

'There's no third act!'

And perhaps no happy ending.

★

It was when she and Dot were having a coffee. That was when Angela learned that people were gossiping about her and Bretts. Dot was telling her about a friend of hers – Dot's – who was having a spot of bother in her own marriage. Her husband was a bit of stuck-on-the-sofa, a telly watcher, whereas Dot's friend liked a spot of socialising.

"This fellow – I won't tell you his name, this is a small town and you probably know him – has been chatting her up. He's bought her a drink a couple of times. He is getting a bit serious, and I admit he is nice. Divorced. I just wanted to ask you for, well, what you think."

"Oh, I see." Angela was flummoxed. What could she say to that? "What makes you think I can help?"

"Well, with you and Bretts, I thought you would have, well, some idea…." The shock on Angela's face halted her right there. Oh dear, Dot thought, what have I said?

"I thought perhaps…." Acutely embarrassed, Dot let her words trail away.

"Me and Bretts?" Angela was not believing this! Dot felt that awful hollow in the pit of her stomach into which people feel they are falling when they have dropped an almighty clanger.

One half of her mind urged her to pass it off as a joke, the other half said an apology was needed instantly. Between the two she floundered, words stuck in her throat.

"Me and Bretts! Dot, what do you mean? Me and Bretts! What are you saying?"

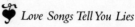

Dot found her voice, or rather, her voice found her. She had little control over anything right now. "No, Angela. No… I meant…" What she meant was that everyone thought Angela was having an affair with the actor. "Angela, I didn't mean anything. But I thought, well…"

"What? Well what! What did you think?"

"Angela, people tell me that you and …" She stopped, distraught. "Oh Angela! Oh, I shouldn't have said anything. It is just gossip. I just thought…" She put her hands to her burning cheeks and kept saying, "No, no, Angela" and "I'm sorry" over and again.

Finally she said: "I just assumed, oh I shouldn't have, I shouldn't have, but him and you, seemed, well…." She shut up and looked even more miserable.

Angela stayed silent for a few moments. Then, frostily: "What made you think that? What have people said?"

The miserable Dot, floundering in a no-win situation, finally just gave in: "Well, Fiona said…"

"Fiona!"

Now all Dot could do was remain silent, looking as though a handy cliff to jump off would be welcome.

"I thought Fiona claimed him her latest conquest!" Angela was beginning to realise a few things even as she spoke. Fiona had boldly set out to bed him, and was quite open about it in her ridiculous way. Then she had been rather tart in her manner to Angela after Bretts had been so anxious to take Angela home that first evening. So that was it. Fiona had not got her man, so she was spitefully spreading lies that she and him were having an affair.

"What has she been saying?"

"Well, nothing. She just joked really. It was just that, well…." Dot just did not know what to say.

"Just joked! And that means everybody believes we are having an affair!" Angela could see it now. Fiona 'just joking', the rest willing to go along, a nice bit of gossip; yaketty-yak, no harm meant, just joking, until they start to believe their own fiction.

The worst bit, Angela realised later as she fumed over what Dot had said, was that the more fuss she made about it, the more people would see fire beneath the smoke. That would not stop her giving Fiona a piece of her mind – a big piece! – but she was still on a hiding to nothing whatever she did. But she would tell Kelly the truth when he came home – before he heard the lies.

Kelly called just at the time she was expecting him to arrive home. Sorry darling, I won't be home tonight. Another rush job had cropped up. He would be away overnight again.

— 43 —

I t had been a lovely day, only a fool would have risked spoiling it. Enter Kelly Webb, the fool. He had made up his mind. Today he would force the issue. Things could not go on as they were.

He had picked up the hire car from the garage on Dorchester road where he was now greeted like a regular customer.

"I'm going to show you something," she said.

Up the zig zag hill, through Dorchester, and after a few miles they drove into a huddle of cottages. It was another of the picture book villages the county possessed in such abundance.

"Cerne Abbas," she announced, like a tour guide. "One of my favourite places."

As they got out of the car, he said: "This is amazing."

"Lovely isn't it."

"You can park where you like. Look, loads of room. No yellow lines!"

"Oh, you Londoners! Somewhere to park and you're happy. That's all you noticed about Abbotsbury. Come with me, and even you will be impressed."

He was. They walked along a street which Shakespeare might have seen exactly as they saw it now, had perhaps been there with his company of strolling players.

They went through an iron swing gate and crossed deep green meadows that had surely never known the plough. She led him along a footpath that climbed steeper and steeper.

Then they were at the top, on a huge, wide-open grassy hill with the village and half of the county miniaturised below. It was a view that filled the soul to overflowing. Words were not needed. They sat holding hands, just gazing at that marvellous countryside. A breeze streamed in silver waves over the grass, making the heat of the high summer sun sweet and comfortable.

They sat in silence, time stripped of importance. There seemed to be no fatal deadlines in their lives. He had no train to catch, nor did she have a family to get back to. The sweet illusion was that all they had to consider was themselves.

She lay back on the grass. "Come to me."

As he kissed her she wriggled. He thought it was because the ground was uncomfortable. "Knickers away," she giggled in his ear, and he saw she had adroitly slipped them off.

"Here?"

"Here."

"You saucy wench!"

Except for erotic endearments, it was the end of talk for half an hour. They were in hundreds of acres of open space. The hill was exposed to half the county. "I hope there were no bird watchers out there with their telescopes," he said when eventually they lay quiet.

"If there are, it'll be your bum that will be in next week's Twitcher's Magazine." She giggled, scoring again. "Come on, I'm starving. There's a nice cafe in the village. Tea and scones!"

"Don't forget your knickers."

It was slide and slither on the way down over the sheening grass. When they got to the bottom they were almost as out of breath as when they climbed the hill.

Gratefully they reached the genteel café that was aromatic with the smell of home-made cakes and pies. It should have been the end of a perfect day and with his growing determination to bring matters to a head he could have ruined it all.

He was foiled.

Something far worse did.

They ordered a pot of tea for two, and scones. They sat at a table in a corner.

"That was lovely, wasn't it. I think I know why you were inspired - up there on the hill." She was looking at him teasingly.

"What?" he asked, puzzled.

"On the way home I'll show you something."

"Right," he said, knowing he was going to have to wait to see what. "It's been a lovely day. I don't want it to end, but ...." She pushed his sleeve back to look at his watch, children's teatime on her mind. "It doesn't have to."

"No..." She was evading him again. "Don't let's...not now."

So as usual he pulled back. But there was something about her. All

day she had been determinedly bright and he had thought she was making the best of the brief time they had.

"Tell me, something's the matter."

Her eyes caught his briefly, then she looked away, the smile suddenly gone. He knew he could ruin everything, but a fool was urging him on, the one who had been on the hill who was blind to reality. Sometime he had to find the courage, why not now?

He tried to gain her eyes, but couldn't. "It doesn't have to end."

"Doesn't it?" She said it lightly, conversationally, as though they were talking about something else. They fell silent while the waitress brought their order.

"No!" The fool would not stay silent.

"Everything has to end."

"No it doesn't. I don't want it to end. Neither do you."

Don't force the issue. You will lose this woman. In a moment the mood had changed unbelievably from glowing happiness to chill gloom.

"Please!" Her eyes were brimming with tears.

He cursed the damn fool in him, and his reckless confidence evaporated.

"It's no good," she said, reaching out to touch his hand. His heart turned to ice.

People at the adjacent table were preparing to leave. Pausing for them to move away before continuing she breathed deep for control, and touched her eyes with a tissue. Now, his fool's courage gone, he tried to think of some way to deflect the moment, to prevent the words he feared being said. She watched the people move out of earshot.

"I'm sorry." Her fingers entwined with his. "You don't deserve this. You have been so good to me." Then the tears were running fast down her face and whatever pain she was feeling, he felt tenfold.

Ineffectually she brushed at her tears. "I do love you. You do believe that, don't you?"

Then why? But he stayed silent. If he did not ask, perhaps even now she would not give the answer.

He reached over and brushed away her tears. "Don't. Don't say anything. Stay with me. Just stay with me."

"No, no." She was shaking her head, and he could not understand what she was trying to say. "It's not your problem. I should not be telling you all this."

"Tell me."

Tell me! I would take on the world for you.

She took time to compose herself.

"Tell me!"

"It's not benign."

She watched him slowly comprehend.

"The lump. It's not benign."

The words darkened the room. Relief that she had not been seeking a way out of their affair was instantly swept away by this terrible news. The silence that followed was very long. He held her hand so tight she had to gently prise it free.

"Your tea will get cold," she said. "You'll need something, after this afternoon." There was a glimmer of a smile.

"You saw a specialist!"

"He said it was benign. But when it still hurt and I wanted to see another specialist he seemed to think I was being - I don't know. A silly woman. He seemed...impatient.. seemed to take the attitude that if I must have another check.... I felt I was being made to doubt his word. It put me off insisting for, oh, I don't know how long. Perhaps too long. Who knows? Anyway, there's nothing to be done now. I went back when it got even more painful and saw another specialist. He recommended a mastectomy."

The tears were gone now. "A mastectomy." She kept his gaze as she deliberately repeated the vile word. "I won't be a complete woman."

No words would come. The chitchat in the cafe murmured on.

"Not complete. A freak. Then what?" The challenge to him was plain.

"I wouldn't blame you."

"No!" How could she even think it? "No!" It will not change anything. "I love you. You! How can you think it would matter?"

His angry response to her challenge went straight to her heart, warm and comforting. No reply was needed.

"We mustn't waste this lovely tea. Have something."

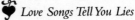

Tea, at a time like this!

She passed him a scone. "Thank you." He started to butter it, something to do as he controlled the fear that had flooded him, the fear of a man who has suddenly lost his way on a dangerous path in a wilderness. He knew only what he felt, but not what to do.

"We'll find a way." What on earth did he mean?

Time flew by as cruel as ever and they had to get back to Weymouth. "Turn right here," she said when they reached the outskirts of the village.

He pointed left. "Weymouth is signposted that way."

"I was going to show you something, remember?"

"What now?"

"Dorset is full of goodies."

A short way along the main road she instructed him to pull into a lay-by and pointed. "That was the hill we climbed."

Above them was the hill and on it a huge carving in the chalk of a phallic giant.

"It's an ancient fertility symbol," she said, the sauciness back in her eyes, watching his face. "I said you would be a new man."

Jokes, even now.

"I didn't see him!"

"You can't, not when you are up there. Too close. You have to be here on the other side of the valley. But you felt his spirit didn't you!"

She was still chuckling about it when they got back to Weymouth. "'Bye," she said. "It is easier, knowing you. Without you..."

He pushed back her sleeve and took the tissue from where she had tucked it. It was still damp from her tears. He inhaled her scent.

"It'll remind me," he said. "Until we meet again."

"'Bye my darling."

"We'll find a way."

The train climbed the incline in an artists' evening light. We'll find a way! If you say it strong enough to yourself, you can actually believe it.

Years later, thinking back over their lives, he would recall the pride he had felt that it was to him she went for comfort.

If only he had known.

She could not give this up. This was what she and all those people who used dating agencies were looking for.

All those years ago, after months of apologetic, guilty, excuses for his frequent absences, he finally dropped the bombshell that he was leaving her. During that bitter, spiteful, row he revealed that he had found with that damn woman what he had never found with her.

"You are cold," he had shouted. "Cold! There is – nothing!" He was angry, guilty knowing what he felt was self-pity, unable to hide his feelings any more; laying blame on her, but still pleading for her to understand.

"Nothing. There's nothing!"

Then he had left, his throat choked with the apology he knew he ought to have made. She was not cold. That had been cruel and untrue. Nothing, that was true; but that was not her fault, nor his. Too late, however, for useless analysis. Everything was in ruins and from then on they only ever communicated in legal language.

She could not give this up. Now she knew what he meant.

★

Bill looked up when Kelly entered the newsroom. "Ah, the wanderer returns! Fellow named Fell phoned. Asked if you would call him back. Said you'd know the number."

"Right, thanks Bill."

"Norman Fell. That the same Norman Fell who is features editor of the Post?" Not much got by Bill.

Kelly gave him a not-answering look.

Bill probed. "Fed up with us Kelly?"

"My face does not fit. You could be Hemingway, Dickens, if your face doesn't fit here, forget it."

★

The face was familiar. Then just as Kelly realised who it was, Norman Fell grinned and offered his hand: "Yes, the same Norman Fell from Brighton."

"Well, I dashed," said Kelly, and apologised. "The name did not ring a bell," he confessed.

Fell had worked on The First Star as a sub when Kelly and Charlie were there.

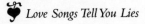

"I guessed you did not realise when you said nothing on the phone," Fell said, waving away Kelly's apology. "There were dozens of staff. I worked in a different room. Anyway, you've done well I see."

"So have you," said Kelly.

"Not bad. Got to keep moving in this game."

His secretary brought in coffees and they talked about Brighton for a while. Soon Kelly felt the job was in the bag and he relaxed.

"I used to sub some of your copy," said Fell, "and the other chap…you were a duo." He chuckled. "The Deadly Duo I called you…"

"Charlie Brown."

"…Yes, Charlie Brown. You two used to enjoy yourselves. I was always a bit envious, but then if you choose to be a sub you can't have the glamour. I figured early that moving to a desk was the best way to get on. It works for some, but you have done well enough."

That led on to the work Kelly would be doing.

"It is tough work," said Fell. "It might be very different from what you have done so far. This is what I would term as news-feature writing, a lot of research and occasionally you will be sent to news trouble spots. OK about that?"

Kelly nodded. It was like a breath of fresh air.

"O.K. We'll give it a shot," agreed Fell and the deal was struck.

"I've got a couple of weeks to go on my contract," said Kelly. "But it might be sooner."

"That will be fine – whatever."

Fell walked him to the door. "By the way, you will find another familiar face when you join us. Remember Tony Church? He was one of the writers in your department if I remember right? He was doing well for a time after you left and got a good job on a national paper, but then got the chop. He's with us now, doing OK, subbing. You two will have a few things to talk about no doubt." He extended his hand in farewell. "Look forward to you joining us Kelly."

On the train home Kelly felt good. Hard to imagine that Buller, Smith or Green enjoyed life as much.

— 44 —

It was late and dark and they sat at a pavement table of an Esplanade café and enjoyed the warm evening. Tonight Kathy acted quite differently. There was no hint of her usual edginess in case they encountered someone she knew. If was as if all that no longer mattered. A waitress brought their drinks and they sat in easy reverie.

This quiet security did not last long.

"A lovely evening."

It was a camp, unappealing, voice. Seated at a nearby table was a portly middle-aged man with an unnaturally large bald head and dead white skin.

For a reply Kelly nodded politely, uninspired by the look or the sound of the man to encourage further conversation. The rebuff however had no effect. Kelly could sense the determination of the sad and lonely to engage strangers in conversation. Apart from the landlady it was the first time anyone in Weymouth had spoken to him and although there was no logical reason for it Kelly felt uneasy. The man was not going to be politely dissuaded and persisted: "On holiday?"

Kelly just shook his head, still hoping to discourage him, but he had not bargained on Kathy's friendly nature.

"No, I live here," she answered for them both.

"I'm from London," the man confided, his voice grating on Kelly's nerves. As Kathy was about to reply Kelly realised with alarm that she might reveal that he was also from London and he sharply cut in with: "We're local" and emphasised this with a warning look towards Kathy.

From her expression he knew he had made a clumsy move, one that underlined all the insecurity of their situation. For the first time in the centre of her home town they had been sharing a relaxed harmony and now it had suddenly vanished, like an illusion. Anger at the intrusion shivered in his gut. Unjustified, but somehow the man raised Kelly's hackles.

"Are you on holiday?" she enquired politely.

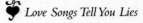

The man shook his head, looking out towards the sands glowing faintly silver in the cheerful Esplanade lights.

"I just caught the train to the end of the line."

Kelly still could not stifle an unease and tried to catch Kathy's eye to indicate they should move on. Now the man seemed to be lost in thought as he stared into the dark.

"It didn't matter where really. Just the end of the line."

Then the man came back from his sad reflection and said to Kelly: "You are a lucky man to have such a beautiful lady."

The lack of a response to this did not deter him; indeed he did not seem to be very much aware of anything other than his own thoughts. He rambled on, almost as though he was alone. "I was lucky once."

Kelly put the money for the bill on the table and ushered Kathy away. They joined the evening promenaders enjoying the Indian summer. Near the Jubilee Clock they stopped and leaned on the railings, looking out into the dark. He held her tight; staying silent. It seemed the safest thing at that moment.

Then, musingly, she observed: "The end of the line. I had never thought of Weymouth like that before. I suppose it is." She looked up at him. Her eyes were bright in the lights but it was incipient tears that made them sparkle. "I suppose it is."

He cuddled her closer and she did not resist, but somehow they did not fit as nicely.

With silent savagery Kelly cursed that stupid man.

Toby Morrison sat staring out over the twilight sea. He was remembering the sweetness of the dream in which he had made love to Catherine.

"Take care of her, or you will lose her," he called out, but the man and his lovely lady had gone. Catherine, his lovely lady, was gone too. Until that lady had asked him, he had not been clear in his own mind why or how he had arrived in this town. The end of the line. That's what he had told her. The end of the line.

Leaving exactly the correct money on the table for the bill he left the cafe and walked out over the sands towards the sea and the endless darkness.

— 45 —

Kelly sat at the kitchen table occasionally sipping his coffee and regarding Angela's face as she spoke. His wife's face was lovely; an honest, warm, loveliness. She was honest and beautiful inside and it showed. Just looking at her – across the meal table, at a party where other fellows invariably tried to hog her company – had always given him so much pleasure, and still did. Inexplicably, it still did.

"You mustn't make a fuss about it," Angela pleaded. "Promise. Please. It will only make things worse. That's all it was," she said when she had finished. "Nothing." Then, with an intake of breath to steady her voice: "I'm sorry."

Sorry! The word cut painfully into Kelly. He could not look directly at her. She could not keep to her resolve to refrain from tears as she continued. She had not mentioned Brett's behaviour after they had got back from London. She just wanted Kelly to know what she had done. It was no good making it all worse than it need be. If Kelly knew what had happened he would kill him – but he did not and would not.

Fiona had called her at the last moment to make up a foursome to the theatre. She had a spare ticket going to waste, she said. Fiona inviting her? Well, perhaps it was an olive branch. It was a play Angela fancied seeing, and on the spur of the moment, said yes.

"Pick you up at six, OK?" said Fiona and before she had time to ask who the other two women were, she hung up.

Then the car arrived and she got in – beside Bretts. The other two were Fiona and her latest conquest. It had been a dreadful evening, with her regretting every moment, and angry knowing she had been tricked.

Arriving back at near midnight, Fiona and the other man were dropped off first and she and Bretts had been left alone. Then when she had refused to go with him to his place he had shown his true colours. It had not been the disappointment of a decent man honestly attracted to her, but that of a lecher denied the easy conquest his vanity had led him to expect. Kelly did not need those details; anyway, nothing had happened.

He had tried to grope but had not even managed to kiss her. He had driven her home when she insisted. He had driven in angry silence. It was not the reaction of a man who had gone too far and who regretted his mistake. It was ugly, vain frustration.

"It was meant to be all of us together, just a group. The others just cleared off, I didn't expect to be left alone with him for half the evening."

If Kelly knew how the actor had behaved it would lead to big trouble, and she knew that she bore some responsibility for the situation, if only for being so naïve.

She looked anxiously at Kelly. "What are you thinking?"

He had stood up and was looking out at the garden. Then he turned and went to her and hugged her. "I was just thinking what a lucky man I am." His hug muffled her sob. Gently he tried to wipe away her tears.

"Luckier than I deserve" he said. Buried in his arms, she did not hear.

"You don't have any doubts, do you?"

"I'm a reporter, remember. I rely on the facts." He leaned back and put on a big grin. "And the facts are that you are a dear, delightful, honest, precious woman and I love you dearly." The woman he had married had that rare and lovely quality of transparent honesty. It had moved him before, moved him deeply, and it did so now.

To cover up his emotions he made a play of looking searchingly into her eyes, from all angles as though checking every corner of her mind. "Yes, you are cleared. You are telling the truth."

She hugged him back, all doubt gone. One thing she knew, he was telling the truth. He did believe her.

"Poor sod."

She looked at him?

"The poor sod thought he stood a chance." He laughed. "But then this town is full of poor sods with no chance!"

Then he picked up the telephone and tapped out a number as she watched, bemused.

"Hello? Good evening. Have you a table for tonight? For

two…good …seven thirty, eight. Eight? – fine. Thank you …goodbye …oh yes, Webb. Mr and Mrs Webb. Thank you."

"What was that about?"

"Dinner for two, you and me."

"Dinner? Lovely! Where?"

"Toffs. Where else? I heard The Dream Factory are putting on a fund-raising do there tonight. Dine and dance sort of thing. What's your friend's number? We'll get her or her daughter to baby-sit."

The Dream Factory. That meant Bretts would be there but Angela said nothing and gave him Ally's number. As he tapped it out he chivvied: "Well, start getting ready! It takes you an hour!"

What was he up to? Angela found out almost as soon as they got to the club.

Kelly pointed. "That him?"

Bretts was at the bar as usual. In fact it was a rhetorical query. Kelly knew it was him and without waiting for an answer strode over to his group, Angela in tow, her heart thumping.

"Kelly!" she whispered anxiously.

Kelly greeted one of the men in the group whom he knew and as they exchanged a few pleasantries the actor shifted uneasily, not looking at Angela.

Kelly turned to leave, then suddenly said: "Oh, I almost forgot. I owe you some money."

"Owe me?"

Kelly deftly slicked four twenties from his wallet. "For the theatre ticket. That should take care of it."

Too surprised to say anything Bretts tried to back away from the money but was hemmed in by the bar and his companions.

"Absolutely not, can't have you paying for her ticket old chap." Kelly deftly tucked the notes into his top pocket and pressed them firmly in, the way some people give a tip. Then he ostentatiously added two more twenties. "Don't want you out of pocket."

Leaving the group rooted in stunned silence Kelly led Angela away to their table. On the way Kelly beamed and exchanged pleasantries with people they knew, the nearest of whom had seen and heard what had gone on. None of them would have understood what it had all been about, but they all soon would!

Angela felt a glow in her cheeks. It was not embarrassment. It was pride.

'And I love you dearly.' How could that be true? It was, although the world and his lawful bedded wife would not believe it. Until now, if he had heard that said by some other husband with the same secret life as his, neither would Kelly.

Angela smiled across the table at the wonderful man she had married, and answering his earlier response to her confession said: "I love you dearly too."

Later, when she reflected on how easy it was to ruin your life, she shivered. You did not even have to try. It was scary. At the slightest excuse people made their minds up about your marriage. Whether they were right or wrong, you suffered!

With his arm around her Kelly drove home one-handed, he steering, Angela changing gears.

As soon as they got indoors he began to undress her, alternating each of her garments with one of his own. They reached the bed leaving their clothes strewn on the stairs and along the landing. He kissed every inch of her, re-discovering her, re-discovering every pleasure. He was on song, and her heart sang to his tune.

If a songwriter could have captured that night in music, he would have made a fortune.

Love songs: such sweet lies.

― 46 ―

S he had been quieter than usual when they met. He had suggested a drink at Sibleys while they decided on where to go but she had insisted on driving off straight away.

The silence was like a stern chaperon between them. In a village close to Golden Cap he turned down a tiny lane sign-posted To the Beach. They parked alongside a pub and took their drinks to a rustic table on a knoll overlooking the beach.

The shouts of children playing sounded a long way away in the wide open space of the shore.

There were only a few holidaymaking families on the beach below them. The spot had an old fashioned, before-the-war simplicity, just pebbles and sand, eddying rock pools and a solitary pub that also sold ice creams, teas and snacks

Their silences had always been communicative, each knowing the other was happy to be there. This silence was very different; a frightening wilderness. Children were noisily building a sandcastle. They cried with alarm and joy when the sneaking tide made it collapse. He could feel the sand shifting beneath his life.

She took a sip of her drink, gazing out into the sea light. Then she reached over and took his hand in both hers and said, without looking at him: "What do you think?"

"Isn't it obvious? Every chance I get, I see you. I come down from London, miles! You could be in China, it would not stop me."

"I know, but can it continue? There's not just us to consider."

"Yes."

"Be realistic!"

"Yes!"

She was not listening. The realism on her mind was her body, cut by a surgeon's knife. She let go his hands in order to sip her drink. Separated from her by the solid table he felt adrift.

He had felt the same way the first time they met after the operation. He had persuaded her to ask her friend for her house again. She had been reluctant, and he guessed why.

"I'm not a complete woman," she had said, refusing to let tears flow.

It was futile bravery. Her distress broke his heart anyway.

"I love you. Nothing has changed."

When they had made love she had tried to keep her bra on. Gently, under the covers he had removed it. Defying her feeble protest he had kissed the scar. For an hour as the man on the radio spun his fantasies there were no more words. Then, with the sun on the east wall and time again to leave her, she said: "You do love me, don't you. You do!"

"Nothing has changed," he said. "Nothing. Nothing. Nothing."

Faith may move mountains, but even love cannot move facts. If they quarrelled there would be no time to let the world take a couple of whirls, no chance to send flowers, leave notes, make telephone calls or get friends to act as cupid.

In reality he still knew little about her, not even where she lived. Even if he knew her house or telephone number, he would not be able to call and be sure she would be the one to answer. If she lived in London or Surrey it might have been easier. So far away, if communication was broken, even by a simple misunderstanding, how could he make contact again?

An honest lover could pursue a woman openly; knock on her door, telephone, write letters. Could he, a secret Romeo, who lived a hundred miles and more distant, just wait at the bridge hoping she might walk by?

That was being realistic.

Suddenly she asked, a faint smile beginning: "How did they know who you wanted when you called the hospital?"

"I asked for Mrs Collins, of course."

"How did you know....?"

"Your surname? When you were in a shop, in Dorchester I think, a sales assistant knew you." He mimicked: "'Hello Mrs Collins!'"

"You clever devil! No one is safe from you reporters are they."

Not with you Kathy. I'm not being very clever there, am I?

⁓ 47 ⁓

"A useful invention, lace curtains," he said.

He had slung his clothes aside eagerly and was quickly in bed to watch her undress. She would keep her bra on, and he would gently remove it under the covers. The sunlight streamed brightly into the room but because of the lace curtains she could undress without closing the night-time curtains. In the bright sunlight her nakedness was wanton.

This time she was not doing her 'knickers away!' routine, and kept her back to him. Then she turned to pick up something from the dresser. Before she turned away again he saw the bulge, glistening white, beautiful and new. With her back to him again she stood in front of the mirror unleashing her rich hair.

He threw the covers aside and came up behind her. He slid his hands gently, lovingly, over her stomach. She placed her hands over his, looking at him via the mirror. He smiled at her, caressing the bulge, slight, but undeniable on a woman who had been so proud of her flat stomach.

He was filled with excitement, a foolish delight. It was madnesss. A baby – his baby, because not for a moment did he consider it was her husband's – was going to bring everything to a decision. That conclusion would be painful, but his reason had been swept away. A shock of urgent, triumphant desire exploded in him.

She shook her hair loose and wriggled away from him. "Bed!" and giggled at his predicament because the warm naked encounter was already hardening him.

"Quick!" she whispered as he joined her under the covers. "Quick," she urged as he entered her and she greedily engulfed him, her cries of pleasure drowning out the man on the radio. Afterwards, as they lay in the sweet damp of love making he put his hands on her stomach again, gently resisting her as she tried to move them.

"Is it mine?"

"What?"

For answer he pulled the covers off her and kissed her stomach. "You had the flattest stomach of any woman of" – he mimicked the

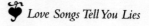

way she chewed up the numbers of her age – "in England."

"Oh, no." She laughed; a forced, nervous laugh.

He said no more, apprehensive as always of the outcome. Was he assuming too much? He felt a flush of embarrassment that his presumption was being dismissed thus, an embarrassment compounded by an outrageous jealousy that he was sharing this woman with her husband.

He placed his cheek against the bulge of her stomach, feeling the erotic warmth.

"I'm putting on weight." She laughed, but seeing his serious expression stopped. "Oh no!" She kissed him. "You silly man!"

On the train on the way back to London he hardened again, just thinking of that moment. Would it bring them together, or drive them apart? Either could be the result, whether or not the child was his.

No, she had joked, I'm putting on weight. But he knew she had been lying.

★

Robert Booth did not become President of the United States. His opponents managed at the last ditch to uncover a reason for not selecting him at the party's candidate. Nothing to do with decency or common sense; they found a rule that the President has to be a natural-born American. Mother and daddy had been living in London when baby Booth arrived. His opponents also managed to throw in the speculation that Mr and Mrs Booth had gone to Britain to have Robert on the National Health to save money. Not natural American! His popularity cooled, but not by too much. At least his loins were hundred per cent American.

Booth hired a platoon of lawyers to take the matter to the Supreme Court for a ruling. It was a certainty that the American public would have overlooked all this given enough chat shows on television, loins being larger than lies in the good old Unlimited Sex of A. But the party leaders decided that they did not want the complication of a Supreme Court case to decide the issue and rejected him as their presidential candidate.

There was the usual consolation. A Hollywood consortium paid him $20 million for the film rights of his life plus two per cent. of the box office.

★

It had been while they were having coffee in Sibleys. A group of women at a nearby table were enjoying a good gossip. Something he said was drowned by their laughter.

"It's a regular meeting for that group of friends," she told him. "They don't know the meaning of quiet!"

He had laughed. "Sounds like the Thursday crowd in the Rendezvous in Reigate. Women enjoying all the gossip."

It was the only time he had given any clue as to where he came from, and she had noted that he had been unaware of giving anything away.

Reigate: she had no idea where that was and looked it up on a road map, just out of curiosity. Then, just out of curiosity, she called directory enquiries. Then she called the number, and enquired about the Rendezvous Thursday Club.

The Thursday Club was in full swing. It was where the friends usually met, Reigate being the most central place for most of them.

As usual Fiona was enjoying being the naughty girl, regaling the others with details of her latest beau. She was in good form and had the others laughing at her stories.

The place only quietened down when Fiona left for a hair appointment.

Angela looked up and caught the eye of a woman seated nearby. She had been there all the while the gang had been in the café. Angela had noticed her smiling privately from time to time, indicating that she had been listening to all their chit chat.

Angela smiled, as nice women do. The woman smiled in return, and remarked: "You friend seems to have men sorted out."

Jill answered that with a chuckle. "Oh, Fiona? Man-eater!"

"It's lock up your husbands in this town then," said the woman.

"Yes, none of them are safe," laughed Angela.

"Oh, you needn't worry Angela," said Jill. "Kelly is Mr Faithful!

"Kelly is her husband," Jill told the woman by way of explanation.

Angela laughed. "He's a darling, isn't he Jill?"

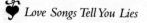

Then the woman said something rather odd. "I'm glad to see he's in good hands."

When Angela and Jill paid their bill ready to leave, Angela said: "If you are still in Reigate next Thursday, you must come and join us. We meet here every Thursday afternoon."

The woman smiled. "Thank you. Goodbye, I am glad I met you."

"She seemed a nice person," said Jill as she and Angela walked down the High Street.

"What was her name?"

"No idea," replied Angela.

"Oh, she seemed to know you."

As she strolled home from the village bus stop enjoying, thanks to the village's enthusiastic flower gardeners, the sweet-scented air, Angela recalled the woman she had just met in the café. 'I am glad I met you'. An odd phrasing. Thank you, madam, whoever you are. Glad to have met you too!

Getting the evening meal ready that evening Angela wondered whether she would take them up on the offer to join them another Thursday. She had been nice. Now she could be a man-eater! Angela smiled to herself. Lucky for us wives she was just passing through!

"What are you grinning at Mum?" demanded her daughter.

"Nothing darling. Just a silly thought."

★

Kathy was glad she had made the journey, crazy notion that it had been. Having met Angela and seen what a nice person she was, she ought to have felt guilty. She did not. It was not something she could explain, either herself or to anyone else, but she felt better. Meeting Angela had made her feel … but she had no words for it, except that she was glad she had met her. Nothing could change things now, but she had made up her mind what to do when… when the time came.

★

Within a week of the Labour Party's New People settling into their offices, two male M.P.s issued a statement that they were homosexual. They posed for pictures with their partners, and the statement underlined the fact that they were regular, long-term, partners. Clever touch, that. The story only lasted one day. All the subsequent comment had been purged in advance. No shock factor, no story. Two days later three women Labour M.P.s made it public that they were lesbians and they too received the same very correct media treatment.

"What are we going to write about?" wailed Frank.

"What sort of journalist do you call yourself?" Bill snorted. "These people will eventually cheat on their partners, just like anybody else."

Frank cheered up. "Thank God for that."

"So what will be the next social sins that will pay our wages, Bill?"

"Oh, still men cheating on women, women cheating on men, then it will be women cheating on women, men cheating on men. The players change but the game will always be played the same. As long as there is sex, there are sales."

"So, like they say, there's nothing new under the sun?"

"No, just new arrangements."

"We'll be all right then?"

"As long as your news nose doesn't lose it sense of smell my boy, you'll be all right I promise. Vice is very varied."

— 48 —

Out of the long tunnel the train emerged high above a poetic muddle of houses and fields bathed in hazy sunshine, then eased down a gentle incline towards the sea. The lake came into view, blazing with stolen sunlight. Did the sun ever fail to shine on it? Somewhere in that prairie of reeds was the path on which they had met. An image came to mind of her knowing smile that first encounter when he had haplessly tried to keep their conversation going.

He saw her right away, at the end of the platform. He walked slowly, to let the other eager-to-be-home passengers go first in case there was someone she knew among them. But she did not wait for the crowd to disperse and went straight into his arms and he held her close, surprised and pleased. So, what the townspeople of Weymouth might think did not matter any more? He was that important to her now?

He pulled back so he could kiss her and then saw she was not smiling. Her face was drawn. The chill of an outsider touched him again. He did not want to ask 'what's the matter?' but had to.

Her answer was tears and, taken aback, he just held her tightly. Eventually pulling away she dabbed her eyes dry, flicked her hair habitually into place and put on a smile.

"Hello my darling, my baby. How are you?"

"Fine, fine. But you're not."

She took his hand and led him from the station. "Come on, let's go to Sibleys."

They ordered coffees and made for their table in the corner. Then she turned back and said it was too hot and would have a coke, then changed her mind again and said coffee would do after all. Then she had another change of mind, and she ordered Dorset apple cake for both of them. He watched as her dithering made both her and the waitress giggle. It was always like that. People around her always smiled.

"You can't take me anywhere, can you," she said as they sat down at their favourite corner table. "Isn't it nice? It's always empty, waiting for us."

They talked about this and that, all the engrossing trivia of people who are good for each other. Then he asked her. He had to, though still afraid of the answer.

"What's the matter? Tell me." Her eyes darkened, but she remained silent.

"What's wrong?" An idiot inside him was making him force the issue.

She looked steadily into his eyes. No tears now.

What was he doing for God's sake, inviting her to finally say it was all over, that it could not go on like this.

She had a family. He had a family. This kind or situation always came to grief. Had he not written about them so often? He was an expert. A bloody prizewinner on the subject.

When she finally answered his question, he was left numb.

Fifty yards from the café was a taxi rank, and he led her towards it. She submitted without argument. His anger had made him purposeful, replacing his weakness. It had been the weakness of a man with all to lose and no ground on which to stand to defend it.

He ordered the taxi to take them to the hire car garage and he took out a car for the day.

"Where are we going?"

"I don't know. Somewhere. We've got to talk."

"What is there to talk about? That's it. No words can change things. Everything has to end."

He drove with an angrily controlled speed, knuckles white on the wheel, the gears slammed in.

She touched his arm. "This won't help."

With an effort he slowed his speed.

"This is Abbotsbury. Let's stop here," she said.

They had arrived at the picture book village that had so amazed him with its olde worlde perfection when he had first seen it. They found a café and ordered tea and scones. Tea and scones!

The café's background music was being provided by a record playing singers and bands of the Twenties and Thirties.

She poured the tea.

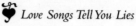

"Your kind of music." Her cheeky mickey-taking grin was fleetingly back.

He took her hand across the table and held it, making her feel his anger.

"I'll find a way." Was it his lot to always be saying foolish things to this woman? To be always ineffectually on the fringe of her life?

"What exactly did they say?"

"Just that. I've got to have an operation."

She told him how the pains in her stomach had got worse, and going back to the doctor to insist on a specialist's opinion. Then the moment she had realised from the look on the specialist's face that that something was terribly wrong.

As he listened to how the ponderous NHS system had made her wait for weeks for the appointment, rage was damming up in him. During those weeks she had said nothing to him, and every day for him had been marvellous.

There was nowhere for his rage to go for release. To everyone in the cafe they were two people talking fondly.

'No,' she had said, trying to stop him believing it was his child, unable to tell him that it was cancer, not new life, that made her stomach swell with specious beauty.

"Isn't this a nice little table, I can touch you so easy." And she did, caressing his cheek. "It will be all right. You are the best doctor I ever had. You cured everything that was wrong with my life. I had a heart problem, and you cured that."

He could not return her smile. He had done nothing for her, had not been there to fight for her. He was a fugitive from both their lives, taking but giving nothing.

The anger knotted his gut again as he remembered that lovely afternoon when he thought she was pregnant, and that the child was his. In his weak and floundering rage he almost demanded to know what her husband had done. He crushed the question. It would have brought someone into the equation he did not want. Truth was he lived a hundred miles away, on the outside.

★

Following the shock at hearing of Toby Morrison's suicide

somehow his old colleagues felt guilty. Some contributed more to the office collection for flowers than they usually did on such occasions. Most gave a token amount. They had disliked him – no, that was too strong, had not liked him – without having any good reason for doing so. How awful, they said to each other. He had just walked straight into the sea somewhere off Dorset. Why on earth did he do that? Nobody had, or ever would have, the answer. He shared his life with none. No one knew him.

It was terribly sad but they did not feel as sad as they felt they ought to.

★

Bill shoved the desk phone over to Kelly. "For you."

Offhandedly, with his mind still on what he was typing he answered the call: "Hello? Kelly Webb."

She was slow to reply and when she did she was hesitant and quiet. "Hello?"

"Kathy? This is wonderful!" He lowered his voice. "How are you?"

"I'm sorry to bother you at the office."

"I'm glad you did. Just to hear you."

"You must be busy."

"No. I'm glad. How are you?"

"All right." Her voice was so quiet, he could only just hear her.

"What made you call?" He had never expected her to call him at the office.

"I'm sorry."

"No! It's O.K. Absolutely fine. I'm glad. It's lovely to hear you. I will ring the hospital every day. Don't forget. Tell them it's all right to let me know how you are. Every day, I promise."

"You had better not ring." Her quietness emphasised the distance between them. He shifted and almost knocked the telephone off his desk. He grabbed it in time, realising with a jolt that he could have cut her off. The fragility of it all was frightening.

"Yes. I will. I want to." Not call the hospital? What was she thinking of? "You had better not."

"Yes!"

Silence again. Then: "I don't want you to."

"Why not?" He was getting frightened. Something was slipping away. Here on the end of a telephone line, a hundred miles away he was helpless and was losing her.

"I'll ring, every day. Then when you are out, we'll…." We will do so many things, please God, so many things. Never again would he be fearful. Now he had the strength.

"When I'm out?" There it was, that 'Oh!' When I am out? What planet are you on?

His head was full of idiotic banalities. Don't worry. You'll be all right.

Instead he just said: "I love you Kathy."

"I know you do. I love you. That's why."

He was not foolish enough to ask why what. That way he might hear what he did not want to hear. She was fainter, further away.

"Every day!"

"Don't. It's no good. You must not come down any more."

"Nothing will stop me."

"Please don't. Please. It had to end. Don't come down."

"I love you." If anyone in the office was watching him, it was just another telephone call, not the end of his world.

"I don't want you to."

"Kathy!"

"Don't forget me will you. I'll never forget you. It's been.." she could not find a word to express what she felt. "I never knew there was so much happiness."

"Kathy!"

"'Bye." A pause. "'Bye my darling. My baby, my darling."

This time the silence did not end.

It took him less than half an hour to track down the hospital she was in, find out when the operation was to be performed and when it was likely to be a good time to visit her. Not for nothing was he a good reporter.

Adroitly he arranged it so when he called again he would get back to the same nurse, so that he would not have to explain everything over again.

"Just ask for me, I go off duty at 4 p.m. every day," said the nurse.

She had a nice voice, a soft Dorset voice, and was superbly understanding. A nice soft Dorset voice.

'Hello my lovely'

The days went by like steamrollers, slow and crushing. How he would manage to see her without any other visitors around was going to be difficult, he knew. Not only her family, but also all those friends she had. That was bridge he would cross when he got to it. Then, if that failed, he would just wait at their bridge. He could not imagine a sun-dazzled morning when she would not walk elegantly into view.

'Oh, it's you again.'

★

Kelly put the letter in front of Bill. "Would you do me a favour, Bill," he said when his colleague looked up quizzically.

"Hang on to that for a couple of days. Then when Green and Smith are nicely wound up, drop it quietly on the editor's desk."

He waited while Bill took it all in.

"When are you leaving?" he asked eventually.

Kelly looked at his watch. "In the time it takes me to get to the front door. But I'd like Green to fester for a while. Just leave it on Chillywinds' desk, and you know nothing."

Bill nodded OK.

"Best of luck Kelly."

"Thanks Bill. We'll have a drink sometime."

★

Astonished, Green repeated what Smith had just told him.

"Resigned?"

"So the editor tells me."

"Resigned! When did he do that? How come I didn't know?"

Smith glared. "How come I didn't know?" That was more to the point.

Green was in limbo. "What were his reasons?"

"No idea. He handed in his letter of resignation to the editor. Presumably he gave his reasons, but what they are I don't know. The editor has not said."

"Well…" Green tried to imply 'good riddance' but with caution.

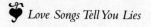

This did not feel right. It was what he wanted, but it did not feel right.

"All I do know is that the editor is very annoyed. Webb was the best in his view. This might cause some trouble, Green." Without a word out of place or hardly a change of expression Smith had distanced himself. In office politics you have got to know when it is the right time to shaft someone.

Green did not like this. Now it definitely did not feel right.

— 49 —

The nurse recognised his voice. He had called the hospital often enough. "Oh, Mrs Collins has left the hospital. She left this morning."

"Oh." His mind raced trying to think of something to keep her talking, to maintain this tenuous link. It was his only contact. "That's good, she must be getting better quickly."

"I hope so."

"Will she return for any more treatment?"

"I don't think so."

Nor more treatment. That must be good. The nurse's voice should have been brighter. He was forced to be open. "I want to contact her. How can I? Has she gone home?"

"No. She has been transferred to the Joseph Weld."

"Ah, I don't know the area well. If you could tell me the telephone number I would be grateful."

The nurse hesitated. They were careful what they gave out about patients, so he had to tread carefully. Even now, caution.

"Never mind, I'll call directory enquiries. The Joseph Weld Hospital. That's in Dorchester or Weymouth presumably?"

"Dorchester. It's the Joseph Weld Hospice."

"Right. Thank you."

He was dialling enquiries when the word hit home.

Hospice. Where people went to die.

Even in her last days he still had to skulk. He called the hospice in the evening after booking into the guesthouse, once a departure point for so many happy days.

"I need your assistance," he said to the woman who answered the phone. "Can I call up today and talk, in confidence, to someone?"

He had expected puzzlement, a query as to what it was about. He had been prepared to remain calm and polite to explain that he wanted to visit someone alone, without anyone else being there. Instead, the woman said of course, and suggested a good time to call to ensure someone in authority could help him. It was very pleasant, strangely soothing, to be asked no unwelcome questions.

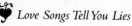

He gave his name and hung up.

Surprisingly the hospice was a bright modern building, with a striking architectural style. He gave his name to the receptionist. She did not ask him any intrusive questions, but called another woman to talk to him. This woman saw his hesitancy and led him to a nearby empty room.

"I need your help," he said. This time there was nowhere to hide.

He drew a breath, and felt a great relief at being able to be truthful and open.

"I want to come and see someone here."

"Of course, there are no restrictions on visiting times. You can come any time."

"It's Mrs Collins."

The woman said: "Oh, Mrs Collins" and smiled. He could see she liked Mrs Collins. "Of course, do you want to see her now? I'll check she is awake."

"Is her family with her?"

"That's all right, we don't have any restrictions on numbers, let me just check."

"No one knows about me."

He was glad of the subdued lighting. The words had made his eyes sting. No one knows about me.

The nurse regarded him for a few moments. He could tell she understood completely, without a query. She understood, but she was a stranger he would never see again.

"Can you tell me a time when no one is ever with her? I can call first, and if…"

"Her family visit every day."

"Can you help? You see, no one knows…" He did not say it again. She had understood.

"They always arrive late morning."

"If I come early tomorrow, can you tell whoever is on the reception – so I don't have to explain?"

"Yes, I will. Just say who you are, that's all you need to do."

"Thank you. If they come while I'm…"

She nodded, no words needed.

"I understand. Don't worry."

"And if you can, let her know that I called, tell her, Kelly, and I will come to see her. Tell her I'll wait for as long as necessary."

"I will."

"For as long as necessary."

"I'll tell her."

★

The approaching winter had been sending drizzle and dullness across England. But the memorable summer was hanging on with bands of bright sunshine still crossing the country. This morning the weather was beautiful. It should have been cold and dark, wintry as his soul.

He had called first thing, and the receptionist only had to learn who he was to know exactly what to do.

"You can come right away," she said.

He drove up the zigzag to the brow of the Ridgeway, the exhilarating start to their journeys exploring the county of which she was so proud. On their return, as they drove over the top, sometimes in dusk's fading light, there was always her delight.

'Home! As soon as I see those lights, that sea, I know I am home. Who would ever live anywhere else?'

On the outward journey the views from the crest of the hill were a very-English pastoral panorama enticing you onward, and on the return they made you wonder why you had ever wanted to leave.

Seeing the streams of molten gold of the streetlights, the dark hulk of Portland jutting volcanically from an evening-gleaming sea, he would agree with her completely.

When he got to the hospice he would tell her how lovely the view was that morning. They would plan more trips. 'You never run out of nice places to go to in Dorset,' she had told him so often with pride. They would have so much to talk about, but so little time.

He was telling himself lies. She was not going to come home. People did not leave a hospice. He knew he would tell her those lies, and they would plan those trips, and they would both pretend. He just gave his name to the woman on the reception desk and she understood. He blessed the nurse who had passed on the message so well. The room was small with just a few beds in it. Screens were drawn around some of the beds. The receptionist led him to one of the screened beds.

"I'll let you know in good time when it is time to leave," she said quietly.

She pulled the screen aside and closed it behind him. For an unreal moment they were in her friend's house, the sun warm and bright through the bedroom curtains. She was lying there waiting for him, knickers away, the man on the radio playing love songs.

Her eyes were closed but she awoke when he sat down beside the bed. There was no surprise in her gaze. She simply lay smiling at him, as though he had been there all along and she had just awoken from one of those naps she could slip in and out of so easily on those wonderful afternoons.

"Hello my darling, my baby."

Instantly his resolve to be strong for her was swept aside.

"Don't cry baby. Don't cry."

There was no fear, just a dreamy peace about her. It filled him with wonder, he who was very frightened; a leaf on a bleak wintry wind.

"Don't cry my darling."

There was no fear in her eyes, just a smiling echo of that mocking look: what are we going to do with you I wonder?

"You shouldn't have come."

He could not speak and did not answer. Nothing would have kept him away.

"You needn't have. I would have understood. I would have known. You love me. I've always known, right from the first time. Remember, on the path? The lake. It's lovely there, isn't it? My favourite walk."

I only walk this way sometimes, if my friend gives me a lift. I live right over there.

Do you mean that I might have missed you?

Right from the first moment it had been that lucky, and that fragile.

"I knew. Right from the start. We both knew didn't we?"

Her voice was far away; but tender, warm. He kissed her, not as hospital patients are kissed but passionately. A lover's kiss. Her mouth was sweet and she murmured. "That's nice." He brushed the covers aside the better to hold her. She glanced down: "Oops, not here! You can't get in with me! What would the staff think!" and there was that chuckle. Her face was gleaming wet with his tears, and they ran down to stain the pillow dark.

"You shouldn't have come. But I'm glad you did."

"Nothing would have stopped me."

She liked that. "I suppose it doesn't matter now, does it."

They both knew that was not true. They both still had families. Innocent families. Even now it still mattered.

"I can't stay long. But I will be staying in Weymouth. I will come every time it's possible."

"Darling, they'll be here all the time. There's no need. I know. That's all that matters. I know. You really do love me. I know."

"I'll find a way." Wasn't he the enterprising reporter? He always found the answer didn't he?

He tried to brush his tears from her face, but it was a waste of time. The flow would never end.

She gazed at him silently for a time, her eyes wide and wondering. They kept closing, as though acquiescing to a sweet, welcome sleep. Then suddenly she came bright awake with that momentary 'where-am-I?' look as when she awoke on those afternoons.

Hour after hour, while the man on the radio played his love songs. Then she would fall asleep in his arms.

You make me feel so safe.

For a few moments she was looking at something in her mind, then she focussed on him. "Hello my lovely."

She reached under her pillow. "I've got something for you. She pushed a paper tissue into his hand. She watched his face as she used to when on impulse she would suddenly buy him a small present, just for the pleasure of seeing his reaction. That was always 'You shouldn't have' but he would still be pleased. It always gave him an excuse to buy her something. "We're daft!" she would say every time.

"Sniff it." It was soaked in her perfume. He breathed deep of it.

"So you won't forget me. You bought it for me, remember?"

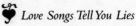

He did, and he also remembered how money increased in value a thousandfold when spent on her.

"Yes, I remember."

She was asleep now. She was going from him but he could not stay. He had to slip discreetly away. Love and courage should go arm in arm, but they don't always.

Don't cry, my baby

She seemed to be deep asleep now, her face shining with his tears. Her pillow was now soaked dark with them.

He breathed deep of her fragrance. Time was ticking. Then a stupidly unimportant thought: he had forgotten the name of the perfume. He would not able to buy any more. Typical! Those eyes would have turned heavenward searching for help for such as he.

"'Bye for now," he said. "I'll be back soon."

There were voices as people passed the annexe door. It was a warning. Recklessly he lingered to kiss her again. Her mouth was as warm and loving as on those lovely afternoons. Oops, not here! What will the staff think! Even now she made him want to smile, causing his tears to flow the more. She murmured 'darling, my baby' against his mouth and he hoped she was remembering those afternoons, as he was remembering. Then she was quiet and did not open her eyes again.

The nurse came into the room and whispered that it was time to leave. He followed her out into the dimly-lit corridor. "Could you do one more thing for me? Before her visitors are allowed in to see her, would you change her pillow please?"

The nurse regarded him for a moment, not understanding, but she could see it was important.

"Of course, I'll do it now," she said and went behind the screen.

The changeable weather was now drizzly, and he walked out into a rain cloud gloom that enveloped him like death.

He called the hospice and the receptionist said, gently as her colleague had explained the situation, that there was no change.

"I'll keep calling," he said, "if that's all right."

"Of course, as often as you like."

The next time he called, the woman said: "Mrs Collins died an hour ago. I am very sorry."
He said: "Oh" Then: "Thank you." Then he hung up.

Cold early evening rain had moved on, leaving the air sharp and clear and the countryside lit by an icy moon and an exultant host of stars. Quite why he had come to Box Hill he could not explain to himself. He had gone as a man who had to go somewhere yet had nowhere to go.

It had always been a happy place. At the lookout built in memory of Leopold Salomons who had given the beauty spot to the nation, he stood where he and Angela and Thomas and Jo used to stand and vainly try and see their home through a pair of old binoculars. On the lookout Meadow Gate was signposted as being five miles away and it was always fun for the children to pretend they could see it.

Far out across England the lights from the warm and secure homes of thousands of families flickered. But he was seeing the lights of Weymouth across moonlit reeds. On that amazing night, thinking of Kathy, he had been the greatest man on earth. Tonight, under a night sky every bit as wonderful, he was not much.

He was not very much at all.

— 50 —

Soaking wet clouds hung over the valley. The earth was clinging to his shoes. Far down in the bottom of the valley black cars were parked outside the church. The service had ended and the mourners were beginning to drift out.

In the hot summer months flowers flourished on this unsullied hill. They had sat in this very spot and within arm's length he had been able to pick her a posy. City-conditioned, he had marvelled how the cornflowers were as fine as flowers growing in a cultivated garden. Irises grew on the valley floor. One time, she said, they had covered it completely in a golden glow.

"And the blackberries, oh, wonderful blackberries!"

The Londoner in him had noticed the brash new houses they had allowed to be built right up to the skyline. With the eye of a critic he noted the road they had built from nowhere in particular to nowhere in particular. All he had thought about was the magic there had been. She had seen the magic that remained.

Drizzly rain started and he instinctively huddled against it. But it was not cold, and the rain was still autumn-warm, pleasant, falling on his face like kisses. It was soft summer rain at the wrong time and place.

Slowly the mourners were departing, and he made his way down the hill and crossed the soggy floor of the valley to the bridge. When he got to the church the mourners had gone. A man, a churchwarden or perhaps from the undertakers, was moving the wreaths. He took no notice of Kelly and soon left.

He sat in a pew. The church was silent and cold as forgotten promises. "It's a beautiful little church," she had said, and it was, for all its sadness. He pictured her as a bride at that altar, brand new, listening radiant-eyed to all those promises.

This image brought back to mind her remark at West Bay when that lovely girl and handsome young man walked by.

Handsome is as handsome does.

What she had meant he had no idea, but it had been spoken with feeling. It did not matter now. Anyway, if he did try to understand he would likely get it wrong. He had got everything else wrong.

He sat for a long time thinking of the summer. In all the time he knew her he had learned so little about her life. All the time he had been anonymous, on the outside.

'Remember the happy times' she had said once. 'Don't let's be gloomy all the time. Life's too long.' She had chuckled at that twist, and here in this church where her funeral service had just been held he found himself smiling.

On the seats some leaflets had been left. He picked up one to see what hymns had been sung but on it was printed Christina Rossetti's desolating poem, Remember. He could barely read the words through stinging eyes.

Nor I half turn to go yet turning stay.

It had taken just a moment to turn both their lives upside down that day near Sibleys when, half turned to walk on, she had stayed.

Better by far you should forget me and smile, than that you should remember and be sad.

He would never return to these reedy, meadowy, seascape places but he would remember. He would remember the woman who was dearly loved and smile.

He put his face in his hands and tears ran through his fingers like winter rain. They were tears that relieved no pain, nor washed reality away.

When he left the church no one was around. He walked away unseen and anonymous.

He walked back past the houses on the hill. Somewhere among those mellow houses was her friend's home where they had made love on those sunlit afternoons. He walked on to the town along the lakeside causeway. The winter was gaining the upper hand. It was raining more heavily and it was now a chill, dispiriting rain. A taxi would have been wise on such a day, but he did not want comfort. That made no sense, as nothing else made any sense. It made no sense to turn off and walk over to the bridge, to stand there and wonder how this cold empty place could ever have been magical. The ducks and pigeons had long since given up hope of any holidaymaker feeding them, and had settled down for the night.

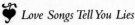

Compared to the ducks' usual indignant row their huddled silence gloomily suited the miserable evening.

As he turned away and headed for the seafront, its skyline etched in charcoal against a dying sky, a single duck suddenly started to quack loudly. It was an ugly, mocking, sound that followed him across the bleak car park like idiot laughter. He was cold and wet through to his shoulders when he arrived at the guesthouse.

Lonely man in lonely town.

There was time to get the last train back to London. He did not want to stay in this sad, damp, town. He was empty of will. He sat on the bed trying to make the simple decision of whether to catch the train that night or wait until the morning.

There was never going to be any blame, no reckoning, for him to face. He was returning to a life a man would kill for. To a woman he loved dearly. No one would judge him. He would not have to make the brutal decision other men in his position had to make. There would be no come-uppance, no expose.

There was a knock on the door.

"There was a telephone call for you, my love," said the landlady, handing him a piece of paper. "Would you call back this evening, she said."

A telephone call? Who could it …? No one knew he was here.

"Everything all right, love?" He must have looked shocked.

"Yes, fine." It was a robot voice answering for him.

"Well, if you need anything, you know where I am." She gave him her nice warm smile, and he wanted her to come into the room and hold him close.

There was no code prefixing the number written on the piece of paper, so it must be local. She? Would you call back this evening, *she* said.

For a long time he pondered, with an uneasy tremor in his stomach, as to who in the town could possibly know him or that he was staying at the guesthouse. It must be some bizarre coincidence, a mix-up. Someone else named Webb they thought was staying at the guesthouse? Yes, that must be it, but he could not ignore the note. That would be worse, never knowing. To avoid using his mobile he picked up the telephone in the hallway. He tapped the six digits to the unknown.

"Hello?" It was a man's voice.

That was unexpected, and he thought of giving a false name. In the same moment he realised how stupid that would be, as the caller who had left the number had known his name. He could just hang up silently. But he had to find out what was happening.

"Hello. My name is Webb. I had a message to ring this number."

"Ah, yes. Just a minute."

A woman's voice replaced the man's. "Mr Webb? Oh, hello. I'm so glad you called back. I'm sorry I did not leave my name. But you don't know me. I'm Kathy's friend." She paused, waiting for this to be taken in.

So it was not the mix-up he had hoped. His mind froze, except, oddly, he was aware that she had used the wrong tense. Kathy was dead. Was Kathy's friend, not 'I am Kathy's friend.'

"You will be puzzled no doubt. Kathy asked to me to talk to you. I'm glad I caught you. I thought you might have taken the train back to London already."

"I see." It was unnerving that this woman – a voice on the phone – knew so much about him.

"Could we meet before you go back. It would be easier."

He was slow to answer. His mind raced. He had thought he was anonymous in this town, safe from exposure.

"I'm going back tomorrow morning."

"Oh. Could we meet before you leave? I'm Lesley James, by the way. I'm doing this all wrong. You must be wondering who I am. Kathy wanted me to talk to you, to explain some things."

"I see."

"It was important to her Mr Webb."

"I see."

"What time do you have to leave tomorrow? Could we meet somewhere – what time is your train?"

Tossed helplessly on to a sea of circumstance he floundered.

"I haven't... It doesn't have to be any particular time. I could meet you in the morning."

"Tomorrow morning? Half past ten? You know Sibleys, the café?"
Sibleys. How strange she should choose Sibleys.
"Yes. Half past ten will be all right. How will I...?
"I will be wearing a red coat. I don't know what you look like
either. But there will not be many people this time of year. I'll look
for someone looking for someone. Half past ten then, Mr Webb."
There was a pause, then again just before she hung up: "It was
important to her."
Then there was silence on the line. Listening to that silence he
heard the sound of loneliness.

The summer kept fighting back. It was another lovely morning. The
sun slanted through the spacious windows of the café illuminating
memories. Lesley James was a big, well-dressed, woman with a
pleasant face. Her fragrance was light and pleasing. Her eyes were
warm and easy to regard. She was exactly the kind of friend Kathy
would have had and he liked her right away.
He ordered coffees.
She opened her handbag and took out a card. It was the guesthouse
visitors' card. "You gave this to Kathy. She gave it to me, hoping you
would stay there again. I called just after she died and they said you
were booked to return at this time."
The waitress brought their drinks. When she had gone, Lesley
continued. With gentle emphasis she said: "Kathy was my best
friend. She had to confide in someone. Everyone does. We talked a
lot, but she told me very little about you personally Mr Webb..."
"Please - Kelly."
"...Kelly. I knew there was someone very special, but very little else.
You need never worry." She looked at him for a moment, to ensure
he understood. She composed herself, then continued.
"She did not want to leave a letter. But she wanted you to know
what you meant to her."
He remained silent, not only because there was nothing to say, but
also because he could not trust himself to speak.
"You knew that, I know. But she knew that you would always
wonder about a lot of things, because she did love you and she

knew you loved her. She knew you meant everything you said. Almost from the beginning it was what she wanted. But soon after she met you she became ill, and then she knew she was going to die."

She had started speaking with careful composure, but had to pause at this point for a moment before continuing.

"I think that if things had been different she would have gone with you. She agonised for a long time. She knew what pain she would have caused....." She chose her words. "....your family. Then...everything changed."

For the second time her calm demeanour faltered and she stopped, looking down. He was glad he did not have to say anything and waited.

After a steadying intake of breath she continued.

"She was so torn between right and wrong. Her heart was breaking, but she realised it was too late when they said the cancer had returned.

"You made her very happy. She was so torn, so torn. 'Everything would be ruined - for what?' she said. She asked me to ... she just wanted you to know that if things had been different ..." Her voice trailed away.

He looked out of the window. The Punch and Judy man had long since packed up and gone. Holidaymakers in daft shorts were nowhere in sight. They too had gone, taking their blobby thighs and bulging paunches with them. The prom - Esplanade! - was almost deserted, with just a few people waiting for a bus. Never again would he see a blobby Brit in shorts without her anguished 'Oh my God!' in his mind's ear.

"Thank you for telling me this." His voice was beginning to obey him. "And thank you for the use of your house. That was ..." He stopped, unable to share those wonderful hours, not even with this warm-hearted woman.

She was looking at him in surprise. "My house?"

"Those afternoons, when you looked after her children." Even as he perceived that she did not know what he was talking about, the truth was dawning on them both. She recovered from her surprise

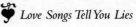

first, shaking her head.

"No, that was not my house. It was her house."

To his unspoken question she said: "I don't know why she said that. Perhaps she thought that if you knew she was alone, you would misunderstand, you would think she did not want – I don't know."

"Alone?"

Lesley regarded him for a moment, debating just what else to tell this man. Clearly he did not know very much. Stay loyal to her dear friend and tell this man only what she had wanted him to know; what would kinder, the truth or the lie?

"Kathy just wanted me to let you know how much she loved you. That it in any other circumstances…"

Then she made up her mind. "There was only herself and the girls."

"She wasn't married?"

A painful anger flooded him: "Then why….?" Kathy had lied to him with her silence.

For a moment Lesley paused, then decided.

"They separated. Several years ago now. Many years. Time flies. Yes, it was her house. It must have been while the girls were visiting their father – they will live with him now of course."

She could see Kelly's bewilderment and pain. "I'm sorry. The truth is they were not right for each other. No one could understand why they parted. None of their friends– it was a mystery to them. They were a wonderfully handsome couple. A golden couple. There seemed to be all the ingredients for happiness, but…"

West Bay. The handsome young man and the lovely girl clinging to his arm. Handsome is as handsome does.

As she continued, he was realising why Kathy had made such an issue of keeping their meetings secret, avoiding friends when they were together, when it should not have mattered who she was with. Why she acted that way was now plain. If her friends had met him it was possible – even inevitable – one of them would have let out her secret. Perhaps she did not want to put him under any obligation.

"You were the only one since, Kelly. It was not from lack of chances. None of her friends ever understood why she never remarried. With you she found what she was looking for."

There had indeed been no lack of offers. Her dear friend Kathy had been created by God to give men a preview of Heaven.

"She knew you would go to her if you knew. She said: 'What can I offer him? He will be left with nothing. No home, no family'. She knew that would be selfish, cruel. She had to let you believe a lie."

There was a questioning movement of her hand. Who can judge?

"It broke her heart."

All around them people were chatting happily. He felt the painful tension in his shoulders as he coped with the need to maintain a public mien.

She attempted some words of comfort. "There was nothing you could have done. Nothing anyone could have done."

What was left of their coffees was long cold. There was not much left to say.

"She had a very good friend in you," he said at last. "Thank you for explaining."

"Kathy was very dear to me. She was very lovable. She had lots of friends." She picked up her handbag and adjusted her scarf. "The town is full of her friends. Although none knew of you. Surprising, in a small town like Weymouth." It was an assurance, given as a kindness.

"Very lovable." There was a smile in her eye as she repeated it. Even in sadness, the memory of Kathy made her friend smile.

"I hope you understand a little better now." She stood up to leave. "Although we may sometimes wonder if we understand anything. Goodbye."

"Goodbye."

The break in the clouds was probably the last warmth before winter set in. The air was still and soft over the lake and people were walking relaxed, coats open, enjoying this unexpected late summer bonus. She would have loved this day, walking high on some Dorset hill.

She was a woman of expensive fragrances, fashionable clothes, a natural habitué of elegant places.

I was born for this! You can't afford me!

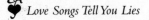

Yet she was never happier than when simply walking the high places on a Dorset coast path, or along a winding lane. Mind you, she would breeze along stylishly, dressed more appropriately for afternoon tea. Stow House. The Harbour Café. Sibleys. The Abbotsbury tea house – *your kind of music!*

And that day on the high hill above Abbotsbury, the view so high they could see the curve of the earth; a day they felt they were the only people on earth, the only ones that mattered. The day they believed anything.

He was not much. A fool and a coward. The fool who had not known what to do. The coward who had done what she wanted.

She had died without having to tell him it was over, that it was an affair could not go on without hurting those who must not be hurt. The end had been brutally decided for them by a malignant fate.

She was a woman of courage and style, and what was he?

What might have been had he not been afraid to assert himself? Now, would he ever know what choice he would have made? Then, in her Dear Dorset he felt he would have given up everything for her. What now, if she were to come swinging along that reedy path through the lake, the last month nothing but a nightmare; Eton jacket jauntily open to the warmth of that wonderful summer? What sort of man he was he would never know.

He wandered round the lake and through town on automatic, missing trains. From the corner where she had half turned to go and, turning, stayed to wreak havoc with all the rules, he walked past Sibleys and along the Esplanade to the Jubilee Clock. Then he turned his back on the sea and caught the London train.

He had no right to the comfort of self pity. He had a perfect life to return to; no recriminations, nothing to pay.

Over the lake the light was now distinctly autumnal. Alongside the station they had put up no-taste shopping sheds. These people who had been handed paradise and had then shoved a road through it were pressing on. The folk from oop north and the London geezers would all feel at home. They would leave mundane surroundings behind and find them again here, along with the same items they could buy at home, or anywhere else.

Never mind, we've still got this.

Nearby passengers were engaged in cheerful gossip. It evoked the memory of those two chatty Brighton women. Only that summer, yet a lifetime since.

"Tell us though, what do you do for a living?"

"Follow fashion."

"That sounds like a good job."

It is ladies, it is, and I am very good at it.

"Hello my darling." The loving voice roused him from his reverie, for a moment as though from a dream; awaking in her arms with the sun streaming through the window.

Seated opposite was a mother with a young child. The child was playing peek-a-boo between her fingers. At each giggling peek from her little girl her mother crooned "Hello my lovely!" Like two women in his life, she possessed that honest, heart-stopping femininity any man would die for; that should make heroes of men. As with this moment, there would always be reminders. An elegant woman passing by. Eyes that ambush. Café tables beside a summer sea.

'Write our story!'

'There's no plot, no third act.'

Could he get anything right? That's all there had ever been. There had been no first or second act. They had walked straight on stage for the third act of The Oldest Story. There had been no plot, no villain, no wicked uncle; just a man and a woman and witless fate.

Nothing would change. Ferocious fashion would continue to move the age. The rights and wrongs of it all were in tomes on lawyers' bookshelves; men and women had no answers.

The train entered the tunnel on its way back to a life to die for.

The End